KILLER *in* HIGH HEELS

GEMMA HALLIDAY

JAICO PUBLISHING HOUSE

Ahmedabad Bangalore Bhopal Bhubaneswar Chennai
Delhi Hyderabad Kolkata Lucknow Mumbai

Published by Jaico Publishing House
A-2 Jash Chambers, 7-A Sir Phirozshah Mehta Road
Fort, Mumbai - 400 001
jaicopub@jaicobooks.com
www.jaicobooks.com

KILLER IN HIGH HEELS
ISBN 978-81-8495-494-4

First Jaico Impression: 2013

Printed by
Snehesh Printers
320-A, Shah & Nahar Ind. Est. A-1
Lower Parel, Mumbai - 400 013

For my mom,
who taught me everything I know about fashion.
And for my dad,
who didn't mind me naming a drag queen after him.

CHAPTER ONE

There are two things in life I hate more than getting shot at. Number one: Birkenstocks, one shoe I am proud to say I did *not* design. And number two: sit ups. The torture routine my best friend, Dana, was currently making me perform on the floor of the Sunset Gym.

"Come on, two more, you can do it!"

I grunted, giving my personal cheerleader the evil eye as I struggled to a sitting position.

"I (pant) can't (pant) do it." My stomach muscles started to shake, and I could feel an unattractive bead of sweat trailing from my blonde roots down to the tip of my chin.

"Come on, Maddie. I know you've got two more in you. Think of how good you'll look in a bikini this summer."

"I'll buy a one-piece," I grunted.

"Think of how great you'll feel knowing you did something good for your body."

I raised one eyebrow, giving her my best 'get real' look.

"Okay, think of this," Dana said, a light bulb moment flashing in her blue eyes. "Think of how bad Ramirez will want you when he sees your ripped abs."

That did it. With one really unladylike grunt I clenched my teeth together and hauled myself into a sitting position.

"Woohoo! I knew you could do it!" Dana stood up and did an end zone worthy victory dance on my behalf. Dana was a 5'7", 36 DD, strawberry blonde aerobics instructor slash wanna-be actress with the kind of body that inspired rock songs. I don't need to add that every male head in the gym suddenly turned our way.

"Thanks," I said. "I needed that."

"No prob. What are friends for?"

"But you do realize you violated The Oath."

Dana bit her lip, getting a guilty look on her face. "Oops."

The Oath was the vow I had made all of my friends and family take to never mention the name 'Ramirez' to me again. Last summer Detective Jack Ramirez, or as Dana had dubbed him, The Panty Melter, showed up at my apartment with a pocket full of condoms. He kissed me. I kissed him. There was a mad frenzy of clothing falling to the floor. We were one Vicky's push-up bra and a pair of Hanes-Her-Way from the bedroom… when his pager went off.

He left me with a platonic kiss on the forehead and a promise to call me the next day. Yeah right. Two *weeks* later I got a message on my machine. "Sorry, been busy. Work. Gotta go. Call you later." And not a peep since.

Men.

Then again what did I really expect? Jack Ramirez was a cop with a big gun, a big tattoo, and a big… well let's just say his BVDs didn't hide much that night. So, I shouldn't really be surprised he wasn't turning out to be Mr. Cleaver material. I had to admit, though, Ramirez was still an improvement over my last boyfriend, Richard, who ended up getting arrested for conspiracy and embezzlement.

Do I know how to pick 'em or what?

"Sorry," Dana said, "but you had to finish the set. Honey, you're doing so good."

Actually, I kind of was. When The Name that Shall Not Be Spoken did his disappearing act last July I did what any other normal, rational, single woman would do when being completely ignored by the object of her affection. I junk food binged. Oh, mama, did I binge. Cheetos, pizza, Oreos, Ben and Jerry's Chunky Monkey by the bucketful and Keebler fudge cookies in every size, shape and variety. Dana finally did a chocolate chip intervention, pointing out that if I didn't cut it out soon I would a) have permanent cheese doodle stains on my fingers, b) not be able to fit into my favorite black Nicole Miller dress, and c) qualify as an official member of the Pathetic Losers of America club. She was right. My Miller was a little snug. Which is why I didn't even protest (much) when she dragged me to the gym and forced me to perform the modern equivalent of medieval torture. Sit ups.

I flopped back onto the blue gym mats, breathing heavily. "Please tell me we're done?"

Dana (who, by the way, hadn't even broken a sweat yet despite the fact we'd been here nearly an hour) put her hands on her hips. "But we haven't even worked your glutes yet."

"If I promise to have lettuce for dinner, can I skip the glutes?" I pleaded. Even though I was actually dreaming of lettuce sandwiched between a sesame seed bun and a quarter pound beef patty.

Dana let a little frown settle between her strawberry blonde brows. But, since she was such a good friend (and I was still panting like a Doberman) she let me off the hook. "Fine. But I expect to see you back here on Saturday ready to do some lunges and squats."

"Aye, aye captain."

Taking pity on me, Dana helped me up, and I dragged my sweaty behind to the locker room.

"So," she asked, "any big plans tonight?"

Considering it was Friday night and the only action I'd gotten in months was from a battery powered rabbit, the answer to that one was a no-brainer. "Nope. Why?"

"I've got a Pilates class at five, but I was going to go shopping after that. Wanna come with?"

Does a bear go poo poo in the woods? "I'm there."

* * *

Twenty minutes later I pulled my little red Jeep up to my second story studio in Santa Monica. Two blocks away from the beach, my apartment was my little piece of heaven. And I do mean little. A fold out futon, a drawing table, and three dozen pairs of shoes had the place at max capacity. I let myself in and even though the half eaten bag of Chips Ahoy was calling to me from the back of my cupboard, I resisted, popping the top on a can of Diet Coke instead while I played my messages.

The first one was from Blockbuster. "The *Sex and the City* DVD you ordered came in," a bored sounding teenager informed me. "The computer also shows that you have out *Pretty Woman, When Harry met Sally*, and…" she paused. And might have even done a little laugh slash cough thing. "…*Joanie Loves Chachi*, the complete set."

Yes, this is what life without a man has driven me to.

I hit the delete button.

The next message clicked on.

"Hi, this is Felix Dunn with The *L.A. Informer*. We're doing a follow up story to your ordeal last summer. I'd like to schedule a time to interview you about-"

Beep. Delete.

Ever since my ex-boyfriend, Richard's, very public arrest, which at one time had included a charge of murder, the press had hijacked my phone number. Okay, I'll admit there had been a little stabbing incident involving me, a homicidal ex-mistress, her popped breast implant and a stiletto heel in the jugular, which had somehow captured the imagination of the media. I'd been featured no less than three times on the cover of the *Informer* since then. Twice with my head superimposed over the body of a slasher movie heroine and once as the bride of Bigfoot. Hmmm… maybe that's why Ramirez hadn't called.

The machine clicked over to the next message.

"Hi honey, it's Mom. Guess what? Ralph finally got our Hawaii pictures printed! You must come see them. They are fabu! Call me!"

Mom had recently come back from an extended Hawaiian honeymoon with husband number two, Ralph. Or, as I liked to call him, Faux Dad. My real dad having run off to Las Vegas with a showgirl named Lola when I was only three. All I remember of Real Dad is a hand, connected to a slightly more hairy than normal arm, waving goodbye out the driver's side window of his '74 El Camino. Needless to say, Faux Dad and I had bonded right away. (And it didn't hurt that he ran one of Beverly Hills' most exclusive salons and offered me all the free manicures I wanted, either.)

The machine clicked and the mechanical voice proclaimed, "End of messages."

Sigh. No Ramirez. No Brad Pitt. No handsome stranger who saw me in line at Starbucks and looked up my number on the internet.

I hated Friday nights.

I finished my Diet Coke and hopped in the shower, washing the gym sweat off my sore limbs. I threw on a pair of jeans, a sparkly pink wrap top with little silver sequins, and brand new, totally kickin' Ferragamo pumps. Which, by the way, had put me in debt (again), but the two inches they added to my 5'1 ½" frame were so worth it. A little mousse and blow-dry number to my naturally (mostly) blonde hair, and I was ready.

Dana picked me up in her tan Saturn and we hopped on the 10. Rush hour traffic had died down, but there were still enough cars on the road to make it light up like a Christmas tree in the early fall dusk. As soon as we pulled into the left lane a blue Dodge Neon grabbed onto our bumper and tailgated us the entire way east to the 405. I looked at the speedometer. We were doing eighty. Only in L.A.

I glanced back to get a look at the driver, but the glare from his headlights was all I saw. I sent him the universal hand gesture for 'back off pal.'

Only thirty minutes, two lewd truck drivers, and one cell-phone related wreck later we were parked in front of our destination.

Sepulveda Guns and Ammo.

"Um, what are we doing here?"

"Shopping," Dana replied.

"This isn't exactly what I had in mind." I took in the barred windows, NRA posters on the door and homeless person peeing on the side of the brick building. "You sure you don't want to go to Macy's?"

Dana shook her head at me. "I need a piece."

"A 'piece'? What, are you Clint Eastwood?"

"Last week Rico told the class we needed to think about protection."

After my 'brush with death' last summer, as my overly dramatic best friend called it, Dana went on this self-defense kick, immediately going out and signing up for a class at the rec center. Surveillance and Protection for the Urban Soldier. The instructor of the class, Rico, looked like a cross between Rambo and the Incredible Hulk. I could see Rico needing a 'piece.' The thought of Dana handling a deadly weapon was, however, mildly frightening.

"Do you even know how to shoot a gun?"

"Yep." Dana smiled with pride. "Rico's been giving me some private lessons."

Considering Dana's uncanny ability to pick up men destined for short term relationships, I could just imagine the kind of 'private lessons' Rico had been giving her.

"I don't know about this." I eyed the store again. The homeless guy zipped up and began yelling at passing cars. "I'll buy you a Wetzel's Pretzel with extra cinnamon sugar if we can go to the Glendale Galleria instead."

Dana got out of the car. "Come on, don't be such a wimp. Rico said this place was the best."

I shrugged. I'd known Dana since we bonded in seventh grade over a shared crush on Corey Feldman circa *Lost Boys*. And I knew once she set her mind to something, I could no more dissuade her from buying a gun in North Hollywood now than I could stop her from FedExing Corey her training bra then. Besides, I guess it wouldn't hurt to pick up a can of pepper spray.

Dana clubbed her steering wheel and locked the car with a backward glance at the homeless guy. He was still busy shouting obscenities at a Ford Festiva on the corner.

The bell over the door to Sepulveda Guns and Ammo jingled as we pushed through the NRA posters, prompting all eyes to turn our way. Two homeboys in low slung jeans and baseball caps were hunkered over an assault rifle in the corner, planning something I *so* did not want to know about. A tall guy with a greasy blonde ponytail and a shirt liberally stained with mustard stopped his inspection of a long range scope and took to inspecting us, his tiny eyes doing a slow up and down thing.

I suddenly needed a shower.

Dana grabbed my arm and steered me over to the woman behind the glass counter, wearing a nametag that read "Mac." She was shorter than me, which put her near the five foot mark, with bushes of frizzy red hair that Carrot Top would be jealous of. And an eye patch. Seriously. A black, Johnny Depp style eye patch that looked like it should come with a parrot. I tried not to stare.

"What can I do for ya', honey?" she asked, her voice rough with years of cigarette smoke. Or maybe just trying not to inhale the homeless guy stench wafting in through the ancient ventilation ducts exposed in the ceiling.

Dana stepped up to the smudged glass counter and did her best Dirty Harry. "I'm lookin' to pack."

I rolled my eyes.

Scary Gun Lady narrowed her good one at us.

"What my friend means," I jumped in, "is that she's looking for a starter sort of gun. Something small. And safe. You know, that won't go off easily."

Her eye narrowed further, and she did a hands on hips thing. "You want a *safe* gun?"

I think I heard Ponytail Guy snicker behind us.

I looked to Dana for help but she was busy scrutinizing the display case full of deadly weapons. I knew that look in her eyes. It was the same one I got when Dior pumps went on sale. My mild fear jumped up a notch.

"Safe-ish maybe?"

Scary Gun Lady gave me a once over, her gaze stopping at my sparkly pink top, which, by the way, would have been perfect for a stroll around the mall.

"Honey, you've never held a gun before, have you?"

No, but I had wicked accuracy with a stiletto heel. "Nuh-uh," I replied.

She shook her head, her red hair flying around her face like Bozo the Clown's. Though, in all honestly, my gaze was still riveted to that eye patch. Why we had ventured into the depths of North Hollywood for guns was still a bit of a mystery to me. I mean, they sell guns in Beverley Hills too.

"I like this one," Dana, said, pointing to a DDA .45 caliber pistol. Neon pink.

The saleswoman did the hands on hips thing again. "Honey, I could sell you that gun. But the first time you pull it out, you know what your attacker's gonna say?"

Dana and I shook our heads in unison.

"Nothin'. He'll be laughing too hard."

Dana nodded solemnly. "Right. No pink." She straightened up and did her serious face, scrunching her eyebrows together like she was thinking really hard. "See, I'm mostly looking for some kind of protection against those smarmy kinds of guys that hit on you in clubs, and then when you turn them down wait for you to go to the bathroom, then slip you a roofie and you wake up in some stranger's bed the next day. Know what I mean?"

Mac raised her eyebrows and looked from Dana to me, as if saying, "Is this chick for real?"

"Okay, look. You seem like nice enough girls, and I don't wanna see you get hurt. How about some pepper spray?"

"What, do we look like amateurs?" Dana asked.

Even I had to agree with the snort of laughter Ponytail Guy let out at that one.

But Dana wasn't giving up. "Listen, Rico told me you could help me find something. He said you were the best."

"Rico?" The woman's face softened and she shifted her defensive posture. "Why didn't you tell me you knew Rico?" She reached into the glass case and pulled out a silver handgun. "Here, this is what you girls need. A Smith and Wesson LadySmith. Semi-automatic, nine millimeter, rubber grips in stainless finish. Hardly any recoil, but it packs quite a punch and fits in your purse."

Dana's eyes lit up like a kid in a candy store. "Can I hold it?"

Gun Lady nodded. Dana picked it up, doing her best James Bond stance. The guys in baseball caps took a couple steps backward.

"There's also the semi-auto, barrel tip." Mac reached into the case again, pulling out a gun in black. "They're lighter, easier to load than a LadySmith. The only disadvantage is they don't retain spent casings. Little harder to explain when the cops show up." She gave me a wink and a nudge.

I did a feeble laugh, trying not to picture how many 'explanations' Mac had spun in her lifetime.

"I like this one," Dana said, still holding the LadySmith, staring down the barrel at her reflection in the smudged glass.

In all honesty, the light in her eyes was getting a little scary.

"I'll take it."

The saleswoman beamed like a proud Mama. "And you?" she asked me.

"I think I'll stick with pepper spray."

* * *

Twenty minutes later I had my mini canister of Pepper Guard and Dana had a trunk full of ammunition. Not only had she laid out her Visa for the Smith and Wesson – which she could take possession of in a mere ten days provided she'd never been arrested for gun running - but she'd also come away with a box full of cartridges, a leather holster, handcuffs (I so did not want to know what those were for!) and last, but certainly not least, a stun gun in the shape of a cell phone. Dana was armed and dangerous.

Miss Guns and Ammo dropped me off at my Santa Monica studio before heading off to class to show Rico her new 'toys'. She tried to get me to come with her, saying they were going over frontal assaults tonight, but I begged her off with the fact I had to get some work done or my employer might threaten to fire me. Again. Which wasn't a total lie. They hadn't been too happy with the way my stabbing incident (not to mention marriage to Bigfoot!) had played across the front page, tarnishing their family friendly image.

Ever since I was old enough to dress Barbie in her pink sparkly ball gowns, I'd dreamed of being a fashion model. Strutting the runways of Paris in slinky couture and designer heels. However, by eighth grade it was painfully clear that even the highest stilettos weren't going to help me achieve fashion model height. So, I did the next best thing, studying fashion design. Specifically shoes. Unfortunately, every failed model studies fashion, and an actual paying job was harder to land than a contract with Cover Girl. Somehow I ended up at the only place that would take me. Tot Trots Children's Shoe Designs. Okay, so it wasn't exactly haute couture, but it paid the bills, I got to set my own hours, and my Spiderman flip-flops were the top selling shoe at Payless last season. I was currently working on the Rainbow Brite jellies for the Spring collection, complete with beaded shoe charms.

Paris, eat your heart out.

I let myself into my studio and checked my machine. The light was blinking. I dropped my pepper spray onto the counter and hit the play button.

"You have two new messages."

Check me out. Maybe my social life was looking up.

I pulled a pint of Ben and Jerry's out of the freezer (hey, shopping burns off a lot of calories, right?) while I listened to the first message.

"This is Felix Dunn with the *Informer* again. We plan to run a piece on you and we'd love to get a quote. Please call me back-"

Delete. You'd think by now the tabloids would have moved on to Jen's newest flame or Tom's latest Scientology weird-out. I mean, I only popped *one* boob!

I waited for the next message to start. There was a pause and some heavy breathing. Then, "I, uh, I'm looking for Madison Springer. I hope I have the right number. I saw your name in the paper. This is Larry."

There was another pause.

"Your father."

I stared at the phone. Spoonful of Chunky Monkey suspended in mid-air as I blinked like mad at my machine. Did he just say what I thought he said?

Then I realized the message wasn't over.

"I know it's been a while. But I, uh, I read about you in the paper. How you helped the police last summer. And I could kind of use your help right now. I, uh…"

Another pause as I held my breath. There was the sound of movement in the background.

"Oh, God… what are you doing… *no*!"

I froze as a loud bang rang out from the machine, reverberating off the walls of my tiny studio apartment.

Maybe it was the evening of learning the difference between a .45 and .40 caliber weapon. Maybe it was the fact that last summer's run-in with Miss Homicide was still just a little too fresh in my mind. Or maybe it was just my overactive imagination at work.

But my mind instantly hit on the source of the sound. A gun shot.

The machine clicked over.

Beep. "End of messages."

CHAPTER TWO

I stared at the phone, my breath lodged in my throat as my heart threatened to pound out of my rib cage. My body immediately remembered the last time I'd heard a gun go off – when it had been aimed at me! – and I went into panic mode. I grabbed the phone and dialed the first number I could think of. Ramirez.

It rang three times. Then I got his voice mail. Damn. I tried to calm my breathing as I waited for the beep.

"It's Maddie. I think I've just been ear witness to another murder. My Dad was shot. Not Faux Dad, the real dad. The hairy one. He got shot. Or he shot someone. I don't know which. But there was definitely a gunshot, and he was definitely there, and he needed my help, and now I think someone's dead. Or dying. Or probably at least wounded. Call me."

I hung up wishing I didn't automatically go into blabber mode when crisis hit. Why couldn't I be one of those calm, cool-headed women that could make a tourniquet out of a tampon and a gum wrapper? Instead I had to freak out like a little kid lost at the mall.

I dialed Mom's number. It rang four times and the machine kicked on. "Hi you've reached Betty…"

"… and Ralph," my stepfather chimed in.

"We're not here right now so leave a number at the beep…"

"…or try us at the salon, ciao!" Faux Dad finished.

I hung up. When Ramirez got my blabbering message he'd probably roll his eyes and make some comment about how girly I was. That I could live with. Mom, on the other hand, would likely call in the National Guard to make sure I was okay. Which, in all honesty, I was.

It was the guy on the other end of the line that was in trouble.

My dad.

I sat down on my futon, absently shoving a spoonful of ice cream into my mouth as I conjured up the image of that hairy arm waving good-bye from the El Camino window.

When I was deep in my teenage-angst phase I'd badgered my Mom into talking about my father. Just once. She said they'd met at a Bob Dylan concert, that he was 6'1", allergic to strawberries, and had run off to Vegas with some showgirl named Lola. When she got to the Lola part she broke down sobbing the kind of racking tears that scared the crap out of my teenaged self. Needless to say, I hadn't broached the subject since, and she hadn't offered.

I wondered if he was still in Vegas? I grabbed the handset and scrolled down my call log. Out of area. Well, that didn't tell me much. He could have been calling from anywhere.

And what kind of help did he need? Was he sick? Did he need a kidney? It would be just like a man to waltz back into my life after twenty-six years and ask for a vital organ.

Only he hadn't sounded sick. He'd sounded… in trouble. In serious trouble if that really was a gunshot. I tried not to picture him wounded or bleeding somewhere.

Maybe I should call 911. But what would I tell them? Someone somewhere might have been shot? I had no idea where he was, or even if it was, in fact, my father calling. I'd gotten more than one crank phone call since my brush with fame. And to be honest, the more I thought about it, the less sure I was that the sound was even an actual gunshot. Maybe it was just a car backfiring?

I shoved another big scoop of Chunky Monkey into my mouth, hoping that the creamy chocolate and banana goodness might calm me down.

Maybe it was a backfiring car and maybe it was a gunshot. Either way, my dad had called me. And first thing in the morning, it was time to take the crowbar bar to Mom's memory again.

* * *

I was in the depths of a dream about being chased by a backfiring car driven by a one eyed woman when the sound of my phone ringing woke me up. I halfheartedly grasped around in the general region of the handset but came up empty. I cracked one eye open to peek at the clock beside my bed. Seven a.m. I groaned. I hated morning people. My theory: if the malls don't open until ten what's the point of being up earlier than that?

The phone rang two more times, then clicked over to the machine. I buried my head under my pillow as I listened to my own voice inform callers to leave a message. The machine beeped.

"Maddie? It's Jack."

I bolted upright in bed, flinging the pillow across the room. Ramirez.

"I got your message last night. What the hell is going on over there?"

I jumped out of bed, diving for the phone. Only the handset wasn't on the cradle. I glanced around my studio apartment. Fold out futon on one wall, drawing table against the other, piles of clothes and shoes everywhere else. Where was the phone?

"What's all this about a gunshot? Are you okay?" He paused. "Look, I may be a little hard to get a hold of for the next few days, so if you're there pick up."

I was trying to! I began digging under my clothes from the night before. I slipped my hands down in the futon cushions, checked under my drawing table, even started opening kitchen drawers. Where the hell had I put the thing?

Ramirez paused. "Well, I guess you're not there. Fine. I'll try back later."

"No!" I screamed at him. Then spied the handset peeking out of a Macy's bag by the door. "Wait, wait, wait," I chanted. I grabbed the handset and hit the 'on' button.

Dial tone.

Crap.

I quickly redialed his number but wasn't surprised to hear it go straight to voicemail again. Crap, crap, crap! I slammed the handset down in the cradle, taking all my aggression out on the poor GE appliance.

Since I was up anyway I made a pot of strong coffee and hit the shower, doing a blow-dry and mousse thing afterward. As a concession to the pint of B&J's I had single-handedly consumed the night before I pulled on a comfortable pair of navy blue gaucho pants, paired with a tank top, navy shrug and knee-high brown calfskin boots. Overall, a pretty decent look for a breezy October day. Breezy translating to 75 and sunny instead of the summer's 85 and sunny forecast. We don't believe in weather in L.A. any more than we believe in public transportation.

After a couple swipes of mascara and a touch of Raspberry Perfection on my lips I was out the door.

* * *

Fernando's salon was located on the ultra chic corner of Brighton and Beverly Boulevard, one block north of Rodeo, smack in the middle of the Beverly Hills Golden Triangle. When Faux Dad had arrived on the west coast from Minnesota he was just plain Ralph, a slightly paunchy, pale, middle-aged hairdresser. Knowing no one in L.A. would get their hair done at a salon called 'Ralph's', he reinvented himself with a fictitious Spanish ancestry, spray on tans twice a week, a salon in a prime Beverly Hills location and voila - Fernando was born, stylist to the very rich and semi-famous.

In addition to his cut and color talents, Faux Dad also had a passion for interior decorating. (Mom swears he's not gay, though I still have my doubts.) Currently Faux Dad was going through a Tuscan phase, painting the walls with a rusty orange glaze and hanging bunches of plastic red grapes and leafy vines from the rafters. Gilt frames surrounding oil paintings of vineyards adorned the walls, and soft classical music mixed with the sounds of blow-dryers, sprayers, and juicy Beverly gossip. All in all, it was an atmosphere that screamed for a glass of pricey merlot.

"Maddie!" Marco, the receptionist, skipped out from behind his slick looking computer as I entered the salon, attacking me with air kisses. Marco was slim enough, pretty enough, and wore enough eye make-up to compete on America's Next Top Model. And probably win. "How are you, dahling?" he asked in an accent that was pure San Francisco.

"Suffering from a Ben and Jerry's hangover."

Marco clucked his tongue. "Awe, poor baby."

"Are Mom and Ralph in yet?"

"*Fernando*," Marco emphasized, chastising me with his heavily lined eyes, "is doing a body wave for Mrs. Simpson." He leaned in, gesturing to the back of the salon. "Jessica's Mom."

"Ah." I looked past the 'crumbling' palazzo walls of the reception area and spotted Ralph talking to a blonde under a beehive dryer. "What about Mom?"

"Your mother's in the back, doing a waxing for that psychic lady."

That 'psychic lady' was Mom's best friend, Mrs. Rosenblatt. Mrs. Rosenblatt was a three-hundred pound, five time divorcee who favored muumuus in neon colors and talked to the dead through her spirit guide, Albert. Eccentric didn't even begin to describe Mrs. Rosenblatt.

She and my mother met years ago when Mom went to Mrs. Rosenblatt for a psychic reading and claimed Mrs. R's predictions came true the very next day. Okay, so the dark, handsome, stranger she was supposed to meet turned out to be Barney, a chocolate lab, but that was close enough for Mom. They've been firm friends ever since, and Mom never goes more than five days without an aura cleanse from Mrs. R.

I thanked Marco and made my way through the humming dryers and chemical smells of the salon to the back room, reserved for fat wraps and facial waxing. At least, I hoped to God she was doing a facial. I'd only had one cup of coffee and witnessing Mrs. Rosenblatt get a bikini wax called for at least two cups. With a couple shots of whiskey.

I gave a tentative knock on the door.

"Uh, Mom? Got a sec?" I asked, slipping into the room painted with a fresco of the Italian hillside along the walls.

I was relieved to find Mom hovering over Mrs. Rosenblatt's mustache, though I cringed just a little at her outfit. I love my mother. I really do. I just wish she didn't insist on getting dressed in the dark. She was wearing electric blue stretch pants, pink legwarmers and a pink sweatshirt with the neck hole cut out over a pair of black high-topped L.A. Gear sneakers, the likes of which I hadn't seen since 1986. I think she was going for Jane Fonda chic but fell somewhere closer to Sweatin' to the Oldies.

"Hi, hon," she greeted me, waving a wax strip in my direction. "What brings you here?"

"You need a waxing?" Mrs. Rosenblatt asked, squinting at my upper lip. "Your mom's a whiz with the wax."

"Uh, no, I'm fine. Thanks."

"You sure?" Mrs. R squinted again. "Cause I could swear I see a little dust up there."

I self-consciously felt my upper lip.

"'Course, you know Albert says there are some cultures that prize hairy women," she continued.

Albert would know. In his earthly existence, Mrs. R claimed her spirit guide was a *New York Times* fact checker.

"But then again, here in Lala-land hairy just means you ain't been to the salon in a while. If I wanna get a date with that fox on the senior bowling league, I gotta loose the mustache." Mrs. R winked at me. "The Fox is Italian. They got them big hands and big noses and big..."

"Okay, hold still now."

I'll say this for my mother, she has excellent timing.

Mom pressed a strip onto Mrs. R's upper lip, thankfully ceasing the flow of too-much-information before she could describe The Fox's other attributes.

"So, what does bring you down here today?" Mom asked, smoothing hot wax down in all directions.

"Well, I, I, uh..." I paused, not sure how best to drop the bombshell that my paternal half had not only contacted me, but might be dead in a ditch somewhere. "See I got this phone call, and..."

Mom looked up, waiting for me to finish, a small frown settling between her thickly penciled eyebrows. "What is it Mads?"

I decided the least cruel way to do it was quick and painless, like ripping off a Band Aid. Or a waxy bit of upper lip hair.

"Larry called me."

Mom froze, her face going a shade of pale Nicole Kidman would be jealous of. Her mouth did an empty open and shut thing like a goldfish, then clamped into a thin tight line. "I see."

She grabbed a corner of the wax strip and yanked with a force that made me cringe.

Mrs. Rosenblatt howled like a coyote.

So much for painless.

"Mom, are you okay?" I asked as she attacked the left side of Mrs. R's face.

"Fine." Mom's lips were starting to turn white from being clamped together so tightly.

I rushed on, afraid she might attack my 'dust' next. "Look, I didn't mean to upset you, but he called last night and left a message on my machine. Only he didn't say where he was calling from or leave a number or anything. He said he saw my name in the papers and… he needed my help."

Mom's lips remained clamped as she ripped the second strip. Tears welled in Mrs. Rosenblatt's eyes.

"*Oy,* I hope that Fox is worth this," Mrs. R wailed, rubbing her lip.

Mom took a deep breath, closing her eyes in a little mini meditation. "What kind of help?" she finally asked.

"I don't know. He… the machine cut him off before he could say." No sense in mentioning the gun shot until I knew for sure that it was one. Besides, Mom was proving to be dangerous with a wax kit in her hands, and despite the reasonable person in me, I was beginning to fear her.

"I see," she said, clamping her lips together again.

I cleared my throat, wishing I didn't have to do this. "Look, I know you two…" I trailed off, her eyes boring into me beneath her 1984 powder blue eye-shadow. "I know he ditched us for a showgirl, which makes him maybe not your favorite person."

Mom made a sound like a snort.

"But despite all that, he is still my dad. And, well, I need to know. Do you know where he might be-"

But Mom cut me off, advancing on me with a fresh wax strip. "Madison Louise Springer, I refuse to discuss the man."

I took one giant step back. When she used my full name, I knew she was serious. Generally my very Irish, very Catholic grandmother was the only person who called me Madison. Mom had only used my full name twice that I can remember. Once in seventh grade when I'd been caught under the bleachers with a high school Sophomore, prompting Mom to explain in exhausting detail about the birds, the bees, and why I should wait until I was thirty to have any contact with the opposite sex again. And the second time was when I'd accidentally maxed out her credit card in a bout of post-breakup shopping when I was eighteen. That had earned me an entire summer working at Hot Dog on a Stick to pay her back. (I still have nightmares about those hats.)

"He left," Mom said. "End of story."

I opened my mouth to protest, but was stopped by Mrs. Rosenblatt laying a thick palm on my forehead.

"Hold on, *bubbee*, I'm getting a vision." Mrs. Rosenblatt rolled her eyes back in her head until she looked like an extra from Michael Jackson's *Thriller* video. "I see feathers and lipstick. Lots of red lipstick." She paused. "Did your father ever work in cosmetics testing?"

Mom and I did a simultaneous eye roll and Mom threw her hands up in the air in surrender. "Maddie, I honestly don't know where he is," she said.

I watched her for a second, trying to decide if I believed her. "But even if you did, you wouldn't tell me, would you?"

She set her mouth in that thin line again and shook her head.

Part of me understood her anger. I mean, the man had left her alone with a young child to raise on her own. And I could only imagine the sting of being left for a five foot gazillion inch showgirl. That had to hurt. I tried to picture how I'd feel if I found out Ramirez had been shacked up with some topless dancer. Not too happy. And we were only dating! (Sort of. If you called one half naked encounter six weeks ago dating. Which, for lack of any other action, I did.) But I honestly couldn't imagine what he might have done that was so bad she didn't want me to even meet him. Just once.

Unfortunately it was clear by the grim set of her mouth that I'd gotten all I was going to get out of Mom.

"Fine," I said, doing a mirror image of Mom's thin lip routine. The two of us did a little stare down thing, which I'm pretty sure neither of us won, and I left.

Fine, if Mom wouldn't help me find my Dad, I'd find someone else who would.

Marco was showing a woman with enormous Lucille Ball red hair a new moisturizing mist product as I made my way back through the salon. I waited for him to finish then approached his desk.

"Can you get online with that thing?" I asked, gesturing to his sleek, black computer.

Marco shot me a look. "What do you think this is, the stone age? This is an 800 MHz FSB Pentium Processor with 4 GB of DRAM. With this baby I can download naked pictures of Brad Pitt before you could even say yummilicious."

Tempting…

"Actually, I was wondering if you could google someone for me?"

"But of course." Marco sat down behind the computer, and pulled up the screen. "What's the name?"

I glanced nervously over my shoulder at the wax room, expecting Mom to appear any minute. "Larry Springer."

Marco typed the name in. "Twelve thousand hits."

Gee, that narrowed it down.

"What exactly are you looking for?" he asked, clicking on the first couple of links on the screen. A web page for a Washington state senator and a link to a memorial page for a clergyman who died in 1842. Neither one particularly helpful.

"I'm not sure," I sighed. "An address or a phone number maybe? Any way to contact him."

"Ah!" Marco danced his fingers over the keyboard with practiced speed, pulling up a white pages directory. He keyed in the name. "Do you know what city?"

I bit my lip, glancing over my shoulder again. "Try Las Vegas."

"Oooo, Sin City. My favorite town, honey." Marco did an eyebrow waggle, adding the city to the search. A page of names and numbers came up. "Okay, we've got phone numbers for three Larry Springers, twelve L. Springers and a couple of

Lawrences. No addresses. Who is this guy anyway?" Marco asked. "New boyfriend?"

I heard the door to the wax room open, and Mrs. R emerged, rubbing at an upper lip that looked like she'd been French kissing sandpaper.

"Uh, no. He's… someone I'm looking for," I hedged. Marco was a sweetheart, but he lived for gossip. Telling Marco a secret is like taking out an ad in Cosmo. Every fashionable woman and gay man in the country would know about it.

"Ooo, is this one of Ramir-" he paused, slapping a palm over his mouth as he remembered The Oath. "Uh, I mean, um, that hottie cop's cases? Oh baby, would I like to work with him." Marco began fanning himself.

"No, it's… personal." I watched as Mom handed Mrs. R a bottle of lotion, motioning to her red upper lip.

"Hey, can you print this page out for me?" I asked, ducking behind the monitor, hoping Mom didn't see me.

"Sure thing, honey," Marco said, as the printer hummed to life.

"Great. Thanks." My attention was still absorbed by Mom and Mrs. R. They were walking toward the reception area, Mrs. R rubbing at her lip, Mom making apologetic motions.

"Here you go, dahling," Marco handed me a sheet of paper, fresh out of the printer.

"Thanks! Gotta go," I said as I made a mad crouching dash for the front doors. "I owe you, Marco!"

"Ciao, bella! Tell Mr. Hottie Pants I said 'hi!'" I heard him yell as I passed through the glass front doors, doing the fastest run in two inch heels that I could.

Despite Dana's best efforts at replacing my Ho Hos with dumbbells, I was out of breath by the time I jogged the block and a half back to my Jeep. Once inside I flipped on the AC and scanned down the list, trying to get up the nerve to whip out my cell phone and begin dialing. At the other end of one of these numbers was my Dad. What would I say to him? Got your message, hope you're not shot, why the hell did you leave before I could make any cool memories of us at the zoo together? I didn't know. All I knew was that until I actually talked to him, visions of that dead in a ditch thing were going to haunt me. I took a deep breath and punched in the first number.

I got an answering machine. In fact, at the first six, I got machines, most of which I weeded out immediately. The first Larry Springer sounded about eighty and the next two machines featured a college kid and a man with a heavy Spanish accent.

I was halfway through the L. Springers when my stomach grumbled loudly enough to make me jump in my seat. Reminding me I hadn't eaten anything since my B&J's binge last night. I revved up the Jeep and hit the McDonald's drive- thru on Beverly and Wilshire, ordering a Quarter Pounder, large fries and a strawberry milkshake. Then threw in an apple pie for dessert. Hey, I figured this was my breakfast *and* lunch.

By the time I'd finished off the last of the greasy fries and my shake had melted into dribbles of watery ice milk at the bottom of my cup, I'd narrowed the list down to two possible Larry's. One number rang and rang and the other was answered by the mechanical voice that came with the answering machine. Either of which could belong to my dad.

What I needed now was some way to match the numbers with addresses. If I had an address, I could call the Vegas police and let them do a casual drive by to see if either of the houses were occupied by conspicuous dead bodies with gunshot wounds.

I looked down at my digital clock. 4:15. Dana's Prenatal Pilates class should be ending soon and if I hit the 405 now, I might be able to catch her before she started her Pole Dancing for Seniors session.

After slogging through the pre- pre-rush hour traffic (Okay, fine, in L.A. the freeways always look like rush hour. But I for one choose to hold onto the hope that there does exist a small window of time where I might actually be able to get from the Citadel to the Beverly Center in under an hour. Never mind that the window is between 3 and 5 am.) I pulled my jeep into the parking lot of the Sunset Gym, a huge concrete and glass structure that housed an Olympic sized swimming pool, seven racquetball courts, and its very own Starbucks. I declined the valet parking, figuring the thirty second walk from my car to the gym could count as my exercise for the day.

The front counter today was manned by none other than Dana's latest ex-boyfriend, No Neck Guy. No Neck had been one of Dana's many roommates at the Studio City duplex she shared with a handful of other actor slash personal trainers. They'd been hot and heavy for about two weeks before Dana caught No Neck hitting on one of the gym patrons. He claimed he was just measuring the size of her pecs, but even Dana didn't buy that one. She gave him the dreaded don't-call-me-I'll-call-you and put an ad in the Penny Saver for a new roomie. Currently residing in No Neck's old bedroom at the Actor's Duplex was Stick Figure Girl, who, rumor had it, had just landed a gig as Lindsay Lohan's body double.

I fished my gym ID out from the deep recesses of my purse (shoved beneath a Snickers bar and an empty M&M's wrapper) and gave No Neck a little wave before scanning the main floor for Dana. I finally found her in one of the group classrooms, leading a handful of pregnant women in cool-down stretches. I did a quick check to make sure I didn't still have strawberry milkshake breath, as the women waddled out and Dana jogged toward me, bottle of vitamin water in tow.

"Hey, what's up?" she asked, taking a long sip. "You here for my pole dancing class?"

"Oh, gee, I left my stripper clothes at home."

Dana ignored my sarcasm. "Come on, it's awesome on your glutes."

"Maybe next time. I just ate." Two hours ago.

Dana narrowed her eyes at me. "Are those French fry crumbs on your shirt?"

Self-consciously, I wiped at my top.

"Maddie, I thought we agreed you were going to take better care of your body. Do you know how bad French fries are for you? They're like injecting fat right in your veins."

I did a deep sigh. "I'll come in tomorrow and do sit-up penance."

"Promise?"

Reluctantly I nodded, feeling my stomach muscles clench around my Quarter Pounder in protest.

"So," Dana said, sipping her water, "if you're not here for pole dancing, what's up?"

"I was wondering if you still have the number of that guy you dated at the phone company."

"Verizon Ted? Yeah, sure. Why?"

I filled Dana in on my freaky phone message and subsequent calling quest as she downed the rest of her vitamin water, her eyes growing bigger as I talked.

"So you think he was shot?" she asked when I'd finished.

I bit my lip. "I don't know."

"I bet it was the Mob. Those Mob guys are all up in Vegas." Dana bobbed her head up and down for emphasis.

"It wasn't the Mob."

"Rico told me the Mob uses forty-five caliber Berettas for all their executions. Did it sound like a forty-five?"

Mental eye roll. "Look, I don't even really know if he was shot. I just think... well, it might warrant a phone call to the police to check it out. Providing I can give them some idea where to check."

Dana shrugged. "Okay, sure. I'll call Verizon Ted right after my pole dancing class and see if he can get us an address."

"Thanks." I handed Dana the numbers as she downed the rest of her vitamin water and trotted off to the group of eighty year old stripper-wanna-bes. I shuddered. Mostly because as they started dancing to the tune of 'I'm Too Sexy' I realized they were more limber than I was even after three margaritas. Depressing thought.

* * *

After seeing Dana I felt just a little guilty about my zillion calorie lunch and decided to do better for dinner. I made a quick stop at the Magic Happy Time Noodle for a double order of moo shoo chicken (chicken was a lean meat, right?) with rice noodles ('cause who can get fat eating rice?) before heading back home to my studio.

As I followed the trail of red brake lights down the 405, I tried calling the two Larry's one more time for good measure. Same thing. Ringing at the first and that mechanical voice at number two. I thought about leaving a message, but I still didn't quite know what to say. Instead I did a fast hang up before the machine kicked in and hoped that Verizon Ted was in a good mood tonight.

I pulled up to my building, parking my Jeep on the street, and started up the steps to my studio, fragrant bags of Chinese food in hand. I was halfway up the stairs when the hairs on the back of my neck pricked up, and I had the oddest sensation of being watched. I slowly turned around and scanned the street, my eyes immediately narrowing in on a blue Dodge Neon with a dented fender parked in front of the building next door. I couldn't be sure it was the same one that had been tailgating Dana and I the day before, but since there where probably only two people in the entire L.A. basin that would be caught dead driving a blue Dodge Neon, I figured it was an odd coincidence.

I walked back down the stairs, doing a causal stroll thing along the sidewalk toward the car. I was a couple of feet away when it suddenly roared to life, squealing away from the curb like some bad cop movie from the seventies. I only got the vaguest glimpse of the driver, just enough to tell it was a guy, before he disappeared down the street, taking the corner so fast his tail spun out behind him.

If I'd believed in coincidences, I'd have said that was a doozy. Even though Mr. Neon was gone, I suddenly felt very exposed standing out in the open. I took the stairs two at a time up to my studio and locked the door behind me. Just for good measure (and because I've seen way too many teen horror flicks) I checked under the futon, behind the bathroom door and in the closet. Predictably no boogie men in waiting. Which, of course, made me realize how foolish I was being. The Neon probably belonged to my neighbor's son. Probably how fast he pulled away from the curb had nothing to do with the fact I was approaching him. Probably it was a totally different car I'd seen following Dana and me.

But I still felt I should probably keep my door locked and my Ginsu knife handy while I ate my take-out. Just in case. (Hey, I'm no dummy. The blonde always dies first in those horror movies.)

After I polished off my Chinese in record time, I spent the rest of the evening doing half hearted sketches of the Rainbow Brite jellies in between calling the Larry numbers again. And again. With the same results each time. I hoped Dana was getting along better with Verizon Ted. Finally after Letterman I did one more round of calls before calling it a night myself. I pulled out my futon and fell into a restless sleep, visions of the Mob al la Ray Liotta invading my dreams.

* * *

I could swear I'd only been asleep for five minutes when the sound of my door being pounded down woke me. Only when I cracked one eye open the sun was up and my digital clock read 7:13 AM. I groaned as another knock sounded. What was it with morning people?

Reluctantly, I rolled over, throwing off my sheets and shuffling in that half-asleep-half-awake zombie walk of those who have stayed up much too late gorging on take-out.

"Coming," I called as Mr. Impatience threatened to rattle my door off its hinges again.

I squinted one half-opened eye at the peep hole.

The sight that greeted me woke me up faster than any grande mocha latte ever could. Dark, tussled hair. Dark eyes with one small scar cutting across his left eyebrow. Tightly set jaw, dusted with sexy day-old stubble and that black T-shirt fairly painted onto a body that instantly made me feel like a dog in heat.

Ramirez.

CHAPTER THREE

Oh, shit! I immediately recoiled from the door as if he could see me through the little peephole. My gaze whipped around my apartment. Clothes on the floor, empty take-out cartons on the counters, lipstick, mascara and drawing pencils scattered everywhere – not exactly Martha Stewart ready for visitors. I hated people who showed up unannounced almost as much as I hated morning people.

Maybe if I stood really still he'd think I wasn't home and come back later. Like, after I'd had a chance to straighten up. I did a quick sniff test of my person. Ugh. And a shower.

"I know you're in there, Maddie. Your Jeep's out front."

Damn. I guess he didn't make detective for nothing.

"Open the door Maddie, or I'll have to break it down."

I was 99% sure that was a bluff. But from the way he was pounding, I didn't think it wise to risk the 1%. Reluctantly, I slipped off the security chain and opened the door.

For a full two seconds we both just stood there staring at each other. He was wearing his trademark faded jeans, work boots, and gun-bulge tucked at his side. A tattoo of a panther flirted with me from beneath the sleeve of his shirt and his dark eyes did a slow sweep of my body that made me very aware I hadn't brushed my teeth yet this morning. I did a dry gulp thing while I tried to decide if I hated him for not calling or loved him for finally showing up on my doorstep.

Finally he broke the silence. "Nice outfit." The corner of his mouth jerked up into a half smile.

I looked down. Just my luck he'd show up the day I throw on yellow duck pajamas.

"Thanks," I said with as much dignity as a grown woman wearing duckies could.

"Can I come in?"

I stepped back, hesitating only a minute. The way we'd last left things was somewhere in that vast limbo land of maybe-relationships. I mean, he'd seen me one inch from naked, and I already knew his condom size. We weren't exactly strangers. Though the fact he hadn't called me in weeks didn't exactly make us a hot item either.

So I opted for a cool, casual air of indifference, leaning against my kitchen counter and crossing my arms over my ducky jammies as I pretended his sexy stubble and Russell Crowe build had no effect on me whatsoever.

"So what are you doing here?" I squeaked out, wishing my voice was just a wee bit better at pretending.

"You didn't return my call."

"Me? *Me*? *Me*!" I sputtered. "I haven't heard from you in weeks!"

He shrugged. "I've been busy."

I narrowed my eyes at him. "Too busy to make a piddley little phone call?"

"Work." He spit out the single syllable then tightened his jaw, doing his silent cop routine. I imagined it was a really effective look for interrogating a suspect, but it wasn't winning him any brownie points with me.

"Uh-huh. And so, what, your schedule just suddenly freed up this morning so you thought you'd pop over and harass me about my choice of sleepwear?"

"You know, you're kind of grumpy in the morning."

My eyes narrowed into fine slits. "You should see me after coffee. I really hit my stride then."

He grinned, his face creasing into his big bad wolf smile. The one that made me worry my panties might be across the room with one little huff and puff. I shifted my stance, reminding myself this was the man who had driven me to *Joanie Loves Chachi*.

"Actually," he said. "I took a personal day. Someone," he gave me a pointed look, "left a message about gun shots and dead bodies on my voicemail. Kind of makes a guy worry. Especially knowing you."

"Ha, ha. Very funny. It was one boob, okay? I popped one freaking implant and suddenly I'm Calamity Jane."

His mouth quirked up again. "Why don't you just tell me about this phone call, huh?"

I hesitated. Yes, I had called him in the first place, but this whole smirky slash sexy slash casual-and-not-even-hinting-at-the-fact-we'd-been-nearly-naked-together thing he had going on was starting to irritate me.

But the way I saw it, I had two options. One, tell him to go to hell for not calling once in six weeks, then having the nerve to show up while I'm in ducky jammies. Or two, swallow my pride, make a pot of coffee, and play the message for him. (I ignored the voice in my head screaming to go with option three, jump his bones right here and now, you idiot! Before he disappears again for God knows how long.)

As much as telling him to go to hell sounded fun, I figured option two was the most productive. So, I set my Mr. Coffee to perk, tossed in some French roast, and played Ramirez the message.

He listened with his unreadable cop face in place. I bit my lip, half hoping he'd say it was obviously a car backfiring even though the more I listened to it the more likely Dana's theory of forty-five Berettas was seeming.

"So?" I asked. "What do you think?"

He sat down on my futon and rubbed a hand over his face. "He said his name was Larry on the tape. Larry what?"

"Springer. Why?"

Ramirez did a deep sigh, his face still a solid wall of Bad Cop. "Nothing. Look, it's probably a prank phone call."

"But we should check it out, right?"

"We?" He gave me a look like I'd just proposed a June wedding, all trace of his previous humor gone. "No, *you* shouldn't check out anything. If you hear from him again, have the police check it out."

"But if he's dead, he can't very well call again. Don't you think someone should investigate?"

"Someone, maybe. You, definitely not."

I was beginning to take this personally.

"I already have his number narrowed down to two possible Larry Springers in Vegas." I showed him my list. "Dana's checking addresses for me."

"Addresses?!" Ramirez's volume shot up about three notches. "Wait, you're not actually thinking of going to Vegas to look for this guy, are you?"

"Well, I hadn't really thought about it, but he is my fa-"

"No! No, no, no, no," Ramirez stood up, shaking his head. "You are staying right here. Look, if that is a gunshot on that tape, I don't want you getting involved. The Vegas PD will handle it. I absolutely forbid you from setting foot in Las Vegas."

I blinked. "*Forbid* me?"

Okay, so here's the thing: I hadn't, in fact, been planning a Vegas trip. As much as the thought of my father lying dead in a ditch bothered me, I wasn't exactly ready to come face to face with the man who had abandoned me without so much as a birthday card for the last twenty-six years. I'd figured once I had a couple of addresses for the police to check out, I would hand the whole thing over to the Las Vegas cops and hope for the best. But the sight of Ramirez towering over me, having the unmitigated gall to forbid me to do anything after pulling a disappearing act for the last six weeks had visions of blackjack tables dancing in my eyes.

"I'm sorry, did you just say you *forbid* me from going to Vegas?"

Ramirez rubbed a hand over his face and muttered a curse. "I am *asking* you very *nicely* to stay home. And since I'm a police officer, I think you might want to listen to me."

"Well, I'd say that since the message is on *my* machine, it is *my* father who called, and last time I checked it wasn't illegal to visit one's own father, I can pretty well decide if I'm going to Vegas or not all by myself."

"I'm warning you, Maddie…"

"Warning me?" I took a step closer, jutting my chest out in a display of mock bravery. "And what exactly are you going to do to stop me?"

He grabbed me by the shoulders. He looked me square in the eye. Then he planted his lips on mine.

For about half a second I was in total shock. I'd like to say I pushed him off, smacked him across the face as I'm pretty sure he deserved, and told him where he could stick his 'warning.' But considering I'd been practicing unintentional celibacy longer than any woman should have to, I melted into a puddle of spineless jelly instead. I suddenly really, really wished I'd had the presence of mind to wear some sexy negligee to bed last night.

Once he'd thoroughly engaged my hormones into overdrive, he stepped back, giving me the puppy dog eyes. "Maddie, please stay away from Las Vegas."

"No fair."

He grinned.

"That was a really dirty trick." I cleared my throat. "And I'm not falling for it." Much.

Ramirez sighed, shaking his head at me. "Okay, tell you what, I'll make a couple of calls to the Vegas PD. If anything turns up, I'll let you know. Okay?"

"Now you're just trying to humor me, aren't you?"

He did that sigh thing again. "A little."

"It's the duckies, right? They make me seem a little crazy, right?"

"No, honey, you do that all on your own."

I did a straight-arm point toward the door. "Out. I have to brush my teeth."

Ramirez sighed and shook his head again. "Look, just promise me you won't go to Vegas, Maddie?"

I fixed him with my best imitation of my Irish Catholic grandmother's evil eye. "Promise me you'll call?"

To which I got nothing but his cop face in return.

"That's what I thought."

And I'm proud to say that at that, I did, in fact, slam the door. Hard enough to rattle my front window in its frame.

Men. One minute they have their tongues down your throat and the next they're forbidding you from meeting your own father and criticizing your fashion choices. Forbid this, pal! I aimed a really unladylike hand gesture at the door.

I poured myself another cup of coffee, hoping the French roast would wipe the memory of Ramirez's kiss out of my mouth, and dialed Dana's cell.

"Hey," I said when she answered. "You busy?"

"I'm on my way to an audition for a baby food commercial. Why, what's up?"

"Did you get a hold of Verizon Ted last night?"

"Uh-huh. I'm actually just leaving his place," Dana said, giggling into the phone.

Great, was everyone getting some except me?

"And?"

"Did I ever tell you about that thing Ted does with his tongue when we-"

"What about the phone numbers?" I said, breaking off before I started to regret sending Ramirez away.

"Oh. Right. Uh… hang on a sec." I heard Dana flipping through her Day Runner. "Here they are. Ted gave me addresses for both numbers. One in Henderson and the other in south Vegas. You think we should call the police now?"

Actually, I'd had it with police that morning. Sure, that would be the logical thing to do. But if I had one more snide man with a badge humor me I think I was going to pop a blood vessel. Besides, after my encounter with Ramirez it was a wake up call that this was the sort of thing the cops would laugh at behind their donuts and coffee. They weren't going to take a maybe gun shot reported from a hundred miles away any more seriously than Ramirez took a lady in duck pajamas. If my dad really was in trouble, I had a feeling that by the time the cops got around to finding him, it would be too late.

"Dana, what does your schedule look like for the next couple of days?" I asked.

More Day Runner flipping. "I've got a class with Rico tonight – Your Body, the Ultimate Weapon."

Luckily Dana couldn't see my eye roll this time.

"But I'm pretty much free tomorrow. Why?"

I took a deep breath. Did I really want to do this? I weighed the idea of coming face to face with the man who'd been largely myth my whole life versus letting Ramirez think he could actually 'warn' me off. I scrunched my eyes up tight and hoped I was doing the right ting.

"Wanna go to Vegas with me?"

Dana did a high pitched squeal on the other end that I'm sure had every dog from here to San Diego howling in protest. "Ohmigod, road trip!"

I held the phone away from my ear. "I'll take that as a yes."

"Yes, totally! It's been like, forever since I went to Vegas. Last time I was there was for that Lil Dawg music video, and we totally spent the whole time out in the desert, and I didn't even get to play like one slot machine. Ohmigod, this is going to be so fun. I'm like totally bringing all my laundry quarters. I heard they even have slot machines in the gas stations, Maddie. The gas stations!"

"Meet me here tomorrow. Say nine?"

"Totally!" Dana yelled. "Vegas, baby! Ohmigod!"

Oh, my God was right. I just hoped I could do this.

* * *

As soon as I hung up, I booted up my laptop and scanned Cheap Rates dot com for a hotel room. I did an eenie meenie minie mo between the Venetian and the New York - New York. In the end, the $69.99 a night room special at the New York won out. I booked a double before I could change my mind. I then spent the rest of the morning cleaning my apartment (in case any other uninvited visitors showed up) and trying not to think about the look on Mom's face when I told her I was going to meet Larry. I was starting to feel bad about the way I'd left things with her, both of us squaring off like stubborn little Napoleons. And I did feel kind of sneaky taking off for Vegas without even telling her. So, after a lunch of a fairly healthy peanut butter (lots of protein, right?) and potato chip (potatoes are vegetables, which are totally healthy) sandwich, I hopped into my Jeep and made the trip back into Beverly Hills.

Marco was in the reception area when I walked in, stringing a row of plastic grapes across his desk.

"Ciao bella," he sing-songed as I walked in. "What do you think? Tuscany Chic?"

I nodded. "Very nice."

Marco beamed.

"Hey, is my mom around?" I asked, giving a wary glance to the back room.

"Sorry, doll, she and Fernando just went to lunch," he answered.

Chicken that I am, I breathed a little sigh of relief.

"Would you mind giving her a message when she gets back?"

"Sure thing, dahling." Marco pulled out a grape shaped pad of paper. "Shoot."

I filled Marco in on my search for Larry Springer, the Houdini of dads, and my upcoming trip to Vegas. When I mentioned where I was staying he did a deep, wistful sigh that could have earned him a Tony on Broadway.

"I always wanted to go to New York."

"Hmm. Well, it's actually in Vegas."

Marco gave me a blank stare. Sometimes Marco had a problem distinguishing fantasy from reality.

"Any-hoo," I continued, "If you could just give my mom the message. And tell her that she can call if she, well, wants to talk or anything…" I trailed off.

Marco patted my hand. "Don't worry, honey. I'll break it to her gently."

I thanked him and left, trying not to picture how tightly Mom's lips would clamp once she found out. But, with any luck, I'd be on the road by then.

* * *

I made a quick detour on the way home, stopping at the Beverly Center for the perfect I'm-going-to-meet-my-dad-for-the-first-time outfit on the chance that a) we did find him, b) he wasn't shot or wounded or… worse, and c) I actually had the courage to go up and introduce myself to him. That last thing was kind of a long shot considering my past record of chickenhood, but I figured I'd play the Girl Scout and be prepared.

Only for the first time in my life, I hadn't a clue what to wear.

As a kid I'd always fantasized about the kind of person my dad might be. When I was six I was certain that he'd left Mom and me to join the circus as a lion tamer. He was brave, strong, and loved animals – an all around great guy if you ignored the fact he'd left his family behind.

By the time I was ten he'd moved on to an illustrious career as a CIA spy, the kind that spent his life overseas drinking martinis that were shaken and not stirred. I figured that was a really good reason for not sending your daughter a birthday card, because of course, if I knew where he was, I'd be in danger. Really he was staying away for my own protection.

When I turned fifteen I was absolutely certain my father was Billy Idol. Of course he couldn't be there helping me with my homework; he was touring the world with his rock band, which everyone knows was no place for kids. Poor Billy. I think I sent him a copy of every one of my high school report cards.

But now, by the age of twenty… somethingish… I had finally accepted the reality that my father was just a jerk who had abandoned his family to get it on with a showgirl.

A jerk I was driving to Vegas to meet tomorrow.

I bit my lip as I stared at a pair of Jimmy Choo slingbacks in teal green. Yet somehow I still wanted him to have the perfect impression of his little girl. I wondered if I should make some more copies of the report cards.

A first for me, I walked away from the Beverly Center empty handed. Instead, I swung by the local Auto Club and picked up a map of Las Vegas before heading home.

I was happy to find only one message waiting for me at my studio. Blockbuster was still on me about not returning *Joanie Loves Chachi*. Yeah, like they had a long wait list for that one.

Instead, I popped it in my DVD player, losing myself in puppy love instead of thinking about what might be waiting for me in the desert tomorrow.

* * *

At seven-o-one I was awakened by a beeping sound that rivaled Mariah Carey's last album in the shrill department. I bounced out of bed, arms flailing, wild bed hair whipping around my face as I fought through my sleep haze for the source. Fire? I blinked a couple times. Didn't smell smoke. I finally realized it was my alarm clock. The one I'd set the night before. I smacked the damn thing with the palm of my hand, thinking for the hundredth time just how wrong it was that mornings had to start so early.

I dragged myself out of bed, made a couple thousand pots of coffee and took a long, hot shower, trying to work the sleepless kinks out of my neck. I threw on a pair of jeans and a long sleeved, white DKNY logo top and my favorite pair of Gucci boots. The ones with the supple black leather finish and teeny tiny hand stitching along the top that only the most discerning eye (which of course, mine was) could see. By the time Dana arrived, knocking on my front door, I was feeling human again and had almost lost my sarcastic morning edge.

I opened the door and took in her outfit. "Who threw up on you last night?"

Hey, I said almost.

Dana was dressed in a classic A-line skirt, black pumps and a white blouse. Covered with green and orange stains.

"Baby food commercial," Dana said, trudging into my apartment. "I had to audition with five different munchkins yesterday, all of whom, apparently, have an aversion to carrots and peas. Got anything to eat?" Dana started going through my cupboards.

"And you're still wearing it because…?"

"I spent the night at Rico's last night. After the audition I needed to get a little aggression out so he met me at the gun range." She paused, scrunching up her nose at my Cap'n Crunch and frosted Pop Tarts. "You know how much refined sugar is in these things?"

"Tons."

She shrugged and put them back on the shelf, taking out a box of Wheat Thins and popping a couple in her mouth as she talked. "Anyway, Rico asked me if I wanted to see his private collection…"

Rico, the master of the double entendre. I did a mental eye roll.

"… and of course I said yes."

"Of course."

"And one thing led to another, and I haven't had time to go home and change yet. You mind if we swing by my place on the way out of town?"

"Fine with me."

After another cup of coffee – which Dana insisted on after the puke comment – we were ready to go. I was giving my studio a last once over for locked windows and irons in the off position when a sound like a dying goose singing Cabaret erupted outside my building. Dana and I rushed onto the porch.

"Hell-oooo dahlings!"

I blinked. Marco was at the wheel of a nineteen sixties mint condition Mustang convertible, sea foam green with white tires. He had on big Donna Karan sunglasses and a scarf tied over his hair circa Miss Hepburn's black and white days. An effect that would have been a tad more classic if he hadn't paired it with a rainbow striped turtleneck and leather pants.

"Are we ready to road trip, girls?"

Dana looked at me, raising one eyebrow. I shrugged.

"Uh, I didn't know you were coming with us," I finally said.

"Well, I just couldn't let the opportunity to go to New York pass me up, now could I?"

Dana raised the other eyebrow at me. More shrugging on my part.

"Don't worry," Marco plowed on, "you'll hardly know I'm there. Besides, I told your mom a much better story than the one you gave me. You're going on a weekend getaway to Palm Springs with that hunky cop. So, shall we?"

I stood there with my mouth hanging open. He'd lied to my mom? I had to admit, though, it was a pretty good lie. Half of me kind of wished I'd come up with it myself.

And he had a point. Mom would be much happier with this version. But, most of all what he had was a nineteen sixties vintage Mustang convertible. What girl could resist the allure of riding through the desert al la vintage starlet?

"Let's get a move on," Mizz Hepburn called from the front seat, "traffic's backing up on the 10 already." He punctuated this by laying on the horn, bringing the singing goose back from the dead again.

"On one condition," I said.

"Yes?" Marco raised his shades.

"Don't touch that horn again."

"Fine, fine." He turned to Dana. "Geeze, she's a little pissy in the morning, huh?"

I gave him the evil eye.

* * *

Two hours later we'd stopped at Dana's for a change of clothes, and at Starbucks for a grande mocha latte that Dana insisted I needed after I threatened to castrate Marco if he played one more Madonna CD.

I sipped in silence as we drove through La Puente and Ontario, finally merging onto the 15 north as we left the city behind us for Joshua trees, sagebrush and the occasional trailer park. We stopped in Barstow for lunch, and I felt only minimally guilty watching Dana eat her fat-free protein bar and fruit smoothie as I wolfed down a Big Mac and fries. And a chocolate shake. And two apple pies. But, everyone knows that traveling calories don't count, right?

As we were merging back onto the freeway I was settling nicely into my fast-food coma when I caught a flash of blue behind a semi-truck to our right. I whipped my head around, that weird tingling sensation breaking out on my neck again. I could swear I saw the dented front bumper of a Dodge Neon disappear behind the truck as we merged into the fast lane.

"Did you see that?" I asked.

"What?" Dana craned her neck.

"A blue Neon. Back there."

"No." Dana shook her head. "Why?"

I bit my lip. I had a sinking suspicion I was becoming paranoid. "Nothing."

Marco peered at me in the rearview mirror. "You okay?" he asked.

"Fine. Dandy. Just peachy," I lied. I peeked behind me again. Just in time to see the Neon dart out from behind the semi truck, exiting the freeway at a rest stop on the right.

I stifled a gasp.

Things had officially just been upgraded from coincidence to creepy.

CHAPTER FOUR

I spent the rest of the trip glancing over my shoulder every three minutes to check for my stalker. No further sign of him. But the tingling sensation on the back of my neck stayed with me all the way up the 15, right into Las Vegas.

"Welcome to Sin City, girls!" Marco said, fairly bouncing out of his seat with giddiness as we exited the freeway onto Las Vegas Boulevard. We crawled past the Excalibur castle and Luxor pyramid, almost crashing into the white limo in front of us when Marco spotted the New York - New York skyline.

"Ohmigod, ohmigod, there she is, Lady Liberty herself," he cried, clutching his hands to his heart.

"Honey, you do know that's not the real Statue of Liberty, right?" Dana asked.

But Marco ignored her, his eyes glazing over as we took a left on Tropicana and pulled up to the front. "Oh, look! The Brooklyn Bridge, New York harbor! It's just like I always imagined it."

Dana and I did a synchronized eye roll.

Marco handed his keys over to the valet in a red uniform, and Dana and I grabbed our carry-on sized bags. Marco reached into the backseat and pulled out a huge, leopard print suitcase big enough to fit a small child.

"How much did you pack?" I asked.

Marco blinked at me. "Honey, this is just my overnight bag." He popped the trunk to reveal three more matching leopard printed pieces of luggage.

Mental forehead smack.

Eventually (after Marco huffed and puffed his luggage onto a rolling cart) we made our way through the lobby. The air was thick with dinging slot machines, cigarette smoke and the occasional holler of "jackpot!" There were no windows in the casino, and it could have been two in the afternoon or two in the morning for all I could tell. The place was packed with an assortment of people ranging from tourists in t-shirts that read 'I heart the Hoover Dam' to women in slinky (bordering on slutty) cocktail dresses and heels. It was like entering another dimension where time, space and tasteful attire did not exist.

The art deco registration counter stood at our left, and after walking through the roped off lines of baggage toting gamblers, we were met by a tall, slim guy with bad acne and a name tag that read, 'Jim.'

"Welcome to New York," Slim Jim said as we approached. Mainly talking to Dana's boobs.

"Ohmigod, did you hear that? His accent is even New York," Marco whispered to me, bouncing up and down on his toes. I didn't have the heart to tell him it was Jersey.

"Maddie Springer," I said. "I have a reservation." I slid my credit card along the counter to Jim. He took it, giving it a cursory glance before returning to his staring match with Dana's chest.

Luckily Dana was too busy salivating over the video poker machines to notice.

Slim Jim did a few clicks on his keyboard. "Yes, I have you down for a non-smoking double, checking out on Wednesday."

I nodded. I hoped that three days was enough time to track Larry down and help with whatever kind of trouble had him leaving gunshots on my answering machine. "We'd like to add a second room, too, please," I said, glancing at Marco and his matching luggage set.

"All right," the Slim Jim said. More clicking. "We have one Marquis suite available on the fifteenth floor."

"Perfect!" Marco clapped his hands together.

Slim Jim smiled. "First time in New York?"

"Don't encourage him," I pleaded.

"Okay, the Marquis will be $495 a night."

Marco stopped bouncing.

"Excuse me?" I choked out.

"Sorry," Slim Jim said, shrugging his bony shoulders. "It's all we have. Bette Midler's performing in the Cabaret Theater this week. We always fill our, uh…" He paused, leaning in close to do a pseudo whisper thing, "…low rent rooms when Bette's in town."

"Ohmigod, ohmigod!" Marco grabbed my arm, his painted black fingernails digging into me. "Bette Milder is here?! I think I'm going to faint. Catch me."

Neither Dana nor I moved.

"I could order a rollaway for your room if you like," Jim offered.

While the idea of sharing a room with the divine Mizz M himself wasn't exactly in my plans, unless I suddenly hit the mega bucks jackpot it was all we could afford. "Fine we'll take the rollaway."

"Okay, here you are. Room 1205, up the Chrysler elevators at the back of the casino and to your right. Enjoy your stay and," he said, clearly addressing Dana's cleavage, "please let me know if there's *anything* else I can do to make your stay more enjoyable."

I grabbed the keys, and Dana and I hightailed it up to our room before Slim Jim stared a hole through her shirt. Marco trailed behind, stopping to stare at a 'street performer' doing *New York State of Mind* on his tenor sax.

* * *

Once we'd huffed our luggage the entire length of the casino (dotted with fake trees, fountains and twinkling lights to look like Central Park) we rode the elevators up to our room and drew straws for the rollaway. Dana lost, grabbing the shortest swizzle stick from the mini bar. She started unpacking while Marco went to the 'little girl's room' to freshen up. I called home to check my messages on the off chance Larry might have called again. No such luck.

The first message was from Mom. She was glad I had let the Larry thing go and hoped I was having a fun time in Palm Springs. I felt just the teeny tiniest prick of Catholic guilt niggling at me. Especially since part of me (the part that hadn't seen any action in so long Scott Baio looked good) kind of wished I was on a getaway with Ramirez. I mean, he did come running at the first indication I might need his help. And as much as I hated to admit it that kiss had been kind of nice. Okay, fine. It had been *really* nice. Nice enough that I was starting to fantasize about a Palm Springs getaway for real. Me, Ramirez, sunny blue skies, a sparkling swimming pool, him in tiny little swimming trunks. Or better yet, no trunks at all…

Only before my wandering libido could get to the good part of that fantasy, my machine clicked over to the next message.

"Maddie? Where the hell are you?"

Mr. Tiny Trunks himself. Ramirez. And he didn't sound too happy.

"I'm outside your apartment right now, and you're not here," he said, his voice doing that tightly restrained growl thing. "Please tell me you're just out getting your hair done or your lip waxed or something."

My hand immediately went to my lip. What did he mean 'lip waxed'? Was I really growing a mustache? I scrutinized my upper lip in the reflection of the brass lampshade.

"Look, call me when you get this, Maddie. I mean it." Clearly an order. Not a suggestion.

I thought about calling him back. For about half a second. I mean, who did he think he was? He'd gone for six whole weeks without calling *me* back. Besides, that wax comment hit below the belt.

I deleted the message, still smooshing my face around in the lampshade reflection, checking for dark hairs.

"Dana, give it to me straight, do I have a mustache?"

Dana paused, pulling a pair of running sneakers from her suitcase. "Of course not."

I squinted at my reflection. "I mean, you'd tell me if I did, right? You wouldn't let me walk around looking like Groucho Marx, would you?"

"Groucho who?" Dana gave me a blank stare.

"You know, that guy with the glasses and the big nose."

"Maddie, your nose is totally not big."

"Mrs. Rosenblatt said I had 'dust' on my upper lip."

Dana put her hands on her hips. "Mrs. Rosenblatt says she sees dead people."

She had a point.

I gave it up, watching Dana unpack instead. She pulled three gym suits out of her bag. Then a curling iron, jumbo can of hairspray and a cell phone.

"Oooo, stylin' phone, honey," Marco said, skipping out of the bathroom. "Is this one of those streaming video ones? I so want one of these."

I narrowed my eyes at the cell. It didn't have Dana's usual pink polka-dotted skins. Uh-oh. Wasn't that…

"Marco, put it down-"

But I was too late. Marco did a little gurgling sound; then his eyes rolled back in his head and he hit the ground.

"Dana!" I yelled, falling to Marco's side. I felt for a pulse.

"Don't worry. It's just a little jolt. He'll be fine." Dana picked up the cell, pushing a red button and buzzing the stun gun to life. "See? Rico said it's virtually harmless."

Virtually being the key word here. Marco's pulse was steady but a little stream of drool was forming at the side of his mouth.

"What were you thinking bringing that thing?" I yelled. I slapped Marco's cheeks to wake him up. His head kind of lolled to the side, his tongue falling out like a golden retriever's.

"Uh, hello?" Dana answered, doing her best 'well duh' face at me. "Your dad was shot by the Mob! I couldn't pick up my LadySmith for another seven days so this was the best I could do."

I closed my eyes. I counted to ten. I did a little prayer to Saint… well, okay, I couldn't honestly remember one saint from the next as I'd been pretty preoccupied in Sunday school by Bobby Tanner who sat two seats in front of me, bore an uncanny resemblance to Kirk Cameron, and wore his Dad's Old Spice at age twelve. But I was pretty sure there was a saint somewhere that granted patience to those whose best friends insisted on carrying concealed weapons around in their purses.

"Dana, just put that thing away, okay?"

She shrugged. "Fine. But I'd think you'd be glad one of us thought of bringing protection." Dana tucked the cell back into her purse. "We're talking about the Mob, Maddie."

I enunciated very slowly. "There is no more Mob in Las Vegas."

Dana shook her head. "Maddie, you are so naive."

I searched my brain for a comeback to that but was spared the need as Marco started to come around.

"Uh appen oo ee," he mumbled, his tongue still lolling to one side.

"You zapped yourself with Dana's stun gun."

"Uhn un?" His eyes grew wide. "What uhn un?"

I helped him into a sitting position as he slowly jerked his limbs back to life and wiped the drool from his chin. Dana got him a glass of water from the bathroom, and after ten minutes of rapid blinking and twitching, he was almost back to normal. Well, as normal as Marco got.

"Is my mascara running?" he asked.

I decided it was kinder to lie. "Nope. You look great."

"I changed my mind. I so do *not* want one of those."

That made two of us.

* * *

Once Marco recovered enough to stand he decided he needed to walk it off. Preferably in the Soho Village shopping center downstairs. As tempting as that sounded, I was anxious to start crossing Larry's off our list.

I made Dana leave the stun gun in the room, and we got back into the sea foam Mustang. The first Larry on our list was L. Springer who lived in South Vegas and apparently didn't believe in answering machines.

South Vegas was populated with apartment and condo complexes with spas, swimming pools, and more palm trees than Florida. We pulled up to a gated complex in a muted orange, dotted with palm trees, birds of paradise and two bubbling fountains.

Unfortunately our L. Springer turned out to be Luanna Springer, a black woman with the longest, most intricately painted nails I had ever seen. She said she worked at Wynn's as a cocktail waitress and had never heard of "this Larry dude." Apart from the name of her manicurist, Dana and I came away empty handed.

We pulled back onto the 15, going north until we merged on the 215 toward Vegas's nearest and dearest suburb, Henderson. Henderson was one new, dusty beige housing development after another, punctuated by the occasional strip mall and Home Depot center. We passed by two parks, both with fields of perfectly green grass that must have been watered ten times a day to grow that uniformly in the desert. The road was dotted with mini vans and SUV's full of car seats, and khaki seemed to be the fashion color of choice. All in all, the perfect family neighborhood. (I'm sure I don't need to add there was no sign of the Mob anywhere. I think Dana was a little disappointed.)

We turned onto Arroyo Grande, and into the Desert Sands Oasis housing development. We took a right on Warm Sands road, then wound around to Hidden Sands Court, going left onto Sand Storm Way, and finally pulling up to 319 Sand Hill Lane. It was a nondescript two story stucco in pale taupe colors that looked like – you guessed it – sand. The yard held a rock garden, punctuated by tall grasses and low maintenance succulents sprouting tiny pink flowers.

I stared. The house looked exactly like the kind of place that bred soccer moms and big wheels. It didn't fit my image of either CIA Dad or Rock Star Dad. It looked more suited to Family Guy Dad. Which begged the question - did Larry have another family? Had he started over with a new wife once he'd left Mom and me? Worse yet… new kids? I bit my lip, my Gucci boots suddenly feeling like they were made of lead instead of Italian leather.

"You okay?" Dana asked, laying a hand on my shoulder.

No. "Fine. Great. Let's go."

Before my overactive imagination could get the better of me, I forced my feet out of the car and up the flagstone pathway to the front door. I rapped three times, steeling myself for the sight of adorable little tow-headed kids in matching jumpers.

Luckily, none appeared. Dana shifted from foot to foot beside me and rang the bell. We waited as the dull, muted sound chimed through the house. Still nothing.

"Now what?" Dana asked.

I bit my lip, trying to see past the lacey window coverings into the house. If my dad was lying dead by the phone it wasn't in the front room. What I could see of the living room dining combo was void of people, just your average oak dining set and an oversize sofa in floral patterns.

"They're not home," a voice called.

Dana and I turned around to find the man holding a garden hose in the next yard over. He was short, balding and had the skin of a shar pei. I put his age somewhere between eighty and a hundred and fifty.

"Car's not in the drive," he explained. "They always park in the driveway."

They. I bit my lip again trying not to picture those tow-headed kids.

"Do you know the people who live here well?" I asked.

He shrugged. "Just to say 'hi' to."

"We're looking for Larry Springer. Does he live here?" Dana asked.

He shook his head. "Sorry. Just a couple of gals live here." His wrinkles parted into a smile. "Real lookers. Think they're dancers or somethin'."

Dancers? My radar pricked up. As in showgirls? "Do you know their names?"

"Harriet's the blonde; she's the chunkier one. Then there's the redhead. Real tall, six footer at least, long legs. I think her name's Lila or Lana or something like that."

My heart sped up. "Could it be Lola?" As in *the* Lola?

His face broke into a smile. "Yeah, that's it. Lola."

"Any idea when they might be back?" I asked.

He shrugged. "Nope. Sorry. But I know they work nights. Like I said, I think they're both dancers."

Dana and I thanked Shar Pei Man and climbed back into the Mustang.

"I guess we'll come back in the morning?" Dana asked.

I took another long look at the house. I wasn't sure why, but I had this feeling of urgency brewing in my stomach. Like the more time I let pass the slimmer my chances of finding Larry alive were getting. Which wasn't wholly logical, but it didn't make cooling my heels in faux New York sound all that appealing.

"Maybe we could find out which club they dance at?" I said.

Dana shrugged. "Okay. So, where do we start looking for two suburban strippers?"

I shot Dana a look. "*Dancers*." I'm not sure why I was defending them except that the idea of my possible step-mommy being a stripper didn't fill me with a whole lot of good feelings.

"What about Jim," she said. "The hotel clerk. He did say he'd help with anything we needed."

I didn't think this was exactly what he had in mind. However, he did look like the kind of guy who knew where to find strip- I mean, dancers.

We flipped the Mustang around and took the 215 back into Vegas. Half an hour later we were in front of Slim Jim again. And he was once again trying to grow ex-ray vision as his eyes focused in on Dana's chest.

"We were wondering if you could tell us about a couple of dancers?" I asked. "Harriet and Lola?"

Jim grinned. "Do you have any idea how many strippers there are in Vegas?"

"*Dancers*," I emphasized.

Slim Jim grinned wider. "Right. Dancers. Look, if you're into that kind of thing," he wiggled his eyebrows up and down, "there's a club up the street. The Kit Kat Bar. Hot chicks, they'll take real good care of you there," he promised Dana's cleavage. "In fact," he continued, his eyes starting to glaze over at the thought of girl-on-girl action, "I get off in a couple of hours. I wouldn't mind showing you around."

I did an internal shudder. Even *I* wasn't that desperate. "We're looking for two specific dancers." I repeated the descriptions Shar Pei had given us. "Any idea where they might work?"

Slim Jim pursed his eyebrows together. "Actually, yeah. I think I know the redhead. Last weekend was my buddy's birthday, and we took him out to this real campy place. The Victoria Club. I don't remember the blonde, but Lola..." He did a low whistle. "Now she's hard to forget."

"The Victoria club?" I asked.

"Uh-huh." Slim Jim nodded. "I had a lot to drink that night, so I'm not totally clear on the particulars, but I know I had a good time. In fact," he said, addressing Dana's cleavage again, "I could show you girls a good time there tonight."

I'm sorry to say for a half a second Dana seemed to be considering it.

"No thanks," I jumped in quickly. "We're kind of in a hurry. Can you tell me where the club is?"

"Fremont Street, downtown," Jim answered, clearly disappointed. "Near the Neon Museum. Not the greatest part of town, but cheap drinks at least."

"Thanks."

"Always happy to help the ladies," he said as we turned away. "And, hey, say 'hi' to Lola for me!"

* * *

After we grabbed a quick sandwich at Broadway Burger (mine a double cheeseburger with lots of melted cheddar and Dana's a soy patty with sprouts that looked like it should be feeding livestock) we hopped back into the Mustang and drove up the 15, past the Strip into the downtown area, the home of Vegas's first casino, the famous smoking cowboy, Vegas Vic, and the largest number of prostitutes on the west coast.

When the mega-resorts started to crop up in the early nineties, the Strip became the face of the family friendly Vegas, and all the degenerates were rounded up and corralled north. In recent years preservationists had started a campaign to restore the historic downtown, adding a touch of glitz and neon with the Fremont street experience. But honestly it was like trying to throw sequins on Keds and pass them off as Jimmy Choos. You dress it up all you like, Fremont was still the bane of Las Vegas. Only now it had a permanent pinkish neon hue to it.

The Victoria club was clearly in the section of town that the preservationists hadn't gotten to yet. Or didn't dare set foot in. And I didn't blame them. As we turned off Fremont the first thing we saw was the flashing blue lights of a squad car blocking the road up ahead. My stomach did that lead weight thing again as I spied yellow crime scene tape and uniformed LVMPD cordoning off a section of the street. Right outside the Victoria Club.

"Uh-oh," Dana said, voicing my exact thoughts.

I took a deep breath, my stomach churning at the thought of what might be happening behind that yellow tape. Or more accurately, to whom it was happening.

Dana parked on the street about a block away from the commotion, between Annie's Escorts and a bail bonds agency. We said a silent prayer that Marco's car would still be there when we got back.

The Victoria Club itself was huge, spanning almost the full city block. It was a shiny mass of building done in art deco black and gold, trimmed with lots and lots of pink neon lighting.

A crowd of people hovered around the police barricade. Homeless guys mixed with teenagers, mixed with tourists snapping pictures with their digital cameras to show the folks back home in Kansas. A uniformed police officer stood behind the line of white barricades and yellow tape, trying to convince them all there was "nothing to see here." Which was obviously a lie, because as I pushed my way past a guy who smelled like he'd just taken a bath in Jim Beam, I got a glimpse of the pavement in front of the club. It was red. A black plastic tarp covered a suspiciously human shaped mound that was oozing red liquid all over the asphalt. I gulped down a dry swallow. Blood.

The scenery swayed in front of me, and I grasped the wooden police barrier for support as a guy in a jacket marked 'Coroner' lifted an edge of the tarp ever so slightly. All I got was one glimpse of an arm, slightly more hairy than normal, then my vision went fuzzy.

My dad.

CHAPTER FIVE

I sat down hard on the curb, taking deep breaths in and out, trying to ignore the oozing form under the tarp. Okay, so it was an arm. I mean, lots of people had hairy arms. That didn't necessarily mean it was Larry's arm, right? Right. So why was I starting to pant like a dog?

"Are you okay?" Dana asked, motioning to sit, then apparently thinking better of it as she weighed her white silk skirt against the well-traveled sidewalk.

"Uh-huh. Sure. Fine. Dandy."

"You're a terrible liar."

"So I've been told." I took another deep breath, peeking between Dana's legs at the scene on the other side of the barricade.

"I'm afraid that's… I mean it might be…" I stumbled, my mouth going Sahara on me as I tried to voice the thousand thoughts bumping through my brain.

Dana followed my gaze. "Larry?"

"Yeah." I started to do the golden retriever thing again.

Dana's forehead puckered in concern. "Hey, how about you just sit tight, and I'll see if I can find out anything, okay?"

I nodded, thankful Dana had come along with me.

She scanned the group of uniformed cops. They seemed to be growing in number. Not good. Finally she picked out one that looked like he'd started shaving yesterday. Dana adjusted her cleavage. "I'll be right back," she said, giving me a little wink before shaking her booty over to Officer Baby Face. I mentally wished her luck, carefully looking everywhere but at that black tarp.

Okay, so in all honesty, if I had really heard Larry being shot on Friday it was unlikely that his body had sat out here in front of the Victoria club for three whole days before anyone noticed. And if someone had gotten away with shooting him three days ago, it didn't make sense they'd then move the body to such a public place. So, really, the chances of that being Larry under the tarp was small, right? (Do I know how to do denial or what?)

Since I was so not looking at that tarp again, I let my gaze wander over the crowd assembled to view the gruesome entertainment. They were lining up two and three deep now to gawk and speculate at the police activity. I noticed one woman pushing forward more aggressively than the rest. A redhead. My internal radar perked up again as I watched her shove her way up to the police barricades. I couldn't see her face from where I was sitting, but I could make out a pair of white go-go boots and matching vinyl mini-skirt. And legs that were longer than the line at Starbucks on Monday morning. Lola.

I shot up from my perch on the curb. "Lola!" I shouted. Which was a mistake. The redhead jerked her gaze in my direction for about half a second before turning and shoving her way back out of the crowd. And being as she was about twice my size, she was much quicker at it than I was.

"Shit," I swore under my breath, jostling between a guy drinking from a brown paper bag and a woman in spandex and an ill-fitting wig. Fortunately, my many years of elbowing my way through after Thanksgiving clearance sales at Macy's worked to my advantage, and I'd nearly caught up with Lola when she broke free of the crowd and starting running. Cursing my choice of footwear, I bolted after her.

"Lola, wait please," I puffed, breaking into a sprint. Which, of course, she paid no attention to. Instead she did a full-on mad dash down the sidewalk, dodging pedestrians with the skill of a quarterback going for one of those big 'H' thingies at the end of the field. (Okay, I admit it. I only watch football for the guys in tight pants. So sue me.)

Half a bock later Lola's lead was increasing, and I was sweating like a fat man in July. I heaved big gulps of air in and out, wondering why all the healthy food I'd been eating lately wasn't helping me. Lola turned left at the corner, and I followed, my lungs burning as she wound down a side street.

I chased her for another half block more before I gave up. Her legs were twice as long as mine, and my heels where twice as high. There was no way I was going to catch up to her. I paused on the sidewalk, watching her disappear around another corner as I bent over at the waist gasping for air like a pack-a-day addict. That's it. I was enrolling in one of Dana's aerobics classes as soon as we got home.

I gave myself a ten second count to get my breathing under control (mostly) and walked the two blocks back to the crowd, now double its size, standing around the flashing lights and crime scene tape.

"Hey, where'd you go?" Dana asked, jogging up to me as I sat down on the curb again. I had a cramp in my side and was growing a blister on my heel. Apparently Gucci wasn't made for jogging.

"I (pant) saw (pant) Lola. (pant, pant)"

I quickly filled Dana in on my redhead chase. She agreed. I needed to get to the gym more often.

"So, what did you get out of Officer Baby Face?" I wheezed.

Dana grinned. "His phone number."

If I wasn't so tired I might have rolled my eyes. "And?"

"And that guy in the street isn't Larry."

I let out a long breath I hadn't realized I'd been holding. Spy, rock star or jerk. I guess it didn't matter. I still cared more about his well being than I wanted to admit.

"The dead guy's name," Dana continued, "is Hank Walters. He performs here at the Victoria in their salute to Hollywood act. In drag."

I raised one eyebrow.

"Uh-huh. And, get this. I asked around, and guess what Hank's stage name is?"

I shook my head.

"Harriet."

"As in Sands Hill Lane Harriet?" I glanced at the tarp again.

"That would be my guess. Officer Taylor said he died from a fall off the roof of the club. They're saying he jumped."

I looked up at the roof. Then down at the body. He must have taken a hell of a leap to land that far out from the building. "So, no gunshot wound?"

She shook her head. "Nope. None that they've found so far. The only other thing he said was that the guy was naked."

My eyebrows headed north again.

Dana shrugged. "I guess people do weird things when they're suicidal."

I watched the guy in the 'coroner' jacket place the tarp on a gurney and wheel it to his black van. I wondered if Hank slash Harriet had anything to do with the gunshot on my answering machine. Did my dad know Harriet? He must know Lola if her phone was registered under his name. And I didn't like the way Lola had run away. Not the actions of an innocent person. Innocent people stayed and talked to the police when their roommates jumped off rooftops.

Since Dana had gotten all she could out of Officer Baby Face, we decided to do a drive by of Lola's house on the off chance she'd run all the way to Henderson.

All the lights were off in the house as we idled at the curb. And the driveway was empty. Just for good measure, I jumped out and peeked in the garage windows. No car.

"What now?" Dana asked.

It was late, I was tired, and one dead body is really my limit in any given day. So, we headed back to the hotel. Besides, now that the police were on the scene, I was feeling just the teeny tiniest bit better. If Larry was in trouble, the cops would get more out of Lola than I could.

If they could catch her.

By the time we arrived at the New York - New York, Dana was still itching to try her hand at the slots. So after we valeted the Mustang, I left her feeding quarters into a video poker machine and made my way up to our room alone. Where I promptly crashed into a deep sleep, punctuated by Amazon women in white go-go boots pushing people off rooftops.

* * *

Somewhere around five A.M. I was awakened by the sound of a foghorn blaring through the room. I opened one eye, peering through the darkness. Dana was spread eagle on the rollaway, her long limbs falling off the sides. Marco was laying on his back in the other double bed, a sleep mask over his eyes that would have made him look like Zorro if it weren't powder blue and trimmed in lace.

I blinked a couple more times and realized the foghorn was Marco. Snoring. I groaned and put a pillow over my head. It didn't help. I got up and put a pillow over Marco's head. Still didn't drown out the sound. Good God, no wonder the man was still single.

I gave up and dragged myself into the shower instead. An eon under the hot water slowly woke me up, then I did a quick mousse and blow dry thing, followed by mascara and lip gloss. I added a little concealer under my eyes to mask the fact I'd been awakened before the sun, but I'm not sure it hid much. Instead I put on some extra high heels to compensate, my silver strappy sandals with the butterfly buckle, paired with a white knit dress and Bandolino jacket. When I slipped out of the room, Marco was still snoring, and Dana had fallen off the rollaway.

I made my way down to the casino level in search of food. Even at this hour the place was full of people. Some were tourists getting a jump on the day, but most were still dressed for the previous night on the town. Whoever said New York was the city that never slept hadn't been to Vegas. Vegas was the city on No-Doze.

I debated for about half a second between a protein infused fruit smoothie at the Mango Hut or the $3.99 pancake feast at the American Restaurant. In all honesty, it was a no-brainer.

After three cups of coffee and a stack of buttery, syrupy pancakes tall enough to rival the Empire State Building, I was feeling a little bit better. Funny how sugar and caffeine can do that for you.

Better that is until my purse began singing the William Tell Overture. I dug around for my cell. "Hello?"

"What the hell are you doing in Vegas?"

I cringed. Ramirez. "Having a girls only weekend?" I said. Only it came out more of a question.

"Jesus, Maddie, I ask you to do one simple thing. Couldn't you listen to me for once? Just once."

Since I obviously couldn't, I elected not to answer that. "How did you know I was in Vegas?" I asked instead.

He paused. "I didn't for sure until just now."

Great. Tricked by Bad Cop. I clenched my jaw, wondering why I thought him *not* calling was such a bad thing again.

"Well you'll be happy to know that Dana's here with me. And we can take care of ourselves. She's taken three of Rico's Urban Soldier classes."

He paused. "Is that supposed to reassure me?"

"I'm fine. She's fine. We're all fine."

"Good. Great. How about you get out of Vegas while things are still fine, huh?"

"I don't get it. What exactly do you think is going to happen to me in Vegas?"

Silence.

I got that weird prickly feeling on my neck again. "Do you know something about my dad?"

More silence.

Then Ramirez let out one of his big exasperated sighs. "Look, I just don't want to see you get hurt, Maddie." And he sounded like he was making an effort to sound sincere. A least a little one.

"I can't leave yet. I haven't found my dad. And… " I paused, not sure how much I should share about last night with Ramirez. But, I figured he was a hundred miles away, so what harm could it do? I told him about the house in Henderson, the Victoria Club jumper, and the bolting showgirl.

Ramirez muttered something on the other end in Spanish that sounded a lot like a dirty word. "Look, just humor me, okay? Go home."

"Did you even hear what I just said? There's something weird going on here."

"Has anyone ever told you, you have a serious stubborn streak?"

I narrowed my eyes at the phone. "It's one of my better qualities."

Again with the Spanish cursing.

"What? What is this Spanish stuff? What are you saying?"

"Trust me, you don't want to know."

He was right. I probably didn't.

"Listen," he said. "I'm serious. I really don't think it's safe for you to be…"

But I had stopped listening. I'd been walking aimlessly through the rows of slot machines in the Central Park casino as Ramirez argued, and I now found myself just inside the front doors of the hotel. Outside I watched a blue Dodge Neon pull up to the curb, drowning out the rest of Ramirez's speech. I quickly ducked behind a life sized cut-out of Bette Midler.

"Uh-huh," I said into the phone, my entire being focused on the Dodge.

"What do you mean, 'uh-huh'?"

I was vaguely aware of Ramirez starting up with the Spanish again, but I was too focused on the Neon to care. I watched the car park in front of the valet station. I couldn't be sure it was the same phantom I'd seen stalking me, but after last night my belief in coincidences was about as great as my belief in finding an authentic Louis Vuitton on eBay. Nada.

A sandy-haired man emerged from the Neon. He was average height, wore a pair of khaki pants with Skechers and a wrinkled white button-down that looked like he'd slept in it. He didn't look particularly dangerous. But as I'd learned last summer, looks can be deceiving.

He gave the valet his key and handed him some money. Probably not enough as the valet made a rude hand gesture behind the guy's back as he walked away.

"Maddie?" Ramirez yelled.

"Right. Sure," I said absently into the phone.

Ramirez made a growling sort of sound, and I could picture that vein starting to bulge in his neck. "Are you even listening to me?"

"Of course. Leave it alone. Go home. Yada, yada, yada."

Neon Guy started walking toward the front door. I quickly skulked into a row of slots out of sight.

"Look, I have to go. I'll call you later," I said into the phone.

"Maddie? Maddie, I swear to God if you hang up on me-" But I didn't hear any more as I quickly snapped my Motorola shut and shoved it back into my purse.

I watched Neon Guy make his way to the registration desk. I crouched down and duck-walked closer, peeking out between two Lucky Seven machines. Slim Jim was on duty again. He and Neon Guy exchanged a few words. Then Neon traded his credit card for a room key. Whoever he was, apparently he could afford more than a 'low rent' room.

"Hey, you gonna play or what?"

I turned around to find a blue haired woman in polyester with a players card dangling from her bony wrist. She glared down at me from behind thick bifocals.

"Oh, sorry. I was just, uh, kind of watching."

"Well, then move over, honey. This machine's giving me nothing but zeros today."

She edged me aside and planted her butt on the vinyl stool, then promptly fed her card into the machine.

"Right. Sorry."

I moved over to the next machine, then glanced back up at the front desk. Empty.

Shit. I'd lost him.

I tried to shake off the creepy feeling as I wondered if I should mention to Ramirez that I had my very own stalker.

* * *

By the time I got back up to the room sleeping beauty and Dana were both awake. Dana was rubbing her shin and Marco was just emerging from the bathroom in a cloud of post shower steam.

"Good morning, sunshine," he sang, folding his pajamas into a tiny square.

I narrowed my eyes at him. "You know, you snore like a lumberjack."

Marco whipped around, his mouth dropping open into a neat little 'o'. "I do not!"

I turned to Dana for confirmation, but she just shrugged. Apparently years of spending the night in unfamiliar beds had trained her to be a heavy sleeper.

"You okay?" I asked, gesturing to her leg. I could see a purple bruise starting to form on her shin.

"Yeah. I think I fell off the bed. This thing's made for midgets."

"I'll take the rollaway tonight," I selflessly offered. At least it was further away from the snoring wonder.

"Well, I slept like a baby last night," Marco said, slipping his pajamas into a drawer.

I narrowed my eyes at him again, making a mental note to check the gift shop for some of those Breathe Right strips. Or a muzzle.

Marco informed us he'd done New York to the fullest last night and today was going to do Gay Paree! (Or at least it would be once he got there.) He planned to spend the day at the Paris hotel's La Boutique using his La credit-card. Dana was up twenty bucks from a productive evening of video poker and was ready to move on to the blackjack tables this morning. And, for lack of a better plan, I decided to go try Lola's house in Henderson again.

How Lola and the deceased Hank slash Harriet tied in to my dad, I wasn't sure. But they were the closest thing I had to a lead at the moment.

So, half an hour later I was parked in front of the house on Sand Hill Lane again. Only this time a white Ford Taurus and a beat up green Volvo were parked in the driveway. This was a good sign.

I took a deep breath and willed myself out of the car and up the front pathway. I rang the bell. I waited. Then rang again. Nothing. I peeked in the windows. Same suburban living room, no sign of anyone inside. I glanced around the neighborhood. Unfortunately, there was no helpful neighbor watering the lawn today. No sign of life at all, everyone either at work or inside watching Regis and Kelly.

I walked along the edge of the rock garden to a wooden gate at the side of the house. With a quick glance around, I tried the latch. It opened right up. Feeling just the teeny tiniest bit intrusive, I slipped through the gate and walked around the side of the house. Two more windows faced this side, both with the blinds shut tight. Staying close to the wall, I rounded the corner into the backyard. More rock gardens, a small patio and a kidney shaped pool beyond. A few dog toys were scattered across the patio. Nothing that screamed suicide. Or gunshot.

The back wall of the house was rimmed in green hedges, beyond which stood a sliding glass door. There I hit the jackpot. No curtains. The back door looked into a kitchen and family room, both immaculately clean and filled with more typical suburban issue furniture. Flowers, chintz and lots of honey oak woods. I wondered again if I had the right house. It hardly looked like a showgirl and a suicidal drag queen lived here. I was just about to try the latch to see if suburbanites kept their back doors locked when a man walked into the family room. (Scaring the bejeesus out of me I'm not ashamed to add.)

I quickly ducked down behind the hedge, hoping the meager leaves gave me cover.

The man was short, with a closely clipped crown of brown hair surrounding a bald palette. He wore a turtleneck, cords, and loafers with little tassels on them. He was either gay or needed to stop allowing his mother to dress him. I was too far away to actually see his eyes, but he seemed to be crying, the backs of his hands swiping at his cheeks as his chest heaved in and out.

Not two seconds later a tall, redhead walked into the room. My heart sped up. Lola.

I scuttled a little closer, leaning into the hedge as the man walked into the kitchen. Lola followed, her back to me. I still hadn't gotten a good look at her face, but she was wearing the same go-go outfit from last night. And she was waving her arms around at Turtleneck Guy. He buried his head in his hands and started crying again. Then he did a few arm waves back.

It looked like they were arguing about something, and I'd be hard pressed to say who was winning. Turtleneck Guy stopped crying and was now yelling in earnest at Lola. I inched closer to the glass door, straining to hear what they were saying. No such luck. The thick glass not only insulated from the Vegas heat, but also from snoopy long-lost daughters. All I could hear was the muffled sound of raised voices.

I moved along the back of the house, hoping to at least get a better look at Lola's face. Only I was watching the argument so intently I didn't see the dog toy laying behind the hedge until my foot came down on it. The loud squeak of my heel hitting a fake squirrel echoed through the yard. Both Turtleneck and Lola froze.

Uh-oh.

Turtleneck made for the back door with Lola close behind him. I turned to make a run for it… then caught my heel in a garden hose.

"Uhn." I did a face plant into the hedge. I scrambled to stand up, but not fast enough.

"Who are you?"

I sheepishly turned around. Caught red-handed.

Turtleneck's face was all purple and blotchy, his eyes swollen and rimmed with dark circles like he hadn't slept. Lola was still inside, though I could see her red hair hovering at the sliding door.

"Me? Oh, uh, I'm the… meter reader?" You would think that with all my years growing up in Catholic school I would have learned to lie a little better than that.

Turtleneck narrowed his bloodshot eyes at me. "Did Monaldo send you?"

"Uh…" I searched his eyes, wondering if that would be a good thing or a bad thing. "Yes?"

Ahnt. Wrong answer. Turtleneck shot a look back at Lola, which I could have sworn held something close to terror. But before I could ponder it more, the barrel of a gun was shoved in my face.

"Whoa, holy crap!" I took an involuntary step back.

"You tell Monaldo we're through," Turtleneck said, waving the gun. "Hank's gone, and we've had enough of him. We're done, you hear me!"

"Hey, I don't even know Monaldo," I said, throwing my hands up in surrender. Why I had to pick that particular moment to become a convincing liar, I will never know. "I lied. I swear I have no idea who you're talking about. I'm just here looking for Larry Springer. I, uh…" I paused, watching the gun barrel waver unsteadily at my head. "I think he might be my father."

Turtleneck Guy blinked, obviously taken aback at this. The gun lowered. He opened his mouth to respond, but before he had a chance Lola stepped out onto the patio.

"Maddie?"

I looked up, for the first time really seeing her face. Strong jaw, long straight nose, face that seemed just a little too wide framed by her long, red hair.

Then I felt my eyes widen as I looked at hers. Round, soft, and a distinct hazelish color that could go golden brown or emerald green depending on how much purple eyeliner you applied.

Just like mine.

CHAPTER SIX

I blinked, realization hitting me like a fat woman diving for the last pair of half-priced mules at a Nordstrom super sale as I stared at Lola. Broad shoulders, slim hips, fleshy cheeks. Adams apple.

I did a couple of dry gulps.

"Maddie?" he said again, this time in a voice that was distinctly male.

I licked my lips and moved my mouth. Only no sound came out. I cleared my throat and tried again. "Uh, yeah." I paused, staring at those familiar green eyes again. "Larry?"

He quirked a corner of his lips. Rimmed in ruby red lipstick. "Most people just call me Lola now."

I nodded, feeling my eyebrows pinch together in a way that screamed for Botox as my brain searched for the appropriate emotion. I'm pretty sure shock would have worked. Or surprise. Maybe even anger. But honestly, all I felt as I stared at my dad in a mini skirt and go-go boots was relief that he wasn't dead in a ditch somewhere.

"What are you doing here?" he asked.

"I got your message." I couldn't help staring down at his boots. Gucci. At least now I knew where I got my fashion sense from.

Lola slash Larry bit his lip, little flecks of ruby red dotting his teeth. "Right. Sorry about that. I, uh, I shouldn't have called. It was stupid. Everything's fine now." Only the way his eyes darted to Turtleneck's in a silent exchange didn't quite jive with his words.

Now that the gun wasn't pointed at me, I noticed how badly Turtleneck's hands were shaking. He shifted the gun from one hand to the other, as if not really sure how to hold it. And he kept glancing around the yard like he was expecting the boogey man to pop out from behind an azalea bush any second.

And Larry didn't look a whole lot more composed. Up close I could tell he was a lot older than I'd originally put Lola. Makeup covered bags under his eyes, his chin was showing a hint of gray stubble, and the distinct outline of a girdle sat beneath his stretchy white top, holding in an unflattering middle-aged spread.

But more than anything I kept going back to his eyes. So like the ones I saw in the mirror every morning that it was kind of unnerving. Okay – it was *very* unnerving. It was almost like seeing the fifty year old version of me if I were ten inches taller and let this mustache thing get out of control.

A million and one questions begged to be answered as Larry and I stood there silently contemplating each other. Were the mini skirt and heels why he'd left Mom and me? Why hadn't he so much as called for twenty-six years? Did this mean he wasn't a rock star? Oh, God. Was my dad a stripper?

And what was with the gunshot? Why had he run away from me last night? And last, but not least, who the hell was Monaldo?

Since I wasn't quite sure I was ready to hear the answers to the other questions, I started with the latter.

"Who's Monaldo?"

"No one," Larry said. A little too quickly. He gave Turtleneck a warning look, and the gun disappeared back into his cords.

O-kay.

"I saw what happened to Harriet last night," I said, switching gears. "I'm sorry."

Turtleneck did a dry sob thing and buried his face in his hands. Larry just bit his lip again.

"Was he your…" I trailed off, my gaze resting on his mini skirt.

"Roommate," Larry supplied. And I hate to admit I was slightly relieved. I wasn't sure I could deal with having two daddies at the moment. Especially when one of them was dead.

Instead, Larry gestured to Turtleneck. "Maurice and Harriet ar- *were* a couple."

Maurice nodded, tears running down his chubby cheeks again.

I gave him the most sympathetic face I could, considering he'd had a gun pointed at my head just seconds ago.

"Look," Larry continued, "I'm sorry you came all the way out here, Maddie. But, uh…" He glanced at Maurice again. "Now's not really a good time. Sorry." And with that Larry turned on his Gucci heels and disappeared back into the house.

"Wait!" I cried. I pushed through the sliding door. Maurice (still sobbing) followed me.

The house smelled like a combination of Clorox and my Irish Catholic grandmother's Glade plug-ins. A bottle of Windex sat on an end table next to a rag, the only two things out of place in the entire room. The house was immaculate. I'm talking Swiffer commercial clean. All the furniture – a chintz loveseat, oak coffee table, and glass entertainment center – was symmetrically arranged, each corner lining up perfectly with the next. It was the kind of room that made me instantly want to take my shoes off for fear of leaving a muddy trail across the pristine tiled floor.

Instead, I charged up the stairs. "Larry?" I called, taking them two at a time with Maurice hot on my heels.

"What are you doing? You can't be in here," he protested, eyeing the bottoms of my strappy sandals versus the white upstairs carpeting.

I ignored him, following the sounds of Lola's movement.

The second floor of the house held three bedrooms and a bathroom decorated in hot pink tiles and a pink and white polka dotted shower curtain. (Who was their designer, Barbie?) The first two bedroom doors where closed. I caught a glimpse of Larry's red wig moving around in the third.

As I entered the room it was instantly clear that Larry was not the resident housekeeper. Larry's room looked like the pictures I'd seen of the Beverly Bloomingdale's right after the Northridge quake hit. Dresses, skirts, blouses, and shoes mingled in disarray on every surface. A handful of long wigs on Styrofoam heads lined the dresser amidst eyeliner, mascara, and – I cringed - the same Raspberry Perfection lip gloss I put on every morning. I averted my gaze, feeling my face scrunch into those Botox worthy lines again.

Instead I focused on Larry, standing in the center of the room zipping closed a black duffle bag as a little yapper dog circled his ankles.

"I need to talk to you, Larry," I said, as Maurice huffed up behind me.

Larry looked up, only mildly surprised I'd followed him in. "I can't. I have to go." He picked up a beaded purse from the floor and slung it over his shoulder.

"So, so... you're just going to leave again?" My voice cracked, images of that hairy arm disappearing from my life overwhelming me. Granted, this was not exactly how I'd always fantasized our father-daughter reunion playing out, but the fact that he was walking away again had me going into a panic.

He must have noticed because he paused again.

"Look, I'm sorry we had to meet under these circumstances. I know how you must be feeling, and I'm sorry this is such a shock to you."

Understatement alert. But shock was good. Shock was one step way from denial, and if I could just tell my mind to make that next leap over the fence, I planned to camp out in denial for a long time. I looked down at his Gucci boots again. A long, long time.

"What about the gunshot Friday night?" I asked, dragging my gaze back up to Larry's face.

He found a piece of lint on his skirt suddenly fascinating. "I don't know what you mean."

"I heard a gunshot on the message you left me."

Larry and Maurice did that silent exchange thing again. "Must have been a car backfiring."

Apparently being a terrible liar ran in the family.

"Look, you said on the phone that you needed help. What kind of help? Does this have to do with Monaldo?"

Larry gave me blank stare. "No. I don't need any help. Everything's fine."

Right. I narrowed my eyes at him. So fine that his roommate had just taken a header off a roof. Not to mention the sobbing gay guy with the gun shoved in his Old Navy cords.

"Larry, if you're in trouble-"

But he cut me off. "Really, I'm fine, Maddie. Everything here is fine." He grabbed his duffel bag and pushed past me, back down the stairs.

"Wait!" I followed, my heels click clacking on the tiles as Larry headed out the front door. I followed him down the flagstone pathway and out to the Volvo in the drive. Turtleneck grabbed the yapper and with a backwards glance at Larry, hopped into the Taurus and roared down the street.

But my whole attention was focused on Larry as he threw his duffle bag into the Volvo and walked around to the driver's side.

"Wait," I said again, that panic rising in my throat. "Can I… maybe call you or something?"

Larry paused, his eyes softening. "It was good to see you Maddie. Tell your mom I said 'hi.'"

And before I could protest being blown off *again*, he had the car in gear and was driving out of my life for the second time. Only this time instead of a hairy arm, all I saw was his long, red wig, flapping in the breeze out the car window.

I stood there in the empty driveway trying to process what just happened.

My father hadn't been shot. He was okay. He wasn't dead, wounded, or bleeding. I should be relieved he was okay, right?

And I was.

Kinda.

Only he hadn't seemed all *that* okay. And I still had more questions than answers. Not even considering his taste in clothing, there was something really weird going on here.

I looked back at the house. Just for good measure I tried the front door. Locked.

For lack of any other bright ideas, I got into the Mustang and drove back to the hotel.

* * *

The first thing I did when I got back to the room was check my messages. Imagine my surprise when I had seven. All seven from Ramirez.

Under any other circumstances, seven messages from an LAPD officer yelling at you to get your butt back to his jurisdiction might not be a good thing. But as I sat there listening to each one, I couldn't help feeling just the teeniest bit of triumph. Who's not returning calls now, huh?

I hit the erase button, and all seven disappeared. Then I flopped back on the bed and stared up at the textured ceiling.

Okay, so my dad preferred lipstick to dip sticks. So he happened to like Gucci boots. (Couldn't really blame him there.) So instead of running off to Vegas *with* a showgirl, he had apparently *become* a showgirl.

The fact still remained he was my dad. And despite his protests, he was in trouble. How much trouble and what kind, I wasn't quite sure. In fact, I wasn't even quite sure I wanted to know. Larry had, after all, just run out on me for the second time in my life. He hadn't exactly exhibited the classic signs of a father happy to see his daughter.

I rubbed my eyes, pushing the fatherless little girl in me to the back of my mind and tried to focus on the practical adult woman. (I knew she was in there somewhere.)

Let's assume that I had, in fact, heard a gunshot in Larry's message last Friday. He'd been asking for help, and someone had taken a shot at him. Three days later Larry's roommate swan dives off a roof. And Larry goes mum. I didn't like the pattern here.

So, what kind of help had he needed? Did it have something to do with this Monaldo guy? Maurice had said they were done. Done with what? Had that been what he and Larry were arguing about in the kitchen? The way they were waving their arms at each other, I couldn't imagine it was over what kind of casket to bury poor Hank in.

I closed my eyes. So, the question was, did I walk away like Larry had so many years ago? Or did I stay and try to help him out of whatever mess he and Turtleneck had gotten themselves into? I wish I could say a brilliant answer came to me, but instead I think I drifted off to sleep.

The next thing I knew, Dana burst into the room with a loud whoop and started jumping on the bed.

"Ohmigod. Ohmigod. Maddie wake up!"

I cracked one eye open, surprised to see the sun setting over the Excalibur castle outside the window.

"What time is it?"

"Time to Par-teee. I just banked at blackjack. A thousand bucks! I am the blackjack queen. Mads, you gotta play this game with me. That clerk, Jim, convinced me to play with him, and at first I was like 'no way,' but then he said, 'it's easy,' and I was like, 'will you show me?' and he was like, 'sure.' So I did. And I like totally hit a ten, and the dealer said, 'now what,' and I totally said, 'hit me,' and he totally said, 'okay,' and then I like totally got a jack and then totally won. A thousand bucks, Maddie. How totally great is that?"

I blinked, cracking the other eye open. "My dad is a drag queen."

Dana stopped jumping up and down. But to her credit she didn't even ask if I was drunk.

"Say what?"

I propped myself up on my elbows and told Dana about my morning in Henderson. And the fact that my dad has been harboring a Victoria's secret all his own.

"Wow," she said when I was done. "I knew a tranny once. Dolly. She worked the corner of Hollywood and Vine."

"Great. Thanks. That really helps."

"Do you think your mom knows?" Dana asked.

I thought about it. If the way she'd gone five different shades of pale when I mentioned Larry was any indication, it was altogether possible.

"I don't know. Maybe."

"Do you think you should call her?"

"No!" I sat bolt upright. "No. There is no way I want to talk to my mom about this. I'm doing denial right now. And if I talk to Mom about it, it's real. And there goes my healthy denial."

"Um, I'm not exactly sure denial is actually considered healthy," she said, her eyebrows drawing together.

I looked her straight in the eye. "Dana, my dad wears go-go boots. Trust me, denial is my friend."

"Okay, if you say so." She sat down on the bed beside me. "So, what do you want to do know?"

My stomach growled, reminding me I hadn't eaten since this morning. "Right now, I want food."

Since Dana hadn't eaten either, being too distracted by her like-totally-banking blackjack streak, we decided to hit Broadway Burger again. And even though the patty melt with extra mayo was calling my name, visions of my father in a girdle drove me to follow Dana's lead and order a soy burger with extra sprouts instead. While the clerk made our sandwiches, I told Dana about the seven messages from Ramirez. She agreed. He was getting what he deserved.

We took our sandwiches to a table near the window, and Dana immediately dug in, making little yummy sounds as she tucked a stray sprout back into her mouth.

"Ohmigod, this is so good," she moaned.

I sniffed my burger, wrinkling up my nose. "It smells like lawn trimmings."

"No it doesn't! Maddie, it's so good for you. It's full of heart-healthy soy and antioxidants."

I sniffed it again. "I don't know…"

"Just eat it," Dana prompted, moaning her way through another bite.

I took a tiny nibble. "It tastes like lawn trimmings."

"It has seventy-five percent less fat than a beef burger."

I looked down at my midsection. Still girdle free. For now. "Seventy-five, huh?"

Dana nodded.

I held my nose and ate the lawn trimmings.

By the time we got back to the room, Marco was back from Gay Paree, loaded down with shopping bags and wearing a jaunty black beret.

"Bonjour my lovelies," he greeted us.

"How was Paris?"

"*Magnifique*! You likey the hat, *oui*?"

"It's totally you," I said honestly.

"Dana, some guy called for you while you were gone," Marco said, pulling a miniature Eiffel tower on a key chain out of a shopping bag. "Roco? Rambo?"

"Rico?" Dana asked, her eyes lighting up.

"Yep. That's the one. Deep voice. Sounded like a total cutie."

"What did he say?"

"He told me to tell you that 'Mac,'" Marco said, doing little air quotes with his fingers, "said your background check cleared, and he'll pick up your 'LadySmith' (more air quotes) for you on Friday."

Dana sighed and clutched her hands to her heart. "How sweet is that? I love that man."

"What's a LadySmith?" Marco asked, planting his hands on his hips. "Is this some new kind of sex toy?"

"It's a gun," I told him.

Marco took a tiny step away from Dana. Considering his run-in with her stun gun, I didn't blame him.

After Marco finished unpacking his Paris souvenirs, Dana and I filled him in on my adventures of *Father Knows Best* meets *Bosom Buddies*. He made the appropriately shocked sounds when I mentioned my dad's go-go boots and the appropriately appalled ones when I mentioned Turtleneck's tasteless loafer.

"So," he said when we'd finished, "do we think Larry killed his roommate then?"

"No!" I said a little more loudly than I'd meant to. "No, I don't think Larry killed anyone. Besides, the police said it was a suicide."

"Oh, pooh." Marco waved me off. "They always say that when they don't know who did it."

While Marco tended to oversimplify things, I wasn't totally convinced he was wrong.

"Monaldo," Dana said, rolling the word over her tongue. "I wonder if that's Italian."

"It sounds kind of Portuguese to me," Marco said. "I dated this Portuguese guy once. Made the best *Polvo* I've ever tasted. I'm talking to die for, dahling."

"No, no. I'm pretty sure it's Italian." Dana crinkled up her brow. "Wasn't one of the guys in *The Godfather* named Monaldo?"

Mental forehead smack. "He's not from *The Godfather*."

"This is just like that pilot I shot last season. *Mafia Chicks*," Dana said. "You know, all these Vegas clubs are run by the Mob," she insisted.

"Oh, my God, Maddie!" Marco gasped. "Is your dad in the Mob?"

"No! My dad is not in the Mob. There *is* no more Mob in Vegas."

Dana and Marco both looked at me. Then each other.

"Oh, honey," Marco said, "you are so naïve."

My left eye began to twitch.

"Look, I'm sure this is all nothing. Just a misunderstanding. Larry was probably just upset about his roommate today. And it must have been a shock seeing me again after so long. I'm sure if I could just sit down with him for a few minutes, Larry would be able to explain everything. Besides, maybe it was just a car backfiring. Right?"

Hey, what do you know? I'd successfully made the leap into denial.

"I think we should go check out that club again," Dana said

Marco squealed. "Vegas clubbing! Oh, can we, please? Pretty, pretty please, Mads?"

I shrugged. It seemed like as good a place as any to catch up with Larry. And who knows, maybe once I got him alone, he really *could* explain everything. "All right. Let's go to the Victoria."

Marco jumped up and clapped his hands. "Eek! Just give me ten minutes!"

CHAPTER SEVEN

Two *hours* later Marco put the finishing touches on his club outfit. Black leather pants and a formfitting purple tank top with three strands of silver chains around his neck. Capped off by the black beret. And I was pretty sure he was wearing more eye make-up than either Dana or me.

"We ready?" Dana asked, adjusting her spangled tube top. She'd paired it with a slinky black skirt and two inch heels. I had my silver strappy sandals on again but had changed into a shorter skirt - black leather - and a fire engine red stretchy top. I had to admit, we looked pretty hot.

"Ready."

We parked the Mustang in front of Annie's Escorts again and walked the short block to the Victoria Club. The yellow crime scene tape was gone, and the only evidence that anything out of the ordinary had happened here last night was the clean spot on the street where someone had tried to bleach the bloodstain away.

A line to get in spanned down the block, no doubt due to the press coverage from last night. I groaned. As much as I loved my strappy sandals, they were three inches high, and the thought of standing around on the sidewalk in them for an hour made my toes curl. Literally.

A big guy covered in muscles from his Doc Martens all the way up to the top of his 6'5" crew cut frame stood behind a red velvet rope separating the waiting crowd from the chosen ones inside the building. He held a clipboard in one hand, no doubt the list of people cool enough to bypass the Line of Shame.

"Hi," I said, giving him my most flirtatious one-finger wave. "Um, any chance we could get in there?" I asked, pointing past him to the club where already I could hear dance music pounding through the walls.

Crew Cut Guy looked at the line of people waiting. Then back at us. "You on the list?" he asked in a monotone that suggested he'd already done this song and dance fifty times that night.

I pursed my lips, making the most of my Raspberry Perfection lip gloss. "Well, not exactly-"

But he didn't even let me finish, instead doing a straight arm point toward the waiting hopefuls. "Back of the line."

"But-"

He gave me a cold stare and pointed again. "Back of the line."

Rats.

I was about to resign myself to numb feet when Dana pushed forward. "Watch and learn," she whispered, adjusting her cleavage until it looked like she was smuggling water balloons in her top.

"Hi, there," she said, approaching Crew Cut. She paused, reading his name tag, "Pete." She flashed him a big smile. "We heard this is *the* hottest club in town. And my friends and I are just dying to see it. You wouldn't want to disappoint us now, would you?" Dana punctuated the statement by batting her eyelashes and coyly touching a fingernail to her plump lips.

Nothing. Crew Cut didn't budge. He just did the straight arm point again.

But Dana, not one to be deterred, just sighed. "All right, Pete. But I don't think your boss is going to be very happy when he hears who you've turned away."

Hesitation flickered in his eyes.

"That's right," Dana plowed on. She turned and gestured to me. "This just happens to be *the* Eddie Izzard."

I nudged Marco. "Who?" I whispered as Pete gave me a head-to-toe. But Marco just giggled.

"No kidding?" Pete asked. He squinted at me. "I thought The Iz would be taller."

Dana waved the comment off. "TV adds six inches."

Crew Cut nodded. "Yeah, right. I think I heard that before."

"Anyway," Dana continued. "We had our hearts set on the Victoria tonight. But, I guess if The Iz isn't welcome here we can always go to the Wynn..."

"Wait!" Pete called, suddenly in a more accommodating mood. "I might be able to make an exception for The Iz."

Dana gave him a smile that was all teeth. "Oh, gee. Aren't you just a doll, Pete," she crooned.

I poked Dana in the ribs as Pete unhooked the velvet ropes and ushered us into the club. "I give up," I whispered. "Who's this Iz?"

She gave me a 'well duh' look. "Hello? Eddie Izzard? *Dressed to Kill*? Transvestite comic? He's like the hottest thing since RuPaul. Honey, you really do need to get out more."

I blinked. "You told him I was a *guy*!?"

Dana turned to me. And I swear stared right at my upper lip dust. "Well, he bought it, didn't he?"

That's it. I was so getting a wax.

I self-consciously kept my head down as we entered the club.

The inside of the Victoria was even bigger than it looked on the outside. There was a dance floor to the right, bathed in strobe lights and gyrating with wall-to-wall bodies. To the left was a glass and neon bar that stretched the length of the wall and held patrons two and three deep vying for a Sammy Davis martini. Behind the bar was a hallway that looked like it held restrooms and offices.

But the main attraction was straight ahead of us. A scattering of tables and tiered booths angled down to a huge stage. Populated by seven women in platform heels, feathers, and yellow sequined leotards. All seven had Adams apples. In the middle of them stood the male version of Marilyn Monroe, singing about diamonds being a boy's best friend.

"I love Las Vegas!" Marco clapped his hands together.

I'm glad someone was enjoying it. Me – I was still doing denial.

As we threaded our way to an empty table near the aisle, I craned my neck around, scanning the crowd for a six-foot tall redhead and a short guy in cords. No luck on either count.

A waiter dressed in early Madonna, complete with silver bangle bracelets and a little painted on mole, approached the table.

"Welcome to the Victoria club. Can I get you ladies something to drink?"

Marco did a little giggle at the term 'ladies' and ordered a peach schnapps. "And may I say," he added, doing an impression of a twelve year old at an Ashlee Simpson concert, "I love your music."

Mental eye roll.

But Madonna ate it up, blushing and autographing Marco's cocktail napkin before taking the rest of our orders. Dana and I both opted for cosmos.

"And would you happen to know if Lola's working tonight?" I asked.

"Sorry. She's off tonight. We only do the go-go number on Mondays and Fridays."

My dad. The go-go dancer. I felt my face do that Botox-worthy wrinkle again. "So you haven't seen her in here at all today?"

Madonna scrunched her eyebrows together. "No, I don't think so. I saw her last night though, right before… " She paused, her eyes casting downward. "Before they found Harriet."

"I'm sorry. Were you close?"

"Oh, I wouldn't say close. We were friendly, but Harriet and Lola have worked here a lot longer than I have. I just transferred over from Caesars last spring. I was a Roman soldier there."

I was never going to look at those togas the same way again.

"Was anyone else especially close with Lola?" I asked.

She shook her head. "No, Lola and Harriet kind of kept to themselves. And Bobbi. The three of them were pretty tight. But Bobbi left last week."

I sat up straighter. "She did? Do you know where she went?"

Madonna shook her head, her blonde wig bobbing back and forth. "Nope. Sorry. She just up and took off one day."

I bit my lip. People seemed to be doing a lot of that lately.

"How about a Monaldo?" Dana piped up. "Does that name ring a bell?"

Madonna's face broke into a smile. "Oh, sure. He's the owner." She gestured to the hallway behind the bar.

"Thanks."

"Uh-huh. Enjoy the show," she said. Then gave Marco a little wink before moving on to the next table.

When she left, Dana kicked me under the table. "See, I told you the Mob owns all these clubs!"

Ugh. "Just because the guy is Italian and owns a club it does not make him a mobster."

"Italian-*American*," Marco corrected me.

"You know," Dana said, leaning in to a pseudo whisper, "I bet you this whole place is crawling with wise guys."

I looked around at the suspicious amount of size thirteen pumps. I seriously doubted it.

"Look, I'm going to go talk to the owner. Who I'm sure is a perfectly nice, normal Italian-*American*," I said with emphasis. "You two stay here."

"You sure you don't want me to come with?" Dana asked. "I took Rico's interrogation and intimidation course. Rico uses the same techniques as the CIA. They totally work, Maddie."

"No! I said I was going to go talk to him, not interrogate him. Sheesh."

Dana pouted. "No stun gun, no interrogation. You're no fun at all."

"Look, you two just… enjoy the show," I said, gesturing to the stage where Marilyn was breaking into a rendition of 'Happy Birthday, Mr. President.'

I left Dana still pouting and Marco still gazing starry-eyed after his Madonna as I weaved in and out of the club goers toward the hallway. I peeked my head around the corner. Three doors to the left, a pair of restrooms to the right. I did a quick over the shoulder and ducked to the left. The first door was marked 'supplies.' The second two had the words 'private' painted on them. I knocked on the first door. Nothing.

Doing another over the shoulder thing, I moved on to the second door. I paused, hearing muted voices inside.

There were two of them. One deeper and slower. I couldn't make out what he was saying, just a low rumble on the other side of the door. The other voice was higher and more urgent. And, luckily, louder. Hearing my Irish Catholic grandmother's lectures on eavesdropping echoing in my head, I put one ear to the door.

The words 'moron' and 'jerk' vibrated through the wood. The guy with the higher voice was pissed. 'Merchandise' and 'Lola' followed. Then the word 'gun.'

I stifled a gasp, adrenaline quickly surging through me. I pressed my entire body up against the door, straining to hear more.

The low-talker mumbled something in response, and the first guy got angry again. This time I had no trouble hearing his response. "I don't care how you do it. Just take care of him."

I froze. The way he said 'take care of him' didn't sound like he meant a pampering foot massage. Suddenly Dana's *Godfather* scenario wasn't feeling so far-fetched. Take care of whom? Larry? My mouth went dry, and my heart started racing faster than a car chase on the 101.

The voices went low again and I strained to hear more. Only all I could hear were footsteps. Unfortunately, I didn't realize they were moving toward the door until it was too late. It swung open, catching me squarely in the face.

"Uhn." The door slammed into my nose, smacking my head against the wall behind me as I crumpled to the floor. I blinked, dazed. Then looked up to find two men staring down at me. One was huge. He seemed to fill the entire hallway with his bulk. And it wasn't fat. This guy was built like a linebacker. He had a long scar cutting across his face and one thick uni-brow that hovered over his eyes like a hairy caterpillar.

But it was the second guy that creeped me out. He was smaller, his features sharp and precise. He was impeccably dressed in a dark, designer suit with close clipped dark hair and olive skin, slightly flushed from his previous shouting match. His eyes were small and black, staring down at me with a kind of cold calculation that sent a shiver up my spine. I'd bet my Blahniks this was Monaldo.

"What the hell are you doing?" he asked, his voice tight with a restraint I could easily see snapping.

"I, uh, was looking for the bathroom."

He looked to the right at the restroom sign, blinking in two foot high neon. Then he looked back at me and raised one perfectly waxed eyebrow.

"Huh," I said. "Guess I had the wrong door."

He narrowed his small eyes. "Wrong door, huh?"

"Sorry, I've, uh, had one too many cosmos tonight." I scrambled to my feet and didn't even have to fake the stumble as I lunged for the ladies' room door.

I locked myself in a stall and sat down, taking big breaths. Ow. Big breaths hurt. I gingerly touched my fingers to my nose, hoping I hadn't broken it. I did a ten count, then came out of the stall to inspect the damage in the mirror. Red, but it wasn't bleeding, and it didn't look terribly swollen. Okay, maybe a little swollen, but at least not Marsha Brady sized. I pulled out a tube of concealer and dabbed some on the red parts as I mulled over what I'd heard.

It was obvious the creepy little guy was pretty pissed at Larry. But why, I wasn't sure. Did it have anything to do with the gunshot I'd heard last Friday? A terrible thought occurred to me. Maybe instead of getting shot, Larry had shot someone else. Maybe that's why Monaldo was so mad. I had a hard time picturing the decked out Lola taking a pot shot at Monaldo while his goon looked on, but I had to admit it wasn't impossible.

After doing the best I could with my rapidly swelling nose, I snapped my compact closed and gingerly peeked my head back out of the bathroom door. The hallway was empty. I could see Unibrow and Mr. Creepy standing at the bar. I quickly slinked out of the bathroom and skittered down the hall. I closed my eyes and did a silent prayer to whichever saint looked after those who committed breaking and entering for really good reasons and opened the office door. Empty.

I mouthed a 'thank you' at the ceiling and jumped inside, shutting the door behind me.

Okay, so, maybe breaking into the office wasn't the smartest idea I'd ever come up with. In fact, it might even be pretty low on the list. But I was fresh out of smart ideas so I went with the only one I had. I didn't quite know what I was looking for. Maybe a gun, a written statement saying Monaldo had pushed Harriet off the roof. Some detailed plan about how they were going to… I did a mental cringe… 'take care' of Larry. Most of all I guess I was just looking for some clue as to why Larry's roommate was in the morgue, and said roommate's boyfriend was going around shoving guns in people's faces. (Okay, and I guess a teeny tiny part of me was actually looking for some kind of plaque that said, "honorary Mob member.")

A desk sat in the middle of the room, flanked by two armchairs in front and a cushy looking office chair behind. Bookcase to one side, a few framed photos, some official looking documents on the wall stating they could sell liquor, and three side by side file cabinets. All in all, your typical office. I started with the file cabinets first. Locked. Damn. I moved on to the desk drawers, turning up rubber bands, paper clips, and a dirty magazine. Nothing terribly helpful there. Except the fact that Monaldo apparently liked his women big and buxom.

I checked the bookcase next, randomly pulling out volumes of employee manuals, binders, and books, checking for anything out of the ordinary. No such luck. I turned my eye to the photos on the wall. Lots of pictures of Creepy doing big cheesy smiles with his arm around people. Mostly men in suits I didn't recognize. Which didn't mean a whole lot. I was usually more apt to flip on *Seinfeld* than the news, so these could have been anyone from politicians to former Mob Dons. In fact the only person I did recognize was Larry. In a pink leotard fringed in peacock feathers. I looked down at his shoes. Silver spangled strappy sandals with a butterfly clip. Mental forehead smack. No wonder I'd passed as a drag queen.

Next to Larry was another man in pink, shorter and chubbier than Larry, with curly blonde hair. He had his arm around Larry's shoulders, and I wondered if this was the unfortunate Hank. Beside them stood Monaldo, doing a big 'cheese' at the camera and pointing up to the Victoria Club sign.

Since staring at a picture of my father in heels and feathers wasn't totally in line with my denial theme, I shook my head and moved on. The only place in the room I hadn't checked yet was the trash. A wire basket sat in the corner of the room, bulging in a way that said Monaldo wasn't much of a housekeeper.

As a general rule, I don't go pawing through people's trash. It's rude, invasive and downright icky. But I was out of options. And quite possibly out of time before the gruesome twosome came back to argue about what kind of cement shoes to order Larry. So, I closed my eyes and shoved my hands into the trash. Luckily, I didn't hit anything too slimy or disgusting. Mostly just discarded papers and receipts. I quickly scanned the first few on top. Nothing jumped out at me. Until I un-balled one piece of paper that looked like a computer print-out of an eBay auction. That alone wouldn't have gotten my attention except the auction, listed last Wednesday by a BobEDoll, was for a pair of pink Prada pumps. In snakeskin leather. New in box with dust bag. I felt a little drool form at the corner of my mouth as I wondered if the auction had ended yet.

I was trying to figure out why Monaldo would be in the market for a pair of pink pumps (Okay, so he did own a drag club, but Monaldo hadn't exactly struck me as the Dude-Looks-Like-A-Lady type. He seemed more like the Dude-has-an-oozi-in-the-closet type.) when I heard the sound of footsteps outside the door. On impulse, I quickly shoved the piece of paper into my purse.

Just as the door swung open.

"What in the hell are you doing?" Monaldo, a.k.a. Mr. Creepy, stood in the doorway, his black eyes flashing at me.

I froze. "Uh… wow, this isn't the bathroom, is it?" Okay, so thinking fast in a crisis isn't my strong suit.

He narrowed his eyes at me, his jaw clenching tightly. "Who the fuck are you?" he asked in a voice that was freakishly calm for how vividly angry his eyes were.

I bit my lip. "All right. You got me. Ha," I faked a laugh. "Okay, here's the truth…" I racked my brain. Quick Maddie, what sounds truthful? "I'm, uh… with the *L.A. Informer*. A reporter. Yep, that's me, reporter gal. Like Mary Tyler Moore. Only without the pillbox hats because the Kennedy chic thing is so overdone. Well, I mean, some women can pull it off, but I'm more of a Sarah Jessica Parker style girl. You know – all about the shoes? Which is why I'm doing a story on…" I bit my lip again, my eyes searching his office. They landed on the photo of Larry's strappy sandals. "Shoes! Footwear fashions for transvestites. It is such an overlooked market don't you think? And I thought maybe I could get a couple choice quotes from you for-"

But he cut me off. "Get the fuck out of here!" he roared.

I didn't think it was wise to disobey. I was across the room in two quick strides. But Creepy blocked the doorway, grabbing me by the arm. "Not so fast."

My heart sped up to the beat of the club music pulsing through the hidden speakers, threatening to pop right out of my ribs and Macarena across the floor. Creepy's eyes bore into mine, black and oddly flat. If eyes were the windows to the soul, I'd swear this guy didn't have one. His fingers gripped my arm so hard I whimpered. Which caused a smile just this side of sadistic to tug the corners of his thin lips.

He turned and yelled over his shoulder to one of the bouncers by the bar. "Bruno! I want you to take care of someone for me."

There was that phrase again. I gulped.

I held my breath, panic starting to rise as Bruno worked his way through the shadowy hallway toward us. Bruno looked solid. Not as big as the linebacker, but he had the shape of someone who liked the gym a whole lot more than I did. I think I whimpered again.

Creepy got close to my face. His nose almost touching mine. I could smell a dinner of garlic and fish on his breath. "If I ever see you near my office again, *reporter* girl," he sneered, "it'll be the last place anyone ever sees you."

I didn't have to worry about my heart beating out of my chest because I think it actually stopped. I nodded, not trusting myself to speak.

"Here," he said, pushing me backwards into the solid wall of Bruno. "Get rid of her."

"No problem."

I froze. I knew that voice.

I whipped my head around, and this time I'm positive my heart stopped as 'Bruno' and I locked eyes.

Ramirez.

CHAPTER EIGHT

Ramirez spun me around, his hands maintaining a tight grip on my shoulders as he marched me down the hallway.

"What the hell are you doing here?" he whispered into my ear.

"Me?!"

"Shhh."

"Me?" I whispered. "What the hell are *you* doing here?"

"Working."

"I didn't know you moonlighted as a bouncer in a drag club!"

"I'm undercover." His breath was hot on my neck, and I could feel his anger bubbling just beneath the surface. "A cover you could very well have blown back there." He turned me left at the bar, muscling our way through the club patrons, heading downward toward the stage. "One little thing," he muttered, as he shoved me in front of him. "I ask you to do one little thing. Steer clear of Vegas. Just stay home. But can you do that for me? No. Just like a woman."

"I'm going to pretend you didn't just say that."

"I'm going to pretend you're going to listen to me this time."

Hey, if he wanted to do denial too, who was I to judge?

He steered me through a doorway in the wall and into a dimly lit backstage area. Women slash men in various states of undress ran between guys in flannels smoking cigarettes and manning pulleys. None of them paid us any attention. I guess they were used to Bruno 'taking care of people' back here.

Ramirez pushed me to a dark corner behind one of the curtains, then whipped me around to face him.

"Look, I don't know what's going on here," I said, "but I-"

But before I could finish, Ramirez's lips were locked over mine, his body pinning me against the wall. Not that I was going anywhere. The second his mouth touched mine any fight I might have had melted faster than a Popsicle on the Venice boardwalk. Man, he was a good kisser. So good, I'd almost forgotten about that sexist comment by the time we finally came up for air.

"Don't ever do that again," Ramirez mumbled onto my lips.

"Do what?" I admit, my brain was a little hazy after he'd just about kissed the pants off me.

"Give me a heart attack by breaking into a family man's office."

"Oh, right, it's okay for you to go undercover as Bruno the Manhandler, but I happen to find one little unlocked office door and- wait, did you say 'family man?'"

Ramirez pulled away, his jaw tightening into that silent Bad Cop routine again.

I gulped. "Please tell me you mean he attends his kids' soccer games?"

No reaction. Crap. I hated it when Dana was right.

"Where are you staying?" Ramirez whispered. He glanced over his shoulder as a couple of the yellow sequin 'girls' walked past.

"New York - New York. Room 1205."

He nodded in the darkness. "I'll be there in half an hour." He didn't wait for an answer, instead pulling open a door behind the curtain and shoving me through it.

Before I knew what had happened, I was standing outside next to an overflowing dumpster and heard the unmistakable sound of Ramirez locking the door behind me. I looked around, trying to reorient myself. It was cold, and I had a pretty good idea that thousands of tiny rat eyes were staring at me from behind the piles of garbage. I did a quick mini-jog back around to the front of the building and hailed the first cab I saw.

* * *

When I got back to the hotel room, I sat down on the bed and stared up at the textured ceiling for answers again. If things had seemed a *little* odd before, they were into Michael-Jackson-odd territory now. It was like I was starring in my own Scorsese movie. Only the goodfellas all wore heels.

Could my dad really be mixed up with the Mob? What exactly *did* Larry do for Monaldo? And what did Ramirez have to do with any of this? He was an LAPD homicide detective; this was clearly out of his jurisdiction.

Did it have anything to do with the gunshot? I wondered. I may not be Miss Police Procedure, but even I knew something was amiss here. I suddenly felt like the dimwitted blonde in the movie theater who spends the whole time asking her date, "Who's that guy again?," "Now, why does he want to kill that other guy?" "And what does the donkey have to do with anything?" I was trying to keep up, honest I was. But somehow none of these scenes were fitting together.

A knock sounded at the door, and I jumped about three feet in the air.

"Who is it?" I called, struggling to return my heart rate to normal.

"It's me," a familiar voice called. "Open up, Maddie."

I breathed a tiny sigh of relief and undid the lock, letting Ramirez in. I hadn't even gotten the door closed behind him before his lips were advancing on mine again.

"Oh, no you don't." I put a hand in the center of his chest, warding him off. And almost wavered as I felt his six-day-a-week-at-the-gym muscles rippling beneath my palm.

Almost.

"Uh-uh. No way, pal. You have some serious explaining to do before there's any more of…" I paused, gesturing between our lips. "…this kind of stuff going on."

He sighed. Then sat down on the double bed and rubbed a hand at his temple. "All right. What do you want to know?"

"For starters, what the hell are you doing in Vegas? And why are you working for Monaldo?"

He paused. And for half a second I thought he wasn't going to tell me, his dark eyes scrutinizing me. Finally he gave in, Lustful Cop for once winning out over Bad Cop. "Okay," he said. "But it doesn't leave this room."

I sat down beside him and held up my right hand. "Scout's honor."

"Two months ago," he started, "the body of a customs agent at the port of L.A. comes floating in with the tide. I got the page that night I was at your apartment. It was pretty clear the way this guy was killed that it was a professional job."

I gulped. "As in mafia?"

"As in not a random act of violence. Apparently the agent had been asking questions about a container that came in from Thailand the week before. The container was stalled in customs. The agent dies, two days later, customs clears our container."

"Convenient."

"Very. We followed the trail of paperwork through a couple of holding companies and dummy accounts, until it finally led us to a name. Monaldo."

"So, why don't you arrest him?" I asked.

Ramirez sighed. "Trust me, I'd like to. Only it seems we aren't the only agency investigating Monaldo.

"The ICE – Immigration and Customs Enforcement – thinks Monaldo is involved with the Marsucci family, an organization that's suspected of having a hand in dozens of criminal activities along the west coast, including importing counterfeit goods and distributing them here in the U.S. Only they haven't got enough proof to link the containers coming in through the port of L.A. to the Marsuccis yet. Monaldo could be that link. They've had him under surveillance for the last eighteen months, but if they want a case to stick against a family like the Marsuccis, they've got to have solid evidence. Monaldo is their best chance at that, and if I arrest him for murder, there goes their case."

My head was spinning. This was all just a little too HBO for me. "So, this is where Bruno comes in?"

He nodded. "If I can get enough proof to link Monaldo to the Marsuccis, then, and only then, can I arrest Monaldo for killing the customs agent."

"What kind of link are you looking for?"

"Money," he said. "If Monaldo is working for the Marsuccis, he'd have to be kicking back their share of the profits from the sale of the counterfeits to them somehow. So far we've scoured all of his accounts and come up empty. He must be handing it over in cash, only we haven't been able to catch him in the act yet. And, trust me, Bruno's been sticking to this guy like glue."

I shook my head. "I don't get it, doesn't murder out rate a few fake items in your justice playbook?"

He gave me a look. "This is more than a few fake items. We're talking ten billion dollars a year worth of fake items."

I blinked. "Wow."

"Yeah. Wow is right."

"What are they counterfeiting, gold?"

Ramirez paused, suddenly not meeting my gaze.

"What?"

He looked down at his hands, rubbing them one over the other. Then up at the ceiling and did a deep resigned sigh. "Shoes."

"Excuse me?"

Another deep sigh. "Shoes, okay? They're importing counterfeit designer shoes and passing them off as originals to retail stores up and down the west coast."

I couldn't help it. I laughed out loud. "Wait a minute - you're telling me that Big Bad LAPD Officer Ramirez can't make his case because of a few *girly* pairs of fake Fendis?" I was enjoying this way too much.

"That's it. Laugh it up, shoe girl." He gave me a playful punch on the arm.

And I was. I was laughing so hard tears were forming at the corner of my eyes, and I was doing some really unladylike snorting. I couldn't have designed better payback for his macho man attitude if I'd tried. "Why didn't you tell me?" I asked, finally getting myself under control. "I *know* shoes. I could have helped!"

His eyebrows knitted together. "Maddie, this isn't SpongeBob slippers. Profits from counterfeit items are often used to fund terrorist activities. The ICE takes this kind of thing very seriously. And you should too. The Marsuccis are not nice people. Not," he emphasized, "the kind of people who take kindly to having girls snoop through their offices."

I pictured the look on Monaldo's face when he'd caught me fumbling around his office. Ramirez was right, it wasn't a comforting thought. Even less comforting was the thought that Larry was somehow mixed up with these kinds of people.

"What about Hank?" I asked. "What does his death have to do with all this?"

Ramirez shrugged. "I honestly don't know."

"Was it really suicide?"

He paused. His Bad Cop face sliding into place again.

"Oh, no you don't," I stood up, crossing my arms over my chest. "Look, if you had just told me this three days ago, I wouldn't have been at that club, and you wouldn't be having to worry about your precious cover being blown. So don't pull this Bad Cop crap on me. I'm a big girl. Lay it on me."

I could have sworn I saw him suppress a smile. "Okay, *big girl*." Yep, that was definitely a smile. "No. We don't think it was a suicide. The trajectory off the building is all wrong. Plus…" He paused again, weighing how much to tell me.

I did my best Bond Girl impression. Hand on hips, eyes narrowed, jaw clenched. Don't mess with me, pal.

Finally he relented. "This is just between you and me, got it?"

I nodded.

"This piece of information isn't being released to the public, but there was a suicide note. Obviously forged. Someone wanted to make it *look* like Hank killed himself."

"Do you think it was Monaldo?"

Ramirez shrugged. "It doesn't matter what I think. It only matters what I can prove."

"So, what do we do now?" I asked.

He shook his head. "See, there you go with that 'we' thing again. Why do I get a very bad feeling every time you say 'we'?"

I narrowed my eyes.

He grinned. "You know, you're kind of cute when you do that."

I stuck my tongue out at him.

"And that." His grin widened into a full-fledged Big Bad Wolf smile, complete with shiny white teeth. "Honey, I've spent the last six weeks surrounded by men in bad wigs. There's not much *you* can do that isn't going to look cute."

I had to admit, all the cute stuff was wearing me down. Especially when he said it with that lopsided grin, showing off the deceptively boyish dimple in his cheek. "So, you've really been undercover this whole time?" I asked.

He nodded.

"All those 'I'll call you's and getting your voice mail. You weren't blowing me off?"

Ramirez took my hand in his and pulled me to him. "I'm sorry. I wanted to call you, but Bruno doesn't get to take a whole lot of personal time."

"So… you do like me?" I asked, knowing I sounded just a little pathetic, but the way Ramirez's warm body was pressed against mine, I really didn't care.

He nodded in response, his eyes going dark and intense as they honed in on mine.

"Are you going to kiss me now?" I whispered as he leaned in closer.

He nodded again.

And then he did. Slowly this time. Taking his time as he nibbled his way from one side of my mouth to the other. I think I sighed out loud.

"Forgive me yet?" he whispered.

I shook my head. "Uhn-uh."

He kissed me again. This time using a little tongue.

"How about now?" he murmured.

"Nope."

His lips dipped back in. This time using a lot of tongue.

"Now?"

"Maybe just a little."

He pulled back, a wicked gleam in his eyes. "Tell you what. Let me *really* make it up to you."

My hormones were suddenly charging like a new MasterCard at Bloomies. I could think of about a hundred things he could do to make it up to me. All of them involving his tongue.

"How about you spend tomorrow taking in a show, doing some shopping…"

I opened my mouth to protest, but he talked right over me.

"…then I'll take you out to dinner tomorrow night."

I shut my mouth. "Like a date?"

"Right. Like a date." He smiled.

Our first date. I bit my lip. He was driving a hard bargain.

"Okay," I felt myself saying. "A date. On one condition."

His smile widened. "Anything."

"Leave Bruno at the club. I want one night alone with you. No pagers, no work."

His smile wavered just a little, but he finally gave in. "Deal. But," he added with a wink, "then you have to do something for me."

Uh-oh. "Does this something involve condoms?"

His grin widened again. "Okay, two things."

Be still my beating heart.

"I want you to stay away from the Victoria Club."

I opened my mouth to protest, but he cut me off again.

"Look, I've spent the last six weeks being Bruno, who, by the way is not a very nice guy, to see Monaldo behind bars where he belongs. Trust me when I say Monaldo is not the kind of person you want to piss off, Maddie. Please, just go home."

He had a point. Mr. Creepy was pretty… well, creepy. Not someone I particularly wanted to meet again.

But there was Larry to consider. It was becoming painfully obviously Larry was involved with some not so nice guys. Maybe even *wise* guys. How involved, I wasn't sure. And by the time Ramirez got enough proof to put Monaldo away, who knows how many other jumpers might have taken a header off the Victoria's roof. Bobbi was missing, and Hank was dead. Odds were stacked against Larry.

"Promise me you'll go home?" Ramirez prompted.

I put my hand behind my back and crossed my fingers. "I promise."

Ramirez looked so relieved I almost felt guilty.

"That's a good girl."

I narrowed my eyes again. Almost. "'Good girl?' What am I, a cocker spaniel?"

That wolfish grin slid across his face again. "You'd rather be a naughty girl?"

I clamped my mouth shut, at a loss for a good comeback to that one. Thankfully I didn't need one, as he leaned in close, and his lips brushed against mine.

Maybe it was the fact he'd actually asked me on a real date. Or maybe the fact he admitted he liked me and hadn't been blowing me off for the last six weeks. Or maybe it was just the fact that the most action I'd seen in months was on *Joanie Loves Chachi* reruns. But as Ramirez nibbled on my lower lip, I suddenly found myself thinking a whole mess of *very* naughty girl thoughts.

I nuzzled closer, running my hands through his thick hair. Ramirez put his hand up my shirt, and I think I blacked out for a moment.

He growled in my ear. "Six weeks is a long time."

Tell me about it.

His fingers were fumbling with the clasp of my bra, and mine were frantically working on his belt buckle. Which, by the way was harder to break into than Fort Knox. I had just given up and was pulling his T-shirt off instead when the door to the hotel room burst open.

"Did you see how Madonna was looking at me? He was so into me, I could totally- Oh. Sorry."

Marco and Dana paused in the doorway. Ramirez muttered a curse in Spanish.

Ditto for me, pal.

"Uh, sorry to interrupt," Dana said, looking from my dangling bra to Ramirez's untucked T-shirt. "But we were worried about you."

I could feel my cheeks filling with heat. Though whether it was a flush of suppressed hormones or embarrassment, I'd be hard pressed to say.

"No problem. I was just leaving anyway," Ramirez said. He shot me a heated look. "Tomorrow night?"

I nodded, not trusting myself to speak for fear of blurting out something totally inappropriate. Like, "Wait. Stay. A couple more seconds, and I swear I'd have that belt buckle figured out!"

"Mmm, mmm! Honey, that man is deeeeee-lish," Marco said, watching him go.

"What is he doing here?" Dana asked. "What about The Oath?"

"Screw The Oath, honey. That man is H-O-T hot! Whew!" Marco began fanning himself.

Once I got my hormones back under control, Dana raided the mini bar, and I filled them in on what Ramirez had told me. Which wasn't technically breaking my promise to him. He had said the information didn't leave the room. And we were still in the room. See? Promise kept. (Sort of.)

Dana was such a good friend she didn't even say 'I told you so' when I got to the part about Monaldo's family connections. Okay, well I might have seen her mouth it to Marco behind my back while I went for that second mini bottle of tequila, but my head was fuzzy enough by then I couldn't be sure.

Once we'd drained the mini bar, I slipped into my ducky pajamas and flopped onto the rollaway. I closed my eyes, visions of Larry in fake Gucci boots overlaid with Monaldo's soulless eyes and the black tarp covering the unfortunate Hank. Worst of all, as I drifted off to sleep, I was assaulted by visions of Ramirez, drippy candles, soft music, and our perfect first date.

* * *

From the depths of a fabulous dream about Ramirez's tongue doing acrobatics across my stomach, I heard the William Tell Overture erupting from my purse. I automatically reached for my cell. Ouch. A pain shot up my left side. I rolled over. A pain shot up my right side. I gingerly pulled myself up on my elbows, rubbing my neck. It felt like I'd fallen asleep sitting up in one of my Irish Catholic grandmother's formal dining chairs. I blinked a few times. No dining chairs. It was worse. I'd slept on the lumpiest rollaway in the entire state of Nevada. I rubbed my neck, cringing, as I pulled my phone out of my purse.

"Hello?"

"Maddie? It's Mom."

Yikes! I sat straight up in bed. Then whimpered as a pain shot up both my right and left sides.

"Uh, Mom. Wow. Hi."

"Hi, sweets. I'm so glad I caught you in. How is Palm Springs?"

"Right. Palm Springs." I glanced around the motel room. Marco was snoring like a little piggy beneath his frilly blue mask, and Dana was sprawled sideways across the other double, her limbs dangling off the side. "It's great. Really. Really. Great." I cringed. I hated guilt.

"Oh, good. I'm so glad you're having a nice time. Did you visit that little boutique on Palm Canyon yet? The one that sells those hand painted abalone shells?"

"Uh, no. Not yet." Which wasn't a total lie, right?

"Oh, you absolutely must. They are so darling! So, what have you seen so far?"

"Oh, not much." Right. If you didn't count the feathered drag queens and shoe trafficking mobsters.

"Well, honey, I'm so glad you decided to do this. You really needed a vacation. And I was just pleased as a pickle to hear that you're out there dating again. It's not good for you to be alone too long."

Tell me about it. But, instead I did a non-committal, "Uh-huh."

"Anyway, I just wanted to call and say 'hello.' I know we had a bit of a... disagreement before you left, and, well, I just... wanted to say 'hello.'"

I cringed, feeling guilt niggle at the back of my mind again. This was about as close to an apology as Mom got. "Mom, about Larry-"

"Right," she plowed right over me, "I'm so glad you've put that behind you." A statement. You *have* put that behind you.

"Uh-huh." I rubbed my neck again. Was the pain actually getting worse?

"And, I'm glad you're having fun. Do you want me to come by and water your plants while you're gone?"

"No, Mom, I don't have any plants."

She paused. "What do you mean, you don't have any plants?"

"I don't have any. They always die, so I have a plastic ficus in the corner. No real plants."

She paused again. "Don't be silly, everyone has plants. I'll go buy you one."

Yep, the pain was definitely getting worse. I tilted my head to the side and groaned.

"Maddie, are you all right?"

"Yeah. I just slept on my neck the wrong way."

Mom giggled on the other end. "I understand. I remember the first time Ralphie and I went away for the weekend together. I 'slept' in all kinds of funny positions."

Okay – ew. "Uh, Mom, I have to…"

"In fact, there was this one time, we 'slept' in this airplane bathroom. Have you ever heard of the mile high club, Maddie?"

Ew, ew, ew! "Wow, gee, I have to go now. I'll call you later, Mom. Bye."

I quickly hung up and flung the phone on the bed as if it had mom-sex cooties. Not the image I wanted to wake up to.

I flopped back down on the pillows and closed my eyes. But thanks to years of Catholic ingrained guilt, I couldn't go back to sleep. Even though I knew it was for her own good, I hated lying to my mother. Mostly because I knew sooner or later she'd find out. I remember one Christmas when I was ten and snuck into my mom's closet to peek at all my presents. I had been so careful to put each and every one back in exactly the same place. Then Christmas morning I awoke to find a note saying Santa didn't like little girls who peeked. I still had no idea how she found out. But somehow she always did.

I sighed, giving up on sleep and hobbled into the shower instead. I spent an eternity standing under hot water, letting the steam and heat ease the tension out of my neck, then threw on a pair of white, cargo capris, a hot pink baby-T and my pink Charles David kitten heels. By the time I'd done the blow dry and make-up thing (heavy on the make-up to compensate for my slightly enlarged nose) I could almost stand up straight. Almost.

"What's wrong with your neck?" Dana asked me, stretching the sleep out of her limbs as she flipped on the casino channel.

"The rollaway," I moaned. "Have you got any aspirin?"

Marco yawned. "You look like Quasi Moto."

I poked a finger at him. "Just for that, you're on rollaway detail tonight, princess."

Marco pouted but knew better than to argue with me before coffee. "Fine. Anyway, I'm off to Egypt today, ladies," he informed us. "I'm going to see Tut's tomb at the Luxor. You know there are real gold replicas of the jewels Queen Nefertiti wore for sale in the gift shop. I'm thinking of a tiara."

I made a mental note to tell Ramirez there was at least one person on the planet girlier than I was.

"Anyway, after Tut's Tomb, I've got a hot date." He did a middle schooler giggle. "With Madonna. He's taking me to the Venetian. Is there anything more romantic than Venice?"

I had a sudden image of Ramirez and myself holding hands in a gondola and tried to shake it off before I turned middle-schooler like Marco.

"Would you do me a favor?" I asked him instead.

"Anything, dahling."

"Would you ask Madonna if she knows where Bobbi lives?" I didn't like how nobody at the club had seen Bobbi in days, but before I went totally paranoid over it, I figured it was a good idea to make sure he wasn't just home with the flu.

"Consider it done."

While Marco headed into the bathroom for his morning ritual of cleanser, exfoliator, and pearl infused moisturizer, I flipped through the booklet of hotel services and found the number of the Regis Salon on the concierge level. No way was I going on a romantic gondola ride first date with Ramirez with an upper lip that looked like a drag queen's. (Yes, I know he'd said 'dinner' and not 'an evening in Venice' but this was my fantasy, and I could play it out wherever I wanted.) A woman doing a nasally Fran Dresher answered, and, after flipping through her appointment book, said she could squeeze me in at four.

That settled, I lay back on the bed and thought about my conversation with Ramirez last night.

From what he'd said, it was clear now that Larry, did, in fact, need my help. Was he working for Monaldo in the sole capacity of a feathered showgirl, or was there something more to it? I wasn't altogether certain, but the way Turtleneck had shoved a gun in my face when I mentioned Monaldo's name didn't speak of the normal employer-employee relationship. Tot Trots for example had only threatened to shoot me once, when

I'd been three weeks late with the Pretty Princess Mary Jane sketches. And, in their defense, I'll admit they were late because my favorite boutique in Venice Beach was having a huge going-out-of-business sale that month and, well, a girl's got to have her priorities.

So, all this left me with the question: what exactly was my dad doing for Monaldo? Or, more importantly, what kind of proof of my dad's involvement with Monaldo were Ramirez and the ICE going to find? As much as I wasn't sure how I felt about Larry I didn't particularly want my next memory of him to be through prison bars.

"Dana, do you still have officer Baby Face's number?"

She looked up from her TV lesson on beating the roulette wheel. "Sure. Why?"

"Do you think you could ask him for Maurice's address?" Larry had been reluctant to talk to me. But I had a feeling that the whimpering Turtleneck might be an easier nut to crack.

She shrugged. "Worth a try."

Dana fished the number out of her purse and gave him a story about wanting to send flowers to the partner of the deceased. I'm not sure if he actually bought it, but apparently he wanted Dana worse than he feared his supervisors, because twenty minutes later Dana had a date to meet Officer Baby Face for drinks that night, and I had a tall latte, two aspirins and the address to a condo in North Vegas.

CHAPTER NINE

Maurice's condo was in an older part of town where the buildings were all a sun-bleached ivory color that might have once been anything from sandy yellow to rosy sand in a former life. The address Officer Baby Face gave us was on the corner of Rancho Drive and Silverado Parkway, a two-story affair with Mediterranean arches and lots of peeling stucco. The walkway was flanked by bunches of dead grass and trampled succulents, and through a rusted gate I could see a courtyard punctuated with two faded lawn chairs lying on their sides. The entire building had a feeling of being dried out and used up. Apparently Maurice's paycheck wasn't quite enough to buy his way into the Sand Hill set.

I parked at the curb and did a quick make-up check in the rear view mirror as I went over what I'd say to Maurice. Considering the last time I'd seen him he'd pointed a gun at me, I wasn't entirely looking forward to this interview. But on the other hand, my father may very well be using his go-go boots to outrun the Mob, so I didn't feel I had much choice. As fortification, I added another layer of mascara and a thick swipe of Raspberry Perfection lip gloss.

"Ready?" I asked Dana as I puckered my lips in the mirror.

Dana pulled her stun gun out of her purse. "Ready."

"Dana!"

She jumped in her seat. "What?"

"What are you doing with that thing?"

She blinked her wide eyes at me. "What? It's just a little protection."

"Condoms are a little protection. That thing is dangerous."

Dana waved me off. "Oh, please. It's harmless. Marco just didn't know how to use it."

I eyed the cell stunner. "And you do?"

"Of course," Dana said, tucking the phone onto her belt. "I used one last year in that sci-fi flick I did with Ben Affleck. I was Alien Girl Number Three."

"And they gave you a real stun gun?"

Well," she puckered her eyebrows. "At first they gave me a real gun. But then there was this little incident, and they said it would be better if I had a prop. But it totally looked like the real thing, and I swear by the end of the shoot I was totally a master of that prop gun."

"Little incident?" I narrowed my eyes at her. "What kind of incident?"

Dana waved me off. "Oh, it was nothing. Just a misunderstanding. Trust me, I know what I'm doing."

Why is it that when someone says 'trust me' I always feel less inclined to do so?

But before I could stop her, Miss Alien Number Three was out of the car and walking up the pathway to Maurice's front door.

I followed her, doing a silent prayer to the saint of stun guns that hers wouldn't go off as I walked between the lawn chairs and dried grass to unit 24A. Dana rapped on the door. I heard footsteps approaching from the inside, but the door stayed firmly shut. As the seconds stretched on, I got that creepy feeling that someone was watching us through the peephole.

Dana knocked again, louder this time. Finally it opened a crack, and Maurice's tiny eyes peeked out.

He was dressed this morning in gray slacks and a black blazer over another turtleneck, this time in somber charcoal. Mourning colors. Though, I noticed, he still wore those hideous tasseled loafers. His eyes held a red rimmed look like he'd been crying non-stop since yesterday, and they darted back and forth, sweeping the area behind us as if we might have brought the fashion police with us.

"You again. What do you want?" he asked, his voice nasally and strained.

"I was wondering if we could talk to you for a few minutes. I'm worried about Larry."

Maurice's eyes shifted from Dana to me, then back again. Finally he shrugged, a sad, defeated little move of his shoulders, and stepped aside to let us in.

It was immediately apparent who had decorated the house in Henderson. The same blend of flowery, stain friendly furniture dominated the living room. Only in Maurice's tiny condo, the bright fabrics and large wooden furnishings looked cramped and out of place. It struck me that Maurice was a housewife without a house.

As in Henderson, everything was immaculately clean and the air held a thick odor of Windex and potpourri. The little yapper dog I'd seen at Larry's bounded out from a back bedroom and began circling our legs. He did a series of high pitched barks and wagged his tail at me like I was the bacon fairy. I had to admit, he was kinda cute. As long as he didn't drool on my shoes.

"Oh, what an adorable doggie!" Dana exclaimed, reaching down to pet the little yapper. "What's his name?"

"Queenie," Maurice said, then choked back a little sob. "He was Hank's baby."

Maurice scooped Queenie into his arms and motioned for us to sit on the chintz sofa. He perched himself on the edge of the matching loveseat, clutching a balled up tissue in one hand and the dog in the other. He was a small guy to begin with, only a few inches taller than I was, but he seemed to have shrunk inside of himself even further since yesterday, as if all the life had been drained out of him.

"I'm so sorry for your loss," I started, genuinely meaning it.

Maurice nodded, pressing the tissue to the corner of his eye. "He was all I had," he squeaked out. "If only I'd known he was so unhappy…" He trailed off, biting his lip as his eyes filled up.

"I'm sorry," I said again, patting his arm awkwardly. "How long had you two been together?"

"Three years," Maurice sighed, swiping at his nose with the tissue. "Ever since I started dancing. Hank took me under his wing and showed me everything he knew." Maurice did a little hiccup gulp.

"So, you're a performer too?" I asked.

Maurice nodded. "At the El Cortez."

That explained the lousy paycheck. The El Cortez was Vegas's first casino and had the clientele to prove it. None of them a day under eighty and all on a fixed incomes. Not exactly big tipper territory.

While I tried not to picture Maurice in feathers and heels, I formulated my next question. The one I was seriously dreading the answer to. "Maurice, I need to know. What exactly did Hank and his friends do for Mr. Monaldo?"

Maurice looked down at the carpet. An olive green shag. Apparently renters couldn't be choosers. "I told you, we're all dancers."

"Then why are you living in a one bedroom and Hank and Larry can afford a house in Henderson?" Dana asked, narrowing her eyes at him.

Maurice pursed his lips and began absently patting Queenie's head. "Hank liked to spend money," he said, careful to avoid eye contact.

"Look," I said, leaning in closer, "you said you were done with Monaldo? What did you mean?"

Maurice looked from me to Dana, but kept up his silent routine.

"Please?" I pleaded. "I don't want my dad to end up like Hank."

That did it. Maurice's shoulders bobbed with a deep hiccup/sigh thing again, and he caved.

"I'm sorry. I wish I could tell you, but I swear I honestly don't know what they were up to." His face took on that sad, abandoned look again. "No one would tell me anything."

"But they were involved in something?"

Maurice nodded. "All I know is that they were doing some work for Monaldo on the side. But I swear to you I don't know what. I tried to get it out of Hank, but he…" Maurice's voice cracked as he trailed off. "We hadn't exactly been on great terms lately."

"Oh?" Dana leaned forward again.

Maurice stared at his hands. "About three months ago Hank started working late at the club. Going in odd hours, when I knew he wasn't on stage. I asked him what it was about. At first he wouldn't answer me. Then one night I saw him coming out of Monaldo's private office. I confronted Hank. I…" He blushed. "I thought maybe they were having an affair. When he came home I accused him of cheating on me, and we fought. He told me he was doing some extra work for Monaldo. He, Larry, and Bobbi. He wouldn't tell me any more than that. But the next day he brought me these as a peace offering."

Maurice held out his arm for inspection. Diamond cuff links twinkled back at us from their spot on his worn jacket. And they didn't look like the home shopping network knock offs. These were genuine, mined in Africa, diamonds. And they were big.

Dana did a low whistle. "How many carats?"

"Two. Each."

Dana whistled again.

Maurice got a sad little smile on his face, and his eyes filled with tears again. "Hank could be very generous."

"So, was Larry working with him too?" I asked, thinking of the beat-up Volvo my dad had driven off in. He hadn't exactly seemed like he was rolling in dough.

Maurice shrugged. "I don't know. I assumed he was, but…" He paused, staring down at the carpet again.

"But what?" I prompted.

His hands twisted around the tissue, making little white shreds of paper dance in the air, spurring the yapper dog to chase them. "A couple of weeks ago, I was at the house with Hank when Larry came home. He was upset about something. He dragged Hank into the den. I couldn't hear what they were saying, but they were definitely arguing. The only word I could make out for sure was 'Monaldo.' Then finally Larry came out and just left."

Figures. His standard M.O.

"Hank was really upset afterward," Maurice continued. "He even went out and bought a gun." He cringed. "I hate guns. When I asked Hank about it, he just said it didn't hurt to be cautious. After Hank died-" Maurice choked back another little sob. "After he passed I took the gun and went to the house to ask Larry what was going on. I wanted to know what their argument had been all about and why Hank had been so scared that he needed a gun. I figured now that he was gone… well, I think I have a right to know why he took his own life." Maurice hiccup-sobbed into the tissue again.

I thought about what Ramirez had told me last night and wished I could tell Maurice it was more likely Monaldo had taken Hank's life. But, instead I asked, "What did Larry say?"

Maurice sniffled. "Nothing. He said he couldn't tell me. He didn't want anyone else to get hurt. I told him it was too late for that. And that's when you showed up."

My crappy timing strikes again.

It was becoming more and more clear that Larry was into something bad all the way up to his cheap wig. Maybe it was time to ask Ramirez for help. I may play Bond Girl, but even I wasn't stupid enough to believe I could protect Larry from the Mob.

"Maurice, have you ever heard the name 'Marsucci?'"

He gave me a blank look. "No. But then again, I'm finding out there were a lot of things Hank kept from me." His eyes threatening to fill with tears again.

"What about Bobbi?" I asked, shifting the conversation before we all drowned in salt water. "I heard he hasn't been into the club in awhile. Have you seen him?"

Maurice shook his head. "No. And Hank hadn't either. He was really upset about it. Agitated."

I bit my lip. And now he was dead.

I digested this bit of worrisome information, wondering just where all this left Larry.

Queenie, apparently tired of chasing Kleenex shreds, jumped up on the sofa beside me and settled himself on Dana's lap.

"Well, hello, cutie," Dana crooned, rubbing Queenie's ear until his tail beat a steady happy-dog staccato against the flowered cushions. "You are just precious, aren't you?"

Queenie's tail began to wave so fast it was nearly invisible. He did happy little wiggles all over Dana's lap, and I cringed as his claws pawed at Dana's Donna Karan sweater. But Dana didn't seem to mind. "You're just adorable," she said in that high pitched cutesy voice used only for communicating with babies, small animals, and retail clerks who look like they might give a cute blonde a break on a full price pair of heels. "Who's the cutest puppy? You are. Yes, you are. You're a cutie boy. A cute, cute, cutie boy. You're a-"

Dana stopped as the dog did a strangled little yelp, then went instantly limp in her lap.

Maurice sucked in a breath. "What happened? What did you do to him?"

"I, I…" Dana looked at the limp dog. Then at the cell gun strapped to her belt.

Mental forehead smack. I quickly grabbed the cell and shoved it into Dana's purse before Maurice saw it.

"Oh, my God, you've killed Queenie!" Maurice started bawling in earnest now, sobbing hysterically as he lifted Queenie from Dana's lap and clutched him to his chest.

"He's not dead," I reassured him. He's just a little… zapped."

"Zapped?" Maurice's eyes went big. Obviously my word choice didn't have the comforting effect I was going for.

"Um, maybe not so much zapped as… sleeping. That's it. He's just sleeping. Dana has a very soothing effect on animals."

Maurice looked at me like I was one cookie short of a dozen.

"See, here's the thing, Dana has this little stun gun…"

"Gun!" Maurice shouted. "You shot my Queenie?!"

"No, no! Not shot. Just zapped. Mac says they're perfectly harmless. And she should know, she owns the gun store. Like with the kind of guns that shoot for real. With bullets and stuff. I mean, not that I know a whole lot about guns. I don't. I hate guns. I don't even own a gun. Neither does Dana for that matter."

"Not for another two days," she added helpfully.

"See? No real guns here. Well, except maybe for the one you have." I paused. "Um, you don't actually have that gun on you right now, do you?" I asked, suddenly a little wary. Maurice just gave me a look. "Right. Of course not. I mean, not that I thought you'd use it. You wouldn't. You're obviously a very nice person. Not that nice people don't own guns, they can. And do. Like you. But Dana doesn't have a gun. Just a stun gun. Totally different. It only gives a little jolt of electricity. A tiny one. See, he's coming around already."

Queenie's hind legs began to twitch as a puddle of doggy drool formed on Maurice's lapels.

"See, he's fine. Probably having a lovely doggie dream about milk bones and fire hydrants and chewing up furniture…"

There was that look again.

"Right. Maybe not chewing up furniture. I'm sure Queenie would never chew up furniture. Certainly not yours. But the other stuff, definitely. Well, okay, I guess we should be going…"

Dana and I backed out of the condo as Maurice watched us, his eyes full of big tears, Queenie twitching in his arms. As soon as we were out the door, it slammed behind us, and I heard Maurice throw the lock.

Well, that went well. I turned to my best friend. "You are a maniac! I don't ever want to see that thing again."

"What?" Dana protested.

"You just zapped a puppy!"

"On accident."

"Right, and as long as the gun stays *in your purse*," I annunciated very slowly, "there will be no more accidents."

Dana pouted. "This is just like the Ben Affleck set."

"Why, did you stun Ben too?"

"No," she said as we got in the car. Then added as an afterthought. "I kind of, *totally* accidentally, stunned his cat."

Never mind fur traders, PETA should be going after Dana.

* * *

After we left the condo, we made a quick lunch stop at Burger King, where I ordered a double whopper with cheese, fries, and a thick vanilla milkshake. I had completely given up on fitting in the Nicole Miller. It was last season's cut anyway. Dana, on the other hand, ordered a side salad and bottled water.

"I can't believe you actually eat those things," Dana said, scrunching up her little ski jump nose at my burger.

"Why?" I asked around a bite of pure heaven. I'm not ashamed to say I was two inches away from a gooey cheddar induced orgasm.

"Uh, hello? Mad cow. Do you have any idea what that burger was fed when it was alive?"

I looked over at her salad. "Probably your lunch."

"Other ground up cows. Antibiotics. Growth hormones. Why don't you just hook yourself up to an IV full of toxins?"

I looked down at my burger. "Because this tastes better?"

Dana shook her head at me and took a bite of her wilted lettuce.

I was just wolfing down the last of my heaven on a bun, when my purse rang. I slipped my cell out as I chomped on a deliciously greasy French fry.

"Hello?"

"Hi, Mads."

Cripes! Mom.

"Uh, hi, Mom."

"How's Palm Springs?"

"Uh… " I glanced around at the full Burger King, hoping she couldn't hear the ding of the slot machine in the corner. "It's great."

"How's the weather out there?"

"Great!"

"And, your fellow? How are things with him?"

"Grrrrrreat," I said, sounding a little too much like Tony the Tiger for comfort. "Everything's just great."

"I'm so glad. Listen, I didn't mean to interrupt, but I just wanted to let you know I bought you a plant."

"A plant?"

"Yes, I went by to water your plants, and I got rid of that plastic thing you had. I bought you a real ficus instead."

Great. Just what I needed. A ficus.

"Now, you're going to have to water it every three days," Mom continued, "but not too much, you don't want to over water. Just until the soil is moist. But don't let it overflow. I got you a dish to set it on, but it could still overflow onto your carpet, so easy on the water. And just a touch of plant food once a month. You can mix it right in your watering can."

I rubbed my eyes, the sleepless nights catching up to me. "I don't have a watering can, Mom."

Mom paused. "What do you mean you don't have a watering can? Everyone has a watering can. How do you water your plants without a watering can?"

"I don't have any plants!"

"Yes you do. You have a ficus. Never mind, I'll go out and get you a watering can tomorrow."

I gritted my teeth together. "Mom, I have to go."

"Sure, honey. I understand. You don't want to keep that man of yours waiting. I know how you young folks are. I was young once too, you know. Of course, with Ralphie, I feel like I'm twenty-three again. God bless those little blue pills." She did a little giggle.

My eye did a little twitch.

"Right. Okay, well, bye now, Mom, gotta go."

I hung up, wondering how much longer I could keep up this charade. Mom may not be the sharpest dresser in the world, but she was no dummy. Any second now I was waiting for her to do the big ah-ha! and realized that not only was I *not* in Palm Springs with the guy I was *not* having sex with, but instead I was running around Sin city zapping puppies and chasing after Larry in a skirt. And I shuddered to think what the punishment would be then. Suffice to say, this was bad enough to make those Hot Dog on a Stick hats look like haute couture.

Once I finished my fries (and added a Hershey's Sundae Pie for desert. Hey, after the conversation with Mom I needed comfort food.) and Dana finished the last of her rabbit food, we hopped into the Mustang and headed back to the hotel. As we merged onto the 15 heading south toward the Strip, I pulled down the visor to check for chunks of Mad Cow stuck in my teeth and touch up my lip gloss. I was applying one last swipe of Raspberry Perfection, when I caught a flash of blue in the mirror.

I whipped my head around. "Sonofabitch."

Sure enough, there in brilliant Dodge blue was my friendly neighborhood stalker, his Neon hanging back one car length in the next lane over.

CHAPTER TEN

"What?" Dana craned around in her seat trying to see what I was staring at.

"That blue Dodge Neon."

"What about him?" she asked.

"I think he's following me."

"Oh, Maddie," Dana did a poo-pooing motion with her wrist and clucked her tongue. "You're just being paranoid."

"That's what I thought, but I swear to you I have seen this same car four times in the last week. First in L.A. and now here. I'm telling you, he's following me."

I kept one eye on the rearview mirror as my hands did a white knuckle grip on the steering wheel. I wasn't sure which was worse, *thinking* someone was stalking me or actually *knowing* it.

Dana craned around again to get a look at the car. "So, who is he?"

"I don't know," I said, accelerating. "But he's really starting to freak me out."

I angled my foot down on the accelerator, surging forward. Then yanked the wheel, veering to the right and cutting in front of a limo with tinted windows. Neon swerved out into the left lane pulling ahead of the limo, then quickly jumped right back onto my tail.

"He's not real concerned about being seen, is he?" Dana asked, still looking out the back window.

No he wasn't. Which was a little unnerving. Either he didn't know how to tail someone, or he was confident we wouldn't be able to pick him out of a lineup later. Like if we were dead or maimed from being run off the road.

I could clearly see the driver now. The same sandy-haired guy I'd seen at the casino. He was wearing tinted aviator glasses and a rumpled polo shirt, to all the world a normal commuter. Except for the fact that his Neon was practically kissing my back bumper now.

I took a deep breath and slammed on the brakes, veering into the far right lane between a pair of semi trucks. The driver of the second one laid on his horn and did a not-so-polite hand gesture out the window. Dana braced herself against the dashboard.

"Whoa! Take it easy, Miss Earnhardt."

But it was too late. I was in serious fight or flight mode, and considering I had trouble keeping up in Dana's low-impact Tae Bo class, I chose the flight option, hoping like anything there weren't any highway patrol cars in the area. (I was already on a first name basis with three of the L.A. county traffic court judges; I didn't need to add Nevada to the list.) Luckily, the Neon driver wasn't dealing with the added bonus of adrenalin fueled reflexes and didn't hit his brakes in time. He zipped past us in the left lane. I quickly veered off the freeway at the next exit, blindly driving surface streets like they were the Pomona Speedway until I was sure my back bumper was Neonless. I pulled the Mustang into the parking lot of a Denny's as the surge of adrenalin receded, leaving my limbs feeling like Jell-o Jigglers.

"Holy crap," Dana said in the seat next to me as she dug her nails out of Marco's Naugahyde dash. "What the hell was that about?"

I would have answered, but it was taking all my concentration just remembering to breath. In, out, in out…

"Who the hell was that freak?"

"I (in) don't (out) know."

Dana turned to face me. "Are you okay?"

"I'm (in, out, in, out) fine." Sure, once I stopped panting and my heart returned to a pace slightly less spastic than a ten year old on Ritalin.

Dana dug around in the back seat and found a discarded Taco Bell bag, which she instructed me to breathe into. The odor of week old Beefy Gordita Supreme was slighting nauseating, but after a few inhale-exhales, the urge to hyperventilate slowly dissipated. As I rhythmically inflated and deflated the fast food bag, I racked my brain to think of who cared enough about my movements to not only follow me all the way across the desert, but ride my butt all over Las Vegas as well. Ramirez? Larry? Monaldo? Not likely, since I'd never even met two of them until yesterday. And I couldn't see Ramirez paying some guy in a Neon to keep tabs on his girlfriend. So who was he? Not surprisingly, I drew a total blank.

Dana offered to drive back to the hotel (probably because she was afraid to ride shotgun with Miss Earnhardt again) and by the time we pulled up to the casino, I'm happy to report that my breathing was once again back to normal. (Though I was totally jonesing for a taco.) Dana got out at the casino entrance, but I declined her invitation of an afternoon at the roulette wheel. With the kind of luck I was having lately, I didn't think it was wise to put money on the line.

I was too keyed up to go sit in the room, not feeling lucky enough for slots, and considering I had a date with Mr. Hardbody tonight, seriously trying to resist the fattening allure of the buffet. I looked down at my watch. I still had an hour before my appointment at the salon. Which, I decided, left me more than enough time to do another quick drive by of Larry's house on the off chance he was spending a quiet afternoon at home. The more I learned about him, the more questions I had. And while the whole Mob angle was just this side of reality TV for me, I had to admit the question topping my list was why Larry'd called me in the first place. Okay, so he'd needed help, that much was obvious. But why <u>me</u>? I admit, the little-girl-lost in me was still holding out hope of that perfect father daughter reunion.

Unfortunately as I pulled up to 319 Sand Hill Lane, it was obvious today wasn't the day for it. The driveway was empty. No sign of Larry's battered Volvo. I parked at the curb and rang the bell just for good measure. No answer. I peeked in the garage windows. No car. No signs of life. No big surprise considering how my day was going so far.

Mr. Shar Pei was outside watering his cactuses again. I strolled over to the row of shrubs that served as a barrier between the two yards and waved. "Hi there," I called.

Shar Pei didn't look up.

I cleared my throat. "Um, hello!"

Nothing. I yelled a little louder. "Hey!"

Finally he glanced up from his hose and gave me a myopic squint. Then turned up his hearing aid.

"Oh, hello again," he said. "Sorry. Wife's been watchin' home shopping all day." He pointed to his ear. "Had to tune Joan Rivers out."

"Ah. Understandable. Anyway, I was just wondering if you'd seen Lar- uh, Lola around today."

He shook his head. "Nope. Sorry. I seen her pull in here last night, though. Went inside there round about when Pat Sajak came on. Then after *Dancing with the Stars* was over, I looked out the window and saw her loading a suitcase into her trunk and off she went again."

Suitcase. That was not good.

"I don't suppose she mentioned where she was going?"

He shook his head again. "Nope. But she looked in a real hurry. Maybe she had a hot date." His wrinkles squished together in an exaggerated wink.

I felt my Mad Cow burger threatening to make a repeat appearance.

"Thanks anyway."

"No problem. Any friend of that Lola's is a friend of mine." He did a couple of eyebrow wiggles that had me clinging to my denial like a security blanket.

I stared up at the house. Well… if Larry was gone, I guess it wouldn't hurt to have just one tiny peek around, right?

I opened the back gate and tippy-toed around the yard to the sliding glass door again, this time careful to watch my step over the dog toy landmines. I peeked in the windows, lifting up on the balls of my feet to see around the bushes. It looked a lot like it had yesterday. In fact, the Windex was even still out on the table. With a quick over-the-shoulder I tried the sliding door. Locked. Well, what did I really expect?

So, what now? I scanned the interior of the house as I thought. Honestly, I was out of ideas. If Larry was involved with the Mob, this was so out of my league. My league was full of children's shoes, Rainbow Brite jellies and Spiderman slippers. My league wasn't even playing the same game as a bunch of Italian-American family men.

On the other hand… I didn't think Larry was really in their league ether. I know, I know, I'd only met the man once. Okay, maybe twice if you count the whole '74 El Camino incident. How could I really know for sure what he was like? Truth? I couldn't. But what can I say? He was my dad. If I wasn't on his side, who would be?

So, telling myself I was really doing Larry a favor, I pulled out my Macy's card and stared at the locked door, trying to remember how Veronica Mars had broken into that guy's house last week. I gingerly slid the corner of the red, plastic card between the metal frame and the door. I paused, waiting for alarms to go off. Nothing. Okay, so far so good. I wriggled the card in a little deeper, until it was wedged in all the way up to the expiration date. Then I slowly slid the card downward until I came in contact with the lock. Hmmm… now what? I wriggled some more. I hated to admit it, but this didn't seem to be doing anything. By now Veronica had been inside the perp's house, had hacked into his computer, and was downloading evidence off his hard drive.

I moved the card up and down a couple more times, silently willing the lock to magically spring free. I gave it a hard downward thrust.

Snap.

Oh, crap. I pulled my credit card out, only coming away with half of it.

"Nooooooo!" I wailed. I stared at my mangled Macy's card. Why oh why hadn't I used my Nordstrom card instead? At least I knew I was already over-limit on that one.

Conceding that I was no Veronica Mars, and not willing to sacrifice my Banana Republic card, I gave up on the sliding door.

Instead, I decided to explore the other side of the house. Who knows, maybe Larry had left a window open in his haste to skip town last night. I followed a neat flagstone pathway around the corner of the building. A line of terra cotta pots and gardening tools stood beside the fence, next to the re-coiled garden hose. This time I carefully stepped *over* it.

There were three windows visible on the top floor from here, and two on the bottom. All five closed (And the bottom ones locked. I checked.) and all five sporting beige mini blinds pulled tightly shut. I might have been discouraged at this point, had I not spied a door leading into the garage at the end of the flagstone pathway.

What were the chances *it* was unlocked? Considering my luck so far, I didn't hold out a lot of hope. So imagine my surprise when the knob turned with ease in my hand. Wadda ya know? Maybe I wasn't a total jinx after all.

With one more quick over-the-shoulder for good measure, I quickly slipped inside and shut the door behind me. It was dark, only a pale stream of light coming from under the garage door illuminating the shadows. I paused a moment, letting my eyes adjust before feeling my way across the space to a door on the far side. As I did, it became clear this was no ordinary garage. This place was clean. I'm talking obsessive compulsive clean. Pristine, white floor to ceiling storage cabinets lined the far wall, neatly stacked side by side. The floor was completely free of any tell-tale oil spots, and I'd dare anyone to find an errant cobweb nestled in the corners. Along the back wall stood a tool bench with one of those pegboard thingies full of tools, each in it's rightful place. I tried to block the mental image of Larry swinging a hammer in his frilly skirts and fake wigs as I gingerly crossed the room and opened the interior door.

I found myself in the kitchen and blinked against the suddenly onslaught of light. Yellow calico curtains hung above the apron sink with a matching calico table cloth draped over a small breakfast table near the windows. Corian counters, whitewashed pine cabinets, and two framed prints of roosters completed the suburban French country look. Standing in the bright, cheerful room it was hard to imagine the owners of this house being into anything sinister.

Since I wasn't entirely sure what I was looking for, I decided to start in Hank's room. He was, after all, the dead guy in all this. Besides, he was the least likely one to mind if I did a little snoop- I mean, *investigating* through his things.

I jogged up the stairs and entered the bedroom on the right. It was clear Maurice had used his magic touch in here as well. Light, airy fabrics mixed with thick, dark woods, and large, mall-store quality prints adorned the walls. Little lace doilies covered the dresser and night stands and if I hadn't known better I'd swear my sixty-five year old Aunt Mildred lived here.

I did a quick scan of his closets and drawers, fighting off a slight case of the heebie-jeebies at touching things that belonged to a dead man. I mean, he hadn't actually died in these clothes, had he? In fact, he hadn't died in any clothes, if I remembered correctly. I made a mental note to ask Ramirez about that.

Due to Maurice's clean-aholic tendencies, I didn't turn up much, other than a few piece of expensive jewelry and a drawer full of size triple XL pantyhose. With a quick glance at my watch (if I limited my snoop- *investigating* – to another ten minutes, I could still make my lip waxing appointment) I moved on to Larry's room.

I crossed the hall and opened his bedroom door. I took one step in and cringed as my eyes fell on that tube of Raspberry Perfection sitting on his dresser.

Here's the thing: I like to consider myself as liberal minded as the next gal. I enjoyed watching *Queer Eye for the Straight Guy* and mourned the loss of *Will and Grace* just like anyone else. I don't begrudge anyone's right to be different, and if a guy wants to wear a wig and pantyhose, more power to him, right? But, just why did it have to be *my* dad in the wig, huh?

It was so much easier to be opened minded when it wasn't happening to me.

Taking a deep breath (and clutching denial in a two fisted death grip) I crossed the room and shoved the lip gloss under a long, blonde wig. There. That was better.

I decided to start with Larry's nightstand, reasoning that's where the contents of my pockets ended up every night. Maybe Larry had left a receipt or matchbook – anything that might tell me where he was now or what he was running from.

I started with the top of the nightstand, unfolding one small piece of paper after another. Mostly receipts from the grocery, drug store, some fast food restaurants. Nothing terribly telling except that he should be eating a lower fat diet. I made a mental note to tell Dana my junk food cravings were genetic.

Coming up zero on the nightstand, I moved on to the closet – not sure my denial cocoon was strong enough yet to withstand the sight of the 'intimates' that might be lurking in Larry's dresser drawers.

I opened the closet door and gasped. Shoes. Dozens of beautiful, shiny, designer shoes. It was like looking in a boutique store window. I knelt down to examine a pair. Michael Kors' last season black satin wedges with rhinestone detail and ballerina straps. If they hadn't been five sizes too big, I would have been in heaven. I turned them over in my hands, letting the long silky straps run through my fingers as I took in every little detail. If these were fakes, I was a rugby player. Whatever Larry's connection to the containers of counterfeit shoes, this wasn't it. These were the genuine $600 a pair article. I did a little sigh and set them back in the shoe rack with all the reverence they deserved.

I stifled a little squeak as I spied the next pair. Jimmy Choo Mary Janes in fire engine red with three-inch heels and gold plated buckles. I had to hand it to Larry, he did drag with style. I pulled the Mary Janes out of the closet and held them up to the mirror. The light from the window shone off the patent leather like glass. I couldn't help myself. I slipped out of my kittens heels and treated my toes to a moment in Choos. I'm pretty sure I moaned out loud. Okay, so I was a small seven and these where a big ten, but I didn't care. They looked fabulous. Beyond fabulous. These were Sarah Jessica Parker-tastic! I did a couple of foot model poses, checking them out from all angles. I was just contemplating how many cotton balls I'd have to stuff in the toes to wear them on my date with Ramirez tonight, when I heard the sound of a door opening downstairs.

I froze.

"Hello?" a voice called out. "Larry? You here?"

I willed myself not to hyperventilate. I recognized that voice. It was the same one I'd heard arguing at the club with Monaldo. Unibrow.

"La-ry," he singsonged. "You here, buddy? Your front door was open, so I thought I'd come pay you a visit."

Liar. If Unibrow had come in the front he was a hell of a lot better at breaking and entering than I was. Not a totally comforting thought.

"Larry!" Unibrow called up the stairs, his voice sharper now. "I've got something here for you. Don't make me come up there looking for you."

Crap, crap, crap! I quickly scanned the room for a hiding place as Unibrow's bulk thump, thump, thumped up the stairs. The closet would have been the obvious choice, had it not been filled to capacity with pumps. Bed, dresser, nightstand – none of which were large enough for me to hide behind. I lifted the leopard printed bed skirt. More boxes of shoes were stacked under the bed. Wow. Aside from myself and Imelda Marcos, I didn't think anyone owned this many shoes. I quickly shoved a stack out of the way and wedged myself in with the shoeboxes and dust bunnies, just as Unibrow reached the landing.

I could hear his labored breathing as he entered the room, but all I could see were his brown wingtips and the hem of his black slacks.

His feet crossed the room to the dresser; then I heard the sound of him opening drawers and tossing the contents. Tubes of lipstick fell to the floor, along with three Styrofoam heads and a handful of costume jewelry. The long, blonde wig fluttered down from the dresser, the Raspberry Perfection lip gloss rolling out from under it, across the carpet, and coming to a stop just inches from my nose.

Okay, why was it fate was taunting me like this? Can you cut a girl a little slack? I'm doing denial here!

Unibrow grunted something and gave up on the dresser. I watched his wingtips moved toward the closet, cringing at the thought of his big meat cleaver hands tossing Larry's precious designer footwear aside. I heard one shoe rack meet it's demise, collapsing with a crash, and felt a tiny piece of my heart break. I was glad now I'd put on the Mary Janes. At least they were safe.

Apparently feeling he'd caused enough destruction, Unibrow's wingtips moved away from the closet. I did a little sigh of relief for the spared pumps.

Then held my breath as he turned toward the bed.

I felt my eyes growing bigger as his shoes slowly came at me. One step after another until the tip of his right foot was inches from my face. I could smell the leather and pungent shoe polish he used, along with the faint scent of Odor-Eaters. I closed my eyes and said a silent prayer to the saint of bad hiding places that Unibrow didn't sit down on the bed. With his bulk, I'd be an instant pancake.

Someone up there must have heard me, because he didn't, instead veering to the left and out the bedroom door.

I did a sigh of relief so big, the dust bunnies in front of my face danced. His footsteps lumbered back down the stairs as I scrambled out from under the bed. I waited until I heard the front door open and shut before kicking off the too-big Mary Janes, grabbing my kitten heels, and taking the stairs two at a time. I padded barefoot across the kitchen to the garage door and slipped inside just as I heard the front door open again. I slid my shoes back on and did a little tippy-toe across the garage in the dark, hoping I didn't bump into anything but too chicken to wait until my eyes adjusted to get the heck out of Dodge.

I only tripped once, over a sack of fertilizer or something that someone had left in the middle of the floor, before I made it to the outside door. I gingerly twisted the handle, cracked the door open and peeked my head out. No sign of Unibrow. I slowly shut the door behind me, trying to make as little noise as possible even though my hands were shaking harder than a 7.2, and jogged over to the side gate. I did another crack and peek. A black Lincoln Town Car was parked at the curb, the trunk popped open. I'd watched enough HBO to know this car had Mob written all over it. I craned my head to the left and right. No sign of its driver. I prayed he was still inside the house. I gave myself a three count, then darted out of the yard and across the street to the Mustang.

It took two tries before I could keep my hands steady enough to fit the key into the ignition. But once I did I wasted no time in punching the gas and squealing my tires down the street, seriously appreciating the zero to sixty qualities of a muscle car with a V8 engine.

* * *

By the time I got back to the hotel room my hands had finally stopped shaking, my teeth were no longer chattering together like castanets and, I realized with a stab of regret, I had missed my appointment at the Regis. Not only was I being followed by a stalker and cornered by Mob goons, I was stuck with my mustache for another 24 hours until the Fran Dresher sound-alike could fit me into her schedule again. (Apparently when Bette was in town not only were the low rent rooms booked, but salon appointments were also in high demand.) After setting up a four thirty appointment for tomorrow, I flopped down on the double bed and stared at the textured ceiling again, trying to make sense of all I'd seen that day.

What had Larry gotten himself into? By now even I had to admit it looked like something just this side of legal. And from what Maurice said, things seemed to have taken a turn for the worse two weeks ago. That's when Larry and Hank had fought, and Hank had started carrying a gun. So, what was it? And what sort of 'something' did Unibrow have for Larry? Had it been in the trunk? Did it have anything to do with the counterfeit shoes? Or was 'I have something for you' code for 'I'm gonna snuff you out execution style'?

I wondered. In fact, I wondered so hard I fell asleep. By the time I woke up the sky had turned into a deep blue and there was a little puddle of drool forming at the side of my mouth.

I rolled over and looked at my cell phone. The display told me I had two new messages. Still holding out a small hope that one of them might be Larry trying to contact me again, I keyed in my pin number and listened to the recordings.

Unfortunately neither, it turned out, were from Larry. The first message was from Mom, telling me about this charming Mexican restaurant on Beech that I had to try. They served the best mojitos in Palm Springs. In fact, she said, she'd had so many of them last time she was there that she'd ended up seducing Faux Dad right there in the backseat of his Caddy in the parking lot. My mother: Queen of Too Much Information.

The second message was from Ramirez. He said he was running late and would meet me at Il Fornaio downstairs at seven. I glanced at the digital clock beside the bed. 6:15. Yikes!

I quickly hopped in the shower, then set to rummaging through my suitcase for something suitable to wear on my very first date with Mr. I-Wanna-Sex-You-Up. The only problem was I'd packed for a father-daughter reunion, not a Vegas seduction. Unless I wanted him to end the evening with a pat on the head and a bedtime story (which, considering my dry spell, was already going into extra innings, I so did *not*) I needed new clothes.

I pulled open Dana's suitcase. Lots of spandex and workout wear. All in size two. I've never considered myself a hefty gal, but there was no way I was going to be able to squeeze myself into her itty-bitties. I made a mental note to skip dessert tonight.

I glanced at the digital clock. 6:45. Not enough time to go buy something in the boutique downstairs. That left only one option. I stared at the matching set of leopard print bags. I quickly pulled one open, hoping to God Marco packed as girly as he shopped.

Bingo.

I found a pink and purple chiffon scarf that was the perfect accent to the low cut, V-neck cashmere sweater tucked into bag number three. Paired with my black leather skirt and Gucci boots, it presented a pretty decent look even if I did say so myself.

I did a smoky number on my eyes with lots of shadow and mascara. With a little blow dry and a lot of mousse, I fluffed my hair into a sexy, just got out of bed, look. (Never mind that I did, in fact, just get out of bed.) And, just in case, I slipped a couple of Altoids into my purse and put on my Vicky's Secret black lace thong. If all went well, this would be a first date to remember.

CHAPTER ELEVEN

Ramirez was waiting for me at the bar. And I had to admit as I approached him my stomach did one of those loop-d-loop things like the roller coasters at Six Flags. He was wearing gray slacks, a blazer, and a white button down shirt open at the neck to show off just a hint of his tan skin beneath. I realized I'd never actually seen Ramirez out of his usual jeans and T-shirt uniform. (If you didn't count that one half-naked encounter, that is.) Bad Cop cleaned up good. Really good. I was glad I wore the thong.

"Hey gorgeous," he said, planting a little kiss just above my ear. He ran one finger lightly along the arm of my sweater. "Soft." His mouth quirked up into a wicked half smile. "I like it."

"Thanks." I didn't tell him I'd stolen the outfit from my gay roommate.

With a hand at the small of my back, Ramirez steered me to a table near the back. A handful of other diners filled the cozy, intimate room, holding hands and feeding each other forkfuls of pasta. Soft, instrumental music played over the sound system, and small, drippy candles at every table completed the air of Northern Italian romance. All in all, the perfect restaurant for a perfect first date. Score one for Bad Cop.

The maitre d' sat us at a table next to an older couple with silver hair and matching shirts that read 'World's Cutest Couple'. And I had to agree. The man was holding the woman's hand in both of his and gazing at her like a newlywed. I looked across the table at Ramirez. I wondered if we had any chance of making it that far.

Ramirez caught my gaze. "You look really nice tonight," he said, his eyes taking on that X-ray vision look as they roamed my body.

I went warm in places I'd forgotten existed.

"Thanks. You're not so bad yourself."

That dimple made an appearance in his left cheek as he pulled out his sexy lopsided grin. He leaned forward, his eyes intent on mine. "What do you say we skip dinner…?" His eyes dipped a little lower to my neckline. "…and go right to dessert?"

I gulped. I had a feeling he wasn't talking about the tiramisu. And I was one second away from agreeing when the waiter appeared at my elbow, asking for our drink order. After a quick perusal of the wine list, Ramirez picked out a bottle of Rutherford Hill Merlot. Nice. I snuck a look at the price. Wow. Very nice. Score point number two for Bad Cop.

Once our waiter disappeared into the back, we both picked up our menus again.

"Decided what you want yet?" Ramirez asked.

"I'm not sure." I looked down at the list of entrées. "Everything looks so good. How about you?"

"Oh, I *know* what I want." I looked up to find him staring right at me. Or more accurately, at the hint of cleavage my Wonderbra was lifting out of Marco's sweater. I did one of those dry gulp things again and hoped I wasn't blushing too hard.

"So," he said, folding his cloth napkin onto his lap. "How was your shopping trip today?"

"Shopping?" I asked before I could stop myself.

He narrowed his eyes at me. "Yes, shopping. You were supposed to go shopping today, right?"

I bit my lip. Oh, yeah. Right. "I, uh, kind of took in some of the local sights instead." I quickly buried my nose in the menu, pretending I was concentrating really hard on the ingredients of the linguini marinara so he didn't see the guilty look in my eyes.

No such luck. Ramirez put a hand over the top of my menu, slowly lowering it. "Local sights?"

"Uh-huh," I said in a tiny voice. Frighteningly like the one I used to use when my Irish Catholic grandmother caught me sneaking cookies before dinner

He narrowed his eyes further. "Such as?"

"Um… Larry's house and Maurice's condo."

"Maurice?"

"Hank's boyfriend."

Ramirez muttered a curse. The world's cutest couple turned and gave us a look.

"What exactly were you doing at Hank's boyfriend's house?" Ramirez asked.

"Just, you know… asking a few questions."

"You don't give up do you?" he asked, rubbing at his temple in exasperation.

"You make that sound like it's a bad thing."

"It *is* a bad thing when we're talking about the Mob!"

The cutest couple gasped.

"Keep your voice down," I whispered.

Ramirez clenched his jaw together. He did a couple of deep breaths, and I could see him mentally counting to ten. Though instead of getting calmer, I think that vein in his neck was starting to bulge.

Luckily I was saved by the waiter appearing with our overpriced Merlot. He uncorked our wine and poured us each a glass. Ramirez downed his in one big gulp.

"Do you realize you just inhaled about $20 worth of wine?" I whispered as the waiter walked away.

Ramirez fixed me with a stare that could stop a charging bull. Then poured another glass. "Okay Sherlock Fashion," he said through clenched teeth. "What did Maurice have to say? Spill it."

So I did. I told him what Maurice had said about the three Manolo-keteers working on the side for Monaldo. I told him about Larry and Hank's blow up, Hank's propensity to carry a gun, Bobbi's disappearance, and Larry's skipping town. I was just about to tell him about my dust bunny encounter with Unibrow's wingtips when the waiter returned to take our order.

Ramirez ordered the steak. Rare. I hemmed and hawed over the linguini marinara or the lasagna with cream sauce, figuring the longer I took the more time Ramirez had to get that bulging vein under control. No such luck. As soon as the waiter left again, Ramirez pinned me with one of his unreadable stares.

"What?" I asked.

He narrowed his eyes. "I'm trying to decide whether to put you on the first plane back to L.A. or take you back to my place, tie you up, and make you forget this whole thing."

I blinked a couple of times. "Do I get a say in this?"

He leaned forward, his face serious. "Maddie the last thing I want to do is be called in to identify your body. Which is exactly what will happen if you don't leave this alone. Guys like Monaldo will hurt you like they're swatting a fly, and not think twice about it. Please go home."

I had to admit, his concern was actually kind of touching. "But what about Larry? I can't just leave him to be hunted down by Monaldo."

"And what exactly do *you* propose to do about it? You can't even squish a spider without freaking out."

I bit back a smart reply as a teeny tiny part of me kind of agreed with him. I was in so far over my head that I could see blonde roots. But Ramirez on the other hand did this kind of thing every day…

"Nothing. But *you* could do something."

His eyes narrowed into cat-like slits. "I don't like the sound of this."

"You've got to put Larry into some kind of protective custody."

"What, I should just lock him up? Maddie, do you know how hard it is to get a legitimate witness into protective custody? Let alone some guy who may or may not know anything, and who, I might add, may or may not even be willing to tell us what he does know?"

"But I think he might be in danger."

"You *think* he *might* be."

"What about Hank?" I asked. "You said yourself that wasn't a suicide."

Ramirez blew a big sigh up at the ceiling. "Look, unless your father turns himself over to the police with information about a crime, there's nothing I can do."

"This is because you want me to leave, right?" I asked, planting my hands on my hips. "You're just trying to discourage me so I'll get out of your hair."

"No," Ramirez said, his voice going tight like he was really trying to restrain himself from lapsing into swearing Spanish again. "I'm telling you the same thing I would say to any concerned citizen."

"But, I'm not asking you as a citizen, I'm asking you as your-" I paused, biting my lip. His what?

Ramirez raised an eyebrow, interested to see how I finished that thought.

"Your… girl you're on a first date with."

He shook his head. "I'm sorry, Maddie, but unless Larry turns himself in, there's nothing I can do. Besides, wherever he is, I'm sure he's fine. I know Larry. He can take care of himself."

I paused and stared at him. My heartbeat speeding up as his last comment sank in. "Wait a minute - what do you mean, you *know* Larry?"

"I've been undercover at the club for the last six weeks, Maddie. I've gotten to know the employees."

I don't know why it hadn't dawned on me sooner, but comprehension suddenly smacked me upside the head. "Oh. My. God. You've known about my dad all along haven't you? You knew he wore go-go boots and didn't tell me!?"

He fidgeted in his seat. And to his credit he even looked a little sheepish. A very little. "Maddie, I didn't say anything because I knew you'd react this way."

"What way?" I said, my volume quickly rising into a range that had the world's cutest couple glancing our way again. "How exactly am I reacting? Like I've been lied to? Like the person I'm supposed to be able to trust is keeping secrets from me? Like everyone else knows about my dad's high heel fetish but me!?"

"Maddie-"

"No, don't you 'Maddie' me." I banged my hand on the table, making the cutest couple jump in their seats. They were openly staring now and I'd wager taking bets to see who won. "How long have you known?"

Ramirez sighed. "Larry had talked about a daughter, but I didn't know for sure it was you until I heard the message at your apartment."

"That was days ago! I can't believe you knew and didn't tell me." My fingers clenched around my butter knife, and it took all my willpower not reach across the table and stab him in his no-good, lying heart with it.

"Maddie, I was undercover. I couldn't tell you."

"I'm sorry, being undercover isn't an excuse for being an asshole. Dammit, Jack, I can't believe you did this. You lied to me!" I paused. "And do you want to know what's even worse than that?"

Ramirez pinched the bridge of his nose. I could tell he really didn't. Too bad. He was damn well going to hear it anyway.

I stood up, throwing the knife down on the table and giving him my best stare down. "You have now officially ruined our very first date!"

Ramirez shook his head, his eyes straying to my Wonder-cleavage again as his voice came out in a wistful sigh. "I'm not getting any again tonight, am I?"

Damn skippy, pal.

* * *

The first thing I did when I got back to the room was raid the re-stocked mini bar for a tiny bottle of tequila and a king sized Snickers bar. Healthy food be damned!

I crunched down hard on a bite of peanuts and nougat, my fists still clenching and unclenching at my sides. I couldn't believe Ramirez had kept my dad a secret from me! What kind of a person would do that? Sure he was undercover, blah, blah, blah. I'd heard enough of his work excuses to last me a lifetime. But this one crossed the line. How could someone know your father wears go-go boots and not tell you? If he could keep something like that a secret, what other things had he been keeping from me? A secret wife? A harem of long, legged Mob girlfriends? A career modeling underwear on the side?

Okay, so I wouldn't really mind that last one too much. But it was the principle of the thing. You are not supposed to keep life altering secrets from your girlfriend.

I paused, Snickers suspended in mid-air. But I guess I wasn't technically his girlfriend. Hell, we couldn't even have one lousy date together. Let's face it, as a couple, we were a disaster. Why was it we were always either fighting or ripping each other's clothes off? What was wrong with us that we couldn't just have a nice dinner together?

I polished off the Snickers bar while I digested this disconcerting thought. I contemplated about going for a second one, but didn't want Marco to accuse me of stretching out his sweater. Instead I checked my messages, figuring I'd given Ramirez ample time to leave me a humble voicemail apology.

No such luck. My in-box was empty. No Dad on the run. No Mom and her travel tips for love birds. No sheepish Bad Cop.

I went for that second Snickers after all.

I was halfway through that one, heading deep into a chocolate and alcohol induced state of self-pity, when Dana burst through the door.

"Ohmigod, ohmigod, ohmigod!" Dana jumped up and down on the double bed.

"What?" I mumbled as I licked a piece of chocolate off my lips.

"I just totally won five hundred dollars at the roulette wheel. Do you know how totally hard it is to win at roulette? Let me tell you, it's hard. See, Officer Taylor and I were having drinks at the Times Square Bar, and then I said I wanted to try that game with the wheel thingy, and he said 'what, roulette?' and I said 'I guess so,' and he said 'do you know how hard it is to win at roulette?' and I said 'how hard can it be?' so he said 'okay, let's give it a try.' And we did. And I was like, '12 black,' and the dealer was like, 'okay,' and then he like spun the wheel, and the ball like totally bounced all over, and then it totally landed on, guess what? 12 black! I am on fire, Maddie! I could so do this for a living. Forget L.A. I'm moving to Vegas, baby. I'm totally going to become one of those professional gamblers on the Bravo network. I am so damn good at this!"

"Good for you." I took another large bite of my Snickers. How is it fair Dana could be lucky with both men and casino games? Me – all I could seem to attract lately was trouble and chocolate.

"You must come play roulette with me, Maddie. It is such a freaking rush!"

She jumped up and down again, her long legs springing her precariously close to the ceiling. The bed let out a low groan of protest.

"Uh, Dana, maybe you shouldn't be jumping-"

But it was too late. Dana did one more bounce, and the springs gave way beneath her with a loud moan.

"Uhn." She rolled off the side, landing face down on the floor as the center of the bed caved in like a 400 pound ghost was laying on it.

Dana pulled her face out of the shag and looked up. "Oops."

"No kidding."

She stared at the ruined bed for a couple beats. Then turned to me. "So, what do you say, wanna go play roulette with me?"

I just rolled my eyes.

While Dana flipped on the casino channel to pick up more tips for delusional gamblers, I called down to the front desk. Slim Jim wasn't there. Instead I got some woman named Shirley who informed me there were still no other rooms available in our 'price bracket.' But, she could send up another rollaway. Since my neck was still aching from the last rollaway I'd slept on, I declined.

Instead, I slipped out of my sexy skirt and thong, more than a little disappointed that I was taking it off myself instead of watching Ramirez do it with his teeth, and crawled into the double bed with Dana. *So* not the person I had planned on sleeping with tonight.

I was just drifting off into a well deserved sleep when William Tell burst out from the region of my cell phone. I fumbled around in the dark.

"Hello?" I asked, steadfastly refusing to open my eyes.

I heard a couple sniffles, and then Maurice's voice came on the line. "Maddie? It's Maurice."

I sat up in bed. "What's wrong?"

He sniffled again. "Nothing, nothing. I, uh, I just wanted to call and tell you that we're holding a service for Hank tomorrow. I… I know he'd want you to come." Maurice broke down, sobbing on the other end.

I suddenly felt twice as bad about zapping his dog. And I admit, I wasn't quite sure what to say. It wasn't as if I'd actually known Hank. To be honest, I didn't even really know Larry. On the other hand, Hank had been Larry's best friend. If Larry was going to come out of hiding anywhere, it would be to pay his last respects.

"What time?" I asked, grabbing a sheet of hotel stationary.

Maurice gave the where's and when's of the service, then hung up with a sniffle and a sob. That poor man. I had a feeling he was going to need a saline transfusion if he carried on much more.

Well, I guess one thing could be said for Ramirez's and my relationship. At least neither of us was dead.

* * *

I was deep into a dream starring Ramirez's six-pack abs when I felt something smack me across my cheek. "Uhn."

I opened one eye. Dana's arm was covering my face. I pushed her off and got a foot in the stomach.

"Ow," I whined.

Dana just grunted and mumbled something about 'frontal assaults.' Then turned over and elbowed me in the ribs.

Note to self: never sleep with an Urban Soldierette. I glanced at the digital clock on the nightstand. 6:20 AM. I groaned, but, due to the imminent risk of bruising, I rolled myself out from under my best friend and took my beaten body into the shower anyway.

I let the hot water rush over me and closed my eyes, trying to shake off the semi-coma state early mornings put me into. Today of all days, I needed my mind to be sharp. It was Wednesday, my last day in Vegas. Unless a) prices in the Marquis suites plummeted into a reasonable (read 'low rent') rate, and b) Tot Trots miraculously decided to extend my deadline for the Rainbow Brite jellies designs (which I'd woefully neglected since I'd first gotten Larry's message), I had only one day left to help Larry.

It was painfully clear at this point that I was in way over my blonde little head. Whatever dealings Larry had stumbled into I had little hope I that could get him out, especially when we threw Mafiosos into the mix. The best I could do was, as Ramirez had said, convince Larry to turn himself in. I hoped Larry showed up at the funeral. Because I was running out of places to look.

As a concession to sleepless night in a row number four, I put on my shortest skirt, highest heels, and more eye makeup than my mother. Or father, for that matter. The look was a little on the slutty side but at least it distracted from the bags under my eyes (which were so big I was pretty sure they wouldn't even qualify as carry-ons anymore). Ten minutes later I was dressed, blow dried, and standing at the front desk before Slim Jim again.

"Checking out today?" he asked, searching behind me for a glimpse of Dana. Or, more accurately, Dana's breasts.

"Yes I am. And by the way, the bed's broken in our room."

He eyed me suspiciously. "How did that happen?"

I shrugged. "Search me."

He contemplated the offer for about half a second. That is, until his eyes rested on my barely-B chest and decided I wasn't worth the effort. "Fine. I'll tell maintenance."

"So, any way I could get a discount for the broken bed?"

He gave me a look. "Don't push it."

I didn't. Instead, I signed the bill (cringing just a little at the total) and told him we'd vacate the room by noon.

That done, I headed in the direction of the American restaurant hoping a big latte, and an even bigger plate of pancakes with gooey maple syrup might help me wake up. I was halfway across the casino floor, picking my way through the fake tress and corridors of slot machines, when my cell chirped.

"Hello?" I answered.

It's a universal truth that no matter how healthy our self esteem, we all have little quirks about ourselves we wish we could fix. Some people wish they could remember names better. Others want to stop smoking or quit biting their nails. Me – I wished like hell that I'd learn to check the caller ID before picking up my phone.

"Maddie! I can't believe you lied to me!"

Ugh. Mom. I rubbed at my temples (where, coincidentally, an instant headache had bloomed) wondering just which lie she'd caught me in this time. "Hi, Mom."

"Maddie how could you. Las Vegas? Las Vegas!?"

Well, that answered that question. "Mom, it's not what you think-"

"Oh, Maddie. After everything I've done for you! I raised you as a single parent, Maddie. A single parent! Oh, how could you do this to me…" She trailed off into a wail that belonged in an Alfred Hitchcock film, and I heard the phone drop from her hands.

A second later Faux Dad came on the line. "Maddie?"

"Hi, Ralph. What's going on?"

"Um, well, your picture was kind of in the *L.A. Informer* this morning."

Again? I smacked my forehead with my palm. What was with those guys? It was one lousy boob! "What was it this time? Wait, don't tell me. I'm engaged to a Martian, right?"

"Actually," he paused, clearing his throat. "There was a story about you getting involved in another murder case. In Las Vegas. There's a picture of you outside some club called the Victoria."

I shut my eyes and thought a really dirty word. They had to pick *now* to print real stuff?

"Listen," Faux Dad continued. "I know how these papers get their facts mixed up sometimes. And I remember how they glued your head onto Pamela Anderson's body when they said you were getting engaged to Bigfoot. So…" he trailed off.

God love him, he was giving me a nice out. But for some reason I was having a hard time taking it. Truth was, I felt funny discussing this whole Larry thing with Faux Dad at all. Ever since he and Mom had started dating, Ralph had filled the role of father figure in a way I never thought anyone would. Okay, so I was a little old for trips to the zoo with him, but he did give me all the free manicures I wanted at his salon. In my book, that spelled love. And now, just by being here, I almost felt like I was betraying him somehow.

Luckily I didn't have to answer as Mom grabbed the phone away again.

"How could you betray me like this?" she sobbed.

Oh, brother. I rolled my eyes.

"Mom. I'm sorry. But I had to come."

"You lied to me, Maddie. Lied!"

"Excuse me," I said, doing a hands-on-hips thing, "but *you've* been lying to *me* for the last twenty-six years. My dad wears go-go boots!" One of the blue-haireds at the *Wheel of Fortune* slot machine looked my way. But only for a second. This was Vegas. Everyone wore go-go boots.

"I can't believe you made up the whole thing about Palm Springs, Maddie."

"Okay, technically it was Marco who made that up. But let's get back to the whole you-never-telling-me-my-dad-was-a-she thing. Do you know how many letters I sent to Billy Idol?"

But nothing I said was going to get through to her. Mom was the guilt master, and she was in her zone now. "I raised you. I fed you and clothed you. I changed your poopy diapers…"

Ew! "Mom, I was just here for a couple days-"

"… and this is the thanks I get. Betrayal! Lies! I would expect this from Larry, but from my own flesh and blood? How could you?" Mom punctuated this with another raise-the-dead wail.

"Mom, I swear I'm coming home today-"

"Where did I go wrong? How did I a raise such a deceitful child?"

"Mom-"

"The trust is broken, Maddie. You've broken my trust and my heart!"

"Look, I didn't mean-"

"And to think, I bought you a ficus!"

"Mom, I-"

But it was too late. The line was dead. My mother had hung up on me. I thunked my head against the side of a mega bucks machine.

"Ow."

I shoved my phone back in my purse and backtracked to the front desk, that headache pulsing behind my eyes with every step.

Slim Jim was checking in a couple with four little kids in tow, all four pointing in different directions and arguing over what they were going to see first.

"Hey!" I called, waving him over.

He gave me a one finger, 'wait' sign, while he handed the harried parents their room keys, then sauntered over. "Yeah?"

"Do you have a copy of the *L.A. Informer* back there?"

"I dunno."

"Well, could you check?" I asked, forcing myself to paste on a smile.

Slim Jim did a dramatic sigh, as if doing favors for barely-B's was so not in his job description. However, he did look behind the counter, popping up a minute later with a copy of the tabloid in his hands.

"Thanks," I mumbled as I grabbed it from him.

I scanned the front page. The headline read "Local Sleuth Snoops into Mysterious Drag Death." Great. Tot Trots was just going to love this! I felt my headache threatening into migraine territory as I read the rest of the story. The reporter started with a blurb about last summer's mishaps and the popped boob, then went on to say I was investigating another suspicious death, this time involving an alleged suicide off a Vegas nightclub roof. He even had the nerve to tell all the Vegas women with implants to stay out of my way.

Beside the story they'd printed two pictures, one of me outside the nightclub and the second was of Dana and me at Maurice's condo yesterday. I stared at them both. Who even knew I was in Vegas, let alone going to Maurice's house?

I scanned down to the byline. Felix Dunn. The same guy who'd left all those messages on my machine last week. And, I realized with a surge of triumph as I looked at his fingernail sized black and white photo, the same guy I'd seen behind the wheel of a certain blue Dodge Neon. Sonofabitch! Neon Guy was a reporter.

"Excuse me," I said, hailing Slim Jim back over.

This time he was in the middle of checking in a short Asian man and a long legged model dressed in an outfit that made me wonder if the New York - New York rented rooms by the hour. Jim shot me an annoyed look and gave the finger again. The 'wait a minute' one, not the other one. Though if he could have gotten away with it, I think he would have used the other one.

Finally he finished with the odd couple and made his way over to me. "What now?"

"I need a room number."

He cocked his head to the side. "Didn't you just check out?"

"No, not for me. I need you to look up the room number of a guest. Felix Dunn."

He shook his head. "I'm sorry, but I can't do that."

"You don't understand. This is an emergency. This is a real story. I'm not the bride of Bigfoot. Tot Trots is going to fire me, not to mention what my mother will do. Good God, I may end up pounding lemons in one of those Hot Dog on a Stick Hats again. Don't you understand, I can't go back to those hats!"

He stared at me. Clearly, Slim Jim didn't understand. Slim Jim thought I was nuts.

"Sorry. It's against hotel policy. We can't give out guests' room numbers. I can get a message to him if you'd like?"

"I don't want to leave him a message. I want to kill him!" Which didn't do much to further my case.

I paused. I counted to ten. Okay, fine, I only made it to five before I started to lose it again. I decided to try a different tactic.

"Tell you what. How about you bend the rules just a teeny tiny bit for me, and maybe I can do something in return for you."

Slim Jim narrowed his eyes at me. "What kind of something?"

I did a mental cringe, hoping Dana would forgive me for what I was about to do. "How about a date with my friend, Dana?"

His eyes lit up. "The one with the DD's?"

I nodded.

Slim Jim did a quick over-the-shoulder supervisor check, then leaned in close. "Think she'd go to the Bette Midler show with me tomorrow night? I've got two tickets right up front"

I crossed my fingers behind my back, and I nodded. "Absolutely." That is if we weren't going to be back in L.A. by then.

He paused. But the allure of a night with a stacked blonde was more than any man could resist. "Okay. But if anyone asks, you did not get this from me." Slim Jim did a couple of quick clicks on his keyboard. "1504."

"Thanks!"

"Hey," he called as I walked away, "tell Dana to meet me here at seven!"

I gave him a wave over my shoulder as I stalked to the elevators with renewed purpose. In the last three days I'd had to deal with not only my so-called-boyfriend showing up undercover in a drag club, but also my mother's tips for the best places to have sex in Palm Springs, my best friend turning into a gambling addict, a dead drag queen, his weepy boyfriend, a zapped yapper dog, my MIA dad's propensity for go-go boots, and, oh yes, last but not least – the Mob! The last thing I needed was for my big fat drag club life to be splashed across the front pages of L.A.'s sleaziest tabloid.

The elevator opened, and I jumped in, slamming my palm onto the button for the fifteenth floor. Well, I might not be able to do much about the Mob or the crappy state of my non-existent love life. Or even the fact that Mom was going to lecture me into a coma, and my employment with Tot Trots was likely to terminate so fast I'd be eating Cup-O-Noodles for the rest of the year.

But I could do one thing about this tabloid guy.

I tapped my foot. I fumed. I tapped and fumed some more. Finally the doors slid open at the fifteenth floor.

I stomped down the hallway, steam starting to come out of my ears as I made my way to room 1504. I rapped so hard on the door my knuckles stung.

"Hang on," a male voice, tinged with a hoity-toity British accent, called from inside.

Then the door was pulled open by Mr. Neon himself. He was wearing the khaki's again, this time barefoot with his shirt open as if I'd caught him in the act of getting dressed. He paused for just a second before recognition him hit.

"Maddie?" he asked, a confused expression washing over his face.

"Felix."

Then I cocked my fist back and punched him squarely in the nose.

CHAPTER TWELVE

"Bloody hell!" Felix staggered back, holding one hand to his face and the other straight out as if to ward off the psycho barging her way into his hotel room.

I slammed the door shut behind me.

"What the hell was that for?" he asked, his accent thick as blood starting to seep through his fingers.

"That," I said, still advancing on him, "was for making my mother cry."

He stared at me uncomprehending. "Lady, you're nuts."

"Thanks to your sleaze factory she may very well disown me now. Stop printing pictures of me!"

He pulled his hand away from his nose. A small trickle of blood still remained on his upper lip. "Sorry, love, I can't. That's what I do."

"No," I said advancing on him again until my index finger jutted into his chest. "You print stories about Bigfoot having the Abominable Snow Monster's love child and Anna Nichole Smith's affair with a three headed alien. You write about the government's secret plot to cover up the Loch Ness monster."

"Don't knock it. I think I'm up for a Pulitzer with that Nessie exposé." He did a slow grin, his eyes crinkling at the corner. On any other day, his brand of self-deprecating humor might have passed as charming. As it was, I fought off the urge to hit him again.

"You work for a tabloid," I said, annunciating as if I was talking to a two year old. "You make crap up. You do not cover real stories about real people."

His Hugh-Grant-blue eyes lit up. "So there is a real story here?"

"No," I quickly covered. "No story. None at all. I'm… here on vacation."

"Funny, I thought you were vacationing in Palm Springs." He broke into a self-satisfied grin, leaning casually against the wall as his arms crossed over his chest.

I narrowed my eyes at him. "How do you know about that?"

"Sweetheart, I know everything about you. I'm a very good reporter, you know?"

"Ha! That's why you work at the *Informer*?"

His grin faltered. "Touché. All right, how about this. I know that last week I got a call from a man who'd seen your picture in our humble little… uh, how did you so charmingly refer to it, 'sleaze factory'? He claimed to be your long lost father and wanted to know how to get in touch with you. Not being able to resist a schmaltzy sob story, I gave him your number. Then followed you around, waiting for the big tearful reunion. Instead, I got a dead body at a drag club. Which, by the way is a very fun angle," he added with a wink.

My hand balled into a fist again.

"And," he continued, "I know that the deceased is reported to have jumped off the roof. Only, any idiot who's ever seen a real jumper could tell you the trajectory was all wrong. Put that together with the fact you've been questioning friends of the deceased, and I've got a headline that reads: Santa Monica's Favorite Amateur Sleuth At It Again."

I felt sick to my stomach. Though, I noticed hopefully, he hadn't mentioned Ramirez or the Mob. Apparently he wasn't *that* good of a reporter. "Leave me alone," I warned him.

He threw on his charming face again, all boyish smiles. "No need to be hostile. In fact, let's make things easier on both of us. How about an exclusive, huh, love?"

"Stop calling me 'love!'"

"Why, are you going to hit me again?"

I was seriously thinking about it.

"Ever heard of slander? Libel? I could easily sue you for that Bigfoot story."

Felix held a hand to his heart in mock horror. "Heaven forbid."

I narrowed my eyes at him. "You're mocking me."

"Indeed, I am."

"I hate you."

"Aw. I'm crushed."

"Listen, pretty boy, if I see one more picture of myself in your little tabloid, I swear to God I will come back here with my best friend who happens to be an Urban Soldierette and knows a hundred and one different ways to make a man sing soprano. And she's not afraid to use them!"

He just smiled. "Ooo. Sounds kinky."

I shot him a look that could freeze the devil himself. (Who I wasn't altogether sure wasn't a tabloid reporter.) "Quit following me!" I stalked to the door and pulled it open so hard it rattled against the wall.

"Lovely to have met you, Maddie," he called after me.

I flipped him the bird as the door slammed shut behind me.

I silently seethed as I rode the elevator back down to the casino level. I went straight to the American Restaurant and ordered a plate loaded with pancakes, waffles, French toast, and crepes that was so high I couldn't see around it. All served with a mound of whipped cream and a river of gooey maple syrup. By the time I was done I felt totally sick to my stomach, but the anger hadn't really gone away. It had just morphed into slow burning anxiety. With Tabloid Boy following me around like a lost puppy, things had suddenly become much more urgent.

If Monaldo saw Felix's story, it wouldn't take much digging for him to put two and two together and realize I was Larry's daughter. I wasn't sure how this fared for Larry's safety, but I didn't think it would endear Monaldo to him much more.

Not to mention me.

Whatever Larry had gotten himself into, I needed to get him out. And fast.

Before Monaldo got to Larry.

* * *

By the time I got back up to the room, Marco was strategically fitting his collection of souvenirs into leopard printed luggage while Dana got in one last poker lesson from the casino channel.

Dana took one look at my low cut tank, liberally dotted with maple syrup, and started clucking her tongue.

"Oh, Maddie. Pancakes? Do you know how many carbs are in those things? Not to mention the refined sugars."

"I only had three." I didn't tell her about the waffles and crepes.

"All that white flour goes right to your mid section. I bet you just ate two hundred sit-ups worth of simple carbohydrates."

I shuddered at the mere mention of the 'S' word. "I couldn't help it. I needed comfort food."

"Why, what happened?" Marco asked, tucking a 'Vegas Vic' coffee mug between a pair of loafers.

I flopped down on the one functioning bed and told them about my morning's series of disasters. How one person's life could disintegrate so quickly, I still wasn't sure. And it wasn't even noon yet!

When I was finished, Marco had stuffed the last of his commemorative postcards into the one square inch of space left in his bags, and Dana was doing a series of "ohmigod," things.

"Ohmigod! That creep! He almost ran us off the road for a freaking picture?"

"Well, he didn't exactly run us off the road," I conceded. In fact, now that I knew my 'stalker' was nothing more than a tabloid hound, the whole thing seemed almost petty.

"What a putz," Dana said. "I ought to go kick his ass right now."

While I appreciated the sentiment, I had a terrifying vision of *that* scene splayed across tomorrow's front page.

Instead, I turned to Marco who was sitting on his carry-on, trying to force the zipper closed. "So, any luck with Madonna last night?" I asked.

Marco got a wicked look in his eyes, dimples creasing both his cheeks. "Tsk, tsk, Maddie. You know I never kiss and tell."

I rolled my eyes. At least someone around here was getting some. "I meant about Bobbi."

"Oh, that! Yeah, sure." He reached into his new 'I heart Vegas' tote bag and pulled out a slip of paper. "Madonna said he lives near the airport. Above this little bar called FlyBoyz. I've got the address right here." Marco handed me the paper.

"I take it there's still no sign of him at the club?"

Marco shook his head. "Nope. Madonna said the last anyone had seen of him was a week ago. He actually left in the middle of a shift. Asked one of the other girls to cover for him and just took off."

"Had he ever done that sort of thing before?"

Marco shook his head. "Never. Bobbi's got two ex-wives and five kids. From what Madonna said, it sounded like he was always behind on child support. He never missed a shift."

I didn't have a very good feeling about this. Hank's funeral wasn't until two, which left us a good three hours to go check out Bobbi's place. So, after we'd thoroughly cleaned the room out of hotel stationary and complimentary mini toiletries, the three of us hauled our luggage down to the Mustang and piled in. Only somehow Marco's luggage had multiplied and there was just one teeny tiny space left in the back seat for me, wedged between his make-up bag and a life sized cardboard cutout of Elvis he'd picked up at the Neon Museum. I tried not to think about riding with The King for the next four hours as Marco pulled out onto the Strip and followed the snail's pace traffic toward the airport.

* * *

The FlyBoyz bar took up the lower half of a faded stucco building located directly across the causeway from McCarran International Airport. A neon sign, dimmed now in the daylight, hovered over a dark, wooden door. Two windows faced the street, though they were both covered in peeling black paint. A dozen Harley Davidsons lined the far side of the lot, punctuated with bumper stickers that read 'Desert Demons.' The upper floors of the building held a series of apartments that would have been great for watching planes take off from the tarmac. Not so great for a peaceful night's sleep. Even as we parked the car in the makeshift gravel lot, the sky above us filled with the underbelly of a 747, and the ground shook with a magnitude 6.4, rattling the blackened windows of the bar.

"Nice place," Dana said, laying the sarcasm on double-stuffed.

Marco just scrunched his nose into an 'ick' face.

Gravel crunching beneath our feet, we made our way around to the back of the building where a set of metal stairs, minus the railing, led to the upper level apartments. There were four mailboxes affixed to the wall at the bottom. Rusted letters on their faces read A, B, C, and D. D was bulging with mail. I gingerly pulled an envelope out. A bill from the water company addressed to Bob Hostetler. A.k.a. Bobbi.

"It looks like he hasn't been here in a while," Dana noted.

"Maybe he's just on vacation?" I asked hopefully.

Dana gave me a 'get real' look. "Who leaves for vacation in the middle of a shift?"

Someone on the run from the Mob, that's who. I forced that thought down as a picture of Larry sprung to mind, and replaced the envelope back in the mailbox.

"Let's check upstairs." Holding onto the wall for support, I gingerly took the first step. The staircase seemed to hold me, so I slowly worked my way up, gesturing for Marco and Dana to follow. Marco did an exaggerated over the shoulder thing before shimmying up the stairs sideways in something that was part James Bond and part audition for *Cats*.

"What are you doing?" I whispered.

He shrugged, palms up. "What?" he whispered back.

"That shimmy thing?"

"I was being sneaky."

"You were being conspicuous," Dana whispered. "Everyone knows the way to be the least suspicious is to act like you belong here."

"Then why are we whispering?"

He had us there.

"Just, come on," I said, reverting to my normal voice.

I led the way up to the top of the stairs (as Marco continued his Broadway Bond routine behind me) where a little landing carpeted in fake plastic lawn opened up to four doors. A and B were on the right, C and D on the left. C had lost its letter, only a dark outline in contrast to the faded paint on the door remained. D's letter had lost its top nail and was hanging upside down. Though, I noticed with a little lift, there didn't seem to be any visible signs of a struggle or break in.

I looked from Dana to Marco, then took a deep breath and knocked, hoping like anything a big hairy lady answered the door.

I waited two beats, then knocked again, shifting from foot to foot on the small landing. I could smell Indian food being prepared behind apartment A's door, and from apartment C I could hear the faint base rhythms of a Black Eyed Peas song. But nothing from apartment D.

I knocked once more for good measure, though I knew deep down it was a lost cause. Either Bobbi was on the run or… well, I didn't want to think about the 'or.' At least not while Larry was still out there in that 'or' limbo land too. Instead, I said a silent prayer to the saint of men on the run that Bobbi and Larry where both holed up somewhere together. Somewhere far, far away from Monaldo and his tweezers-challenged goon.

"I don't think anyone's home," Marco whispered, voicing my thoughts.

"You want me to pick the lock?" Dana asked.

I turned on her. "You know how to do that?"

She shrugged. "How hard could it be? I watch Veronica Mars. All you need's a credit card."

"Yeah, that's what I thought," I muttered under my breath. But, considering our combined experience in breaking and entering consisted of five episodes of a teenage detective and one mangled Visa, I persuaded Dana to leave the lock be.

"Well, maybe we could check his mail? Rico says you can tell a lot about a suspect by going through his mail."

I shrugged. Might as well. Though I was pretty sure the Mob didn't send death threats via US postal service.

We clanked back down the stairs and converged on box D again. With a quick over the shoulder to make sure the local postmaster hadn't suddenly appeared at our backs, we each took a stack of mail and began sorting through it.

Mine was mostly bills and a couple of envelopes from Clark County Child Services, no doubt wondering where little Bobbi junior's monthly mac and cheese money was. Electric bill, credit card bills - two of them stamped past due. And a handful of catalogues for 'hefty' women's fashions. I took it Bobbi was not a slight man.

"Check out this dress," Marco said, holding up a 'Big Lovely Ladies' catalogue featuring a pink and black polka dotted off the shoulder in size 3XL. "This out to be outlawed."

"Oh, yeah, I'll one up you," Dana countered. She held out a catalogue page featuring a teal green poncho with bright yellow daisies on it. "Why not just walk around in a shower curtain?"

Me – I was quiet. As I was pretty sure my mom owned that same poncho.

Bobbi's bad taste in clothes aside, there wasn't anything terribly telling in his mail. No subscription to *Mobsters Monthly*, no indication of where he might be now. Though, Marco pointed out that the earliest postmark was the middle of last week. Bobbi hadn't been back to pick up his mail since then.

"You want to go check out the bar?" Dana suggested.

Marco and I eyed the blackened windows and row of Harleys.

"Nuh-uh," Marco said, shaking his head violently. "Do you know what they do to guys like me in places like that?"

"Don't worry, princess. I'll protect you," Dana said, taking Marco's arm and steering him toward the door.

The interior of the FlyBoyz was just about as appealing as the outside, and I immediately wished I hadn't confiscated Dana's stun gun. The painted windows gave the place a cave-like feeling, not mitigated by the shadowy crowd gathered around scarred tables and an ancient jukebox playing a George Thorogood song. The men (and a couple of beefier ladies) were dressed in various versions of the leather chaps and biker vest look, some going with the grubby bandanna over the shaved head while others opted for the I-combed-it-last-week mullet look. All of them looked way overdue for their monthly bath. And smelled even worse. The air held the distinct odors of beer, sweat, and a cloyingly sweet scent that I wasn't about to try to identify. Clearly this was not the Vegas advertised in flashy posters at your neighborhood travel agent.

The air was so thick with cigarette smoke that I could hardly see where I was walking as we made our way to the bar.

Which might be a good thing. I didn't even want to guess what the sticky substance all over the floor was.

"Excuse me," Dana called to the bartender. He was bald, had full tattoo sleeves on each arm and a long goatee that reminded me of a nanny goat.

"Yeah?" he grunted. He gave us a once over, his eyes squinting at the corners as they rested on Marco.

I think I heard Marco whimper.

"We're looking for the man who lives above you in apartment D," Dana continued.

Nanny Goat Guy just gave us a blank look.

"Bob?" I prompted.

A slow grin spread out on Nanny's Goat's face, showing off a row of stained teeth. Most of which were still there.

"Big Boy Bob," he drawled.

"Big Boy?" I asked, remembering the hefty women catalogues.

Nanny chuckled. "Yeah. It's kind of a pet name. The fruit's always comin' in here dressed like a chick." Nanny paused with a sideways look at Marco's beret.

Marco gave him a feeble one finger wave.

"Uh, anyway..." I cleared my throat. "When was the last time you saw Bob around?"

Nanny stroked his goatee. "Not sure. Been a few days though. He missed karaoke night on Friday, and Big Boy never misses that." He did that gap toothed grin again. "He always does *Pretty Woman*."

I tried not to picture the shower curtain poncho to go with that audio track.

"Say, what do you want with Big Boy anyway? Who are you?" Nanny asked, his eyes going from Dana to me... then resting on Marco again.

This time I'm sure I heard him whimper.

"Who are we?" I asked, my voice going about an octave higher as Nanny narrowed his eyes at us. "We're, um, well...."

I hesitated to tell him. Unibrow had already searched Larry's place. I didn't particularly want my name coming up should he make a visit to Bobbi's as well. I was racking my little brain for a good fake name, when Dana came to the rescue.

"Hey, is that a cobra?" she asked, pointing to a snake tattoo making its way up Nanny Goat's left forearm.

He nodded. "Yeah. Got it in the Gulf War."

"No kidding?" Dana leaned in closer. "Because my friend, Rico, has the same one."

Nanny Goat's face broke into a smile. "Rico Moreno?"

"Ohmigod, yes!"

"Hell, Rico and me go way back. Used to run around San Bernardino together with this group called the Hellcats when we was kids. After I joined up, we served together in Kuwait. That's where I got this beauty," he said, gesturing to his arm again. "Why didn't you tell me you all was friends of Rico's?" He reached across the bar and slapped Marco on the back.

Marco lurched forward from the impact, steadying himself on the counter with another whimper.

"What a small world," Dana mused.

"Hell, in that case I don't mind tellin' you, you ain't the first people come lookin' for our Big Boy."

"We're not?" I asked, visions of Unibrows dancing in my head.

"Nope." Nanny leaned back, crossing his arms over his chest. "About a week ago his ex was in here looking for him. Said he missed his child support payment this month. Nothin' new though, that guy is always behind."

"So we gathered. Anyone else stop by?" I asked.

He nodded. "Yep. Couple days before that. Big dude. Built like a tank. Real hairy eyebrows."

I gulped. "What did he want?"

"He was looking for Bob too. Gave me some line about Bob owing him on a gambling debt. I didn't buy it though."

"Why not?"

"Like I said, Big Boy was always behind. Any extra cash he got went to those ex-wives of his. No way would he gamble any of it away. The dude was odd, but he wasn't stupid."

"Thanks," I said, though it wasn't really the news I wanted to hear. Apparently Monaldo was sending his goons to pick off the drag brothers one by one. It was only a matter of time before they worked their way down to Larry's name.

I pulled a pen out of my purse and wrote down my cell phone number on a cocktail napkin. "If you see Bob, would you mind giving me a call?"

"No prob," Nanny said, depositing the napkin in his pocket. "Like I said, any friend of Rico's is a friend of mine."

After Dana and Nanny exchanged a few pleasantries about what the old 'dirty dog' Rico was up to lately, we made our way back out into the assaulting sunlight.

Marco, who'd been quiet save for the whimpers, let out a long breath as we reached the car. "That was the most scary place I have ever been," he said, fanning himself with his beret. "I seriously need a drink. Anyone want to stop for a cranberry-tini?"

CHAPTER THIRTEEN

In lieu of cocktails, we pulled into a McDonald's on Maryland and after a Quarter Pounder, Diet Coke, and hot apple pie (hey, I did go for the *diet* soda) we changed for Hank's funeral. I paired my mostly-clean black leather skirt with the most demure white blouse I'd packed and a dark blazer I borrowed from Marco. Topped off with a pair of casual black Cavalli pumps, I looked conservative enough to blend at a memorial service.

I wish I could have said the same for Marco. He emerged from the men's room wearing a pair of gray slacks with an iridescent purple sheen to them, a skin tight black shirt and the jaunty black beret again. And to think this was the man worried about being conspicuous.

Dana followed my lead, doing a little black dress thing with a black leather jacket over the top. Okay, so our hemlines were a little higher than true mourning called for, but hey, this was Vegas.

And, as we entered the church at Alta and Campbell, I realized that a Vegas funeral has a whole different meaning than a Beverly Hills funeral. Vegas funeral made West Hollywood on Liberace's birthday look tame.

While the church was a subdued stained glass affair with dark pews, light flower arrangements, and soft organ music, the inhabitants of the large room were anything but.

The first couple of pews held what I assumed were Hank's family – an older couple in grays and navy blues, a man in a dark suit, and two squirmy children probably glad they'd got to miss school for 'Auntie' Hank's funeral. But the pews behind them were a mix between the circus and a soap opera audition. Three full rows of aging drag queens in unrelieved black. Long, lacey dresses, wide brimmed hats (one with an ostrich plume sticking two feet into the air), and somber black veils. The handful whose faces were visible were fully made up, big fat tears running a marathon down their powdered cheeks as they sobbed into little white hankies. Oh, boy, did they sob. Not a dry eye in the house. And none of this dainty eye-dabbing stuff either. These ladies were doing the kind of sobs usually only heard from toddlers at naptime. Big, full blown body-sobs that echoed under the high ceiling like a symphony of dying geese. Punctuated by the occasional nose blown loud enough to shake the stained glass windows.

I tried to look past the veils and hankies to see if Larry was among them. But, honestly, I couldn't tell one from the other. A different wig, a different girdle, and I wasn't sure I'd even recognize my father.

Beside the painted ladies sat Maurice. His face looked like it had aged a couple hundred years since I'd last seen him. And the somber music wafting in through the sound system didn't do anything to mitigate the grief lines etched around his eyes. He reminded me a little of Eeyore from *Winnie the Pooh.* His eyes downcast, his skin taking on a little of a gray color that perfectly matched the suit he donned in lieu of his trademark turtleneck. I wondered if he'd slept at all since Hank died. His bags looked bigger than mine.

Across the aisle from Maurice sat Monaldo and his line of henchmen. To his right was Unibrow and to the left, Ramirez.

Marco, Dana and I settled into an empty pew behind the painted ladies. Luckily, Monaldo didn't notice us.

Unluckily, Ramirez did.

He craned his head back, letting his eyes casually scan the room until they met mine. Then they went all big and round as his jaw did a little drop open thing like it was on over-oiled hinges. He blinked a couple of times, then mouthed at me, "What are you doing here?"

I just smiled and shrugged. What else could I do?

Ramirez pulled his jaw into a tight Bad Cop face and narrowed his eyes, staring me down. I could feel them boring a hole right through me. I hoped I'd never have to face him across an interrogation table. I had a pretty good idea I'd crack.

We all settled into our places as a white-haired priest took to the pulpit and began waxing poetic about Hank's life and the hereafter. I admit, I kind of tuned him out, instead searching the sobbing painted ladies again for any sign of Larry. Unibrow kept glancing behind him, toward the open church doors, doing, I supposed, the same thing. I felt like I was on a Where's Waldo hunt, and the first one to spot Waldo's miniskirt won the prize of Larry – dead or alive.

The ceremony was short, thankfully, then we all shuffled out of the church to drive single file the short distance to the cemetery. On the off chance Monaldo and his crew might recognize the Mustang, we held back. I noticed Ramirez scanning the crowd for me. I ducked behind the woman with the ostrich feather until Monaldo motioned him into the long, black Lincoln and shut the door behind him.

Since we'd brought up the rear of the parade, most of the crowd had already assembled at the gravesite by the time we arrived. Hank's eternal rest would be under a large tree, atop a small, manmade hill, covered in a lawn that must have used half of Lake Mead to water in the summer. We parked the car on the gravel road and hiked to the top where the coffin sat, now laying next to a tarp covered pile of dirt. Carnations, roses, and fragrant lilies of the valley lay on the polished mahogany surface. Maurice started bawling as he lay a single red rose on the pile. Which of course set off the painted ladies (who would take any excuse to pull out a hankie), and pretty soon everyone was in tears again.

Except for Monaldo. While his face was a placid mask, I was pretty sure on the inside he was celebrating having just gotten away with murder.

Beside him Ramirez just glared at me, his eyes silently cursing at me in Spanish. I tried to ignore him, instead focusing on the priest as he said a final few words over the gravesite.

Something about funerals always depresses me. Usually it's the idea that my own end is somewhere in sight. It raises the big scary question of what is there after this life? Do we really ascend, as the priest promised, to a beautiful magical plane where there is no pain, sorrow, or shoes that pinch your toes five minutes after you put them on? Or do we simply die, turn to dust, and that's all she wrote?

Only today, the questions of the universe were taking a backseat to questions about my father. I wondered where he was. I wondered if Monaldo might have already gotten to him. I wondered if I'd ever be able to picture him again without thinking of red lipstick.

I scanned the faces of the mourners for Larry again. Most were the same from the church, though a few had opted to join the group here. So far none was six feet tall in a red wig.

Once the priest said his final 'ashes to ashes' the crowd began to disperse, lingering in small groups to console each other. I casually mingled amongst them, searching each veiled face for any signs of my father. It had been a long shot that he'd even show up, but I hated to let go of that small hope I'd see him once more.

I was circling a group of painted ladies (still sobbing into their hankies) when the hairs on the back of my neck stood up. I felt him before I even heard him. That's how hot the anger radiating off his body was.

"What are you doing here?" Ramirez growled in my ear.

I froze. "Paying my last respects."

"You are supposed to be on your way back to Los Angeles," he said in a tightly restrained whisper. I was pretty sure that if I turned around now I'd see that vein bulging in his neck again.

"Maurice invited me. It would have been rude not to come."

Ramirez muttered something in Spanish. But before I could figure out which creative swear word he was employing now, he grabbed me by the arm and pulled me down the hill and into the back of Monaldo's Lincoln.

"I swear, I'm leaving right after-"

But I didn't get to finish. As soon as he had the door shut behind us, Ramirez grabbed me by the shoulders and planted his lips on mine.

I shuddered from the impact. Or maybe it was from the volcanic heat instantly settling south of my belly button.

"God, you look sexy in black," he murmured, coming up for air.

"I'm wearing Marco's clothes."

Ramirez looked down. Then shrugged. "It's been six weeks. You'd look sexy in anything."

I was about to protest, but he didn't give me a chance, taking my lips in his and thoroughly kissing me again.

"Or better yet," he amended, "nothing at all."

He slid his hand up my shirt, his fingers closing around the clasp of my bra.

"Whoa, boy!" I pushed him away, both hands flat against his chest. "You're kidding, right? You want to do this *now*?"

He paused, looking around the backseat. "What? The windows are tinted."

"We're at a funeral!"

"So... is that wrong?"

I'm ashamed to say that with my hands still glued to his rock hard pecs, I actually thought about it for a minute.

"Yes, of course it's wrong. And by the way, have you noticed that every time we're together we're either ripping each other's clothes off or fighting?"

"Yeah, we should do a lot less fighting."

"I'm serious."

He flashed me his big bad wolf smile. "So am I."

I rolled my eyes. "Why can't we just have a normal conversation like normal people in a normal relationship?"

"So, you wanna talk *now*?"

I crossed my arms over my chest. "Yes."

He sighed. Then tilted his head from side to side, as if working out tension kinks that magically appeared whenever I did. "Okay. Fine. Let's talk."

"Good."

Then we both stared at each other. Silent.

Great. Turns out we had nothing to talk about.

"So..." I said, grasping for anything. "How was your day?"

He raised one eyebrow at me. "My day?"

"Yes. This is what normal couples talk about. They talk about their day. So, how was your day?"

Ramirez rubbed the back of his neck, relieving a little more of that tension. "Okay. My day was fine."

I threw my hands up. "No, that's not how it goes. You're supposed to tell me what you did, where you went, who you talked to. You're supposed to tell me how you felt about your day so I can be all supportive and stuff. Like, here I'll go first. I had a call from my mother. She's pissed, and I feel like crap for lying to her and am pretty sure she's going to either disown me or at the very least take back my new ficus. After that I punched my stalker in the nose, which felt a lot better than it should have. Then we went to FlyBoyz which just made me feel like I needed a shower. There. That was my day. Now your turn. What did you do today?"

Ramirez just stared. "Whoa. Back up – stalker?"

Whoops.

"Did I say 'stalker?' Okay, well, see he's really more of a *follower* than a *stalker* to be honest. He just kind of follows me around town and occasionally takes pictures that he occasionally prints in his newspaper."

"A reporter?!" he shouted. That vein started to bulge in his neck, and I wondered if maybe I should have stuck with the stalker story instead. "You're telling me you have a reporter following you?"

I did a deep sigh. This was so not how normal couples had conversations. But it was too late to put that horse back in the barn. Instead, I told Ramirez all about my encounter with Felix and the many Dodge Neon sightings I'd been privy to in the last week, ending with the *Informer*'s piece this morning.

When I finished he did one of those foreign curses again, and I made a mental note to sign up for Spanish class at the rec center.

"Don't worry," I reassured him. "The worst has already happened. Mom saw it."

"Maddie, I'm not worried about your Mom," he said, the vein staring to pulsate now. "I'm worried about Monaldo! If he sees this, how long do you think it will take before he puts two and two together? He saw you at the club. He knows your face, and if he sees that paper he'll know your name and where to find you."

The thought sent a cold chill right up my spine. "I didn't think of that."

"Obviously."

"Hey, it's not like I asked to have my picture in the paper."

"Yet somehow the other ninety-nine point nine percent of the population can manage to stay the hell out of things that don't concern them."

"Larry's my father. It concerns me!"

Ramirez rubbed his neck again. "Look, just leave it alone, okay? Go home, design a few SpongeBob boots or whatever it is you do and let *me* do *my* job, okay?"

While his tone was way over the border of condescension, making me want to quote last quarter's sales figures for my 'whatever it is you do' shoes, I knew he was right. The best thing for me to do was get out of town before I messed up his investigation any more than I already had. The sooner he put Monaldo behind bars, the sooner I could breathe easily abut my father's safety. So, instead of taking a stand for shoe designers everywhere, this time I let the comment go.

"Fine. But," I added, "just so you know, we're doing it again."

He paused, a blank look on his face. "Doing what?"

"Fighting. See?"

He took a deep breath, then looked toward the sky as if asking for patience from some where above. "I told you we should have just had sex."

I crossed my arms over my chest. "Hmph." It was the best response I could come up with because I was kind of thinking he might be right. "Look, I'll go away and let you do your job, but just promise me you won't let anything happen to Larry while-"

But he cut me off, shoving my head down in his lap.

"Um, hello? Ever heard of foreplay?" I mumbled against his thigh.

"Shhhh. Someone's coming."

I shifted my body down to a crouching position on the floor mats as someone knocked on the other side of Ramirez's window. I held my breath, trying to make myself as small as possible.

Ramirez cracked the window open. "Yeah?"

"There you are, Bruno."

That arctic freeze tickled my spinal column again as I recognized the voice. Monaldo.

"Yeah, I'm here," Ramirez answered, doing an Oscar worthy impression of cool, casual Goon Number Two. Even though I could feel his legs muscle tense beneath my palms.

"What's going on in there?" Monaldo asked.

I scrunched my eyes tight, my fingers digging into Ramirez's thighs as I willed the bad man to just go away.

"Nothin'," Ramirez answered, in a lazy, drawl. "I just had enough of the bawling, you know?"

Monaldo was silent for a moment. And I was on the verge of wetting my pants when he finally said, "Fine. Were leaving in five minutes."

I did an internal sigh of relief.

"You're the boss," Ramirez responded; then I heard the sweet sound of the window being rolled back up.

I let out a long breath as Ramirez helped me back up onto the seat.

"Those are some claws you've got." He rubbed his leg where I could see the distinct impression of my fingernails in his slacks.

"Sorry," I said, still shaking a monster case of the heebie-jeebies off me.

"No problem. Just promise me you'll file those things down before our next 'normal conversation.'"

And with that, he opened the door and gave me a little push out of the car. Punctuated by a swat on the bottom, before shutting it again behind me.

Sadly, it was the most action I'd gotten in months.

I straightened up and smoothed out my blouse, wiping the carpet lint off my skirt as I scurried across the dirt road lest Monaldo catch a memory-jogging glimpse of me.

The painted ladies were still chatting graveside with the reverend, most still leaking from the eyes, though I noticed as they lifted their veils, they'd invested wisely in waterproof mascara. I spotted Marco standing under a tree chatting up the Madonna from the club – resplendent in knee length black lace, leather ankle boots, jelly bracelets up both arms, and crimped hair that added a full six inches to her height. (Sigh. Part of me, the part that barely makes the height requirements on the Six Flags rides, still yearned for the big hair days of the eighties.)

Dana was off to the side of the group, chatting with the Crew Cut bouncer from the club. Okay, maybe 'chatting' wasn't the right word. Shamelessly flirting might better describe the pouty-lipped, jutty-chest thing she was doing. After his non-interest the other night, I'd say Dana was on a mission to prove the powers of a 36 DD aerobics queen.

Off to the side of the cemetery were a few mourners in pairs, talking quietly, consoling each other, some stopping to smell the fragrant bouquets of flowers flanking the gravesite. I watched as one mourner leaned down to sniff a gardenia, her hat tilting ever so slightly forward on her head to reveal a hint of red hair beneath.

I froze. Larry.

My instinct was to sprint the short distance between us, but I didn't want to scare him off. I already knew he could outrun me. Instead, I casually strolled across the lawn, adrenalin pumping through my veins with every step. I clenched my teeth together to keep from calling out his name, as the closer I got the more sure I was it was him. The same tall frame, same slightly paunchy middle, and the same impossible shade of red hair, just barley visible beneath the long, opaque veil covering his face.

I was a mere three steps away when a light flashed from the trees to my right. Larry saw it too, quickly straightening up like a deer in the headlights. The flash went off again.

Larry looked up, our eyes connecting for one brief second before he took off like a shot, disappearing behind a stone mausoleum.

"Wait!" I called, dashing after him. I rounded the stone building and saw a flash of black take the corner, dashing through a grove of trees down to the road where the line of waiting cars sat. "Please!" I pleaded. I hated how desperate I sounded. I tried to tell myself it was for Larry's safety, but part of me just wished my father would quit darting in the opposite direction whenever he saw me. It was enough to give a girl a complex.

Instead of following him into the grove of trees, I cut across the lawn, taking a more direct route to the cars. I was almost to the road when another flash of light went off, this time so close it momentarily blinded me.

"Uhn." I did a perfect ten-point face plant into the grass, my torso skidding like I was on a Slip 'n' Slide as my hands splayed out in front of me.

I heard a car engine turn over and regained my fuzzy vision just in time to see a beat up Volvo pulling down the road.

Damn! I pounded one fist on the ground.

Then saw that flash of light behind me again. I twisted around on the ground and looked up to find a pair of blue eyes smirking at me.

Felix.

"A bit out of shape, aren't we, love?" he asked. He was dressed in the same rumpled khaki, today paired with a blue striped button down, opened at the neck as he casually leaned against a tree, his camera dangling from one hand. Though, I was satisfied to see, his blue eyes were rimmed in purple today, a white bandage taped across his nose.

"You!" I said, pointing an accusatory finger at him. "I should have known." I stood up, trying in vain to wipe the grass off of me. I had a nice green skid mark down the front of my once-white shirt, and a deep scratch punctuated the leather skirt, spanning from my hips all the way down to the hem.

"You all right, love?" Felix asked. Though I noticed he didn't stop clicking that damn camera.

"I'm fine," I said, blinking away the little points of light dancing across my vision. "No thanks to you."

"Now, now. Don't blame it all on me. You're the one tottering about in those ridiculous shoes."

I sucked in a shocked breath. "Ridiculous? I'll have you know these are Roberto Cavalli, Italian calfskin pumps worth more than your monthly salary, pal. These are not ridiculous. They're fabulous," I said, with as much dignity as a woman in a ruined skirt and a grass stained blouse could muster.

His eyes roved down to my feet. "They don't look very fabulous to me."

I looked down. He was right. One sad little heel was jutting out at an unhealthy angle. "Noooo!" I wailed. This day just kept getting better and better. I stood up and took my shoe off, inspecting the damage. There was a slim possibility it could be repaired by a professional, but it would require major surgery.

I was just contemplating whether my MasterCard had enough room on it for a replacement pair when Felix took a picture of the poor damaged victim.

"No pictures of my shoes!" I yelled.

"Shhhh," Felix said, putting a finger to his lips. "You're boyfriend might hear us." He gestured to 'Bruno,' now lounging against the side of the Lincoln.

"He's not my boyfriend," I argued. Which was, sadly, only too true. We couldn't even have a conversation together, let alone a relationship.

"No? Because I could have sworn I saw you and he making a little time in the back of that Lincoln there."

Damn. This guy didn't miss a thing.

"We weren't making time. We were…" Arguing about reporters? Discussing an on going investigation? "I mean, he was…" Undercover? Ordering me back home? "Well, I was kind of…" Hiding from a mobster with my head in his lap?

Felix raised one eyebrow. "Indeed."

"Look, it's not important."

"It's not?"

"No. He's nobody."

"Nobody?"

"Nobody."

"So, you routinely hop into the backseat with nobodies?" he asked.

"No! Look, maybe I kind of know him, but not like that. Not like you're thinking. He's not… and we're not… and there's nothing going on. I mean, we haven't done anything. I haven't done anything in months. So long that I'm three weeks over due with *Joanie Loves Chachi* and at this rate Blockbuster's going to make me pay for a new one."

Felix raised the other eyebrow. "Indeed." Then he snapped another picture of me.

"I swear to God if you take one more picture of me, I'm going to kill you."

He grinned, showing off his slightly crooked teeth. "Can I quote you on that, love?"

I felt my left eye starting to twitch. I took a deep breath and counted to ten. Then counted to ten again. I was pretty sure that strangling him with his own camera strap would be bad funeral etiquette.

"What are you doing here anyway?" I asked instead.

Felix shrugged. "Paying my respects."

"You didn't even know Hank!"

"Did you?" he asked, leaning in.

I narrowed my eyes. "Oh, no. No. you're not getting a story out of me, pal."

"Too late." He grinned. Then shot another picture.

"Stop that!" I yelled, waving away the little flying specks of light. "I'm going to go blind."

He cocked his head to the side, narrowing his eyes as he stared at me. "You've got a little something…" he trailed off, pointing to his upper lip.

"Yes, I know! I'm growing a mustache. Okay? So freaking what? You want to make a story out of that? Oh, I know, how about calling me the hairy yeti woman of Los Angeles; that oughta sell copies for you. Hey, maybe you'll even be up for a Pulitzer. So, go ahead, take a picture of me with my big, fat, hairy lip. I dare you."

Felix's lips quivered, threatening to explode into full blown laughter any second.

"Uh, actually, I think it's grass."

"Huh?" I put my hand to my lip. Sure enough, I came away with three little blades of green grass. Mental forehead smack.

"Oh."

The laughter broke free, and Felix shook with it, his entire body spasming as he clicked away, taking a series of pictures he'd have to caption "Woman dies of embarrassment – police investigating the role of lip hair in her untimely demise."

Before I could make any more of a fool of myself in front of the press, I turned and hobbled over to where Marco was chatting up his Material Girl.

"I have to go," I whispered. "*Now*!"

* * *

I waited while Marco and Madonna exchanged phone numbers, hugs, jelly bracelets, and a series of air kisses, then dragged him and Dana back to the Mustang where we all piled in. (Me behind the wheel this time, as I still had an indentation of cardboard Elvis's microphone on my tush.) I pulled the car back onto the main road and out to the 15. True to my word, we were leaving Vegas. But… I had one quick little stop to make first. Regis's Salon. I had a four-thirty lip waxing, and after the embarrassing monologue I'd given Tabloid Boy about my yeti lip, there was no way I was going to miss it this time. I glanced down at my watch. 4:22. I eased the gas pedal just a little further down, zipping by a sports car in the left lane.

"Slow down," Marco whined. "Dahling, this car is a classic. She's not a dragster."

I ignored him, passing a pick-up on the right. It may be a classic, but I was on a mission.

"Seriously, Maddie, slow down. Elvis keeps falling in my lap," Dana whined from the backseat.

Nothing doing. We were two exits from the Strip with a minute and a half to spare. I could make it this time. The next time Ramirez pulled one of his surprise lip-locks, I was going to be smooth as a baby's behind.

Then the unthinkable happened. Blue lights flashed in my rearview mirror.

Marco turned around. "Uh-oh."

'Uh-oh' was right. I spun my head around. "Shit!" A police car was glued to my bumper. He turned on his siren and motioned for me to pull over.

"I told you to slow down," Macro said.

I gave him the death look as I eased the car over to the right shoulder.

The police car parked behind me. I looked at my watch. 4:29. Shit, shit, shit!

The highway patrolman motioned for Marco to roll down the passenger side window. He was in his late thirties with a pronounced mid-section and wore mirrored aviator glasses and a little brown Magnum P.I. mustache. He placed his hands on his hips and popped a piece of gum between his teeth. "License and registration, ma'am."

Marco opened the glove box and fished around for the registration while I searched my purse for my driver's license.

"I'm sorry, was I going too fast?" I asked, batting my eyelashes at him.

"License and registration," he repeated. Clearly he was not into the flirtatious blonde routine. Damn. In L.A. that shtick killed.

Marco finally found the registration and handed it over to the officer. I was still searching.

"Look, maybe I was going just a teeny tiny bit too fast, but I had a really, really good reason. See, I'm late for an appointment, and I can't miss it this time."

I looked up. No sympathy at all.

"I mean, it's very important," I said, still rummaging through my purse as I pleaded my case. "I have a waxing I'm late for. I'm not sure if you've ever had one, but they're essential to preventing a mustache."

Officer Magnum twitched his upper lip and did a little grunt.

"Oh! I mean, not that some people might not want a mustache. Mustaches can be wonderful. You for instance look stunning in one. Very hip. Right, Marco?"

Marco nodded. "Right."

"See, on you it looks fantastic. But on a woman, well, not the same effect. Women have to wax. Take your mother, for instance, I'm sure she waxes all the time."

He clenched his jaw and gave me a hard stare.

"Not, of course, that your mother needs to wax. I mean, I'm sure she's not at all hairy. She's probably a very hairless woman in fact. I mean, not totally hairless because then she'd be bald, which wouldn't be very attractive either. Which I'm sure your mother is. Attractive that is, not bald."

Officer Magnum took off his mirrored glasses and narrowed his eyes at me. "Li-cense and reg-is-tra-tion," he said, sharply annunciating each syllable.

"Right." I dumped the contents of my purse onto my lap. Bingo. My license fell out, and I handed it to him.

"Hairless mother?" Dana asked, poking me from behind as the officer walked back to his car with my ID.

"What?" I shrugged. "I was nervous."

Marco just shook his head at me.

I looked down at my watch, watching the digital numbers tick by. 4:32. 4:33. "Come on, come, on, come on," I chanted. If he would just write me the dang ticket already there was still a chance I could make it to the salon before the next appointment.

Finally Officer Magnum got out of his squad car again. He put his shades back on and made purposeful strides to the driver's side window, one hand on his utility belt.

"Ma'am, I need you to get out of the car."

Marco and I looked at each other. Huh?

"Why? Is something wrong?"

"Ma'am please step out of the vehicle." His hand hovered over his revolver.

"Look, I'm sorry for the crack about your mother. I'm sure she's a very lovely person. Really. Just the appropriate amount of hair."

"Ma'am, please don't make me ask you again."

"Maddie," Marco whispered. "I think he's serious. You better do it."

I bit my lip, feeling my heart sink down to the tip of my toes as I realized I might never see the end of this upper lip 'dust.' I slowly opened the driver's side door and stepped out.

"Look, officer, I'm sure that whatever this is about-"

But before I could finish, Officer Magnum had my arms twisted behind my back and was clicking a pair of handcuffs on my wrist.

"Hey!"

"Hey!" Marco and Dana echoed in unison from the car.

"What's going on here?" Dana demanded.

"Maddison Springer," the officer recited as he clicked a second cuff on my wrist. "You're under arrest."

"Under arrest! For speeding?" Ray Liotta I asked, my voice going into mezzo soprano range.

Officer Magnum spun me around to face him, his mirrored glasses reflecting the look of fear and confusion on my face.

"No. You're under arrest," he repeated, "for the murder of Bob Hostetler."

CHAPTER FOURTEEN

In a place where both laying down your life savings on twenty-two black and selling your body at the rate of thirty bucks an hour are legal, you have to do something pretty bad to end up in the Clark County lockup. Which didn't make me feel terribly comfortable around my cellmates. (My cellmates! Ugh! A phrase I could have happily gone my whole life without using.)

A homeless lady wearing a head full of dreads (and not the sexy Lenny Kravitz kind but the matted-with-gobs-of-who-knows-what kind) sat on a sparse wooden bench in the corner talking to herself. Next to her was a 200 pound black woman who looked like she'd gone three rounds with Oscar De La Hoya. And lost. If she was the one in prison, I shuddered to think what the other guy looked like. She was wearing a red pleather mini skirt and stained white bra. Nothing else. I tried not to stare as I sat down on the opposite side of the holding cell, next to a thin woman in a Motorhead T-shirt scratching at the imaginary bugs on her arms.

After Officer Magnum had handcuffed me and shoved me into the back of his squad car (with a 'watch you're head, ma'am,' the sole response to my frantic questions of, 'what the hell do you mean, murder?') I was transported to the Clark County holding, where I was fingerprinted (and now had black smudges on my blouse next to the grass stains), photographed, then searched from head to toe by a woman who was the spitting image of Jim Belushi (talk about someone in need of a waxing). Then they'd taken my purse, cell phone and, worst of all, my shoes, citing the heels were high enough to qualify as weapons. Instead, they gave me these little blue paper booties to stick over my feet before shuffling me off to my cell.

All in all, it qualified as the most embarrassing incident of my entire life. Even winning out over the junior high school Valentine's dance where I shared my first French kiss with Benny Winetraub. During which our braces got stuck together, resulting in a metal lip-lock that lasted until the principal called Benny's orthodontist to cut us apart. On a scale of one to ten, the Benny incident ranked a nine for most embarrassing moment ever.

Being booked for murder was a thirty-five.

"Springer!" Mizz Belushi called.

"Yes!" I jumped up so quickly my itchy friend yelped.

"Let's go."

"Oh, thank God," I said as she unlocked the door and led me out. "See, I told you this was all just a big mistake."

She smirked. "Hmph. We'll see about that."

Then, much to my disappointment, instead of leading me back down the hall to the room where I'd abandoned my pumps, she walked me through a series of doors into a tiny room with peeling gray paint and buzzing fluorescent lights overhead. It held one long table, four metal chairs, and a huge mirror covering the length of one wall.

Uh-oh. I watched *Law & Order*, I knew this room. This was where they shined those bright lights down on people and fed them soda after soda without letting them go to the bathroom until they finally cracked and confessed to everything.

I hesitated in the doorway.

"Don't I get one phone call?" I asked.

Belushi snickered. "You watch too much TV." Then she sat me down at the peeling laminate table. "You wanna soda or something?" she asked.

Gulp. See, what did I tell you? "No, thanks."

She just shrugged, then walked out, shutting the door behind her.

I cautiously looked around the room. No bright spotlights. No video cameras in the corner. The only thing that screamed 'interrogation' was the big one-way mirror. I stared at it. I admit, I was curious. Of course I'd seen these things a hundred times before on TV, but I'd never actually seen one in person. I slowly stood up and walked over to it, wondering if there was anyone watching me from the other side.

"Hello?" I whispered, doing a little wave at the reflective surface. No answer. I took a couple of steps closer, squinting to see if I could make out anything on the other side. Nothing. I put my nose right up to the glass and smushed my face into it. Still couldn't see a thing.

Unfortunately, Belushi picked that moment to come back into the room. I jumped back from the mirror as the door popped open.

"What are you doing?" she asked.

"Nothing." I pulled my sleeve down and rubbed a nose print off the mirror.

"Uh-huh," she said, believing me about as much as I believed no one was watching this whole exchange from the next room. She gestured to the table and I obediently sat down in one of the metal chairs as two men entered the room. The first was a short guy in brown slacks and a short sleeve button-down that looked like it came with a free pocket protector. His bald head and sparse mustache bore an uncanny resemblance to Detective Andy Sipowicz from *NYPD Blue,* and his round figure just barely made it through the door.

But my gaze didn't stick with Sipowicz for long, my attention immediately falling on the second guy as his broad shouldered frame walked through the door.

Ramirez.

I had never been so glad to see anyone in my entire life. I would have jumped up and hugged him had he not been giving me the death look.

Ramirez and Sipowicz sat down on the opposite side of the table, the portly detective placing a lined, yellow notepad out in front of him.

"My name's Detective Romanowsky," he said, doing a Jersey accent. "You already know Detective Ramirez. We need to ask you a few questions about your activities over the past two days. Before we begin, can I get you a soda?"

"No!" I blurted out.

Sipowicz jumped in his seat.

"Uh, I mean, no thank you." I bit my lip, looking to Ramirez. He wouldn't actually let them do the soda-no-bathroom routine on me, would he? I searched his face for any sign of leniency, but he just stared back doing his stony Bad Cop.

"Okay, then. Let's start with your whereabouts this afternoon," Sipowicz said, pen poised over the notepad.

I swallowed, my mouth feeling like sandpaper. "I went to a funeral and was on my way to the salon, and after that I swear I was going to leave Vegas," I said, addressing Ramirez's poker face.

Sipowicz raised one eyebrow. "So you were on your way out of town when the officer picked you up?"

"No, wait. I mean, I didn't try to *leave* leave. Not like I was skipping town 'cause I did something bad or anything. I was just going away. With a totally guilt-free conscience. Okay, well, maybe I feel a little guilty for lying to my mother about the whole Palm Springs thing, but that's a whole different kind of guilt. I mean, that's the I'm-going-to-have-to-endure-dinner-at-her-house-for-a-month-straight-to-make-up-for-it kind of guilt. Not the someone-died-and-I'm-not-taking-the-rap-for-it kind. Not that I *want* to take the rap for this. I don't. Because I didn't do it. Which is why I wasn't fleeing at all. I was just leaving. Slowly. No fleeing."

Sipowicz raised the other eyebrow.

I looked to Ramirez, desperation bubbling into my voice. "You believe me don't you?"

But all I got in return was Bad Cop.

See, here's the thing: last summer when I kind of got involved in that murder investigation, Ramirez had, for a fraction of an instant, believed I had something to do with it. In his defense, I did suspiciously keep turning up in the vicinity of dead bodies. But I'd hated the fact that he doubted me, even for a second. And now that our tongues had done the mambo together, I hated that blank, give-away-nothing stare of his even more.

My hands fidgeted in my lap as I waited for him to say something. (Anything!)

Finally he broke his silence, turning to Sipowicz. "Could you give us a minute?"

The balding detective looked from Ramirez to me. Then shrugged. "All right. I'll be outside."

I waited until the door clicked shut behind him before pleading my case again. "You have to believe me," I blurted out. "I didn't kill anyone! You know I wouldn't do that."

Ramirez sighed, rubbing one hand across his face. "Of course I know that. Jesus, Maddie, why can't you just go shopping or get your hair done like a normal girl?"

I did an internal sigh of relief. Okay, so the comment was sexist on *so* many levels, but at least someone knew this was all a big mistake. "Then why am I here?" I asked. "What happened to Bobbi?"

"Bob Hostetler's body was found this afternoon in your father's garage."

"But that's impossible," I protested. "I was just-" I paused. Oh, my God, the bag of fertilizer! I suddenly felt sick to my stomach. I hadn't tripped over a soil treatment. I'd tripped over Bob!

"You were just what?" Ramirez leaned his elbows on the table, his eyes narrowing in on me.

"I was just… talking about Bobbi the other day."

Ramirez shook his head. "Look, now is the time to come clean with me, Maddie. Your fingerprints are all over that house, and the crime scene unit found half a credit card with your name on it wedged in the back door."

Damn! My Macy's card! In my haste to slip past Unibrow, I'd forgotten all about it.

"And," Ramirez continued. "… the shoe print of a size seven high heel was found next to the body. Any guess whose?"

"Jimmy Choo's?"

Ramirez ground his teeth together. "Yours."

"Okay, I can explain."

"Oh, I bet you can."

I put my hands on my hips. "Hey, what's that supposed to mean?"

Ramirez tilted his head from side to side, working a whole new set of kinks out of his neck. "Nothing. Go on."

Considering he had handcuffs and I was currently a ward of the state, I let it go. "Okay, well, I just went to the house to talk to Larry. Only he wasn't there so I thought I'd have a little look around, so I tried to get in the back door, but picking a lock with a credit card is a lot harder than it looks on UPN, and it broke. So I tried the side door, and that one was open, so I went in and looked around. That's how my prints got there."

Ramirez stared at me. "Do you realize you just admitted breaking and entering to a police officer?"

"I didn't break and enter! My credit card broke, so I entered through an open door. Totally different."

Ramirez looked up at the ceiling. I wondered which saint he was praying to. Probably the one that looked over men who had to endure babbling blondes.

"It wasn't me," I said again for good measure. "They're framing Larry, don't you see?"

"Who's framing him, Maddie?"

"Monaldo and Unibrow!"

His eyebrows knitted together. "Unibrow?"

"That big guy who works with Monaldo. He was at Larry's house yesterday, too."

Ramirez sat forward, all ears now. "You saw him with the body?"

"Well, no, not exactly. But I saw him in Larry's house and then saw his car outside, and the trunk was open. That must have been how he transported the body."

"So, let me get this straight." Ramirez rubbed his temples again, as if following my train of thought gave him a headache. "You actually saw Unibrow in Larry's house."

"Yes. Kind of."

"Kind of?"

"I was hiding under the bed at the time. But I saw his shoes."

Ramirez threw his hands up in the air. "Jesus," he muttered.

"But I could totally pick them out of a line up though. They were chocolate brown, soft leather, wingtips, thin rubber soles, with a tiny detail on the back like a diamond shape."

Ramirez gritted his teeth together again. "We are not doing a shoe lineup."

"But you've got to believe me. You know I didn't do this!"

Ramirez sighed, blowing a big breath of air up at the ceiling. "I'm sorry, Maddie," he said, his voice a little softer, "but it doesn't matter what I know, it only matters..."

"... what you can prove," I finished for him. He was starting to sound like a broken record.

He nodded. "Look, I'll see what I can do to get you out of here. But I'm telling you, the DA has enough to hold you over for arraignment. This is murder they're talking about. I can't just make this go away because I like you."

I bit my lip. I know I should have been plummeting into despair at the thought of going back to my friends in holding, but instead I was fixated on that last part of the sentence. Ramirez liked me. He really liked me.

I reined in my Sally Field impression, instead asking, "So, about Bobbi. How did he... you know, expire?"

"The cause of death was blunt force trauma. Someone hit him over the head."

Not a gunshot. I let out a breath I hadn't realized I'd been holding. Okay, I know I told Ramirez Larry was being framed, but until he'd said that a teeny, tiny part of my mind had been replaying the sound of that gunshot on my answering machine.

"So where has he been for the last week?"

Ramirez shook his head. "I don't know. Look, this isn't even technically my case. I should be with Monaldo right now."

"Sorry," I said, hanging my head. Just when I'd vowed to stay out of Ramirez's way, here I was jeopardizing his case all over again.

He reached across the table and put his hand over mine. It was big and warm, and I had the sudden urge to feel that same comforting grip wrapped around my whole body. Tears stung the back of my eyes at the thought of him leaving me alone here again.

"It's going to be okay," he promised. Had anyone else said it, I would have told them they were full of donkey doo. But somehow, coming from him, I believed it.

Instead of letting the sting develop into full-fledged tears, I sniffed and nodded in what I thought was a pretty brave display, considering the circumstances.

"Here," Ramirez pushed the notepad across the table to me. "Write down everything you just said to me. Though," he paused and shot me a lopsided grin. "You may want to leave out the whole breaking and entering part."

I nodded. "Right." I picked up the pen and tried to put down the events of the last two days in a semi coherent fashion.

"I'm going to tell Detective Romanowsky he can come back in now," Ramirez said, standing up.

I nodded. Then did a little wave at the mirror.

Ramirez paused halfway across the room. "What was that?"

I pointed at the mirror. "I was waving to the detective."

He cocked his head to the side and gave me a funny look.

"You know," I continued. "On the other side of the glass."

The corner of his mouth quirked up ever so slightly, his eyes crinkling at the corners. "That's just a mirror."

"But on *Law & Order* they…" I trailed off as Ramirez shook his head at me, that quirk turning into a full-fledged grin.

"Honey, you watch way too much TV."

I ducked my head back down to the notepad, feeling volcanic heat blush my cheeks as Ramirez did a low chuckle out the door. I think I just hit an embarrassment scale seventy-five.

* * *

After I finished my written statement, then verbally repeated the whole thing to Detective Sipowicz, I was escorted back to the holding cell where Buggy and the Bra Lady were still waiting.

There were no windows in the cell, and since my watch had been confiscated along with my shoes (I was still trying to figure out just how my Fossil could be used as a weapon.), I had no idea how long I sat there. But it felt like an eternity. Especially since I hadn't used the bathroom since before the funeral and despite refusing every soda offered, now had to pee like a racehorse. I eyed the very public commode in the corner. Even overlooking the fifteen million germs lurking on it's steely metal surface there was no way I was going to do my business out in the open for all to see. I crossed my legs and prayed Ramirez got me out of here soon.

In the meantime I replayed my encounter at Larry's house over in my head again. After listening to Ramirez, I was sure Unibrow had killed Bobbi then planted the body in my dad's garage. What I wasn't sure of was if the LVMPD could ever really prove it. So far Monaldo had gotten away scot-free with Hank's killing, and by the looks of things – me in a jail cell! – he wasn't doing much worse with this one. Which begged the question: which was worse, my father being on the run from the Mob or on the run from the police?

I uncrossed and re-crossed my legs again, wondering just how long it took for a bladder to burst. I was pretty sure I was seconds from finding out when Mizz Belushi finally came back in and called my name. I almost wept for joy when she opened the doors and said I was free to go. Almost. Instead I pleaded with her to point me in the direction of the nearest bathroom.

After using the facilities (which honestly weren't a whole lot better than the one in the holding cell) I splashed a little water on my face and went in search of my belongings. Specifically – my cover up. My eyes no longer qualified as bags. These were steamer sized trunks I was packing.

Belushi escorted me to a little metal cage where a guy in a uniform handed me a plastic baggie with my personal belongings. I was instructed to check to make sure everything was there then sign my name on a slip of paper in triplicate. They were, including my broken heeled Cavallis. I put them on anyway. Broken or not, they were better than the paper booties. Besides, they went perfectly with my grass stained blouse and mangled skirt.

Before I left, Sipowicz met me at the door where he informed me in no uncertain terms that I was not to leave Clark County. Even slowly.

I stepped outside into the cool, night air and did a big deep breath. I felt like I'd been locked up for days instead of hours. The sun was long gone, the sky a dark blue, and above the layer of Vegas lights there might have even been stars twinkling. I wrapped my arms around myself against the chill in the air, feeling the weight of the last twenty-four hours sitting on my shoulders like a tension headache just waiting to explode.

Part of me had hoped that Ramirez would be waiting for me when I got out, but the only people on the steps of the Clark Country Regional Justice Center were a couple of homeless guys and a man handing out flyers for a strip club downtown. I was torn. The fact he was working meant he was that much closer to putting Monaldo behind bars and my father out of harm's way. But the fact that he'd chosen work over me, yet again, didn't speak well of whatever sort of non-relationship relationship we were attempting to have here. I tried not to think about it (lest I incur the wrath of that tension headache). Instead I sat down on the stone steps and pulled out my cell to call Dana for a ride.

But before I could hit send, the phone rang in my hand.

"Hello?"

"You were arrested!" came the screeching tone of my mother's voice.

Why, oh, why couldn't I remember to check the caller ID before I picked up?

"Hi, Mom."

"Oh, my God, please tell me it's not true. Tell me that my baby is not in jail!."

"Okay. I'm not in jail." Which, as of five minutes ago, was actually the truth.

"Oh, Maddie, how could you do this to me? Last time Vegas, now Marco calls and tells me you've been hauled off to jail!"

Great. Leave it to Marco to spread news faster than a grassfire in the Hollywood Hills.

"Mom, I'm okay, really."

"Where did I go wrong, Maddie?" she asked, ignoring me. "What did I do to turn you to a life of crime?"

Mental forehead smack. "Mom! I didn't do it."

"Of course not. And we'll get you the best lawyer in town to prove it. Let's see, Mrs. Rosenblatt's second husband was an attorney. Of course, he's dead now, but I'm sure she knows someone from his firm who will take our case. Oh, I know! Al Weinstien has a brother who knows a man who did time for mail fraud. Maybe we can call his lawyer…"

"Mom!" I interrupted before she started calling names from the yellow pages. "I'm fine. Look, this is all just a big misunderstanding."

"They didn't hurt you, did they, Maddie? I saw this Barbara Walters special last month about how those guards take advantage of female prisoners. They didn't take advantage of my baby, did they?"

"No, Mom. I'm fine. The officers were very nice."

"Are they standing right there? Are they making you say that? Cough twice if they're making you say it?"

I seriously hoped Dana had an Advil in her purse because the tension headache had just started flirting with migraine territory.

"I'm fine, Mom. F-I-N-E."

"This is all your father's fault. He dragged you into this. I could kill that man." She paused. "Woman. Whatever."

I rubbed my temple. "Let's not bring Larry into this, okay?"

"Oh, my sweet, sweet, sweet baby. You always were so protective. So caring. So loving."

So in denial.

"But don't you worry, Maddie," she continued. "Mommy's here. It's okay if you want to cry."

"I don't want to cry." What I wanted was an aspirin with a tequila chaser.

"Oh, my brave baby! Don't worry, honey, we're going to take care of everything." Then I heard a funny sound in the background. Almost like an announcement over a loudspeaker.

"What was that?" I asked.

"Oh, nothing. Just the 317 in from Dallas."

I froze, pure dread washing over me. "Mom," I said very slowly. "Where are you?"

"The airport, of course."

No, no, no!

"Mom, please don't tell me…"

"Don't worry, honey, Mrs. Rosenblatt got us tickets on the first flight out. We'll be there in no time. Just hang in there, and don't admit to anything!"

"No, Mom, you don't need to-"

"Mommy's on her way, baby!"

"Mom, please, I'm-"

"Oh, they're calling our flight. I've got to go."

"No, Mom, wait-"

"Hang in there Maddie. Keep the faith alive! We won't let them lock you up. Freedom!" she cried, doing a bad imitation of Mel Gibson in a kilt.

Then the line went dead.

I stared at my cell. In the past twenty-four hours I'd been to a biker bar, a drag funeral, and a prison. I'd been lied to, photographed, and arrested. I'd had a reporter follow me, my wig-wearing dad run from me, and both the mafia and the LVMPD threaten me. And now Mom and Mrs. Rosenblatt were on a plane to Vegas.

I dropped my head into my hands, wondering what else this day could possibly throw at me.

And then I found out.

A black SUV pulled up to the curb, and the passenger side door opened. Ramirez was sitting at the wheel, his face covered with a sexy growth of day old stubble, his eyes dark and dangerous.

"Get in."

CHAPTER FIFTEEN

I got in. With just the tiniest bit of reluctance on my part as I settled into his passenger seat.

I know, I know, just minutes ago I'd been hoping he'd be here to pick me up, and here he was. Wish granted. Only in Maddie's perfect world I'd envisioned him giving me a big hug, a tender kiss on the lips with maybe even a little tongue action. (Tender tongue action. You know like, I-missed-you-and-worried-about-you-every-second-you-were-in-jail tongue.) But instead, I'd gotten a barked order. Get in. Not exactly the words of endearment every girl longs to hear. Which left me wondering – was I a girlfriend? A suspect? Or just a girly blonde who kept messing up his case?

But, like I said, I didn't argue.

I buckled my seatbelt silently as Ramirez pulled away from the curb.

"Thanks for getting me out," I finally said, as he rounded the block.

"You're welcome." Then added as an afterthought, "Just don't make me regret it."

"Who me?" I asked in mock innocence.

He pinned me with a look. Right. Not in the mood for prison humor.

"Um, so where are we going?" I asked instead as he navigated the darkened streets.

"Back to my place."

Despite the totally un-sexy day I'd had, I felt my hormones zing to attention. "Your place?"

"Uh-huh." He nodded. "The only reason you're not sitting in front of a judge right now is that I convinced him to release you into my custody. So," he said, giving me a dark look. "I want you where I can keep an eye on you."

"You mean you don't trust me?"

He smiled a slow, crooked smile. "Nope."

I should have taken offense, but honestly, I couldn't say I blamed him.

I sat in silence as Ramirez wound us through downtown, ending up two streets over from Las Vegas Boulevard in a neighborhood populated with motor inns, convention centers, and low cost buffets. Amazing how just two blocks over from the Strip the price of prime rib plummeted to $3.99 a plate.

Ramirez pulled his SUV into the parking lot of the Lucky Seven Lodge, a twenty-unit motel done in peeling turquoise paint and rusted wrought iron. A kidney-shaped swimming pool, drained of water, sat next to the street while a neon sign over the front office advertised free HBO. Or rather 'Free H_O.' Their B was on the fritz.

"This is your place?" I asked as he parked and shut off the engine.

"What can I say? Bruno doesn't get paid a whole lot."

"Yeah, but you're not really Bruno."

He shrugged. "Okay, I don't get paid a whole lot either."

We got out of the car, and Ramirez led the way up to unit 13, a room on the second story that overlooked the parking lot. I could hear Metallica pounding from the room next door and a group of college kids yelling and drinking two doors down. Not exactly what I'd call homey, but it beat sleeping on sheets that read, 'Property of the Clark County Jail.'

Ramirez plopped down on a pastel, desert-motif double-bed that took up most of the room, then proceeded to whip out his cell phone. "Checking in," he explained, keying in his pin number.

I followed his lead, digging my cell out of my purse. The little battery symbol was flashing a 'low' sign, but hopefully it would be enough to let Dana know where I was. Luckily she picked up on the first ring.

"Hey, it's me," I said.

"Ohmigod Maddie! Are you okaaaaaaaaaay?" she shrieked into the phone.

I held it away from my ear, sure that tiny dogs all the way from here to San Bernardino were yapping in protest. "Yes. I'm fine." Sort of.

"Ohmigod, after they took you in, Marco and I went straight to the Victoria and told Ramirez about your arrest, but we've both been worried sick about you. What happened?"

I quickly filled her in on my brush with the law, the discovery of Bobbi's body and my theory about Larry's frame up. She made the appropriate shrieks and gasps (especially when I told her how they'd confiscated my shoes) and, when I'd finished, asked, "So, what do we do now?"

"I don't know." And I honestly didn't. I was fresh out of ideas, good or otherwise.

"Tell me where you are," she said, "and we'll come pick you up."

"Oh, well, I, uh…" I looked over at Ramirez, jotting notes down on a pad of motel stationary as he listened to his messages. "I'm actually kind of still in police custody."

Ramirez turned his head and raised an eyebrow at me.

What? It was mostly the truth. And to be honest, I was tired. I mean *really* tired. I couldn't even remember the last time I'd had a full night's sleep. And between Marco's snoring, the rollaway neck cramps, and Dana's middle of the night beatings, that big double bed in the middle of the room was looking nice. *Really* nice. (And, I'll admit, the sexy cop lounging on it didn't look so bad either.)

"Oh, okay," Dana replied, though I could hear the question in her voice. "Well I talked Slim Jim into giving Marco and me a discounted room for the night, so call me in the morning. Oh, and by the way, did you know I have a date to see Bette Midler with him tomorrow night?"

Oops. "Sorry. I forgot about that. I thought we'd be long gone by then."

"No prob," she replied. "Actually, it might be kind of fun."

I paused. "Seriously?"

"What?" she asked, her tone going defensive. "I think he kind of likes me."

Or more accurately, certain parts of her anatomy. But, considering I wasn't one to be giving dating advice, I let it go, instead promising to call her in the morning.

I hung up and turned around to find Ramirez watching me. He'd abandoned his phone and was lying on the bed, one elbow propped up beneath him. His eyes were dark and intent, trained on me with a predatory look in them. Like at any minute he might pounce on the blonde in the mini-skirt.

I cleared my throat, my mouth going total Sahara on me.

"Come here," he commanded, cocking one finger at me.

Well, who was I to argue with a cop? I sat down on the bed facing him.

His eyes did a slow sweep of my face, roving over each inch until I was sure I was blushing like a virgin. He lifted one hand to my cheek and softly tucked a strand of hair behind my ear.

"What am I going do with you?" he whispered, his mouth so close to mine I could taste the coffee and Dentine on his breath.

At the moment I could think of about a hundred things he could do with me. All of them naked.

But he didn't wait for a reply, instead leaned in closer, brushing his lips softly over mine. I melted on contact. I swear this guy could apply for a PhD in kissing. He was *that* good. So good, I was seconds away from being that 'Free H_O' myself.

His hands slid up to the nape of my neck, burrowing into my hair as his five o'clock shadow tickled my cheek, leaving a tingling sensation that spread clear down my spine.

Then settled into somewhere south of my belly button.

He wrapped his arms around my middle and laid me back on the pillows, his six-day-a-week at the gym body pressing against mine. Hard chest, long legs, thickly muscled arms. I closed my eyes and said a silent 'thank you' to the saint of totally ripped bodies, instantly reminded me of how long it had been since I'd been with a man. Never mind a man as rock solid as Ramirez. (And I wasn't just talking about his pecs here.)

He broke away from my lips and dragged a wet line of kisses down my throat. I arched my back and bit my lip to keep from laughing as his lips tickled my super-sensitized skin. One warm hand came down on my knee, then slowly slid up my thigh, flirting with the hem of my skirt.

My eyes popped open. Oh, crud, had I put on those ugly high-cut hipsters this morning? They were great for preventing leather mini-skirt chafing, but the stretched out elastic and faded blue horizontal stripes didn't exactly scream 'sexy mama.'

"Um, could we turn off the lights please?" I asked.

Ramirez paused. "Sure." He leaned over and switched off the lamp on the nightstand. The room plunged into semi darkness, the lights from the 'Free H_O' sign casting a pinkish hue through the thin curtains.

Much better. Ramirez leaned in close again, his hands resuming their upward accent on my hipsters. I prayed he couldn't feel how full-coverage they were in the dark. Something, as it turned out, I didn't have to worry about. With one quick flick of his wrist, he had them off and across the room before you could say 'Hanes Her Way'.

The sudden cool breeze in my hoo-ha region left me panting just a little. Something that multiplied exponentially as Ramirez lowered his lips to the inside of my thigh. He made a low, growling sort of sound in the back of his throat, doing butterfly light kisses along my inner thigh. His hands slid up to my waist, lifting my leather skirt until it could double as a belt.

I suddenly realized he was wearing way more clothes than I was. I made short work of his T-shirt, pulling it up and over his head, revealing that Budweiser worthy six pack. I tried not to drool as I ran my hands over his stomach. Okay, I admit, I didn't try very hard. I was goo, absolute putty in his hands. I'd never seen a body like this outside of a Brad Pitt movie.

He leaned into my touch, his fingertips flirting with my thighs as he did a low growl into my ear. I suppressed a giggle, his hot breath on my earlobe sending shivers down my spine. I felt goose bumps raise the hairs on my arms.

And legs.

Damn! I hadn't shaved my legs this morning. Had I even shaved them yesterday? I couldn't remember. I self consciously wiggled out of his grasp, gently nudging his hand away from my bare, stubbly thighs.

Okay, so as long as the lights stayed off and he didn't touch my legs, I'd be fine. I tried to reassure myself and relax back into his touch as his lips broke from my earlobe and began nibbling their way south. Down my neck, across my collarbone, into the deep vee of my blouse. I closed my eyes again and sighed out loud, arching my back as his warm breath penetrated the thin fabric of my shirt.

He slid one large hand beneath the hem, moving upward until he reached the lacy edges of my Vicky's Secret. I couldn't help wriggling beneath him like a schoolgirl as his fingertips pulled the lacey fabric away and closed possessively over my barely B's. You know, I was beginning to think that being arrested wasn't all that bad. There were the perks of being patted down by the LAPD's resident sex God. A status which Ramirez sealed for himself as I heard the zipper on his jeans give way and got a first hand glimpse of what a lacey Vicky's Secret could do to a man.

Oh. My. God.

My throat did that Sahara thing again, and I wouldn't be surprised if a little drool traveled down my chin.

This so beat an evening with my battery-powered rabbit.

Ramirez seemed oblivious to my stares of admiration, fully consumed with popping the clasp on my bra. Not that I was complaining. The rasp of his warm hands against my bare skin was enough to make a girl forget her own name. I was seriously two seconds away from ripping the thing off myself when I finally felt the clasp give way and Ramirez do another satisfied growl against my neck.

"This has got to go," he mumbled, tugging at my blouse.

And then he started to undo the buttons. With his teeth. Did this guy have moves or what? I was in total heaven. I was one touch away from being a puddle of melted hormones on a motel room bed.

I felt the first button release, then the second, Ramirez's hot breath tingling against my bare skin. Button number three gave way, and I braced for the feel of his warm, wet kisses along my peaked barely B's. Only I didn't feel any. In fact, he shifted, pulling away from me.

I opened my eyes and looked up to find him propped up on one elbow, picking something out of his teeth.

"Are you okay?" I asked.

His eyebrows hunched together as he blew air out through his lips in a spitting motion. "I think I just got grass stuck in my teeth."

I looked down at my shirt. Sure enough, there were little bits of dirt and grass from my lawn dive stuck in the grooves of my formerly white buttons.

I let out a big sigh. Fine. I give up. Fate obviously had it in for me.

"This is so not working."

"What's not?" Ramirez asked, running his tongue over his teeth.

"This!" I sat up, shifting my skirt back down. "This isn't the way this is supposed to happen. I smell like a jail cell, my legs aren't shaved, I'm wearing day old underwear, and I'm in desperate need of a lip wax. Look at me," I gestured down at the lawn on my shirt and busted Cavalli's dangling off my feet. "I'm a mess. I can't have sex with *you* looking like *this*."

Ramirez stared at me, blinking. "I think you look fine?" he said. Only it came out more of a question.

I narrowed my eyes. "Was that a statement or a question?"

Ramirez bit the inside of his cheek. "Which is the answer that will get us back to the kissing part?"

"Don't you care that this is our first time?" I asked, doing a hands-on-hips pose. "Our first time is supposed to be special. It's supposed to be at your place with scented Illuminations candles and Enya playing in the background. I'm supposed to be wearing a cute little lace camisole and matching panties from Fredericks of Hollywood. I'm supposed to look sexy. This," I gestured to my ruined outfit again, "is not sexy."

Ramirez rolled over onto his back and blew a long breath up at the ceiling. "You're killing me here; you are aware of this right?"

I bit my lip. "Sorry." And as I stared at his six pack abs, I was. Very, very sorry. Sigh.

"Fine," he said. "If you want to wait, we'll wait."

"Thank you."

He raised one eyebrow at me. "You are *sure* you want to wait?"

No. "Yes."

Ramirez blew out another sigh. "Okay. In that case, I'm taking a shower." He stood up and crossed the room in one long stride. "A very *cold* shower," he added, zipping up his fly and sending me a look that was all heat. Then he shut the bathroom door behind him.

I flopped my head back on the pillows again as I heard the water start to run, trying really, *really* hard not to imagine Ramirez's naked body standing beneath it.

I was *so* gonna get Fate for this.

* * *

I spent the night tossing and turning and trying really hard not to let my stubbly legs come in contact with Ramirez's. Was there any worse torture in the world for a woman who's gone *this* long without sex to be sleeping next a man like *that*? If there was, we should be using it on the terrorists because by the time the sun finally peeked through the paper thin curtains, I was ready to tear my hair out.

Ramirez got up first, and I could hear him getting dressed, though I steadfastly refused to open my eyes. One look at that body, and I knew I'd be a goner. Hairy legs or no hairy legs, I'd jump him. By the time I felt it was safe to look, I heard the door to the room shut and popped my head out of the sheets to find him gone. There was a little note on the nightstand written on the back of a KFC napkin: Went for coffee, be right back. R

Okay, so maybe he didn't sign it with a heart or an XOXO, but the man was going for coffee. Gotta love that.

I took the opportunity to drag my tired self into the shower and in lieu of my usual mousse and blow dry routine, twisted my wet hair up into a French braid. I scavenged in the closet and found a T-shirt and pair of sweats and plopped back down on the bed. I'd just flipped on *The View* when Ramirez came back in with two Starbucks cups in one hand and a bakery box in the other.

"Bless you," I said, taking one of the steamy cups. I sipped it. A tall mocha latte with whipped cream. Oh, I *liked* this guy.

"I thought you might be hungry." He lifted the lid on the bakery box. Krispy Kremes. I *really* liked this guy.

"So," he said as we sat on the bed eating the doughnuts picnic style. "Do you want the good news or the bad news first?"

"Hmmm... always the good news," I said around a bite of crispy, sugary dough and oozing cherry filling. This so beat Dana's box o' bran breakfasts.

"Okay." Ramirez swallowed a bite. "I talked to Detective Romanowsky. They did an autopsy on Bob last night, and it turns out he did not die yesterday. The ME found signs of freezer burn."

"He was frozen?" I asked, amazed that even talk of a dead body wasn't making these doughnuts any less delicious.

Ramirez nodded. "Which makes it a little harder to pinpoint actual time of death, but taking into account the condition of the body and the last time anyone saw him, Romanowsky thinks we're looking at sometime on the twelfth."

I did some mental calculations. Today was the twenty-first, so counting backwards that would make the twelfth… last Wednesday. I perked up as I realized the significance. "That was before I was even in Vegas!"

He nodded again as he licked a bit of jelly off his fingers. "Exactly. So, he says you're cleared to go home as long as you make yourself available for further questioning."

Which should have made me happy. I was in the clear, right? Only the idea of going home didn't fill me with a whole lot of good feelings. Now that I knew not only had both of my dad's friends been murdered, but also that the Mob was trying to frame Larry, I knew he needed help more than ever. I wasn't sure what I could actually do, but I knew leaving town wasn't it.

"Does the good detective have any idea who did off Bobbi?" I asked, hoping all signs pointed to Monaldo.

Ramirez shook his head. "Nothing concrete. At least not that he would share with me."

I took another bite, letting the gooey cherry goodness ooze onto my tongue. Last Wednesday. Why did that date ring a bell with me? I racked my little brain as I took a steamy sip of mocha latte. Then it hit me. The eBay auction I'd swiped from Monaldo's office. BobEDoll had listed his pair of Pradas the same day our Bobbi had bit the dust. I wasn't totally sure what one thing had to do with the other, but it was quite a coincidence.

"I have something to show you, but I don't want you to get mad," I said, setting my doughnut down and wiping my fingers.

Ramirez paused, coffee halfway to his lips. "Great. What now?"

I narrowed my eyes at him. "Well if you're going to be like that, maybe I won't show it to you."

He put down his cup and relieved a little more neck tension. "Okay. Fine. I promise not to get mad."

"Swear?"

"I swear."

"Double pinky swear not to get mad?"

"Jesus," he muttered. "Fine, I double pinky swear." He held up his little finger. "Now what is it?"

"I kind of took something from Monaldo's office."

"Jesus, Maddie!" he yelled, his pinky clenching into a fist. "What the hell were you thinking?"

"Hey, you promised you wouldn't be mad."

He ran a hand through his hair. "I'm not mad."

"That mad vein in your neck is bulging."

He gritted his teeth together. "What did you take?"

I crossed the room to my purse and pulled out the listing, handing it to Ramirez. "I found this in Monaldo's trash can."

He stared at it. Then looked back up at me as if not comprehending. "An eBay listing?"

"Not just any listing," I pointed out. "One for Prada. And, the seller is going by the name BobEDoll. Get it? Bobbi, *Bob*-e-doll. And," I said, pointing to the listing date. "Same day Bobbi died. Kind of a coincidence, right?"

He looked at the paper a minute longer, then folded it and put it in his pocket. "Coincidence? Yes."

"Significant?" I asked, hopefully.

He did a noncommittal shrug. "Maybe. Proof," he added before I could question, "definitely not."

I pouted.

Ramirez smiled and leaned in, planting a little kiss on my protruding bottom lip. "You know, you're kind of cute when you do that."

"I'm wearing your sweats and my hair is in a wet braid."

He cocked one eyebrow up. "Which means?"

"This is not sexy either."

"You know," Ramirez said, pulling away. "A person can only take so much."

Tell me about it.

"So, what's the bad news?" I asked, reaching for a second doughnut. Hey, if I wasn't going to have sex I was damn well going to load up on fat and sugar.

"The bad news is Monaldo wants Bruno back at the club this morning. He's got a meeting with a vendor, and he wants his muscle there while he negotiates. Which means I want you to stay here until I get back."

"But-" I started.

"No, no buts. For once, please just humor me and do what I say? Don't make me come bail you out of jail again."

"You're not going to let me live that one down, are you?"

He grinned. "Nope."

* * *

After he downed the last of his coffee, Ramirez left, promising he'd be back in a couple of hours and making me double pinky swear that I'd be here. I finished off the last of the doughnuts while I watched the end of *The View*. I was halfway into Maury's surprise paternity show when my eyes strayed to my empty Starbucks cup sitting on the table.

The thing is, that latte was good. Really good. And between sexual frustration torture and lack of sleep I really wanted another one. More than that, I really wanted a fresh pair of underwear. I know Ramirez had said to stay right here, but I'm sure he wouldn't mind if I made a teeny tiny little trip to the hotel for a change of clothes and a mocha whipped cream latte. Besides, it was only a couple of blocks away. I'd be back before he even knew I was gone.

So convincing was my logic that ten minutes later I was in a yellow cab pulling up to the front doors of the New York - New York. I crossed the casino floor to the elevators and pushed the up button, waiting with a family wearing matching shirts that read 'Wheeler's Vegas Vacation '07'. Finally the doors slid open, and the Wheelers got in. I was one step behind them when someone barreled out of the elevator straight into me.

"Uhn."

"Ohmigod, Maddie!" I looked up to see the *someone* was Dana, her strawberry blonde brows pulled together in a tight line as her voice went into dog whistle territory again. "I am so freaking glad you're here. We've got to go!" She grabbed my hand, steering me away from the elevators.

"Wait – what? Go where?"

"It's your mom, dahling," Marco said, hot on Dana's heels.

I groaned. I'd almost forgotten about the post menopausal Bobbsey twins to the rescue. "Oh, no. Mom's here?"

"No, that's just it," Dana said, her voice tinged with hysteria as she hustled us back out of the casino. "She's not here."

She paused, putting both hands on my shoulders and spinning me around to face her. "Maddie, she's gone after Monaldo!"

CHAPTER SIXTEEN

"What!?" I yelled so loud a passing blue-hair shushed me.

"We tried to stop her," Marco explained, his mouth moving a mile a minute as he handed his car ticket to the valet. "But she was out for blood. She said she was going to kill Larry for turning you into a criminal."

"But then we explained that no one knew where Larry was," Dana cut in.

"Right, so then we told her about Monaldo and the shoes and the whole frame up thing and how you mistakenly ended up in jail over it."

"And that's when Mrs. Rosenblatt had the vision."

"Right, the vision." Marco nodded.

The vision. This just kept getting better and better. "I know I'm going to regret this, but what vision?"

Dana took a deep breath. "Mrs. Rosenblatt said she saw an Italian guy-"

"Italian-*American*," Marco corrected.

"Right. Italian-American guy. With a gun. She said he had teeny tiny eyes, a teeny tiny heart and a whole cloud of negative emotions looming over him. He was turning your aura a muddy brown."

"Your mom was not happy about that." Marco shook his head. "Brown is very bad for the soul. Very bad."

"She said she wanted to teach this guy a lesson," Dana continued. "And then my cell phone rang. It was Rico." She paused, a goofy smile spreading across her face. "He picked up my LadySmith for me from Mac's. Isn't that just the sweetest thing you ever heard?"

I shook my head. "Wait. Let's get back to my mother and the mobster."

"Oh, right. Well, as soon as I hung up with Rico I turned around, and they were gone."

"Poof, just like that," Marco said, doing a jazz hands thing.

"And you just let them?" I cried. "Where were you?" I asked, turning on Marco.

"Little girl's room."

I rubbed my temples, the tension headache from last night returning full force. "So, let me get this straight. My mother is now on her way to teach a lesson to a member of the mafia because Mrs. Rosenblatt had a vision of my aura?"

"Kind of," Dana said, biting her lip. "But that's not the worst of it."

What could be worse? "Oh, it gets better?"

"Well, see, before Rico called, your Mom was kind of admiring my cell phone. And well, when I noticed they were gone I checked my purse. The phone was gone too.

"Wait." I held one hand up to silence her, tilting my head to the side as I tried to wrap my throbbing brain around this. "If they left while you were on the phone, how did they take it?"

Dana bit her lip again. "Um, yeah, see, they didn't take *that* phone. They took the *other* one."

"What other one, you only have…" And then it hit me. The stun gun phone!

I smacked the palm of my hand to my forehead. If there was one thing in the world more dangerous than my mother in lecture mode, it was my mother in lecture mode with a weapon.

I whipped out my own cell and dialed Ramirez's number, in hopes he could head off the impetuous seniors. But, of course, it went straight to voicemail. So, we all quickly piled into the Mustang and made tracks for the Victoria.

My bags were still in the trunk, so while Marco navigated the Strip, I did a quick change in the backseat from Ramirez's sweats into a pair of black cargos, a rhinestone studded tank, and my silver slingbacks. And tried not to picture Mom being stuffed into a mobster's freezer.

Unfortunately, there was a wreck on the 15, and it took us another twenty minutes before we pulled up in front of the club. We dove out of the car and scrambled to the front doors. Since it was barely noon, there was no line to get in, the door left unguarded by the Crew Cut gatekeeper. We quickly pushed inside, blinking as our eyes adjusted from the Vegas sunlight to the windowless interior.

The dance floor was less crowded than before, though a few die-hards still shook their tushies to a techno beat from the nineties. The big stage was empty, save for a lone Whitney Houston look-alike doing a baritone "I Will Always Love You" to a sparsely populated room of convention goers. Half the barstools were empty, the other half filled with hard core AA dropouts who didn't care if it was ten in the morning or ten at night. No sign of Mom or Mrs. Rosenblatt.

"Maybe they're not here?" Dana said.

Marco nodded. "Maybe they changed their minds."

Maybe Monaldo already had them bound, gagged, and fitted for cement loafers.

"Come on," I motioned for Dana and Marco to follow as I wound my way to the hallway of offices. Dana clickety-clacked on her heels, Marco did his Broadway Bond slink, and I tried to make myself small so no cranky, sex-deprived cops noticed me breaking my pinky swear. We passed the bathrooms and the first 'Private' door, heading straight for Monaldo's office. I was just about to put my ear to the closed door when I heard a loud thud on the other side.

I sucked in a breath. Oh, God. Mom!

My heart leapt into my throat, pure panic racing through my veins as I grabbed the handle and twisted the door open.

The first thing I felt was relief. Mom and Mrs. Rosenblatt were standing in the middle of the room, unharmed, un-shot, and generally un-victimized. (If you didn't count the crimes of fashion being perpetrated by their wardrobes. Mom was wearing denim knee-length, elastic-waisted shorts paired with a long sleeve purple paisley printed shirt and hiking boots. Mrs. Rosenblatt had opted for her hibiscus printed muumuu in an orange and avocado color scheme that hadn't been socially acceptable since nineteen seventy-three.) My relief wavered, however, when I saw they were standing over a pile of crumpled man on the floor, who looked suspiciously like one very not-nice mobster. The relief disappeared completely when I saw the stun gun dangling from Mom's hand.

"Mom!" I shouted, rushing at her like a linebacker and tackling her in a big bear hug. "I'm so glad you're okay."

She was shaking like a leaf, and the stun gun dropped from her hands as she hugged me back. "Oh, Maddie, I think I just killed him!"

Mrs. Rosenblatt nudged Monaldo with the toe of her orthopedic sneaker. "I don't know. He doesn't look dead to me. My third husband, Alf, he died on the living room sofa watching *Jeopardy!*. When he hadn't gotten up after Pat Sajak came on, I poked him in the arm. And, I gotta tell ya', his skin was a lot more rubbery than this guy's."

"I only meant to scare him," Mom muttered, her eyes kind of dazed. "I didn't mean to kill anyone."

"What happened?" I asked.

Mrs. Rosenblatt gave Monaldo another poke. "He was making your aura brown, so your mom and I decided someone had to talk to this punk. No one messes with our Maddie."

I might have been touched by this had we not been standing over the motionless body of a mafia member.

"And," Mom added, "after we saw Dana had two cell phones, we thought we'd take-"

"*Borrow*," Mrs. Rosenblatt corrected.

"Right. Borrow one just in case things got out of hand."

"Which they did," Mrs. R cut in, poking Monaldo with a finger that resembled an Oscar Mayer cocktail sausage. "We told this guy to leave you alone and he says. 'Oh yeah, and who are you?' and we said, 'Maddie's Mom, that's who,' and then he says, 'Who the heck is Maddie?' Okay, well, actually he didn't say 'heck,' he said a word a whole lot worse than heck, but seeing as I'm a real lady, I won't repeat what he *really* said. So, then your Mom says. 'Maddie, Larry's daughter," and then he gets this grin like he's got some really bad gas or something, and then he just starts laughing and says, 'You married that fruit?' And, well, you can imagine how your mother reacted to that one."

From the look of Monaldo on the floor, not well.

"She may have called him a couple of names."

"Schmuck," Mom supplied. "Putz. Jerk. Motherfu-"

"Okay, I get the point." Apparently Mom wasn't as worried about being a real lady.

"Any-hoo," Mrs. R continued, "this clown starts yelling how he's gonna tear us limb from limb, so your mom pulls out the phone to call 911, and the next thing you know, he's out like a light." She paused to nudge Monaldo again. "That thing don't work like any cell phone I've ever seen."

"Honestly, I didn't mean to shoot him," Mom said, her hands still shaking.

"You didn't shoot him," I reassured her. "He's just a little zapped."

She looked at me, her voice going into soprano range. "Zapped?"

"Don't worry, he'll be fine," Dana said. "Rico said the jolt only lasts for a couple of minutes. Right Marco?"

Marco shuddered as if he only knew too well.

"Well, I've got a feeling he's not gonna be too happy when he wakes up," Mrs. R said, scrutinizing Monaldo's face. His legs did a little jimmy thing.

"In that case, I suggest we go *now.*" I dragged Mom away by the arm, her eyes still glued to the crumpled form on the floor, and ushered our little band of accidents waiting to happen out the door.

I'd like to say we made an inconspicuous group as we made a beeline for the club's front doors, but between Marco's slinking, Mom's state of catatonic shock and Mrs. Rosenblatt's three hundred pound frame clad in shower curtain chic, we might as well have been carrying a flashing sign that read 'suspicious people here.' Luckily, this was Vegas, and, though we incurred a couple of stares, no one tried to stop us.

We were almost to the front doors when Mom snapped out of her stupor and yelled, "Wait!"

We all halted, Marco running into the back of Mrs. R with a little moan.

"What?" I asked.

Mom pointed to the office. "I left the cell phone in there."

"Don't worry, we'll buy a new one," I said, pushing her toward the door. Just a few more feet, and we were home free. Monaldo would wake up none the wiser, and Ramirez would never know my pinky swear was worth less than flip-flops on a Payless clearance rack.

"But my prints are all over that one!" Mom protested.

I paused. Damn. She had a point. Not that Monaldo looked like the type to keep fingerprint dust in his back pocket, but Ramirez might. And I knew for certain Detective Sipowicz did. Considering the way I'd already gotten on the LVMPD's bad side, I wasn't sure I wanted to chance another encounter with Mizz Belushi and the soda-pushers.

"Fine," I conceded. "I'll go get it. You guys go to the car, and I'll meet you there."

Mom nodded, letting Dana lead her out the front doors and into the sunlight again. I waited until I saw Mrs. Rosenblatt bring up the rear, waddling to safety, before I spun on my heels and ran as quickly as my strappy slingbacks would allow back to the office.

I paused a moment outside Monaldo's door, putting my ear to the wood and listening for any signs of movement inside. Nothing. I did a two count before reassuring myself he was still out and slowly pushed open the door.

He hadn't moved from his crumpled heap on the floor, though his limbs were convulsing like he'd stuck a finger in a light socket. Which, I guess technically, he kind of had. I tippy-toed into the room, carefully stepping over Monaldo's twitching form, and grabbed the stun gun, slipping it into my purse. Then I tippy-toed back out, keeping one eye on the drooling wise guy. I shuddered to think what he'd do if he woke up. The phrase 'limb from limb' came to mind.

I shut the office door behind me and skittered back down the hallway, out onto the main floor of the club again. I was just gearing up to sprint the last few feet to the front doors when I felt a hand clamp down on my shoulder.

"What the hell are you doing here?" he growled into my ear.

Oh, crud. But with the way my luck was going, I shouldn't have been surprised. In fact, I was starting to think they should rename Murphy's Law, Maddie's Law. Anything bad that could happen, did happen. And usually to me.

I slowly turned around to find Ramirez giving me the death glare – arms crossed over his chest, vein in his neck bulging, jaw clenched so tight he could crush diamonds with that thing.

"Uh… hi?" I did a little one finger wave at him.

"Hi!?" he gritted through clenched teeth. "Is that the best you can do?"

I gulped. "Hi there, handsome?"

He looked to the ceiling and muttered something in Spanish. Probably praying to the saint of ditzy blondes again for the patience not to strangle this one.

"See, I can explain," I said, knowing I was gonna have to talk fast to get myself out of this one. "I was going to stay in the room. I really was! But then the latte was so good, and I really needed a change of underwear, and it had been such a long night with the tossing and the turning and the trying not to maul you with my leg stubble. So I went to the New York - New York, and I was just going to be a second, but then Dana told me about the visions, and we had to stop Mom, but we were too late, and she'd already zapped Monaldo."

Ramirez narrowed his eyes at me, that vein in his neck pulsing double time. "*Zapped* Monaldo?"

I nodded. "Just a little. He should be waking up soon."

He opened his mouth to say something (which I'm pretty sure involved more naughty words) but was interrupted as the cell phone on his belt chirped to life.

He looked down at the readout. "Shit. Monaldo."

I gulped, my eyes instinctively going to the hallway where any minute I expected to see a red faced, jimmy-legged mobster with a gun.

"See, I told you he'd be waking up soon," I said, trying to put a positive spin on things.

Ramirez ignored the comment, instead doing another growl slash glare thing and grabbing me by the arm. He steered me around the bar, carefully avoiding the private offices, and through the maze of mostly empty tables, toward the back of the club.

"Where are we going?" I asked as I stumbled over my feet, trying to keep up with him. Hey, not all of us have 6'1" long, I-can-leg-press-a-Buick strides, you know.

"*I* am going to convince Monaldo he was not just zapped by some nosy blonde's mother," he answered, not slowing his pace any. "And *you* are going to wait for me. Then I am going to drive you to the airport and personally put you on the first plane back to L.A. Got it?"

"But what about Hank and Bobbi and Lar-"

But Ramirez cut me off, giving me that death look again.

Right. Never mind.

He pushed me ahead of him through a door in the back of the club leading out into a small parking lot behind the building. A handful of cars filled the spaces, mostly second handers spotted with an impressive variety of dents and dings. Two long, black town cars that I recognized as Monaldo's preferred method of transportation were parked in the spaces up front. In the back corner of the lot sat Ramirez's black SUV. He marched me in front of him and unlocked the doors with his remote before shoving me into the back seat.

"You," he said pointing a finger at my nose, "stay."

I crossed my arms over my chest. "I'm not a puppy, you know."

His eyes narrowed again. "No, you're not. You're a little pain in the ass that's driving me up a wall. And, by the way, you're also running precariously close to being hauled downtown for obstruction of justice, assault with a semi-deadly weapon, and pissing off an officer of the law."

"You made those last two up."

His eyes narrowed into fine slits. "Don't try me."

I gulped. Trust me. Trying Bad Cop's last nerve was not high on my list of to-dos.

"I'm sorry," I said instead.

His eyes softened just a little, his jaw relaxing as he rubbed one hand over his eyes. "Maddie, you make me crazy, you know that?"

"I know. And I'm sorry," I said again.

He shook his head. Then let a little half smile play at the corner of his mouth. He reached one hand out and fingered a lock of my hair. "It's a good thing you're so cute, you know it?"

Generally I'm not fond of being called 'cute.' Cute is for drooling babies, dogs in sweaters and cartoon teddy bears with rainbows on their bellies. I prefer 'beautiful', 'sexy'; even 'da bomb' worked in certain situations. But somehow, delivered with Ramirez's husky growl and dark bedroom eyes, the word 'cute' instantly switched my lever from cold to hot in two seconds flat.

Suddenly being in the backseat of his car didn't seem like such a bad thing.

His hands left my hair, snaking around my middle as his lips moved in slow motion toward mine. The heat from his body suddenly washed a menopause-worthy hot flash right through me. His tongue brushed against my lower lip and he let out a low groan. Or maybe I groaned. I wasn't sure which. In fact, I wasn't sure of anything except the warm, wiggly feeling settling somewhere in my panty region and the fact I was a freaking idiot for not sleeping with this guy last night. Seriously, what was I thinking?

His hands slid down my arms, encircling my wrists as his thumbs caressed slow, small circles on my skin. He was kissing me in earnest now, and I was so engrossed in the heady rush of hormones Mr. Big Guns had coursing through my body that I didn't even realize what he was doing until I heard the unmistakable click of metal on metal.

"What the-?"

I broke our lip-lock just as I felt something cool circle my left wrist. I looked up. Ramirez had handcuffed both my hands to the headrest of his car.

My turn to give the death glare. Remember that whole cold to hot thing? I could go the other way too. Much faster.

"What the hell is this?" I yelled, jingling the two inch metal chain between my wrists.

"This," he said, gesturing to the handcuffs, "is to make sure you're still here when I get back."

I stuck my chest out, mustering up as much indignation as a woman handcuffed to an SUV could. "Are you saying you don't trust me?"

Ramirez pinned me with a look. "You've got to be kidding me, right?"

And with that he shut the car door, and I heard the automatic locks click down as he walked away.

Great. Oh, this was just *great*!

I admit, in those lonely weeks of waiting for my phone to ring, I'd played out more than one scenario involving me, Ramirez, and a pair handcuffs. But none had ended like this! That was it, this whole couple/non-couple thing we had going on was so not happening. If he thought he could treat me this way and still get a sneak peek at my sexy Fredericks lingerie, he was more delusional than both Mrs. Rosenblatt and her spirit guide!

Men. They were nothing but trouble anyway. I mean, really, look where the men in my life had gotten me. Handcuffed, fingerprinted, jailed… then handcuffed again! That's it. I washed my hands of the whole lot of them. In fact, I was actually looking forward to flying home, sitting in my cozy studio and spending the evening alone with Joanie, Chachi, and the Keebler elves. Now those were my kind of men.

Minutes ticked by, during which my hands grew increasingly numb, and my list of tortuous ways to get back at Ramirez grew increasingly longer. I was up to number five (stuffing rotten eggs down the seats of his precious SUV) when my purse rang on the seat beside me. I looked up at my hands. Crap. I shimmied my butt over to the far side of the seat and lifted the purse strap with my foot. Had I actually attended Dana's Power Yoga classes instead of just signing up and blowing them off in favor of a pint of Chunky Monkey, I might have been able to lift my purse high enough to grab the phone with my teeth. As it was, I made it to my belly button before the strap slipped off my foot, and the bag fell to the floor. Luckily, my cell spilled out onto the floor mats. I slipped off one slingback and managed to hit the 'on' button with my big toe.

"Hello?" I shouted in the direction of the floor.

I leaned as far down as I could to hear the response. It was faint, but I could make it out.

"Maddie, it's Felix."

Fabulous. Speaking of men I'd like to seek revenge upon.

"What do you want?" I shouted, stretching my head down between my knees to hear the response.

"I need to talk to you." He paused. "Are you alone?"

I looked around the backseat. Unfortunately.

"Yes. Why?"

"Because I have someone here that wants to speak to you."

I heard noise as the phone was passed. Then an all too familiar voice rose up from the floor mats. "Maddie, honey?"

I froze.

Larry.

CHAPTER SEVENTEEN

"Larry!" I shouted, leaning so far south metal cut into my wrists. "Where are you?"

He hesitated. And I feared for a minute I'd lost the connection.

"Larry? Can you hear me?" I asked, my voice starting to go hoarse from shouting.

"I need to talk to you," he finally answered, so quietly it was barely more than a whisper. "But I don't want to do it over the phone. Can we meet somewhere?"

I looked back up at the handcuffs.

"Uh… I'm kind of tied up at the moment. Can't you just tell me what's going on now?"

"No. No, it's too… I'd feel better doing this in person."

I sighed. "I'm not exactly mobile at the moment." Understatement alert.

"Fine," Larry responded. "I'll have Felix come pick you up."

"No, I-"

But he'd already handed the phone back to Felix. "Maddie, where are you, love?" he asked.

"No," I shook my head at the phone. "No, you can't come here. Ram- uh, Bruno will be out any second."

Felix paused. "What's going on over there?"

I sighed. "I'm handcuffed in the backseat of Bruno's car."

I wasn't sure being so far away from the earpiece, but I could have sworn I heard Felix laughing. "Kinky."

"No, not kinky. False imprisonment. And quit laughing!"

I think I heard him snort. "Okay, where exactly is this car?"

"The employee parking lot of the Victoria Club."

"Give me five minuets."

"No, Bruno will be back any-" But he'd already hung up.

I hit the end button with my big toe. So much for my date with the Keebler boys.

I watched the numbers on Ramirez's dash clock crawl by, all the while keeping one eye on the back door of the Victoria. If Ramirez came out before Felix got here, I had no doubt he'd make good on his promise to shove me onto the first flight home, and I'd miss my one chance to see Larry. Maybe for ever. I wondered what Larry wanted to tell me. Hopefully something bad about Monaldo. Really bad. As in bad enough for the Feds to arrest him and end this whole *Godfather* meets *Tootsie* my life had become. Then I could go back to my *real* life where my biggest worries included finishing the Rainbow Brite jellies on time (which, the longer I stayed in Vegas, was becoming a bigger worry), sitting in traffic on the 405, and when those adorable wedge sandals were going on sale at Macy's.

I was just wondering exactly when the sales clerk *had* said those wedges would be on sale when a blue Dodge Neon pulled into the parking lot and killed its lights. I waved the best I could with my foot (since in addition to being immobilized, my hands had completely fallen asleep), and finally Felix spotted me. He pulled the Neon into the empty space beside the SUV and got out. He allowed himself a little smirk for my benefit before trying the door handle. Not surprisingly, it didn't open.

"It's locked!" I shouted through the tinted windows.

Felix nodded. Then went back to his car and returned with something that looked like a long nail file. With a little maneuvering, he wedged it between the doorframe and the window of the passenger side. I kept one eye on the back door of the club, knowing that if Ramirez caught him tampering with his car, Felix was a dead man.

The nail file wiggled and twisted, making a couple of awful grinding noises that I prayed weren't the sounds of black paint being chipped away. Finally the door locks popped up. I was so happy I could have laughed.

Felix opened the door. He took one look at the handcuffs and *did* laugh.

"It's not funny."

"No, not at all," he responded, starting to snort again.

"Just get them off, smartass."

He pulled a pocketknife out of his khakis and flipped it open. To my surprise, it didn't contain scissors and bottle openers, but a series of different sized and shaped files. He fit one in the keyhole of the handcuffs, and after doing the same sort of shimmy and wiggle thing he'd done with the giant nail file, one metal bracelet finally popped off my wrist.

I could have hugged him. That is if I'd had any feeling left in my arms whatsoever. I shook my hand, feeling little pins and needles race over my skin as the blood surged back into my limbs. Felix made short work of the second bracelet, and as soon as I was accessory free, I jumped out of the SUV and into the Neon's passenger seat.

"Let's go!" I shouted as Felix tucked his handy-dandy lock picks back into his pocket. "Trust me. You do not want to be here when Bruno sees this." While no paint had been actually chipped in the making of this great escape, the little rubber strips between the car door and his window were kind of stretched out. And bulging. And there might have been one or two teeny tiny marks on his windows. Those, coupled with the fact that an empty pair of handcuffs was dangling from his passenger seat, were enough to put Bad Cop in a really bad mood. We're talking back-in-a-holding-cell bad. Not something I wanted to be around to witness.

Felix seemed to get my drift, sliding behind the wheel and gunning the engine. I kept my eyes on the back door, chanting a little "please don't open, please don't open, please don't open" thing as Felix flipped on the lights and pulled out of the parking lot, heading west on Fremont.

I heaved a sigh of relief as the Victoria shrank in the rearview mirror, glad that at least one thing had gone my way today.

"So was that a reporter thing back there?" I asked, rubbing the feeling back into my hands.

"What?"

"Breaking into cars. Picking locks."

He grinned. Then did a non-committal, "Maybe."

"Not that I'm being judgmental or anything. I'm actually quite impressed. I know how hard it is to open a locked door.

Trust me, that whole credit card thing they do on TV – doesn't work."

Felix raised an eyebrow at me. "Been doing some breaking and entering of our own lately, have we?"

I shrugged and mimicked his, "Maybe."

"Touché," he muttered.

"So, where *did* you learn how to do that?"

"Liverpool."

I gave him my 'and…' look, gesturing for the long version of that answer.

"Tell you what," he said, turning to face me as we stopped for a red light. "I'll answer your probing question if you answer one of mine."

Uh-oh. Never good when a reporter used the word 'probing'. But, then again, I reasoned, what did I really have to lose? This guy already knew everything about me. Besides, it wasn't every day a girl ran into someone with their very own lock picking set outside of HBO's primetime lineup. I admit, curiosity won out over good judgment. (And for those of you keeping track, yes, this was a recurring theme in my life.)

"Deal," I said.

Felix swiveled back in his seat as the light turned green. "All right then. When I was a kid, my friend Rodney's father owned a towing service. When we got bored we used to borrow his tools and break into parked cars."

"You're a car thief?!" Okay, I knew tabloid reporters where pretty low on the food chain but hadn't figured I was actually riding with a criminal.

"No, no, no." He shook his head. "We just borrowed them for a bit. Always put them back."

"More like a car borrower, then?"

"More like, yes."

"So, did you ever get caught?"

Felix shook his head at me, doing a tsk, tsk, tsk thing with his tongue. "That's two questions, love."

"Hmmm." I sat back in my seat, pretty sure I wasn't getting the whole story out of him.

"My turn," Felix said, his eyes twinkling.

"All right, what do you want to know?"

"You and that Bruno fellow. What's really going on there?"

"Nothing," I said. A little too quickly.

"Nothing?" Felix gave me a sideling glance.

"Absolutely nothing," I replied. Which, was almost the truth. (Almost.) From Ramirez I got no sex, no trust, no respect… see? Nothing.

"So," Felix prodded, not any more satisfied with my answer than I had been with his. "The words 'boyfriend,' 'dating,' not entering into this situation at all then?"

I shook my head until whips of blonde hair smacked against my cheeks. "Nope. Not at all." The whole truth and nothing but the truth this time. Ramirez hadn't uttered either one of those words. And I had a sinking feeling it would take an event more miraculous than the Red Sox winning the World Series to make it happen. Happily-ever-after wasn't looking like it was in Bad Cop's repertoire. Hell, we couldn't even do happily-sleeping-together-just-once.

"Hmmm," Felix said, taking his eyes off the road to give my barely-B-hugging tank top a healthy stare. "Interesting."

I shifted in my seat, not sure I wanted to probe what that 'interesting' might mean. "So, uh, where are we going anyway?" I asked instead, clearing my throat.

Felix gave me a little half smile, and I could swear he was enjoying how uncomfortable his attention made me. "The New York - New York. Larry's waiting for us in my room."

"What's he doing there?"

"He called me about an hour ago, trying to get hold of you again. Said he needed to see you."

"Any idea what about?"

Felix shook his head. "No. But he seemed rather shaken up about something. I almost didn't want to leave the poor fellow alone, but he said there was no way he was going near the Victoria again. Apparently some bad blood there."

I cringed, thinking of Hank's swan dive. Felix didn't know how true that statement was.

Ten minutes later we pulled up to New York - New York. Felix slowed down at Tropicana, and I could see him mentally debating between the valet and the mile long hike in from self-park that saved a whopping two dollars.

"I don't get it," I said. "You can afford the Marquis suite, but you're too cheap to pay for parking?"

Felix shot me another one of those crooked smiles. "What can I say, Maddie. I'm an enigma."

"Hmmm." I narrowed my eyes at him.

"Family money," he confessed, pulling to the right as he opted for the valet after all. "From my father's side," he explained. "The *thriftiness*," he emphasized, with a look that said he did not appreciate my cheap comment, "is from my mother's side. She's Scottish."

"So you're a stingy rich guy?" Okay, I admit, I kind of enjoyed making him uncomfortable, too.

He let my question go without comment, instead handing his keys over to the valet as we got out of the car. He didn't wait for me to follow before making quick strides through the casino to the elevator doors. We rode up in silence. Once we got to the fifteenth floor, Felix unlocked his door with a keycard, and I got my first glimpse of Larry.

He was sitting on the edge of Felix's bed, fidgeting worse than a heroin addict. He looked like he'd aged fifteen years in the last three days. His eyes were bloodshot, his girdle twisted around his waist revealing an unflattering paunch (that made me instantly suck in), and his pantyhose were running a marathon all the way down to his scuffed heels. All in all, he looked so pathetic I couldn't help myself. Despite my earlier vow to let all men rot in Hades, I ran over and gave him a big hug.

Larry hugged me back, his arms wrapping tightly around my middle, and I got a warm, fuzzy, Hallmark moment feeling.

"I'm so glad you're okay," I said, my voice threatening to crack as I pulled away. Only he didn't look all that okay. To be honest, he looked terrible. "Larry, what's going on?"

He did a deep sigh. Then looked from me to Felix.

"I'm in big trouble, Maddie."

Well, duh. "Tell me," I said instead, sitting down on the flowered bedspread beside him.

He sighed again and looked down at his hands as he spoke, picking at his flaking ruby red nail polish.

"I don't even know where to begin."

"Start with what you told me," Felix prompted.

I shot him a hurt look. My dad had confided in Tabloid Boy first?

Larry nodded. He took a deep breath, did a little more nail polish picking and finally started in a shaky voice. "I've been dancing at the Victoria club for about five years now. Before that I was on the Strip, but, well, you know how it is when we girls get older. Weight starts climbing, things start to sag, there's more shaving…"

"Got it, moving on," I interrupted, fighting the urge to stick my fingers in my ears and chant, "I can't hear you! I'm doing denial!"

"Right. Anyway, Hank and I both moved to the Victoria. The pay was all right, not Strip good, but all right. It might have been enough but… well, see, I've got this little problem."

Uh-oh. Here it was. I was going to find out I was genetically predisposed to alcoholism or a gambling addiction. "What kind of problem?" I asked. "Drugs? Gambling? Booze?"

"Shoes."

Mental forehead smack.

"Shoes?"

Larry nodded. "I can't help it; I just love shoes. I see a pair of heels, and I can't stop myself. I need to have them. Pumps, slingbacks, mules – it doesn't matter. I love them all. And let me tell you, finding heels in a size eleven wide is not cheap. But I can't stop. You don't know what it's like. I buy them, and it's like a rush of happiness just courses through me."

Sadly enough, I did know what it was like.

"Okay, so you were in debt over shoes. What happened next?"

"Well," he said, "one day Monaldo said he had a delivery to make and would Hank and I like to do it for a little extra cash. I was about to have my car repossessed over an adorable pair of ballerina strap wedges in lime green, so I jumped at it. It was simple, really. Monaldo gave us a handbag that we took to one of Monaldo's warehouses out in the desert. We handed it off to these two Italian guys in business suits, then we came back to the club. Simple."

Right. Simple. Somehow the Italians in business suits would have tipped me off, but then again, I wasn't in shoe debt. (Okay, at least not *that* much shoe debt.)

Though, I had to hand it to Monaldo, the plan was brilliant. The last place Ramirez and the Feds would be searching for Monaldo's payoff to the Marsuccis was in a bunch of drag queen's handbags.

"What then?" I asked, almost giddy that I'd finally found the proof Ramirez needed to put Monaldo away for good.

"Well, the next week Monaldo had another errand for us. This time he sent me and Bobbi. Pretty soon it became a regular thing. We'd trade off, whichever of the three of us wasn't on stage that night, we'd go make the run. Worked out great for a couple of months."

"So, what went wrong?"

Larry shook his head and sighed again. "One day the guys in suits were late. It was Bobbi and me out there. We got bored waiting, so we started looking around the warehouse. We opened a couple of boxes and found out they were all filled with shoes. Bobbi and I…" He paused, looking sheepish. "We each took a pair. I know it was wrong, but we honestly figured no one would miss two little pairs. The place was filled with them. I mean, thousands of designer shoes, Maddie. Can you imagine?"

I tried not to salivate, reminding myself they were probably all fakes. "So, you took the shoes?"

"Yes. I took a pair of Dior pumps, and Bobbi chose some black Prada stilettos. Then when the suits showed up we gave them the bag like always and went home. It was a couple of weeks later that Bobbi decided he could raise some extra money by selling his pair on eBay. Being that they were Prada, he figured he could get a whole month's child support out of them. Only when he put the auction up, the lady he tried to sell them to said they were knock-offs. I looked more closely at my pair, and sure enough, they were fake, too. Look, if we had known that Monaldo was dealing in fake designer shoes, we never would have gotten involved."

Mobster, he didn't blink an eye at. But fake shoes were where he drew the line. I would have rolled my eyes if deep down I didn't kind of agree with him.

"So, what did you do?"

"Nothing," he said, his eyes filling with tears. "Bobbi disappeared the next day. I didn't know what to do. I filed a missing person report, but the officer didn't seem to think anything had happened to Bobbi. He said these dead beat dads skipped town all the time. So, I told Hank everything we'd found and told him I was going to tell the police about the shoe warehouse. Hank didn't want me to do it. He..." Larry paused. Then looked down at his hands again. "Well, Hank liked the money too much. He didn't want it to stop. That's when I decided to call you for help. I'd seen your picture in his paper," he gestured toward Felix, who had been silently standing near the door this whole time. "I read how you got your boyfriend out of trouble last summer and helped put a murderer behind bars. I thought maybe, well, maybe you could do something here. Only as I was dialing, Hank came into the room waving a gun. He was talking crazy, about how he couldn't afford to go back to a dancer's salary. We fought and the gun went off. Blew a hole right through Hank's favorite chair."

At least that explained the gunshot I'd heard. "Then what happened?"

"I promised Hank I wouldn't tell anyone if he'd put the gun away. We went back to work like nothing had happened. Then three days later, Hank got pushed off the roof." His eyes teared up again.

"Do you think it was Monaldo?" I asked, slowly, watching Felix out of the corner of my eye. His expression was placid, but I'd bet anything he was mentally taking notes like a fiend.

Larry nodded. "Who else would it be? He must have killed them both."

I chewed on a fingernail, the hamster running overtime in my little wheel as I tried to digest all he'd said. I could see Monaldo wanting to silence Bobbi. Advertising their counterfeit merchandise on eBay probably wasn't good for business. But it sounded like of the three, Hank was most happy to keep his mouth shut. So, why go after him? I admit, so many pieces of random information were swirling through my brain that I was having a hard time connecting the dots.

And then Larry gave me another one to add to the mix.

"That's not all," he said. "Monaldo called me." He paused, his eyes shifting to Felix again. "And he wants me to do another drop for him."

"Another drop?" I got a bad feeling in the pit of my stomach.

Larry nodded. "Uh-huh. That's why I wanted to talk to you. Monaldo left me a message a couple of hours ago. I don't know what to do."

"When is it?"

"Tonight."

I bit my lip. "You have to tell the police, Larry."

He shook his head, his red wig swishing back and forth. "Unh-uh. No way. I wouldn't last a second in jail. Look at me!"

He had a point. I saw *OZ;* I knew what those places were like. Inmates weren't exactly the most tolerant bunch of people around.

"Maybe you wouldn't have to go to jail," I reasoned. "Ramirez said if you testify against Monaldo, you could be put into some kind of protective custody."

"Ramirez?" he asked.

Oops. I shifted my gaze from Felix (who had suddenly become much more interested in our conversation) to Larry. "Uh, he's a police officer I kind of know. Not important. Point is, if you go to the police they can protect you."

Larry looked down at himself. Then up at me. "I don't think I'd exactly blend in witness protection, do you?"

I wrinkled my forehead. "Well maybe if you…" I looked down at his shoes. Pink Mary Janes. Okay, bad place to start. I moved my gaze upward. "If you just changed the…" Pink pleather skirt? Ruffled white blouse? Sparkly red two-tone nail polish?

I sighed. Forget it. He was right.

As much faith as I had in Ramirez, it would take a Lance Burton sized illusion to hide Larry from Monaldo. I mean, how many six foot tall redheaded drag queens were there? Besides, once Larry went into protection it was out of Ramirez's hands. And into the hands of the Feds. After the way they'd handled this case so far (not to mention short changed me on my tax return the last two years in a row) I didn't have a whole lot of faith in *them*. All it would take was one little slip, and my dad would be flying off a building or stuffed in with the frozen peas.

As much as I'd had a martini shaker of mixed feelings about Larry in the last few days, seeing him sit across from me – his pantyhose run, his mascara smudged, and his love handles drooping out the side of a too tight girdle – I wasn't ready to let some Mafia shoe runner rob me of the chance to get to know my dad. Instinctively I leaned over and caught him in a hug so fierce it surprised even me.

"Don't worry, Dad, we'll think of something."

Larry pulled away, shock mixing with a faint smile on his face.

"What?" I asked.

"That's…" he paused, his voice choking up. "That's the first time you've called me 'dad.'"

He was right, it was. I hugged him again, feeling that warm, fuzzy Hallmark thing wash over me again.

Only this time, it was mixed with dread.

* * *

After promising Larry we'd find a way to get him out of this, I sent him into the bathroom to shower, change, and (denial, denial, denial) touch up his make-up. Felix booted up his laptop, his fingers flying over the keypad as he typed out the story of his career. Visions of tacky headlines danced in my head, but there wasn't much I could do to stop him at this point. Instead, I pulled out my cell and dialed Dana's number, filling her in on where I was and giving her the abridged version of Larry's monologue. She assured me she had Mom and Mrs. R under control, showing them the finer points of blackjack while Marco bought everyone 'Viva Las Vegas' T-shirts.

I hung up and stared out the window at the shapes of the Excalibur, the MGM Grand, and the Luxor shining in the distance. Everything about this town seemed larger than life.

Including its problems. I watched the endless stream of tourists glide down the moving walkways as I mulled over Larry's options. All the while listening to the constant hum of Felix's keyboard.

"Some story, huh?" I asked.

Felix didn't look up. "Uh-huh."

"What if I could give you an even better one?"

He cocked an eyebrow my way. "I don't quite see how it could get better than this."

I paused. See, here's the thing: As Ramirez had said over and over again, it all came down to proof. If Larry wasn't willing to testify about being the missing link between Monaldo and the Marsuccis, we needed some other proof of what had gone on. Like pictures. And I knew one person who had a knack for snapping photos of the unawares.

"What if I promised you an exclusive?"

"An exclusive?" He looked up, giving me his full attention now.

I nodded. "If…"

"Aha. I knew there was a catch."

I ignored him. "If you help me."

He narrowed his eyes. "Help you do what?"

"I'm going to do the drop for Monaldo."

"Pardon?" he said, giving me the 'this chick's crazy' look.

"I need you to call Monaldo and pretend to be Larry. Tell him you'll do his little errand for him. Only you're really going to be taking pictures of me while I dress as Larry, go get the bag from Monaldo, and take it to the Marsuccis."

"Who?" Felix asked, scanning his notes.

I bit my lip. I felt a little bit like I was making a pact with the devil himself, here. I weighed the possibility of Larry being wed to a cell mate named Bubba versus the amount of Spanish I was going to have to learn to translate the onslaught of Ramirez's curses when he saw my name splashed across the *Informer*'s front page. Again.

I looked from the steamy bathroom door to Felix.

What the hell.

"The Marsuccis are an organized crime family," I said.

Felix did the one eyebrow raise again. "As in mafia?"

I nodded. Then, to the tune of his fingers furiously typing out his golden story, I told him everything Ramirez had shared about the dead customs agent, the Fed's investigation, the containers of counterfeit shoes, and the link to Monaldo's club.

"I knew there was something fishy about that Bruno," he said when I'd finished. "You didn't strike me as a bouncer's girlfriend."

"For the last time, I'm not his girlfriend. I'm just his… Look, that's not important. What's important is that we have enough pictures to hand over proof of Monaldo and the Marsuccis' connection so that Monaldo goes to prison, and Larry doesn't end up doing a pancake impression on the asphalt. So, are you in?"

Felix stuck the end of a hotel issue ball point in his mouth, chewing thoughtfully. "It sounds a little dangerous," he finally said.

I put my hands on my hips, thrust my chest out, and put on my best tough chick voice. "Look, I'm a grown woman. I can handle this. Why is it everyone thinks I'm just some girly little shoe chick who can't do anything except wait for the big boys to work this stuff out? I left it to the big boys. Look what happened? Hank's dead; Bobbi's dead. I am not - you hear me? N-O-T," I spelled out for him, "going to sit around while my dad gets picked off like some sitting duck in heels just because you think it's too dangerous for the girly blonde. Well, let me tell you something, pal. I'm no little girl. I'm a big bad woman!"

Wow that felt good. Okay, so it might have felt even better had I actually been saying it to Ramirez, but I had a picture of his face in my head the entire time, so it was sort of like he was there. I could feel all my anger and frustration disappearing, leaving a big bubble of confidence that I could feel filling the entire room. I was woman; hear me roar!

That is until the corner of Felix's mouth began to quirk upward.

"Actually, love," he said, laughter escaping him, "I was thinking it was a bit dangerous for <u>me</u>."

Pop. There went my bubble.

"Oh. Right."

"But," he said, actually making an effort to control his giggles, "If you're that determined-"

"I am."

"-and you really do agree to an exclusive, complete with pictures and everything-"

I cringed, hoping at least he used my own body to go with my head this time. "I do."

"-then, you have yourself a deal. I'll be your photographer." He stuck his hand out. I shook it, half expecting his hidden horns and forked tail to come popping out.

I didn't waste time, knowing Larry would be out of the shower any minute. I quickly dialed information and got the number of the Victoria club.

"You can do an American accent, right?" I asked, handing the number to Felix.

He grinned. "Ya'll don't have nothing to worry yo' purty little head about, darlin'," he drawled, doing a bad John Wayne.

"Uh, maybe this isn't such a good idea after all..."

"Just give me the phone," he said, snatching my cell.

I held my breath as he dialed, crossing both fingers and toes and saying a little prayer to the saint of deception and fake accents. Luckily someone up there was listening, as Felix did a perfect Californian into the phone. Okay, so maybe he was a tad more Keanu Reeves than Larry's natural voice, but it seemed to pass muster with Monaldo.

I kept one eye on the bathroom, where steam from Larry's shower was still seeping under the door, as I listened to Felix's side of the conversation. It was brief and to the point. Basically a lot of 'uh-huh's and 'I'll be there's. My stomach played host to a butterfly convention as Felix asked Monaldo to remind him of the address, taking down the information on a pad of hotel stationary.

Finally he hung up.

"Well?" I asked.

"Tonight. Eight o'clock."

The butterflies formed a conga line.

CHAPTER EIGHTEEN

Since I had less than four hours to transform myself from a five foot tall woman into a six foot tall woman pretending to be a man pretending to be a woman, I needed help. Luckily if anyone was up to the job, it was Marco. I found him downstairs in the I Love NY-NY gift shop eyeing a pair of novelty shot glasses.

"Maddie, dahling!" he cried when he spotted me, going for a two-cheeked air kiss. "Where on earth have you been? I was worried sick about you!"

"Ramirez caught me. Handcuffed me in his backseat."

"Kinky." Marco wiggled his perfectly waxed eyebrows up and down.

"Humiliating was more like it. Anyway, I need to ask you a favor, Marco."

"Anything, for you sweetie," he said, thumbing through a stack of postcards.

I briefly filled him in on Larry's troubles and my plan to save his Prada wearing hide. When I got to the part about needing platform shoes and a wig, Marco clapped his hands with glee.

"Oooo, this is gonna be so fun. A drag make-over!"

Necessary, yes. Fun I wasn't so sure about. "I only have until eight tonight," I warned as he grabbed me by the arm and headed straight for the Off Broadway Costume shop.

Two hours and three dozen bad wigs later I was decked out in true Drag Queen Chic. I stood in front of the mirrored closet doors of Marco's hotel room staring at my reflection. He had gone with a long black skirt that covered my slightly-less-stocky-than-Larry's (thank God!) legs, a long sleeve corset-waisted red top that covered my slightly-less-hairy-than-Larry's (thank God!) arms, and a long red wig that was almost the exact duplicate of Larry's (which honestly didn't look half bad on me. Who knew I could do redhead?). Knowing that even in the highest heels I couldn't fake nine inches, Marco chose a clingy Lycra material for the skirt which, along with the vee necked top, gave the illusion of longer lines. And, I'm happy to report I did manage to add at least five inches to my frame with a pair of truly hooker-esque patent leather platforms.

Marco offered to use some charcoal eyeliner and putty-like cover-up to 'age' my face to match Larry's, but I declined, instead going for a huge pair of black J Lo sunglasses and a gauzy black veil that reached down to my chin. Though I did let Marco cake on some thick foundation and blush a hint of five o'clock stubble onto my chin. All in all, it was as close to fifty something transvestite as I was ever going to look (thank God!).

"Honey, you look divine!" Marco stood back, clasping his hands to his breast as he admired his work. "That wig is so you."

"Let's just hope Monaldo thinks it's so Larry."

"So," Marco said, leaning in close, a co-conspiratorial twinkle in his eyes. "What's the plan, spy girl?"

I adjusted my butt-length wig in the mirror as I recited the directions Monaldo had given to Felix over the phone.

"The plan is we drive to the Victoria, slip backstage and look for a red, crocodile handbag sitting at Larry's make-up station. Then Felix and I take the cash out into the desert for our rendezvous with the Marsuccis. I'll drop Felix off a few yards away to set up surveillance, then I'll continue on to the warehouse and hand the payoff over to the bad guys while Felix takes pictures of it all."

Hmmm… somehow saying it out loud made it all sound so improbable. Rendezvous? Surveillance? Payoff? Who did I think I was, James Bond?

Though, Marco didn't share my misgivings. "This is so freaking James Bond! I love it! Wait until I tell Madonna about this."

"No!" I spun on my platforms to face him. "No, you can't tell anyone. If Ramirez finds out about this, he'll skin me alive. Not to mention what my mother would do. Good God, can you imagine her traipsing after me with stun gun in hand? You have to promise me you are not going to tell a soul."

"But-"

"Promise!" I commanded, planting both hands on hips. And being as I towered over him by a good two inches now, he conceded.

"All right." He thrust his lower lip out in an exaggerated pout. "I promise."

I made him double pinky swear and felt a little bit better about it. Just a little. Swearing Marco to secrecy was about as effective as using a sharpie to cover up scuffs on my favorite black pumps. A temporary fix at best. But, I had no choice. I could only hope Marco sat on the gossip of the century long enough that Felix and I could get to the desert, and it would be too late for either Mom or Ramirez to stop me.

Okay, part of me hoped that. As I stared at my made-up reflection in the mirror the other part of me, the one that preferred all my limbs exactly where they were, was silently chanting, 'somebody stop me!'

* * *

Felix met me at the valet parking at exactly seven-o-two. If all went according to plan, he wanted to be in place long before the Marsuccis showed up. He took one look at my outfit, and I could see him mentally warring between a dozen ready-made snide comments.

"Don't start with me," I warned. "These are five inch heels. I could kill a man with these."

His grin widened, but he held up his hands in a surrender motion and wisely refrained from comment. Instead he handed the valet his ticket (and a fifty cent tip. Cheapskate.) and ten minutes later we were on the road.

I fidgeted nervously in my seat as we motored up the 15, my stomach tying itself in enough knots to macramé a plant hanger. The thing is, I wasn't the world's biggest fan of undercover work. Once, last summer while investigating the disappearance of my ex-boyfriend, Richard, Dana had convinced me to go undercover as a hooker. As if the neon spandex she'd made me wear wasn't bad enough, the evening had ended with a dead body. And considering I was currently the only player in this little drama without a gun, I really hoped tonight wasn't a replay.

I was chewing the Raspberry Perfection off my lips, debating whether I could tell Felix to turn around and forget the whole thing, when we pulled into the employee lot of the Victoria. The two Town Cars were still parked up front, and the lot was populated with half a dozen more rent-a-wrecks than it had been earlier in the day. Though, I was relived to see Ramirez's SUV conspicuously absent. I prayed Bruno had the night off. (Or was spending it out trying to find one escaped blonde.)

I stared at the back door as Felix killed the engine. Okay, I could do this. I was a tough chick. I was dangerous. On a mission. Take no prisoners.

"You ready?" Felix asked, grabbing his camera case from the back seat.

"Hell yeah!" Only somehow my pep talk hadn't convinced my body. My feet had turned to lead, and my butt was glued to faded seat.

"So… you want to go in, then?" he asked.

I nodded. "Nuh-unh."

Felix paused. "You know, it's not too late to change your mind. If you don't feel comfortable with this, we can call it off."

Did I feel comfortable with it? No. But neither did I feel comfortable in my gorgeous four inch, leather, Gucci logo pumps that angled in at the tip until my pinky toes turned blue. But if I could survive cutting off circulation to my feet for fashion, I could survive a knotted stomach for my father.

"No, I'm fine," I lied. "Let's do this."

Somehow I pried my booty off the seat despite feeling like it was covered in Elmer's and crossed the few feet of pavement to the back door. All the while feeling the heat of Felix's camera lens at my back.

The steady beat of dance music vibrated through the thick walls of the building, spilling out into the night as I opened the door. I blinked in the dimly lit interior, wishing I could take my dark glasses off. I took a moment to orient myself. I was in the backstage area. To my right was a panel of levers and pulleys, behind which sat a guy in a John Deere cap with a cigarette hanging out one side of his mouth. To the left, a changing room, the sounds of clacking heels, hairdryers and catty gossip mingling with the dance rhythms.

I went to the right, trying to look as inconspicuous as I could. The changing room was a small ten by ten affair, crammed with vanities topped by mirrored lights. Makeup bags and wig stands littered every surface and a rolling wardrobe rack sat by the door. Luckily, no one really seemed to take much notice of me. A skinny black guy in a Tina Turner outfit rushed past me yelling about her cues, and two of the yellow sequin 'girls' sat at one of the vanities, trying to get their feathers pinned on their heads and gossiping about someone named 'Molly'. (Who, apparently, had slept with half the men in the club.)

I scanned the room for a red crocodile bag and came up with pay dirt next to the vanity at the far end of the room. Ducking my head down, I stepped over discarded shoes and costumes on the floor, quickly grabbing the bag and ducking out again before the sequin girls could question me.

The bag was a lot heavier than I had expected, and I needed two hands to carry it as I backtracked to the outer door. By the time I reached it, my heart was pounding in my ears, and my stomach had knotted itself an entire afghan.

I stepped back out into the night, letting the door close on the club music behind me and did a quick scan to make sure a black SUV hadn't miraculously appeared while I was inside. None had, so I jogged (which in five inch heels was more like a series of baby steps on speed) to the Neon and quickly slipped into the passenger seat.

"Go, go, go!" I commanded as Felix put down his camera. He did, pulling out of the parking lot and taking a quick right onto Fremont. I heaved a sigh of relief that was much too big considering Operation Mafia Takedown was only halfway done. Getting the bag had been the easy part, the hard part would be coming face to face with the living breathing models for the *Sopranos* out in the desert where God knew how many generations of 'accidents' were buried in shallow graves.

I shivered and flipped on the heater.

To distract myself, I looked down at the bag in my hands as Felix drove south on the 15. It was a soft, crocodile skin dyed a deep burgundy color with little gold buckles and a bamboo handle. Actually tre chic, if you asked me. My hands shaking only slightly, I peeked inside. It was filled with wads of hundred dollar bills. I did a low whistle. As I may have mentioned, Tot Trots was not the Rodeo Drive of shoes. I made enough to cover my rent and keep me in Top Ramen and heels, but this was way more money than I'd ever seen in one place before. I put my nose down in the bag and inhaled deeply. The unmistakable scent of cash mixed with leather. This must be what real Pradas smelled like.

Fifteen minutes later we'd passed by the Mandalay Bay, the Bellagio, and the Treasure Island and were heading into the no-man's land between Vegas and Los Angeles. Tumbleweeds began to replace casinos until we spied the sign for Lone Hill Road. Felix turned off the highway, onto the roughly paved, two lane. Two more turns and we were reduced to a dirt road which might have been fun to navigate in my four wheel drive Jeep, but was just plain bumpy in a late model Neon. We bounced about three more miles in silence before a building came into sight on the horizon of the sparse, rocky terrain. Felix pulled the car over to the side.

"This is where I get off," he said, his voice betraying a hint of the jangling nerves I felt.

I nodded, not trusting myself to speak. For fear something like, "Don't leave me! I'm just a little girly girl!" would pop out.

"You sure you're going to be okay alone?" he asked and in the rapidly settling dusk, I could have sworn he actually looked concerned.

I nodded again. Hoping he couldn't tell what a bad liar I was.

Apparently not, since he grabbed his camera case and exited the car, doing a quick survey of the landscape before settling into position behind a rock formation. He gave me a thumbs-up sign, which I guess was supposed to reassure me as I slid over to the driver's seat.

I gave myself a little mental pep talk again, watching Felix's form disappear in the rearview mirror as I continued down the dusty road alone. Only the closer I got to the squat building in the distance, the less convincing I became.

I flipped the radio on to fill the silence. After playing with the dial I finally found a station playing '60's hits. It's hard to be freaked when you're listening to the Beatles. I tried to sing along to 'Good Day Sunshine,' but I found my eyes darting to the rearview mirror every three seconds, watching for black Town Cars.

This was it. If this didn't work... I didn't even want to think about it. And, I had to admit, I was beginning to seriously question the wisdom of not telling Ramirez about this plan. Sure, he would have nixed it from the get go, but maybe he could have sent one of his operatives to do this? Maybe he could have convinced Larry? Maybe we could have had sex at least once before I drove to possible maim-ment and death in the desert.

By the time I pulled up to the warehouse, my hands were sweating, my lips had been bitten raw, and I was beginning to get a nervous tick in my right eye. If I didn't already have a bag full of cash sitting beside me, there's no question I would have turned around and fled right then and there.

Instead, I parked the Neon in front of the warehouse. It was a nondescript building, square and large with concrete sides and a corrugated metal roof. Around it was a whole lot of dusty nothing.

No other cars were visible.

I sat there for a full two minutes, trying to talk myself into getting out of the car. I was halfway there. I had the cash, I was at the meeting place. So far so good. All I had to do now was hand over the bag, and all was well. (What can I say, I was becoming a pro at this denial thing.)

I opened the door and stepped out. The night air was cool and eerily quiet. Not even a cricket chirping anywhere. Picking my way over the hard packed dirt, I slowly made my way to the warehouse, the crocodile bag clutched so tightly my knuckles where turning white. Three loading bays spanned the length of it, with a smaller door off to the right. I tried the knob. Unlocked. I'd been expected.

I took one more deep breath for good measure and slowly pushed the door open. I felt around on the wall until my fingers came up against a light switch.

The interior of the warehouse was filled with tall, metal shelves like the ones Mom had in her garage for storing Christmas decorations and Tupperware tubs of my childhood mementoes. They spanned from floor to ceiling, each filled with big cardboard boxes. Exposed pipes and ducts ran the length of the ceiling, and the same corrugated metal décor covered the walls. It gave the feeling of being in a huge tin can. With about the same acoustics.

"Hello?" I called out, hearing my voice echo back to me in triplicate. No answer. I gingerly took a few steps inside, my platforms sounding like firecrackers on the cement floor.

I walked to the metal shelf nearest the door, and, with a quick glance over my shoulder, pried open a box on the lower shelf. Inside it were a dozen smaller boxes. Shoe boxes.

I gingerly pulled one out. Michael Kors. I'd love to say I slipped it back in and left it at that, but of course, I couldn't resist. What can I say? I'm my father's daughter. I popped open the lid. A perfect copy of last season's snakeskin pumps in chocolate brown, right down to the brass buckle detail on the face. I had to remind myself they were fakes to resist trying them on right then and there.

But the sound of tires crunching on the gravel outside snapped me out of it fast enough. I quickly replaced the lid and turned down the flaps of the box, taking two giant steps away from the shelves as the sound of a car door slamming shut echoed throughout the warehouse. I skittered across the cement floor, stepping back outside. And into Felix's line of vision. If we were going to get any decent shots at all, the exchange had to take place outside.

A black Range Rover had parked next to the Neon. (Apparently they were prepared for the rough terrain.) Two men in black suits stood beside it, both wearing tinted aviator glasses and looking like bad imitations of the Men in Black. I was about to approach them when a third man stepped out of the car. He was smaller than the other two, his suit a gray color, though he wore the same tinted glasses. Must be standard Mob issue. In addition to the eyewear, he was sporting more gold jewelry than Joan Rivers, including a large gold medallion around his neck and pinkie rings on each hand. His hair was slicked into a perfect black helmet over his too-big-for-his body-head. All in all the only thing missing were a pair of shoe spats and an Uzi, and he'd be the spitting image of the Italian family man.

The three of them slowly approached me, the Men in Black flanking Shortie.

"You have something for us?" the little guy asked, his voice a dead-ringer for Joe Pesci as he gestured to the crocodile bag clutched in my vice grip.

I nodded, clearing my throat to make my voice as low as it would go. "Yes," I answered.

Shortie took off his glasses and squinted at me. "What's with the veil?" he asked.

My panic meter rose about fifty notches. "Uh… I'm in mourning." I lowered my eyes to the ground. "Hank passed away."

Shortie nodded, pursing his thin lips together. "I heard about that. Tragedy."

Somehow I had the feeling these guys encountered 'tragedy' on a regular basis. A thought which did nothing to lower my panic reading.

But instead of saying anything, I just nodded again.

Shortie motioned to the bag and the taller Man in Black stepped forward to take it from me. His hand brushed mine as he did, sending a cold fear prickling up my neck as his tinted eyes settled on my face.

I cleared my throat again and studied my shoes, hoping he mistook my fear for grief. For one long, terrible moment, I thought the jig was up. He'd seen through my woman pretending to be a man pretending to be a woman ruse, and I'd soon be swimming with the fishes. (Or freezing with the peas as the case may be.) But instead of fitting me for cement slingbacks, he took a step back into formation beside Shortie and opened the bag. Shortie took a quick peek inside, pushing the bundles around to check that I hadn't slipped a hundred on top and filled the rest with hay. He nodded at Goon Number One, apparently satisfied.

Shortie turned back to me. "You tell Monaldo that we's sorry about his associate's untimely passing," he said, just two notes short of sincere.

I nodded.

Shortie kept his eyes on my face for one more agonizing beat then slipped his glasses back on, apparently satisfied.

I felt every muscle in my body sigh in relief as he walked back to his car. Goon Number One held the back door open for Shortie, then got in the back seat himself as Goon Number Two got behind the wheel.

Adrenalin laced sweat dripped down my back, but I stayed rooted to the spot as I watched them do a three point turn and drive back down the dirt road. What do you know; I was good at undercover work after all. No dead bodies. No angry mobsters. Not even a cranky cop to muddy the waters. I felt glee rising up in the back of my throat as I pictured the look on Ramirez's face when I handed him the proof that would crack his case wide open. Not so girly now, huh?

I squelched the urge to jump for joy, lest the Men in Black see me victory dancing in the rearview mirror. Instead, I waited until their tail lights disappeared down the road, then waved in Felix's general direction.

I could have sworn I saw the flash of his camera lens in response against the dark night sky.

But that was the last thing I saw.

A crack of thunder exploded inside my head, and the desert landscape instantly folded in on itself as the ground rushed up to meet me.

Then everything went black.

CHAPTER NINETEEN

Once when I was in college at the Academy of Art University in San Francisco, I went out with a group of my friends after spring finals. Linda, who was majoring in film production and had just landed a job with DreamWorks, suggested we go to the Golden Gate Club to celebrate. She insisted news like a DreamWorks job called for Apple Pie shots. This sounded like a great idea to me considering a) I'd just spent the last three nights staying up until 2 AM writing essays about the difference between kitten and stiletto heels and b) who didn't like pie? That is until I realized that Apple Pie shots consisted of schnapps, followed by vodka, followed by more schnapps. I'd like to say I had a wild night to remember. Only I couldn't. Remember it, that is. The last clear memory I had of that night was showing some guy named 'Snake' how I could touch the tip of my nose with the tip of my tongue.

I woke up the next morning with stale gym socks breath, sand paper tongue, and Tommy Lee drumming a pounding beat between my ears. It was the Brangelina of headaches, the Mt. Everest of headaches, the worst aching-eyes, throbbing-temples, ringing-ears, pounding-head, so-bad-you-want-to-throw-yourself-in-front-of-a-bus-just-to-stop-the-pain headache to end all headaches.

And this was worse.

I groaned, the pressure of a sixteen wheeler pulsating through my brain with every breath I took. My mouth felt scratchier than polyester pants in August, and my eyes ached like they'd been glued shut. I slowly did a mental check of my person, wiggling first my toes then fingers. All ten of each seemed to be functioning. Though, as I moved on to wriggling my hands, I noticed they didn't have quite the range of motion I was used to. Mostly because they were bound together. I rubbed my wrists together, and something sharp and plastic bit into them. Ditto my ankles. I wiggled my butt, feeling a hard, cold floor beneath me.

I gingerly opened one eye then the other. It was dark, and I continued the painful practice of blinking, trying to bring the shadows into focus. It looked like I was in some sort of storeroom. Cardboard boxes were stacked along the walls, and a couple of empty wardrobe racks sat off to one side. I could hear a steady thump, thump, thump of music from somewhere just beyond the plaster walls, echoing through my head, where I felt a serious goose egg trying to take hold.

"Hello?" I called out. Okay, I should say *tried* to call out. It was more like a pathetic little squeak, my throat dryer than my mother's elbows in January. And, I realized, useless. Over the music no one could hear me anyway unless they were in the same room.

As I sat there, immobile, slowly letting my eyes adjust to the darkness, I tried to remember how I got here. Or, for that matter, where here even was. Had I passed out? Fainted? Had one too many dessert themed shots again?

I looked down at my bound feet, clad in five inch patent leather platforms. Then in a flash it all came back to me. The Drag Queen Chic look, the Men in Black, the warehouse in the desert.

The ground meeting my face.

Someone had whacked me on the head! I hated it when people did that. Just when I'd thought everything had gone so well, too. I'd passed as Larry, the Marsuccis had their money – everyone should have been happy. I just hoped Felix had gotten a shot of the creep who'd hit me.

Felix!

My only hope. He must have seen the whole thing. Maybe he followed me. Maybe he was, at this very moment, corralling the troops to break in and rescue me…

A fantasy which was cut short as I heard a groan from the other side of the room.

"Uhn. Bloody 'ell."

Great. So much for my rescue.

"Is that you?" I asked, squinting through the darkness.

"Maddie?"

"Yeah. What happened?"

He groaned again, and I heard movement, then another 'bloody hell,' as he realized that, like me, he was bound. "I don't know. The last thing I remember, I was popping off a shot of those Italian blokes taking your bag, and now here I am." He paused, groaning again. "With a hell of a headache."

On the up side, at least he had gotten the shots of the Marsuccis.

"Where's your camera now?" I asked.

He groaned again, this one louder and sadder. "No clue."

So much for the up side.

I leaned my head back (carefully, to avoid the goose egg) and felt tears prick the backs of my eyes. Ramirez was right. I was an idiot for not staying in L.A. when I had the chance. Mobsters, goons, Mafiosos – what did I know about these kinds of people? Nothing. Less than nothing. Negative nothing. So nothing that I'd flubbed the one chance of proving Monaldo's connection to the Mob and gotten myself and Felix both kidnapped in the process. Not only that, but I had a feeling that when whoever was responsible for the goose eggs came back, they weren't just going to cut our bonds and let us go. I had a feeling my last moments on earth were going to be dressed as a fifty something drag queen.

But do you want to know what the worst part was? The worst part was I was going to die without ever having sex with Ramirez! This thought was so depressing the tears escaped my eyes, rolling down my cheeks in big fat droplets.

"Are you crying?" Felix asked from across the room.

"N-n-n-no," I sobbed.

He shifted on the floor. "Er… there, there. It's going to be all right," he said awkwardly.

"N-n-no it's not!" I wailed. "You're just saying that to m-m-make me feel better."

"It's not really working very well, is it?"

I sniffed, doing a sob slash hiccup thing. "We're going to die, and it's all my fault!"

"No, no," Felix said. He shimmied across the floor like an inverted inch worm until he was sitting beside me. "Look, this is as much my fault as it is yours. I should have been watching you better. I was too focused on my lens to notice anything else. It's my fault we're here."

I sniffed again. "You're right. It's your fault."

"Well, you didn't have to agree with me quite so quickly."

I looked up to find Felix doing one of his self-deprecating grins again. Maybe it was the darkness, or maybe the impending death, but it seemed just a fraction more charming this time.

"So," he said quickly, "any guesses where we are?"

I looked around the room again. "A storeroom of some sort."

"The warehouse?"

I shook my head. Then regretted it as the pounding between my ears went into double time. "I don't think so." My eyes had adjusted to the windowless room, and I could make out faint writing on the sides of one of the cardboard boxes nearest me. Budweiser.

"The club!" I cried. "We're at the Victoria."

Felix nodded beside me, putting it together at the same time. "Someone must have followed us from here. They must have seen you drop me off."

"Monaldo." I felt my previous tears quickly turning into anger. That guy was really starting to piss me off. First he gets me arrested, then whacks me over the head. Who did he think he was? I was suddenly wishing Mom had stunned him a little harder when she had the chance.

I was about to let out a string of curses aimed at the creepy little weasel, when the sounds of someone outside the room froze me in place. Felix heard it too, going stiff beside me as both our eyes riveted to the door on the far side of the room.

"If this is the end," Felix whispered beside me, "I'm sorry I pasted your head on Pamela Anderson's body."

"And I'm sorry I broke your nose," I whispered back.

"Apology accepted."

I held my breath as the door swung open, the sudden light from the hallway momentarily blinding me. I blinked, squinting at the huge form silhouetted in the doorway.

The door slammed shut behind him, and overhead fluorescent lights flickered to life. Again I felt my pupils contracting harshly as I blinked at the man, now bathed in greenish flickering light. Unibrow. And he wasn't happy. The hairy caterpillar hovered over his eyes in a menacing line as his beady eyes bore into me. Only that wasn't the scary part. The scary part was the gun he had pointed at my vee necked top.

I bit my lip, for once willing myself not to open my big mouth as Unibrow's threatening gaze bounced between Felix and me.

But apparently, Felix felt no such compunction.

"Where's my camera?" he demanded.

Unibrow narrowed his eyes at him. "We don't like people that takes pictures."

"I'm a member of the press," Felix retaliated. "You can't hold me here. I demand our release immediately."

His eyes narrowed further. "We ain't too fond of press either."

Since Felix was only serving to piss off the man with the gun, I jumped in with a different tactic. "Please, please, please let us go?" I pleaded, throwing on the best innocent little girl face I could while being bound hand and foot amidst cases of longnecks. "Look, we don't know anything. And we won't tell anyone anything. Because we don't know anything. Where are we? I don't know. Who are you?" I shrugged. "I don't know. See, I'm just a dumb blonde. I couldn't give a description of anyone or anything to anybody."

If it wasn't effective at least my speech had entertainment value. Unibrow laughed, letting out a quick, dry cough. "I don't think so. Monaldo was very specific about what to do with you."

I gulped. "Um, so what *are* you going to do with us?" I squeaked out. Even though the gun leveled at my chest gave me a pretty good idea.

"Don't worry" he said, a twisted smile distorting his ugly features. "We'll take care of you."

Oh, lordy. There was that phrase again.

"Like you took care of Bob Hostetler?" Felix piped up beside me.

Unibrow's caterpillar hunkered down in a frown again. "Shut up!" he growled.

I nudged Felix in the ribs. Why was he dead set on antagonizing the man with the gun? Ix-nay on the urder-may.

"Or what about Hank?" Felix asked, not giving in. Even under threat of thirty-eight special in the schnoz he was all reporter.

"I didn't do nothing to Hank," Unibrow protested.

Felix smirked. "That, my hulking friend, is a double negative. You *didn't* do *nothing* implies that nothing was not done, which means that the opposite of nothing, which is something, was, in fact, done by you. So, in essence, you just admitted that you *did* do something to Hank. Something quite nasty, I'd venture to guess."

Unibrow hunched his caterpillar down low in a perplexed stare. "Huh?"

"You see, it's really a quite simple rule of grammar-"

"Shut up!" Unibrow growled again, shoving the tip of his gun against the white bandage covering Felix's nose.

Felix snapped his mouth shut with a click.

"I've had enough of you," Unibrow said, his voice low and scarier than a Wes Craven villain.

I heard my breath come out in deep ragged gasps as I held myself rigid against the wall. I heard the gun cock, the chamber loading. Oh God, he was going to shoot Felix!

Then, as if to prove me wrong, he added, "But ladies first." He swung the barrel of the gun to the right, catching me squarely in the chest.

Oh God, he was going to shoot *me*!

I closed my eyes, feeling hot tears run down my cheeks again. Images of Mom, Faux Dad, Larry, and, oddly enough, Ramirez flickered through my head at lightening speed as I silently said a prayer to the saint of hopeless causes. Saint Jude. Funny that I should remember that now. But I did, with crystal clarity. So, I prayed with all the desperation of a woman who hadn't been to Sunday mass in years, promising to give money to the poor, to volunteer with sick children, to stop having unholy thoughts every time I watched Ramirez walk across the room in his butt hugging jeans. Anything! As long as the next sound I heard wasn't the shout of a gun redecorating the sparse walls with my innards.

I waited, my breath hitched in my throat, my eyes clamped shut, my lips pursed into a thin white line.

Only the gun didn't click. Instead, I heard the sound of glass breaking just outside the door.

I popped my eyes open. Unibrow had heard it to. He froze, his entire pea brain focused on listening to the commotion outside the door. Which was growing. Something thudded against the wall, and I heard voices, all yelling incoherently. Unibrow took a step toward the door. Then paused looking back at Felix and me, his one eyebrow hunching down in concentration. Apparently it was a big decision – shoot the blonde first, or go break up the bar fight?

Luckily, Unibrow was not the sharpest stiletto on the rack and chose option number two. Two lumbering strides and he was at the door, hand on knob. Only he never quite got the opportunity to turn it as the door came bursting off its hinges, slamming toward Unibrow like a battering ram was on the other side. Unibrow stumbled back before regaining his grip on the gun. He may have been slow-witted, but years of mafia experience had made him quick on the draw. Before I could yell out a shout of warning to our would-be rescuers, he had his hands around the trigger and was squeezing off shots that cracked against the door jam, sending splinters of wood flying into the air. Crack, crack, crack. He got off three shots in a row, before one really loud bang echoed from the doorway, and Unibrow fell backwards, a bright red stain spreading across his chest.

I screamed. A long, loud, roller-coaster worthy scream that echoed in my own ears even after I ran out of breath to sustain it. I looked from the toppled giant to the doorway, expecting to see police, the Feds, Ramirez, the LVMPD and good old Detective Sipowicz.

Instead I saw a smoking black LadySmith attached to the shaky hands of my best friend. Dana.

I think I screamed again. Only this time it was more like the second time you ride the roller coaster, when you realize that as long as your harness actually does hold you in, those dips and rolls are actually kind of fun.

Behind Dana the cause of the commotion came pouring into the room - the Nanny Goat bartender from FlyBoyz, a whole army of bikers in black leather, Mom and Mrs. Rosenblatt holding broken beer bottles out like weapons, Marco (cowering behind Nanny Goat) and a guy who looked like The Rock's bigger brother. Rico.

He put a hand on Dana's arm, lowering the LadySmith as she stared at the stain now seeping onto the concrete floor. Her eyes were as big as Maybelline compacts, her mouth dropped open into an 'o' of surprise.

"Did I get him?" she asked, her voice cracking.

I nodded, tears of relief mingling with the tears of terror still staining my cheeks. "Yes, honey, you got him."

Dana blinked, looking from the gun clutched in her white knuckled grip to the big hole in Unibrow. She licked her lips. "Wow, Mac wasn't kidding. This baby packs quite a punch."

CHAPTER TWENTY

For once I was glad to hear that Marco hadn't been able to keep his big mouth shut. After he'd left me, he'd gone down to the casino where he'd found Mrs. Rosenblatt at the Big Apple Bar. One comment on his fishy aura and Marco had broken down like a '73 Pinto going up a steep hill. He'd told her all about my plan to play Larry (which Mrs. Rosenblatt had immediately said was not a good idea for a person with karma like mine); then Mrs. Rosenblatt had tracked Mom down at the craps table and told her. Mom had nearly fainted (which cost her thirty-two dollars when she'd hit the table for support and the dealer had mistaken this for a bet on a hard eight), but once she'd recovered, Mom called Dana to see if she was with me. Obviously, she wasn't. Dana had been on her way to the airport to pick up Rico who had surprised her by flying in to personally hand deliver her new LadySmith and 'compare hardware.' (And I wasn't entirely sure we were talking guns here.) Dana did a few 'ohmigod's, then told Rico, who then called his friend the bartender who had then gathered the entire patronage of FlyBoyz.

Long story short (I know, too late) Unibrow hadn't been the only one following us into the desert. Twenty minutes behind him had been Marco riding with Mom and Mrs. Rosenblatt in their rented Dodge mini-van, Dana and Rico in the Mustang, and a whole slew of Harleys bringing up the rear. By the time they were traveling down Lone Hill Road, they passed a long, sleek Town Car speeding in the opposite direction. Dana had recognized it and, on instinct, followed him to the Victoria where her impeccable timing had just saved me from becoming fish food.

Once Rico pried the gun from her hands, Dana started alternating between crying and shaking, swearing she was never touching that thing again. And considering it was now evidence, it didn't look like she'd have the opportunity anytime soon anyway. When the police finally did arrive, Dana's hands were swabbed for gunshot residue; then she and Rico were escorted into one of the back rooms for questioning by Detective Sipowicz, though we were assured it was just a formality and that considering the circumstances no charges would be brought against them. Just in case, Mrs. Rosenblatt stood at the ready to call her dead second husband Carl's law firm at the first sign of handcuffs or extraneous sodas.

Somehow in all the commotion, Felix had slipped away, no doubt rushing to summarize his version of the event before the Associated Press picked up on the story. Mom, Mrs. R, Marco, Nanny Goat, the lot of burly looking bikers, and the 'girls' in feathers were all corralled onto the main floor of the club where they were called one by one to give statements to a team of uniformed police officers that now outnumbered the drag queens two to one. The room looked like some sort of weird costume party gone bad - leather chaps mixed with sequined leotards mixed with Mrs. Rosenblatt's neon pink and blue spotted muumuu. I had a feeling this was what a bad acid trip was like.

As for myself, I was parked on a vinyl barstool, wrapped in an ugly green blanket, wondering when my teeth would stop chattering. The paramedic who first arrived on scene told me I did, in fact, have a mild concussion, but other than that I was physically okay. Mentally, however, was another story. It wasn't every day a girl saw her best friend blow a hole the size of a softball through someone's chest. And while I wasn't mourning the loss of a scumbag like Unibrow anyway, the sight of gooey red stuff pooling around his head was permanently etched in my brain. Trust me. The real deal was a lot more disturbing than a *CSI* episode.

"Maddie!"

I turned to see Ramirez hailing me from the front doors. He flashed his badge to one of the uniformed LVMPD, then pushed through them, making a beeline toward me. I quickly swiped a finger under my eye to check for black smudges. With the way

I'd been crying that night I was sure I had mascara streaks clear down to my chin. I swiped the other eye and fluffed my hair a little. Hey – I was shaken up, not dead.

"Maddie!" he said again, then grabbed me in a hug so fierce I thought he might crack a rib. He held me there for a long minute, not saying anything. "Don't ever pull a stunt like that again," he finally whispered into my ear. Only this time there was no Bad Cop in his voice. This time it was, dare I say, almost tender.

"Sorry," I mumbled against his chest.

He released me and stood back to get a good look at me, doing a quick check of my person for broken bones with his hands. Though I admit as his palms skimmed over my thighs, I went warm in a totally inappropriate way considering the circumstances. "Are you okay?" he asked, his fingers moving upward to gently probe the goose egg at the back of my head.

"I'm fine." I paused. "Okay, maybe fine is a bit of a stretch. But I'm not dead."

He blew out a big breath, running one hand through his black hair. He looked down at my outfit, taking in the platforms and drag queen chic bustier. "Jesus, Maddie, what were you thinking? You know, I almost had a heart attack when LVMPD called me."

"You did?" I asked, my body doing that inappropriate thing again at the concern lacing his voice. "Really?"

"Yeah, I did." He reached a hand up and tucked a strand of hair behind my ear, his knuckles brushing softly against my cheek. "I hate it when I miss all the action." His mouth quirked up at the corner.

"Ha. Ha. Very funny, tough guy."

He grinned, though his hand lingered in my hair, making little goose bumps break out on the backs of my arms.

As my body continued to equate near-death-experience with horny-teenager-worthy-hormones I cleared my throat and forced myself to ask after the one person conspicuously absent from the night's activities. "So… what happened to Monaldo?"

Ramirez stopped doing the hands-in-hair thing, and I could see him mentally switching back into cop mode. "He's been taken into custody."

I let out a long breath I'd been holding since I first stepped into Larry's shoes.

"The Feds picked him up a few minutes ago outside his penthouse, and he's being processed as we speak," Ramirez continued. "No formal interviews have been conducted yet, but the minute he heard he'd been under surveillance, he started squealing like a stuck pig, naming at least three Marsucci family members in the counterfeit shoe ring. He even said he'd cop to killing the customs agent and Bob Hostetler if we pleaded down to manslaughter and promised him protective custody. The Feds are so happy I think I saw one do a cartwheel."

"What about Hank?" I asked.

Ramirez shrugged. "Monaldo still says he had nothing to do with Hank's death, but I think he's just holding out for a better deal. Honestly it doesn't really matter. Any way you look at it the Marsuccis are going down, and Monaldo's going to jail for a long, long time. Everybody wins."

Except Unibrow, I thought, remembering the sickly red stain.

"So, what now?" I asked.

He took my hands in both of his, his voice taking on that tender quality again. "Now you go home and get some sleep. You've been through a lot tonight, you need some rest."

I felt the heat of his touch pulse through my palm. I licked my lips. "And you?"

He looked down at me, his eyes like two melted pools of Hershey's Special Dark. But instead of promising to spend the night showing me a hundred and one new uses for those handcuffs of his, he glanced at the front door. "I've spent the last six weeks living this case, Maddie. I'd really like to be there when they question Monaldo."

I felt my heart sink. Work. Again.

But, considering I had a personal stake in seeing Monaldo disappear into maximum security for a very long time, I didn't complain. Much.

"You're leaving?" I whined.

He glanced from the door to me. "Look, if you need me to stay, I will," he said. Which I took as a small victory. At least he was *pretending* he'd put me before work. That was a start.

"Go. I'm fine," I lied.

"You sure?" he asked. Though he was already pulling away.

"Yes. Go. I'll be okay, really."

He placed a quick kiss on my forehead. "Get some sleep, and I'll call you as soon as I'm done. I promise." Then he spun around and stalked back out of the club with purpose.

I watched his denim clad butt walk away, my inappropriately charged body sighing in disappointment. Then I slapped both hands over my eyes. Hey, I had promised Saint Jude, hadn't I?

* * *

The sun was rising over the horizon by the time Detective Sipowicz finally told us we could go home. But considering home was 100 miles away, and the New York - New York was just a few blocks, Mom, Mrs. Rosenblatt, Marco, Dana, Rico and I caravanned back to the hotel instead. We were making our way across the casino floor, the ding, ding, ding of the slot machines making my goose egg throb like a trombone in my ear, when Slim Jim caught my eye.

"Hey!" he called. Then pointed at Dana as he rounded the reservation desk and advanced on our merry little group. "Hey, where were you last night? I waited over an hour for you to show up. I completely missed Bette's opening act. I can't believe you stood me up!"

Mental forehead smack. With everything else that had been going on I'd totally forgotten that I'd pimped my best friend out to Mr. Walking Acne Commercial for the night.

Dana looked from me to Slim Jim, then to Rico, whose eyebrows were angling downward.

"What do you mean she stood you up?" Rico asked.

Slim Jim crossed his arms over his sunken chest. "I had a date to see Bette Midler with this chick, and she totally blew me off."

Rico's eyes narrowed as he turned on Dana. "You had a date with this pencil neck?"

"Hey!" Slim Jim yelled.

"Uh…" Dana said, biting her lip. "Well, kind of…"

"You're not here one week, and you're cheating on me with *this* guy?"

"Hey!" Slim Jim said again. "What's wrong with *this* guy?"

"You know," Mrs. Rosenblatt piped up, "this is just like the time my third husband, Rory, thought I was foolin' around with the dry cleaning guy. Only that time-"

But she didn't get to finish. Before anyone could stop him, Rico swung one meaty fist in the air, missing Slim Jim's jaw by millimeters.

"Holy crap!" Slim Jim yelled, ducking. Rico came in for another try, swinging his left fist this time. Slim Jim crouched behind a Lucky Seven slot machine. "Holy freakin' crap!" he yelled.

"Rico, no!" Dana cried, grabbing onto the back of Rico's shirt. It ripped as he lunged for Slim Jim again, looking frighteningly like a scene from *The Incredible Hulk* as Rico's bared muscles flexed, his fist making another dive at Slim Jim. Jim skittered behind a fake tree.

"Somebody call the police!" Marco shouted.

Dana pulled out her cell and dialed 911. But before she could even get the call out, two security guards came rushing up. They each grabbed one of Rico's arms, which was almost effective in holding him back. Almost. Hey, the guy was about a thousand pounds of pure muscle. He charged at Slim Jim again, a security guard dangling from each arm like puppets. Slim Jim ducked behind a street sign, one of the guards called for back-up, and Marco screamed for Dana to call the police again.

She did. And this time they arrived. Five minuets later I was treated to my second Vegas PD encounter of the evening as three uniformed officers pushed their way through the growing crowd of onlookers. Much to the relief of Slim Jim who was starting to look tired of bobbing and weaving. I didn't blame him. Actually, I was kind of impressed he'd lasted three rounds with Jolly Green-with-jealousy Giant.

The first two uniforms helped the two security guards restrain Rico. The third stared at Dana, uncomprehendingly.

Because, of course, with our luck, the LVMPD had sent us Officer Baby Face.

"Dana?" he asked. "What's going on?"

Dana looked like a deer caught in the headlights, her gaze whipping from Rico to Slim Jim then back to Officer Baby Face.

"Uh..."

Ever helpful, Marco stepped in. "See, Dana had a date with this guy Jim, but she totally forgot about it because Maddie set it up for her, and then her boyfriend, Rico, got into town-"

"Boyfriend!?" Officer Baby Face yelled, clearly hurt. "You have a boyfriend?"

"Uh..." Dana said again.

I elbowed Marco in the ribs. "Not a *boyfriend* boyfriend. More like someone she just dates occasionally."

"You went out with me when you were dating someone else?" Officer Baby Face asked, and I feared he was on the brink of tears.

"You went out with this guy, too?" Rico growled, his face going red, steam starting to pour out of his ears.

"Uh..." Dana looked from Rico to Marco and me. "A little help here?" she pleaded.

"Oh, come on, fellows," Marco said, stepping up. "What happens in Vegas stays in Vegas, right?"

Three pairs of angry eyes turned his way.

Marco whimpered and jumped behind me.

"Okay, clearly this is all just some big misunderstanding," I said, trying to diffuse the situation. "See, I'm the one that-"

"Wait!" Mrs. Rosenblatt cut me off, slapping her palm over the bulging veins on Rico's forehead. "I'm having a vision!"

Oh. Good. Lord.

Mrs. Rosenblatt rolled her eyes back in her head, doing her *Dawn of the Dead* impression. "I see... a donkey. A big, strong donkey." Mrs. Rosenblatt snapped her eyes open. "You got a pet?"

"Ha!" Slim Jim said, popping out from behind the Lucky Seven machine. "She thinks you're an ass."

Rico growled and lunged for Slim Jim again, dragging the security guards and LVMPD with him. They may have held his arms, but his legs were free. And considering Rico was trained in fifteen different forms of marital arts, this was a huge oversight on the LVMPD's part. Rico coiled one foot back like a snake, then shot it out toward Slim Jim, catching him squarely in the face.

"Uhn." Slim Jim rocketed backwards, bouncing to a stop against a Deuces Wild machine.

"All right, that's it. You're all asses!" Dana yelled. She turned to Officer Baby Face who was looking like he was trying to remember if this had been covered in the manual. "You," she said, pointing a finger at him. "Yes, I'm seeing Rico."

Office Baby Face opened his mouth. "But-"

"But," Dana continued, "I went out on *one* date with you. One! It's not like I promised I'd marry you. I mean, hello? Does this look like the body of a married woman? I don't think so."

Officer Baby Face clamped his mouth shut and found a piece of dirt on the floor suddenly very interesting.

"And you," Dana continued, turning on Rico, who now that he'd made contact with Slim Jim's face seemed freakishly calmer. "Who do you think you are that you just go around picking on poor defenseless little wimps like that?"

"Hey!" Slim Jim called from his crumpled position on the floor.

But Dana ignored him. "Rico, that was the worst display of jealousy I have ever seen. And I work with actors! You are a grown man, not some little boy playing soldier."

Wow, I was impressed. She was taking tough chick to a whole new level.

"What about me?" Slim Jim asked.

Dana rolled her eyes. "Hello – you talk to my breasts. Get a grip!"

Slim Jim pouted. Either that or his lip was swelling.

"Now," Dana said crossing her arms over her chest, "You three children can go on squabbling if you like, but I just shot a man, and I'm tired. I'm going upstairs to get some sleep." Dana turned around and marched toward the Chrysler elevators. "Maddie?" she called over her shoulder. "Are you coming?"

Considering the testosterone level down here, that was a no-brainer. "Wait up," I called, doing a mini jog across the casino floor to catch up to her. Marco, Mom and Mrs. Rosenblatt followed close on our heels.

By the time we made it upstairs, I was beyond exhausted. Dana and Marco took one of the double beds and Mom selflessly fit her five-foot-one frame onto the rollaway. Which left me sleeping with Mrs. Rosenblatt. Or, more accurately, occupying the sliver of bed left over after she rolled her 300 pound frame into bed. But I honestly didn't care. I closed my eyes, hit the pillow, and fell into the first good night's sleep I'd had in weeks.

* * *

I awoke the next morning to the sounds of Marco getting into the shower. I rolled over and checked the digital clock radio display. 10:15. God I loved sleeping in. I rubbed my eyes and stretched as I sat up in bed. Dana was on the other double, watching a show on beating the blackjack dealer.

"Where are the gruesome twosome?" I asked, yawning.

"Your mom and Mrs. R? They went to breakfast across the street at the $4.99 pancake buffet. Why, you hungry?"

I nodded. Actually, I was. I realized as my stomach growled that I hadn't eaten anything since yesterday morning. Dana dialed room service and ordered a fat free yogurt cup with strawberries and granola for her and bacon, hash browns, and French toast with extra whipped cream for me. (Hey, I'd almost died last night. Life was too short for health food.)

While we waited for our dome covered trays, I plugged my cell phone into the wall and checked my messages. There were so many my inbox was full. The first batch was from last night, Dana and Mom both calling frantically to find out where I was and if I was okay. The next was from Tot Trots, saying that if I didn't turn in my designs for the Rainbow Brite jellies by Monday, I could kiss my job goodbye. I did a few mental calculations, figuring that if we left first thing in the morning, didn't hit any traffic, and I stayed up all night, I might still be employed next week. Maybe.

I tried not to picture my silver slingbacks hoofing it to the unemployment line as the next message came on. Ramirez. In fact, the next *seven* were from him, alternating between swearing in Spanish (when he found the dangling handcuffs) and *lots* of swearing in Spanish (when he heard about Dana shooting Unibrow).

My last message was from this morning. It was Larry, saying Felix had filled him in on last night's excitement and was I okay? I could call him back at home, since, thanks to Monaldo's arrest, he was back in Henderson.

I stared at my cell contemplating that little LCD screen. I knew I should call Larry back. And I would, I decided. Later. Now that imminent danger and threat of life had been taken off the table, I wasn't really sure what to say to him. All that were left were the biggies. Why had he run off? Why had he abandoned that three-year-old me? What kind of relationship did I want to have with him now? All questions that were too deep for a woman with a mild concussion to contemplate.

Instead, I ate my breakfast, threw on a tank top, denim skirt, and my Gucci boots, and headed downstairs.

Slim Jim was at the check-in desk, his lip swollen to collagen standards, his nose covered in white bandages and both eyes rimmed in purple. I would have felt sorry for him if it weren't for the two Swedish tourists in mini skirts and tube tops fawning over his injuries. Apparently being pummeled had its perks.

"Hey," I called down the counter. "I don't mean to interrupt, but do you have a copy of today's *Informer*?"

Slim Jim pulled a copy out from under the counter and gave me a shooing motion as he turned back to the busty Swedes.

I pulled the tabloid open. The headline read, "Local Reporter Busts Open Counterfeiting Ring". Hmmm… not exactly how it went down, but then again it was closer to the truth than ninety percent of the stuff the *Informer* usually published. I scanned the rest of the article. I admit, I was actually kind of impressed. Given an actual story to work with Tabloid Boy didn't do half bad. And he even kept my head attached to my own body in all the photos. Maybe that Pulitzer loomed in his future yet.

At the end of the story was a smattering of pictures – Hank's tarp-covered body outside the Victoria, Monaldo being led away from his penthouse in handcuffs, mourners at Hank's funeral. The last was a shot of Maurice, sobbing over Hank's casket, a tissue clutched in one hand. Poor Maurice. I felt my heart go out to him. No matter what happened to Monaldo now, it couldn't bring Hank back. I wondered if anyone had even told him about Monaldo's arrest. Ramirez and the Feds had seemed pretty focused on Monaldo last night. I had a feeling no one even remembered the broken hearted partner Hank had left behind.

I stared at the picture. After zapping his dog, the least I could do was give him the peace of mind that Monaldo wasn't still out there somewhere. I left the paper on the counter and hailed a cab.

Twenty minutes later I pulled up in front of Maurice's condo. The same lawn furniture was overturned in the courtyard, and in the late morning, I could hear *Judge Judy* and *All My Children* echoing through the thin walls from the units surrounding his.

I knocked on the door of 24A, and a few beats later Maurice appeared. The dark circles under his eyes had gained momentum, making him look older and more sunken than the last time I'd seen him. His gray pallor hadn't improved, and he was still wearing somber, unrelieved black – a black turtleneck, black slacks and a black sweater vest. And those hideous loafers.

Queenie danced around his legs, yapping a greeting.

"Maddie," Maurice said, his voice hoarse like he'd been crying non-stop since the funeral. "Please, come in." He stepped back to allow me entry. "What can I do for you?" Maurice motioned for me to sit, then took a spot on the loveseat opposite.

I cleared my throat, the potpourri and Clorox combination making the air feel thick in his tiny living room. "Have you seen the papers today?" I asked.

Maurice shook his head. "No. I haven't been out much. Why?"

"Monaldo's been taken into custody," I said, laying a comforting hand on his arm.

Maurice's eyes teared up, and he pulled a tissue from the box on the coffee table, holding it under his nose. "He has?"

I nodded. "The police arrested him last night."

"Oh, thank God!" Maurice heaved a sigh of relief, his shoulders sagging as if a huge weight had been lifted off of them. "You don't know how nerve wracking the last few days have been. Not only loosing Hank but knowing that monster was out there somewhere."

I patted Maurice's hand again. "I'm so sorry about Hank."

Maurice sniffled into his tissue. "Thank you. And thank you for coming to tell me about Monaldo, too. You're a good person, Maddie."

I smiled. "It's the least I could do." I didn't add, especially since we'd zapped his dog.

"So, has he confessed?" Maurice asked. "Monaldo, I mean. Has he admitted to killing Hank?"

I shifted in my seat. "Well, no, not exactly. But I'm sure he will. He's confessed to being a part of an organized crime ring, and from what the police say, he'll be going away for a very, very long time."

Maurice nodded, sniffling and dabbing with the tissue again. He shrugged. "I guess it's possible he really didn't kill Hank. You know, Hank was a very sensitive soul. Maybe it was all too much for him. Maybe he really did kill himself. There was a note after all."

I nodded. "Maybe."

I watched as Maurice twisted his Kleenex into oblivion, Queenie yapping at his heels for attention, the scent of Clorox heavy in the air. Silence stretched between us as his last comment replayed in my head. Something wasn't right. The hairs on the back of my neck prickled as realization crept over me.

"Wait - what did you say?" I asked.

Maurice blinked at me. "That Hank was a sensitive soul."

"No, not that," I said, feeling my lips moved slow motion as puzzle pieces rapidly dropped into place. "About the suicide note?"

Maurice slowly looked up. Our eyes locked.

Ramirez had told me no one knew about the suicide note. They weren't releasing that information to the public. There was only one other person who could have known that the police found a note.

Hank's killer.

CHAPTER TWENTY-ONE

I swallowed, my mouth going drier than the Santa Annas as I stared at the man across from me. Suddenly his red rimmed eyes held more malice than grief.

"I said Hank left a note," Maurice said slowly, face searching mine for hidden meaning.

"You're right," I said quickly. "He did. So, it was probably a suicide after all."

I had to get out of there! I had to call Ramirez. I had to leave. Now!

"Anyway, I'm sorry for your loss, and I have somewhere to be so I guess I should be going." I grabbed my purse and stood up, making quick strides toward the door. Which would have been a whole lot quicker if Queenie hadn't been dancing between my legs, begging with a little yap, yap, yap for a pat on the head. If it weren't for her, I might have made it to the door before I heard an unmistakable click behind me.

I froze. I was beginning to know that sound all too well. The clinch of a bullet sliding into the chamber. For the second time in as many days I spun around to find myself face to face with the barrel of a gun. Maurice took a wide stance, both hands wrapped around Hank's .38 special. Tears trickled down his cheeks, and his hands were shaking, the gun barrel bobbing between my forehead and my chest.

"I'm sorry, Maddie," he said, sniffling again. "I liked you. I really did."

His use of the past tense was not reassuring. "Maurice," I said slowly, trying to keep the panic out of my voice. "Let's talk about this."

He shook his head. "I'm sorry, Maddie, there's nothing to talk about. It's over. It's finally all over. They're both gone now. Don't you understand? It's all over."

I gulped. I didn't understand. He wasn't making a whole lot of sense, and his tears were bordering on hysterical territory. The one thing I did understand was the gun pointed at my barely-B chest, which at the moment I wanted to keep just the way it was, thank you very much.

"Maurice, just put down the gun, and we'll talk." My eyes searched wildly around the apartment for anything within reach that could be used as a weapon. But, thanks to Maurice's compulsive cleaning tendencies, the surfaces were not only free of clutter, but free of anything sharp, heavy, or useful as a projectile. Damn!

He shook his head at me. "I'm sorry, Maddie, I can't do that." He started crying even harder, big racking sobs. But, surprisingly, his grip on the gun seemed to be growing more steady. Not a good sign.

"So, you wrote the suicide note?" I asked, stalling for time. Not that I was sure what good that would do. No one knew where I was or even that I'd left the hotel, for that matter. But the longer I could delay getting shot, the better in my book.

Maurice nodded. "I had to. I didn't want anyone else to go to jail for killing him. I didn't want anyone else to suffer."

"Just Hank?"

More tears flowed and his nose starting running, only this time Maurice's face contorted with anger. "He deserved to suffer! He cheated on me! Me! That jerk thought he could treat me that way. He was going to break up with me, move that big hairy ape of his into the home that I'd created for him. Sleep on my sheets, eat off my china, sit at the dining table I polished every week. I couldn't let him do that. I couldn't let him bring that Neanderthal into my home."

"What Neanderthal? Monaldo?" I asked, confused. Maurice had mentioned he'd seen Hank coming out of Monaldo's office. Maybe it had been more than a business relationship after all.

Maurice shook his head. "No. That goon of his. The one in need of a waxing."

Unibrow! "Unibrow was gay!?" I asked, unable to keep the disbelief out of my voice.

Maurice narrowed his watering eyes at me. "Yes, he was gay. We're not all delicate little flowers, you know."

I mentally rolled my eyes. The man with the gun was lecturing *me* on political correctness.

"So you pushed Hank off the roof?"

Maurice nodded. "Don't you see, I had to? He was going to ruin everything with that big hairy monster of his."

"Why naked?" I asked, remembering the little detail that had been bothering me from the start.

Maurice gave me a 'well duh' look. "He was wearing an off the shoulder vintage Dior evening gown. It would have gotten blood all over it. There's no way you could get those kind of stains out."

Good point.

"Where is the dress now?" I asked. Though, honestly, I could care less. I was fishing for anything to buy time, to distract him. I slowly eased one hand into my purse, dangling at my side. If I could just get my fingers around my cell phone…

"What are you doing?" The gun popped up from my chest to catch me smack between my eyes.

A wave of pure panic surged up from my belly, every muscle in my body going tense as he took a step forward.

"Nothing," I squeaked out in a voice almost as shrill as Queenie's non-stop yapping.

"Drop your purse. Throw it on the floor."

I did as I was told, slowly slipping the thin strap off my shoulder and letting my one hope at rescue drop to my feet.

"Now kick it toward me," he commanded.

I did, the contents spilling out the top as it bounced across the olive green shag. Queenie immediately pounced on the new toy, and I cringed as her pointy little teeth dug into the Italian leather.

"Now what?" I asked, half dreading the answer.

"Now walk down the hallway," Maurice said, gesturing with the tip of the gun. "Slowly."

"Where are we going?"

"The bathroom," Maurice responded. "I'm going to shoot you in the bathtub. Easier to clean up."

I felt the gun barrel at my back, poking and prodding me down a narrow hallway, into a small bathroom. The floor and tub were tiled in rosy ceramic squares, the walls a nauseating teal. The room smelled like someone had plugged in fifteen different air fresheners all at once. I gulped back the sickeningly sweet scent as Maurice spun me around.

"Hold your hands out in front of you," he commanded, the gun barrel mere inches from my face.

What choice did I have? I held my hands out, palms up, wrists together. Maurice reached into a bathroom cabinet, all the while keeping the .38 pointed my direction, and pulled out a roll of duct tape. Using his teeth he pulled at the end, then wrapped the sticky gray stuff around my wrists until I was immobilized. That panic started to build again, and I felt tears pricking my own eyes.

"Maurice, please, let's talk about this," I pleaded.

Maurice ripped off another piece of tape with his teeth, then gave me a sympathetic look. "I'm sorry, Maddie. I truly am. But I have to do it." Then he stuck the tape over my mouth, smoothing down the edges until any hope of making a sound more than a whimper was lost.

And, I'm not ashamed to say, I did in fact take the opportunity to whimper. In fact I whimpered so piteously as Maurice nudged me into the bathtub that Queenie bounced down the hallway to see what was happening. She still held the strap of my purse in her teeth and cosmetics, credit cards, tampons, and change trailed behind her. She padded into the bathroom, her little nails clicking on the tile, and rubbed against Maurice's leg. He reached down absently and gave her head a pat. So grateful was she for the attention, that Queenie dropped the purse strap and started yapping a 'thank you' up at Maurice. As my favorite leather handbag hit the floor, a cell phone tumbled toward the edge of the tub. My eyes grew big, and I was glad the duct tape stifled my gasp as I saw it wasn't *my* cell phone. It was Dana's *special* cell phone.

The stun gun.

"Now, Maddie, please make this easy on both of us," Maurice directed, sniffling and biting his lip as he held the gun in a straight-arm pose, taking his aim. "Don't move. Just stay right where you are."

Not on your life, pal.

I took a deep breath, gave myself a two count, then lunged for the cell. My bound hands clamped around it just as I heard the gun erupt. The bullet whizzed so close to my ear that I felt it ruffle my hair before it embedded itself in the shower tiles, sending chips of rose colored ceramic spraying in the air.

"Look what you did!" Maurice shouted, aiming down at the floor where I was wriggling toward him like a snake, cell stunner shoved out in front of me, hoping to God I pushed the right button.

"It's too late to call for help, Maddie," he said, popping off another shot. This one bounced on the tile beside me, sending Queenie into a tizzy. She bounded up and down like a yo-yo, thankfully springing between me and Maurice's gun as I edged closer. Just a few more inches…

"Move, you mutt," Maurice yelled, squinting one eye shut as he tried to aim around the yapper.

One more inch…

I wriggled closer, reaching my arms out as far as they would go, then closed my eyes and hit the red button.

Maurice did a strangled little cry, then crumpled to the ground, his head landing inches from mine as his tongue lolled to the side.

I did a sigh of relief and went limp myself, staring at the teal colored ceiling, taking in big deep breaths of air and basking in the glory of being alive.

I gave my self a couple more beats of basking, then traded my stunner for Maurice's .38 and backed up against the far wall. Holding the gun in one hand, I grabbed a corner of the duct tape covering my mouth and ripped.

"Holy mother of God!" I cried. My eyes welled up with tears, my hands instinctively going to my throbbing upper lip. I think I ripped off a layer of skin. Or two. Well, on the up side, at least I didn't have to worry about that mustache thing anymore.

Trying to ignore the fire smoldering on my upper lip, I quickly grabbed my real cell phone from my purse and dialed Ramirez's number.

For once, he picked up. I tried to explain where I was and what was going on without giving him another heart attack, though I'm not sure I completely succeeded. He was quiet for a second then let out a whole string of curses, some of which I had to give points for creativity. Once he ran out of curses, he said he'd be right there. I hung up just as Maurice began to twitch on the floor.

Shit. I grabbed the roll of duct tape and, with my own hands still stuck together, awkwardly wrapped it around Maurice's ankles and wrists. Then, just for good measure, I smoothed a piece over his mouth too. Which, knowing how much that sucker was going to hurt to take off, was rather evil of me. But what could I say? Being duct-taped put me in a vindictive mood.

Once I had him bound, I propped him against the tub, then scooted to the far wall and picked up the .38 again, pointing it straight at Maurice as his eyes flickered open in surprise.

He looked down at his bound hands, then up at the gun, his eyes going wide and weepy.

"Sorry Maurice," I said, keeping the gun aimed at his bald head. "I had to do it."

* * *

As I may have mentioned before, there are two things in this world I hate more than getting shot at. Birkenstocks (which no matter what kind of pedicure you wear them with, always make a girl's feet look like they should be drenched in patchouli at a Grateful Dead concert) and sit-ups (the cruelest form of punishment still currently legal). But, I realized as Ramirez tugged at my wrists, I had a third item to add to the list.

Duct tape.

"Owww!" I whined, watching the evil gray strips rip the peach fuzz off my arms.

"Don't be such a baby," Ramirez said, dropping another piece on the floor.

"But it hurts!"

"We're almost done. Just one more piece." He shot me one of his lopsided grins, then ripped the little sucker off.

"Owww!" I wailed.

Okay, I admit, I was playing up the baby thing just a little. But the way Ramirez had fawned over me ever since he burst through Maurice's bathroom door, I'd be an idiot not to. The first thing he'd done was grab me in another rib-crushing hug that lasted so long I feared I'd pass out. Then he'd promised he was not letting me out of his sight again. *Ever*. Okay, so probably a little heat-of-the-moment and unrealistic, but it made my heart go all mushy inside anyway.

After the LVMPD had arrived and taken Maurice into custody (sobbing all the way to the squad car) Ramirez had held my hand while the paramedics checked me out, and Detective Sipowicz (who was looking a little peeved at seeing me yet *again*) took my statement. Then, Ramirez packed me into his SUV and drove me back to the New York - New York where he was currently removing the last remainders of my latest encounter with the homicidal Mr. Clean.

"There," he said, pulling one more bit of sticky tape from my arm. "All done."

I rubbed my wrists. "It still hurts," I whined.

Ramirez got a wicked look in his eyes, and his lopsided grin grew to Big Bad Wolf proportions. "Maybe I should kiss it and make it better."

"Seriously? I just almost get killed – again – and you're thinking about sex?"

He grinned. "I'm male. I'm always thinking about sex."

"Oh, brother." I rolled my eyes.

"Come on. You. Me. A quiet hotel room." He looked down at the double. "A big bed…"

Hmmm… I had to admit, he made a persuasive argument. Which became even more persuasive when he grabbed my hand and brought it to his lips, whispering a soft kiss along the inside of my wrist.

I closed my eyes, my temperature rising about fifteen degrees.

"Feeling sexy yet?" he murmured against my skin.

I shook my head. "Unh-uhn," I lied.

His mouth traveled upward, nibbling at the inside of my elbow. "How about now?"

I swallowed back a sigh as his sexy day-old stubble skimmed over my skin. "Nope."

He wrapped one arm around my middle, pulling me flush against his rock-hard body. His mouth hovered over mine, so closely I could feel his hot breath on my lips. "Now?" he whispered.

"Okay, maybe just a little."

He grinned, showing off that deceptively boyish dimple. "I knew you'd come around," he growled, his deep voice vibrating against my lips. Then his mouth closed over mine. Softly, slowly, igniting an instant fire that started somewhere in my belly and quickly spread south.

I kissed him back. Hard. Okay, fine, I was female. Around Ramirez, I was always thinking about sex too. So much so that right at the moment, I didn't care if my legs weren't shaved, if my underwear didn't match my bra, or that my upper lip was still red and swollen from my duct tape facial. Screw it. We were all alone, the bad guys with guns were behind bars, and Ramirez was kissing me. *Oh boy*, was he kissing me.

I shuddered as his hand snaked up my thigh, sliding past the hem of my denim skirt until I was praying to the Gods of prophylactics that Ramirez carried protection in his wallet. I wrapped one leg around his solid body, pulling him close, my fingers seeking out his button fly. I was just popping button number two when the door to the hotel room burst open.

"Maddie, guess what," Marco cried, prancing into the room. "Madonna got us tickets to see Bette Midler! I'm going to see the divine Mizz M in person tonight. I am in heaven, dahling, absolute heaven! I am so-" He paused. "Oh. Am I interrupting something?"

I glared at him. If looks could kill, Marco would be one dead duck.

Ramirez did a primal growl that belonged on Animal Plant, then stood up, adjusting his jeans.

"Oops. Sorry," Marco said doing a sheepish grin. "My bad." He looked down to the pile of duct tape on the floor.

"What's with the tape?" he asked. Then got a wicked gleam in his eyes. "Is this something kinky?"

"No, it's not kinky. Sticky and painful is more like it," I reassured him. Then filled him in on my run-in with Maurice while Ramirez re-buttoned his fly. By the time I was done, Marco's jaw was dragging on the floor.

"Oh, honey, you are amazing! You're the shit. You are the fabbest lady I know. You totally took down a cold-blooded killer!"

I hoped Ramirez was getting all this. "Well," I said modestly, "Dana kind of helped. It was her stun gun after all."

"Oh, no honey, it was all you. Oh!" He clapped his hands together. "We have to celebrate. Drinks tonight after the show?"

"Absolutely," I agreed.

"Fab! Well, I'm going to make like a cheap stocking and run. I've got to find something to wear to fawn over Bette. I'll, uh, leave you two to your private celebration here then," he said with a wink before skipping back out of the room.

As soon as the door closed behind him, Ramirez grabbed my hand and pulled me to him again, wrapping one arm around my waist, the other hand caressing the back of my neck. "Now," he growled, "where were we?"

He didn't give me a chance to answer as he zeroed in on my lips. This time more urgently, with purpose. Not that I minded. I had to admit as my hands roved up to his six-pack that belonged in a Cool Water commercial, my hormones switched into urgent mode, too. Ramirez groaned as my fingers moved south to that button fly again. He leaned me back on the bed, falling on top of me. Whoa. Was that a colt .45 in his pocket or was he just happy to see me?

I was two buttons away from finding out when the hotel room door popped open again.

"Sonofabitch," Ramirez swore.

"Ohmigod, yes, that's totally the spot!" Dana staggered in the door, giggling and flushed as Rico nibbled on her neck. "Oh!" She paused when she saw us. "Whoops. Looks like this room's already occupied."

I cleared my throat as Ramirez rolled off me, muttering something about strangling the blonde. "Uh, kind of. I mean, we were just…" I trailed off, blushing too hard to finish the thought.

"Uh-huh, us too." Dana giggled again as Rico pinched her behind.

"So, I guess you two made up then?" I asked, even though the hickey forming just below Dana's ear answered that question clearly enough.

Dana nodded. "Rico called me this morning after Officer Taylor released him from holding. Can you believe Slim Jim's pressing charges? Anyway, Rico apologized for getting all jealous, and I apologized for totally overreacting, and now we're going to…"

"Make up?" I supplied before she could venture into too-much-info territory.

"Uh-huh," Dana giggled. "Besides, I couldn't stay mad at my little love guns," Dana crooned, smooshing Rico's cheeks until his lips puckered out.

"Awe," he cooed back in baby talk, "I wuv you my little bullet baby."

Ugh. Urban Soldier endearments.

"Hey, what happened to your wrists?" Dana asked, looking down to where the sticky tape residue had mingled with lint from Ramirez's jeans, leaving me looking like I had Smurf bracelets on.

"Long story," I answered. So, I gave her a quickie version, highlighting the attempt on my life and the good fortune of a dog that liked leather purses.

"Ohmigod!" Dana yelled when I'd finished. "I knew that stun gun was a good idea!"

"Yeah, well, for once it zapped the right guy. Anyway, we're meeting Marco for drinks to celebrate tonight. You in?"

"Totally!" Dana said. Then shot a glance at Rico. "If I'm not otherwise engaged."

"Speaking of which… " Rico said, catching Dana's eye.

"Right. Well, I guess we'll leave you two alone," Dana said as she and Rico staggered out the door in a lip-lock.

Ramirez slammed it shut behind them, then turned his dark eyes on me. "You have way too many friends."

At the moment, I had to agree.

In one long step he crossed the distance between us, and we were engaged in a lip-lock of our own. And this time urgency was definitely the name of the game. His hands were everywhere at once. Tugging at the hem of my skirt, sliding up my belly, fumbling with the clasp of my bra. And I was keeping pace. This time I had all five buttons undone before you could say 'BVDs'. We were on a mission. Nothing was stopping us now…

"*Oy*, I tell ya', that game was rigged. There's no way that dealer coulda had a run like that unless he was- Oh. Sorry, Mads."

…nothing except Mrs. Rosenblatt.

I closed my eyes and thunked my head against the headboard, wondering what a girl had to do around here to get laid.

"Mads?"

My eyes popped open. "Mom?"

Ramirez stood up, pulling his hand out of my shirt like it had been bitten by a snake. "*Mom*!?" he squeaked out in a falsetto. Mobsters he could handle, but my mom, now that scared him.

"Uh, sorry to interrupt," Mom said from the doorway. "It was time for Mrs. Rosenblatt's blood pressure pills, and she left them up here in the room. But had we known you had company…" Her eyes strayed to Ramirez's un-done fly.

"Shit." Ramirez turned around and re-buttoned. Again.

"Yeah, you shoulda put a sock on the doorknob or somethin'," Mrs. R said as she crossed the room and dug into her suitcase. "Then we'd know you had some lovin' going on in here."

"Duly noted," I muttered.

Mom cleared her throat, looking from my askew bra to Ramirez, standing awkwardly in the corner.

"Oh, Mom, this is Jack Ramirez."

"Oh, so you're *that* detective," Mom cooed, grabbing his hand and pumping it up and down. "Maddie's told me so much about you. And, between you and me, I'm relieved she's dating again. It's been too long. It's not good for a girl to go that long. I know. Once Ralphie had to go away to this wig convention in Sarasota, and I was all alone for the whole week, and well, I saw this commercial for this little thing they called a pocket rocket-"

"I got em'!" Mrs. Rosenblatt said, raising a pill bottle above her head.

Ramirez and I did a simultaneous sigh of relief. Nothing like visions of your mother with a vibrator to kill the mood.

"Come on, Betty," Mrs. Rosenblatt said. "We got a good hour of Keno left before our flight leaves."

"Okay. Nice to have met you," Mom called as the door closed behind her.

I flopped back on the bed and stared at the ceiling.

Ramirez lay down beside me and let out a big sigh. "You do realize that I'm going to have to shoot the next person who walks through that door."

I nodded. "I think you could probably claim self-defense at this point."

He sighed again, wiping a hand across his face.

"So, I guess you're not in the mood anymore, huh?" I asked.

"Honey, I'm male. I'm always in the mood. I'm just waiting for the next crazy to walk through the door before I go through the trouble of doing my fly up again."

"Okay, here's a thought," I said, rolling over to face him. "What do you say we go away somewhere?"

"Go away?" He raised one eyebrow.

"Yeah," I said, sitting up. "I know, it's a bold move seeing as we're not even really… I mean I'm not officially your… I mean it's not like we've ever even…" I paused. I took a deep breath. Then I went for it. "I hear Palm Springs is lovely this time of year."

"Oh, yeah?" Ramirez propped himself up on his elbow.

I nodded. "Very romantic."

"Oh, so you want romance, do you?" he said, grinning until that dimple dropped into his cheek again.

"I wouldn't mind a little romance," I answered coyly. "Besides, think of it, you and me alone. No work, no *nosey friends*," I added with emphasis, pointing to the door. "Just the two of us. What do you think?"

"Sounds won-der-ful," he said, drawing out the word.

I felt myself go giddy.

"There's just one problem."

I frowned. "What?"

Ramirez got up and crossed the room to Mrs. Rosenblatt's open suitcase. He grabbed one of Mrs. R's purple and pink polka dotted socks and handed it to me.

"I don't think I can wait that long," he said. He leaned in close, his eyes doing that dark and dangerous thing, his voice going middle of the night husky. "Lock the door."

NEXT IN HIGH HEELS MYSTERY

UNDERCOVER IN HIGH HEELS

Gemma Halliday

CHAPTER ONE

"Wait, Chad, don't leave. I... I have something to tell you."

"After all your lies and deception, there's nothing you can possibly say to make me stay now, Ashley."

"Chad, please! You know I love you. I only did what I had to to keep us together. Besides, you can't go now... I'm carrying your baby!"

I gasped, grabbing another handful of popcorn as the TV switched to a commercial for deodorant.

"Oh my freaking God, the baby is the gardener's?" my best friend Dana shouted from the sofa beside me. "Her husband is gonna freaking flip."

"Don't worry," I said, taking a sip of Diet Coke. "He's still in that coma, remember? He'll never know."

"Oh, right. I missed that episode. So, does that mean the lady that hit him with the car went to jail?"

I shook my head. "No, her husband blackmailed the D.A. to get the charges dropped, but only if she checked herself into rehab. But instead of going to rehab, she shacked up with her sister's husband at his place on the lake."

"Oooooooh," Dana said, drawing out the word. "So that's why the sister is poisoning the husband."

I nodded. "Shhh, it's back on."

Dana and I went silent, our eyes glued to the screen as Chad and Ashley fell into a passionate embrace. I'm not ashamed to admit it. I was seriously hooked on this show. *Magnolia Lane* was the hottest prime time soap to hit the air waves since Brandon and Brenda moved to the 90210, and I was powerless against its junk TV spell.

My cell rang from my purse.

"You're ringing," Dana said.

I waved it off. "Commercial," I mumbled around a bite of popcorn, my eyes glued to the screen as Chad asked Ashley just how sure she was the baby was his and not her comatose husband's. While, of course, Ashley's nosey neighbor listened at the bedroom door, catching the whole conversation.

Just as they switched to a shot of Ashley's husband in the coma ward, my purse rang again.

"You sure you shouldn't get that?" Dana asked.

I shook my head. "Are you kidding? Ashley's husband is about to wake up."

I ignored the William Tell Overture trilling from the region of my Kate Spade, instead grabbing another handful of popcorn as Nurse Nan leaned over the comatose Preston Francis Barton the third. Considering she was his wife's secret evil twin sister, I figured we were in for two options: she was either going to smother him or pull the plug.

She leaned in closer. Her hands reached for the plug.

Dana and I did a collective gasp.

Then the screen went to a life insurance commercial featuring a baby boomer in leather pants air-guitaring a Jimi Hendrix song.

"I hate it when they do that!" Dana said, throwing a piece of popcorn at the screen. Hers, of course, was minus the butter, oil, fat, salt, and flavor. Dana was an aerobics instructor slash wanna-be actress with the kind of curves that caused car crashes on the PCH. Her body was a temple. Mine, on the other hand, required regular sacrifices from the natives of double stuffed Oreos, cheeseburgers, and popcorn with lots of bright yellow butter flavoring made of things I couldn't pronounce. My theory? As long as my favorite Cavalli jeans still fit, I was doing okay. (Fine, so they were a little snug around the waist lately, but I could still zip them up!)

While Dana tossed another kernel of popcorn at the television, I reached into my purse and checked my cell readout. Two missed calls. Both from the same number, one that had me doing a little happy squirm in my seat. Ramirez.

Detective Jack Ramirez was not only the LAPD's hottest cop, but as of last fall he was also mine. All mine.

Okay, so he hadn't exactly officially said that I was his girlfriend yet, but I'm pretty sure that just last week he used the words "girl" and "friend" in the same sentence. Which was a start. Ramirez wasn't exactly your typical Happily Ever After material. He was a homicide detective with a very large gun, a very large tattoo and some very dangerous moves in the bedroom. More of a bad-boy Russell Crow than a home-and-hearth Ward Cleaver. Not, mind you, that I was complaining. (See bedroom reference above.)

We were supposed to meet for "drinks or something" later after he got off shift. Me, I was wearing a black lace Vicky's Secret thong under my Capris in hopes of the "or something."

I keyed in my pin number and waited for my messages while the *Magnolia Lane* theme song played and credits rolled over a backdrop of manicured lawns and a picture-perfect neighborhood.

"Hey, Maddie, it's me," came Ramirez's voice. "Listen, something came up. I've got to meet someone at the Cabana Club, so I can't get together later after all. Sorry. I'll call you tomorrow."

Great.

Ramirez's fatal flaw, as you may have noticed, was his tendency to make and break plans. Or, worse yet, not make them at all. Even though I was seconds away from actual girlfriend status, I hadn't seen Ramirez since last Friday night when a dinner and movie at City Walk had turned into appetizers and me in a cab when he got a call about a gang shooting in Compton. And now, true to form, he was blowing off our "or something" again. I narrowed my eyes at my cell, wondering what kind of *someone* he was meeting instead?

"What's up?" Dana asked, watching my face fall.

"Ramirez. He's canceling on me." Again.

"What, again?" Dana asked, voicing my thoughts.

"I know! He said he has to meet someone. What does that mean?"

Dana shrugged. "I dunno." She popped another piece of popcorn into her mouth.

"I mean, are we talking a work-related-someone or a personal-someone? 'Cause if it's a personal someone, why not just ask them to join us for drinks? Why cancel on me? What, is he ashamed of me? He doesn't want his friends to meet me? That's bad, isn't it? It means something really bad. He's having second thoughts about this whole relationship thing isn't he? I knew it. I knew it wouldn't last. I knew he'd never settle down. I mean, not that I'm asking him to settle down. Oh, God, do you think he thinks I want him to settle down? Is that it? Am I smothering him? Am I too needy? I'm not too needy, am I?"

"Whoa. Take a breath, Gilmore Girl. No wonder he needs a night off."

Dana was right, I was beginning to hyperventilate.

"Look, he's probably just out with the guys or something tonight. You know how those cops are. It's a total boy's club."

"You're right." I took a deep breath. "Right. He probably just needs a night out with the guys. It's not that he *doesn't* want to be with me. I mean, of course he wants to be with me. Why wouldn't he want to be with me? I'm so not smothery." I paused. "But, just in case, how about we go on a double date this weekend?"

Dana shot me a look. "Double date?"

"It's way harder to smother someone on a double date. Beside, it'll be fun. Me and Ramirez, you and…" I paused, unsure which flavor of the month Dana was presently working her way through. As much as I loved my best friend, even I had to admit she had an uncanny ability to pick men destined for short term romances. Case in point, her last boyfriend, Rico, a self-proclaimed Urban Soldier who'd ended up joining a group of mercenaries in Afghanistan searching for the last remnants of the Taliban. Dana was still nursing a sore ego at being dumped for a bunch of dusty caves halfway around the world.

She bit her lip as a little frown settled between her strawberry blonde brows. "Sorry, Maddie, I can't do a double date."

"Please! It's not like I'm asking you to actually have this relationship for me; I just need a buffer."

Dana shook her head. "No, no. It's not that. I can't date. I'm off men."

"Oh, no. Please don't tell me you're trying that lesbian thing again," I said, sipping my Diet Coke.

Dana shook here head. "No, it's not like that. It's… well… I can't have sex." She put her hands on my shoulders, turning me to face her as she put on her serious look. "I have a problem."

"A problem? What, like an STD?"

She shook her head again. "No, Mads. This is worse."

I arched an eyebrow. "Okay, I'll bite, what's worse than an STD?"

"I'm addicted to sex."

I rolled my eyes. "Oh, good. I thought this was something serious." I laid on the sarcasm double stuffed as I grabbed another handful of popcorn.

"This *is* serious!" she protested.

"Dana, you are hot. Men like you. Since when is that a problem?"

"That's not true, Maddie. I'm sick."

"You're lucky is what you are. You know how many push-up bras I own just to have half your cleavage?" A lot. I was pretty sure that Jack Black and I were the only people left in L.A. that still wore B cups.

Dana ignored me. "Sex can be like any other addiction. It's a disease. One I have to accept and learn to manage one day at a time. I'm practicing positive sexual sobriety."

I crunched down hard on a popcorn kernel to keep from laughing. "Positive sexual sobriety?"

Dana nodded. "Uh-huh. Therapist Max says it's the only way to break the cycle of addiction."

I blinked. "Therapist Max? You're seriously taking advice from a guy named 'Therapist Max?'"

Dana nodded again. "Yes, Maddie. We're all first names at SA. Even the therapists."

I knew I was going to regret asking. "SA?"

"Sexaholics Anonymous."

Mental forehead smack. "And I thought *Magnolia Lane* was over the top."

"Oh, Maddie," Dana said, her eyes lighting up, "you should totally come with me to a meeting. There are tons of hot guys there, and they're always super nice to new girls."

I'll bet. "Thanks, but no thanks. Besides, I have a boyfriend. Sort of," I added ruefully, thinking of my Vicky's thong going to waste tonight. "You sure Ramirez isn't blowing me off?"

Dana opened a bottled water and took a long drink. "Positive."

"All right. Then I promise not to freak out about it anymore tonight. I mean, if he wants to go with the boys to the Cabana Club, I'm not going to be one of those whiny kind of girlfriends about it."

Dana's head snapped up, and she did a little cough/choke thing with her water. "The Cabana Club?!"

Uh-oh. "Yeah... why?"

"Maddie, have you ever been there?"

I shook my head. To be honest my idea of a night on the town started with dinner on Ventura and ended with a turn around the Beverly Center and a new pair of pumps. I wasn't exactly a regular on the club circuit.

"Ohmigod, Maddie. It's a total hook-up place. You didn't tell me Ramirez was going *there*!"

Oh, shit. I felt my stomach bottom out, fizzy Diet Coke mixing with fake buttered popcorn mixing with pure dread. "Oh, God. This is it. He's totally dumping me, isn't he? It was all about the chase, wasn't it? Now that he's got me where he wants me, he doesn't want me anymore! I'm stale, Dana. I'm like that day-old bagel no one wants. Oh, God, what am I going to do?"

"I'm sorry, hon." Dana laid a hand on my arm and sent me the same pity look she'd been giving me ever since my mother insisted on giving me a bob with bangs in seventh grade. "Look, I'm sure it's nothing. I'm sure he's just..." She trailed off, unable to come up with an adequate lie.

"Right." I took a big gulp of my Diet Coke, the carbonation burning all the way down my throat. "But just in case, you feel like grabbing a drink?"

* * *

The Cabana Club was a large, brick building on the corner of La Brea and Sunset, painted pink and flanked by flashing neon flamingos. Since it was Friday night there was a line to get in, but luckily Dana knew every bouncer in town (most on a more intimate basis than I knew my gynecologist) and we were inside before you could say "Lindsay Lohan."

As my eyes adjusted to the dimly lit interior, punctuated by pink and green flashing lasers, I realized Dana was right. The placed reeked of hook-up. A crowded dance floor to our right held L.A.'s hottest bodies – actress-slash-waitresses, model-slash-waitresses, a bunch of CW actors, and that girl from *Survivor* that everyone hated – all gyrating together in a way that couldn't even air on HBO. Tables to the left were filled with groupings of men and women doing the heads-bent-together thing and drinking tall cocktails while grabbing each other under the table. The bar straight ahead was two people thick with singles looking to score a martini and a phone number. I squinted through the darkness, praying my boyfriend wasn't one of them.

"This is *so* not a boys night out," I shouted over the techno beat pulsating off the walls.

"This is *so* not the place a recovering sex addict should be spending her Friday night." Dana eyed a guy at the bar wearing leather pants, an unbuttoned shirt and a "how you doin'" smile.

He winked at her.

Dana bit her lip.

"Let's find Ramirez and get out of here fast before I do something I'm going to regret," she said.

Fine by me. We wove our way through the crowd, circling the bar. I got elbowed by an Olsen twin look-alike, and a guy in a cowboy hat spilled a margarita on my Capris, but I didn't care. I was on a mission. I had been patient with Ramirez. I had given him his space. I had even waited a record two months before having sex with him. (Not entirely by choice, but that was beside the point.) I had done everything known to woman to make this relationship work. And what did he do? Blow it all for a night in hook-up heaven. Woman scorned didn't even begin to describe the anger surging through me as I scanned the club.

Then I spotted him. He was sitting at a table near the back, a half empty glass of beer in front of him. I gnashed my teeth together, my vision going red as I stared my worst fear in the face.

Ramirez was sitting next to a woman. A *tall* woman. If there's anything in this world that my 5'1 ½" self hates more than being dumped, it's being dumped for someone tall.

Her legs were almost as long as I was, tucked under the table beneath a barely-there leather mini. And her top didn't cover a whole lot more. A plunging neckline dipped almost to her belly button, showing off cleavage that was obviously man-made. Over her shoulders was a little red shrug jacket, more for fashion effect than actual coverage, and her long black hair was loose, flowing down her back, giving her that dark, exotic look that a blonde Irish/English mutt like myself could never pull off.

And then she put her hand on his thigh.

I felt my nostrils flare, my hands balling into fists at my sides. That's it, police officer or no, I was gonna kill him.

I vaguely heard Dana yelling something along the lines of, "Maddie, wait!" but I couldn't have stopped if I wanted to. My body was moving all on its own as I marched straight toward the happy couple.

"You sonofabitch!" I yelled once I was in earshot.

Ramirez turned around, his dark eyebrows hunching together at the sight of me. Despite my anger, my hormones did that little happy sigh they always did when he was around. Ramirez had perfected the tall, dark and dangerous look - his black hair just a little too long, his dark brown eyes just a little too hard, and a sleek panther tattooed on his arm, just a little too big to hide beneath the sleeve of his black T-shirt. His tan skin was interrupted by a thin white scar running through his left eyebrow and a perpetual dusting of rugged stubble across his chin. The Bad Boy slash Sex God effect of it all was almost enough to stop a girl in her tracks.

Almost.

"I can't believe you blew me off for this!" I yelled, gesturing to his Amazon woman. She gave me a startled look, her eyes darting from side to side as if trying to figure out where I'd come from.

"Maddie, what are you doing here?" Ramirez asked, his eyebrows still drawn together in confusion.

"I could be asking the same question." I poked a finger at Ramirez's chest, coming up against his hard, six-day-a-week-at-the-gym pecs. "Who the hell do you think you are that you can lead me on then just blow me off like this for another woman?"

"Maddie," Ramirez said, his voice low and commanding. "Go home. I'll explain later."

"Oh, right! I'll just go home and let you finish your date with Slut-zilla here." I was yelling loudly enough now that even over the pounding dance music, the couples at the adjacent tables were staring.

"Who is this?" Amazon's eyes ping-ponged between Ramirez and me. "I told you to come alone."

"Maddie," Ramirez said again, his eyes shooting daggers at me. "Don't do this."

"Don't do this? Don't *do* this! I'm sorry, what exactly am I doing? Because it sure as hell isn't dating some abnormally tall chick when you were supposed to be doing 'or something' with me!"

"Ramirez?" the Amazon asked, shifting nervously.

"Maddie," Ramirez warned.

"Jerk!" I yelled.

Then I picked up his half-empty glass and tossed the contents in his face.

"Jesus," he sputtered, jumping from his chair and blinking Budweiser out of his eyes.

"And as for you…" I said, turning on Amazon Woman.

But I didn't get to finish that threat.

She bolted from her chair and before I could register what was going on pulled a gun out from her little red shrug (which, I now realized was clearly not *just* for fashion's sake) and grabbed me by my blonde roots. I let out a strangled cry as she wrapped one arm around my neck, holding me in a vice grip.

"All right, nobody move!" she shouted, commanding the shocked couples at the nearby tables, their mouths hanging open as they watched the scene unfold.

Then Amazon Woman pushed the barrel of the gun against my temple.

"Or blondie dies."